Any Other Time

G000129084

Mary Kennelly
Ahalahana, Moyvane

JOHN TROLAN
ANY OTHER TIME

BRANDON

A Brandon Original Paperback

Published in 2000 by Brandon
an imprint of Mount Eagle Publications
Dingle, Co. Kerry, Ireland

10 9 8 7 6 5 4 3 2 1

Copyright © John Trolan 2000

The author has asserted his moral rights.

ISBN 0 86322 252 8
(original paperback)

This book is published with the assistance of
the Arts Council/An Chomhairle Ealaíonn.

This book is sold subject to the condition that it shall not, by way of trade or
otherwise, be lent, resold, hired out or otherwise circulated without the
publisher's prior consent in any form of binding or cover other than that in
which it is published and without a similar condition being imposed on the
subsequent purchaser.

Cover design: id communications, Tralee
Typesetting: Red Barn Publishing, Skeagh, Skibbereen
Printed by The Guernsey Press Ltd., Channel Islands

To the memory of beauty that was Mick, Caroline and Barney

THE LAST TIME. Why? Because he was never going to get caught again, that's why. And two months on remand was long enough for anyone. Mind you, it had almost been worth it, if only for the look on O'Toole's face when District Justice O'Dálaigh said, "I am afraid I've already warned those solicitors representing the DPP that if the Book wasn't ready for the defendant's court appearance today, then all his charges would be dismissed. You are free to go, Mr Byrne."

Proper fuckin' order too, thought Davy Byrne. His solicitor had told him O'Dálaigh, being a stubborn old bastard, would not issue new arrest warrants on the same charges. Davy was confident for a different reason: the police couldn't prove a thing.

When Mickey Hughes got bail, Davy worried he had grassed. Now he chuckled at the occasions when he cursed Mickey from a height. He would catch up with him later and hear what exactly had happened. First things first though, he had to get to Ballymun.

Where the warped North Circular Road crosses Dorset Street, Davy decided to walk down to Drumcondra. From there, it was easier to run for whichever bus came first, a 36 or a 13. He would need to explain to the driver he had only got out of the Joy and he hadn't got a shilling to his name.

He felt anxious. He always did when he had just been released, frightened that the police might arrest him before he reached the relative safety of his own territory. Something was required to relieve the self-obsession, the rawness, the feeling of overwhelming susceptibility. He relaxed when a familiar face beamed at him on Drumcondra Bridge.

"How a'yeh, Davy? Are yeh oney out?"

"How a'yeh, Johnny. Yeah, I just got out now. Wha's the story?"

"Not bad. Jaysis, you're after puttin' on some weigh'."

"Yeah, I know. I wasn't usin' tha' much in the Joy, d'yeh know? Listen, is there any gear in the Mun?"

"I haven't a clue. I got a job last month and I haven't used since then."

"Is tha' righ'? Well seein' as you're workin', can yeh lend me ten bob for me bus fare?"

"Jaysis, Davy, sure. Here's a fiver, get a few smokes as well."

"Nice one, Johnny. I'll fix yeh up later."

"Don't worry abou' it, Davy, don't worry. Mind yourself now," said Johnny, and he continued walking towards Dorset Street.

A single-decked bus rolling towards a stop on the Drumcondra side of the bridge forced Davy to run. It was a 36 and would get him to Ballymun quicker than a 13. The bus arrived at the stop before him, but the driver had seen Davy running and waited until he caught up. Davy didn't bother to thank him, or an old man he bummed a cigarette from, but walked to the back of the bus where he sat and tried to decide what he would do when he got home. Should he go straight to Breen's flat or should he go to the snooker hall in the shopping centre? Fuck it! He would try Breen's flat first.

Davy's mind bounced between obsession and annoyance: frequently, he felt like leaving his seat to urge the driver to go faster and he cursed every red light. His anxiety increased when the bus, at last, turned and entered the dual carriageway that led to the estate. Despite being desperate to get there, his heart always sank a little when he saw the first of the tower blocks rise like a concrete centurion. Jaysis! How he hated the kip, and every snivelling little grasser and tapper in it. But it was the most difficult place in Dublin to get captured by the police. This was home.

Eventually the bus reached the stop nearest to Breen's flat. Davy, first to get off, leaped from the platform and almost ran to the block where Breen lived. When he saw that the lift was not on ground level, he ran up the five flights of stairs, taking the steps two and three at a time. Breathless when he arrived at the right landing, he tried to compose himself, while waiting for his knock to be answered.

Barefooted and scrawny, with dark, dishevelled hair, Breen wore clothing so casual, it seemed temporary. His loose, unbuckled jeans threatened to fall down and a light blue cotton shirt seemed to have dropped on him. He stood in the doorway, the pupils of his eyes like pinpoints and when he spoke, he mauled his nose with one of his hands.

"How a'yeh, Davy? Wha's the story? Are yeh oney out?"

"Listen, a'yeh doin' any dike?"

"I've only a few. How many a'yeh lookin' for?"

Davy took a deep breath. "Lay seven on me and hold seven for me until me oul' wan gets in from work. She has a few bob belongin' to me, so I'll pay yeh this evenin', Tony, for the fourteen of them."

Anguish filled Breen's face, then uncertainity, and both fought with his fear of Davy. "I oney have seven to sell so I'll lay four on yeh now and hold three until six this evenin', okay?"

Desperate for the Diconal, Davy agreed, but he had to spend another couple of minutes persuading Breen to allow him to use his flat and his syringe.

"A'yeh sure yeh haven't got the germ, Davy? This is the oney works I have."

"Of course I'm fuckin' sure. Wasn't I tested in the Joy? A'yeh sure you haven't got it?"

"Well I can't be sure, I've never been tested."

"Don't worry then, I'll go first."

Davy calmly now, but authoritively, recited a list: toilet paper, an empty cigarette box, the syringe, warm water and, of course, the dike.

Breen's hand reached down into his crotch and brought out a small, white-capped, brown pill bottle. Carefully, without revealing how many pills were in the bottle, he handed four to Davy, who turned them in the palm of his hand, reassuringly, while he waited on the other items.

When Breen returned, Davy expertly, with a seemingly pious respect, laid what he had asked for on top of a small chest of drawers beside the bed. The room was scruffy with a mangy, dank carpet and only three distinct items of furniture, one of which was a large brown wardrobe that seemed to come to rest upon a corner of the room. A single bunk bed which had once been part of a pair was covered in bedclothes uncannily similar to the carpet. The small dirty white dresser Davy now used like an altar. He was oblivious to everything except the ritualised preparation. Even Breen, while quiet, was ignored as he sat on the end of the bed carelessly witnessing the all too familiar scene.

Davy folded the four pink pills into the cigarette carton for protection while he crushed them to a fine pink powder with his teeth. As he was pouring the Diconal into the barrel of the syringe, Breen muttered to him, "Jaysis, Davy, I hope yeh don't keel over."

The remark was contemptuously shushed. Having poured all the powder in, Davy put the plunger of the syringe back into the barrel and sucked some warm water from the tumbler on the dresser. Having covered the small hole at the top of the syringe with his finger, he began swilling the contents gently at first, then vigorously, until he was sure that as much of the powder which would dissolve had dissolved. Controlling himself, despite the sense of urgency he felt, he pulled his jeans down below his knees and placed a green-based needle on top of the syringe, before respectfully raising it with both hands to the air and checking it was clear of any air bubbles. As confidently as any medic he squirted a tiny amount skywards and licked the needle clean, before searching for and quickly finding the small crater-like tunnel at the top of his groin, where constant using had created easy access to his femoral vein. He hesitated a moment while he uttered a quick prayer that he wouldn't hit an artery, and then turned and bent his right leg slightly at the knee and slowly, horizontally, slid the needle in as far as it would go, feeling its steel slide through worn flesh. When he drew back the plunger and saw the dark red blood mingle slowly with the pink liquid in the syringe, he thanked Jesus for locating the vein so easily. Surrendering to the urgency, he smiled as he flushed the mixture as quickly as possible into his body. He sensed the journey of the warm concoction as it sped through his vein and towards his heart. Then the impact; the collision-like sensation; the hit.

He stood, crouching from its effect, until he was aware of Breen pleading with him, "Jaysis, Davy, get it together, will yeh? I told yeh me oul' wan'll be in soon and yeh know she'll take a bluie if she sees you here, especially in tha' state. For fucksake!"

"Alrigh', Tony," Davy mumbled, "alrigh'. Where's the tissue?" When Davy felt the tissue being placed in his hand he removed the syringe from his groin and immediately covered the wound to stop the blood seeping down his leg. Minutes later, he was saying good-bye to Breen as he was urged towards the door, and he didn't forget to promise he would be back by six that evening for the other three dike.

As Davy left, he passed the lift and used the stairs, walking slowly and steadying himself by gripping the handrail tightly. Halfway down, he became aware of a warm liquid spraying from the metal banisters and the concrete steps above his head on to his face and hands. He paused, puzzled, and glanced back up through the slit which separated each stairway and ran the height of the block. A few flights up he saw a young boy of about ten pissing down through the gap. Davy jumped back from the handrail and roared, "Yeh little bastard. If I get me hands on yeh, I'll cut the prick off yeh." Hearing the child's laughter fade away, he used the sleeve of his denim jacket to wipe where he had been splashed. He worried about smelling of piss for the rest of the day. He *was* only out. Embracing the fresh March air which greeted him as he left the block, he thought, these kids are getting fuckin' worse.

He walked to the snooker hall. It wasn't long past two o'clock and Davy's ma wouldn't be home until about half-past four. Still having the best part of the fiver Johnny gave him, he could afford twenty cigarettes and a few games of pool. When he arrived at the snooker hall, which was at one end of a four mall shopping centre, Davy noticed a few familiar youths lounging around outside. He spat a "Fuck off" at the first two who asked him for odds. One of these he offered a few games of pool.

"Get the balls, Yako, and set them up while I do a piss," said Davy.

The youth had the table ready when Davy returned. As the effects of the opiates wore off, Davy began to feel more agitated, intolerant. Although still stoned, the rush had long gone and the remaining sensation only left him with an itchy nose and a growing anger. After they had played for half an hour, Davy had enough. He paid for the pool table and gave Yako a quid towards his cough bottle bill.

"Aw, nice one. Thanks, Davy."

As he left, Davy decided to visit his brother Billy. When he reached the flat his sister-in-law, Deirdre, answered his knock, her expression switching instantly from placidity to pain. "Jaysis, Davy, I didn't expect to see you."

"Yeah? Well me charges were struck out this mornin'. Where's Billy?"

"He's gone in for his labour and he won't be back until abou' four."

"I'll hang on for abou' an hour then," said Davy, and as he hadn't been invited in, he brushed past her and walked through the corridor of the hall to the living room. He saw their child there, an infant of about twelve months.

"How a'yeh, Jason? Jaysis, you're getting huge, nearly as big as your Uncle Davy. C'mon and I'll put yeh into your cot while I talk to your ma."

"Leave him there, Davy," said Deirdre, a plea in her tone. "He's not doin' any harm."

Davy ignored her and asked where the baby's bottle was. Deirdre, muttering something, fetched the bottle and filled it with a mixture of milk and warm water. Davy took it from her, brought the baby to his bedroom and sat him in his cot with the bottle. When he returned to the living room, Deirdre was standing with her back to him, amongst the toys.

"A'yeh not deligh'ed to see me, Deirdre?"

"Yeh know I hate to see anyone locked up," she answered.

"Wha' kind of fuckin' answer is tha'?" In the scant seclusion, with less regard and without any warning, he struck her across the side of her head with his open hand and almost knocked her on to a sad, Formica-topped coffee table which centred a black leather, multi-punctured suite of furniture.

"Please, Davy," she begged. "Yeh said yeh wouldn't do this again. Yeh promised."

Davy turned her to face him and, sneering, told her "Yeh were a little more eager when our Billy was locked up, weren't yeh?"

"Jaysis, Davy, I was drunk, and yeh know how I felt afterwards, please. . ."

Davy looked at her, but his hesitancy, any reluctance, was cancelled, abandoned, postponed until the next time. He pushed her against one of the walls and calmly began to open her blouse. Deirdre put her head in her hands and began to sob. He didn't bother to open her bra, but instead pushed it over and around her breasts, and then the assault began in earnest, with a zealous squeeze and a token suck. Lifting her skirt he pulled her pants past an area where fear imploded, thighs trembled, pulled on down to her ankles, "C'mon, Deirdre?" he asked kindly, and she lifted one foot out. He rose and opened his jeans, pushing them to his knees for the second time that day.

Deirdre cried.

Davy lifted her skirt again, a wine coloured, three-quarter length made of corduroy and extended by a hemmed imitation slip of lace. It was an armful his elbows held aloft to enable him to proceed with fistfuls of gropes and grabs while his silence amplified her sobbing.

Other sounds drifted in from Jason's room. Him kicking gently the cotton sheet entangled round his feet while a bare plastic mattress rustled and cot bars creaked, bearing witness to his effort. Hooked in one hand, a bright pink and yellow crochet blanket, daubed with stale baby rusks, trapped like a net a couple of long discarded ginger nuts. In his other he swung a bottle by the teat while he talked to the mobile butterflies which dangled from the ceiling above his head. The message was unmistakable: he offered some milk and at the last moment cruelly shoved the rubber teat into his mouth. His giggle, both a gorgeous shriek and a careless spit of milk dribble, made him cough, almost choke, and changed his tone. Serious, sincere, and then a gesture. The bottle was flung from the cot. He had something to say, so he told the butterflies, blue wide-eyed and with intimate awe. His thin, top lip sought shelter behind its chubby, bottom companion, while his big blue eyes swelled up with tears. There really was something he wanted to say. Dragging himself up, he grabbed hold of the cot bars and shook and hammered for all he was worth, focusing attentively on his bottle all the way down on the floor.

Deirdre lay against the wall like she may have lain upon the floor. Davy pulled his jeans back up and thought of a final humiliation. He began to bruise-suck on one of her breasts. She sobbed hysterically. He smiled, and wondered how she might manage to hide it from "Our Billy". One more smack silenced her sobbing as she stood holding the wall, sucking like a child with no tears left, those sharp, short, involuntary breaths which are always exhaled as one. Davy didn't look at Deirdre, or speak to her again before leaving, stopping only to say good-bye to the child and hand him back the fallen bottle.

BALLYMUN IS HARD. The flats are much the same, concrete cell-like structures where the walls are hostile to nails. The Byrnes lived in a three bedroom flat on Silloge Road. There, they had a long hallway and a bathroom, having moved when Davy was four, from a room they rented in Summerhill. In Summerhill they had no bathroom, only an outside toilet they shared with other families from the tenement and long brown canal rats that came with the dark.

To help them move, Uncle Jack had driven his turf truck into the city from his home in Ballyfermot, and with Davy's da, used it to transport the furniture. Then they came back to collect the family. It was late. They had stopped to wet their tongues, his da said. Drowned them, by all accounts, his ma said. Davy sat in the back of the open truck on one side of his da and Billy on the other. There was only enough room in the front for his ma, fat with another child, and baby Jojo. Davy would never forget his first impressions of the estate, the height of the road lights at the central roundabout in the dual carriageway. The tower blocks, standing majestically, with authority. He had gazed at them from beneath his da's overcoat. He didn't understand anything: how they stood? How people lived in them? Questions he hasn't bothered to ask himself since.

After their first night they were all woken early, even his da, by the noise of a plane coming to land at Dublin airport. They all thought it was going to crash into the flats and had a great laugh trying to find out who was frightened the most, after it missed. His ma admitted she was, because she was a girl. But his da had nearly shit himself as well. Billy began waving to the planes after that and swore he could see people waving back. His da told him they were American tourists coming to Ireland to look for children that they might adopt. From then on, Billy smiled when he waved.

They got used to the planes quickly, but the central heating took longer. It made all of them sick for over a week. The hardness took a while too. Acting the gobshite was life threatening. If they banged their head on the floor, it was more likely to lead to a fractured skull than a bump, or at least a severe concussion. No more floorboards and no more soft, damp plaster walls. When his ma asked his da to hang a picture of the Sacred Heart, he glued it to the wall, because he would have needed a jack hammer to drill a hole for a nail.

Davy had four brothers, and eight years separated the eldest from the youngest: Billy was twenty-three; Davy two years younger; then Jojo at eighteen; Whacker seventeen; the youngest, Simon, was fifteen. They all, whenever they could, took drugs in some form or another. None of them had ever been employed except, reluctantly, in prison. Their mother was the only member of the family who worked and she had three jobs, all of the cleaning variety.

Kathleen Byrne was reliable, punctual, so Davy knew she wouldn't be home when he knocked at the door of the flat. The flats on Silloge Road are eight storeys high and the Byrnes lived on the sixth floor of one of the middle blocks. Nothing much had changed during the seventeen years he had lived there. Nothing had changed in the two months he had been away. From the balcony he could see, to his left, Sandyhill Avenue, Sandyhill Gardens, and beyond them Poppintree, the housing estate which sprang up in the mid-seventies. Below him to his right, stood his old school, the Holy Spirit, which he had finished without learning to read or write. Beyond that, Balbutcher Lane, and to the far right, one of the tower blocks, Joseph Plunkett, looked down upon them all.

Jojo opened the door and muttered a greeting to the brother he least got on with, but had to because they were more alike than any of the others. Davy was polite; he muttered a reply.

"Have yeh any gear?" said Jojo. When Davy shook his head, Jojo asked, "Have yeh any money?"

"Fuck off, will yeh? I'm oney out."

Jojo picked up a beige bomber jacket and left the flat sulking.

Davy walked the length of the gloomy hall to the kitchen and caught the smell of his da as he passed a bedroom. Glancing in, he saw him dozed on a bed with *The Daily Mirror* open on the racing page and spread across his chest. His da's smell wasn't that strange, it wasn't that unique. Davy associated it with most men over forty; with wire-hard chin stubble, fat stomachs, porter farts and dark moist socks.

The kitchen was tight, packed, and the utilities ran round the wall: electricity for the fridge, gas for the cooker, water for the taps. To the side of the sink sat a large cupboard behind which was the kitchen window. All the windows in all the flats were of standard size, about five feet by three. They were impressive because of the drop which lay beyond them. Davy had sometimes experienced a fear of standing too close, in case not only the window fell out but the rest of the wall too, taking him with it. It was a secret fear, illogical, terrifying, embarrassing, but real enough not to risk it when the danger threatened.

Jojo had left uneaten on the table half a plateful of baked beans, a half-eaten piece of toast, an unfinished mug of tea. The table wasn't so big as the kitchen small, so only two people at a time had room to eat there. His mother liked that table. When her sister visited, it was where they sat and drank sherry.

Davy walked from the kitchen to the living room and out on to the balcony which gave a view from the rear of the block. To his left, Silloge Avenue, the four storey flats, and between him and them a tarmacadam football pitch, scorched by fires and littered by broken glass. Ahead he could see Pinewood and Glasnevin, private houses whose residents had built a seven-foot wall to deny access to the people from the flats. It wasn't enough and hundreds of trees and thick bushes augmented the intention. It seemed if the people from Glasnevin couldn't see the flats, they could pretend they didn't exist, though the flats did their best to taunt. In front of the foliage, a seven-foot high wire fence had been erected and ran the length of the perimeter of the estate—just in case.

Davy looked down on the Berlin wall and smiled as a few kids jumped the wire, darted through the bushes and climbed and dropped into Pinewood. They were about ten or eleven years old. He had made similar excursions when he was that age, with Mickey and other kids. They would go over the wall in gangs of four or five, bully kids, rob apples, shout obscenities at women. Sometimes the police were called, but they usually got away.

He laughed, remembering another time. About five of them again. They all took turns to shit into a sheet of newspaper, which must have taken them a couple of hours. When they were ready, they wrapped it like a parcel and then all sat on the wall, except one. He took the paper to a doorstep they could all see and set it alight, before banging on the door and running back to the others. A man came to investigate the commotion and saw the burning paper. It was wrapped tight, so the flames were low. Instinctively he stamped and jumped on it, trying to extinguish the flames before they could mark his tiles. The shit squirted everywhere. The boys, they laughed so hard they almost pissed themselves, and Lar Dempsey fell off the wall and broke his arm.

Poor Lar. He could whistle through the gap in his front teeth but he was never lucky. He was the one who got caught, about a year later, when they had matured enough to snatch handbags. Because they were new to it, they snatched one just inside Pinewood. Davy grabbed the bag and threw it to Mickey. As he caught it, Davy was passing him and heading for the wall. Mickey threw the bag to Lar and followed Davy. A man who had been passing saw what happened and began to make chase. The woman whose handbag it was stood frozen, shocked, where they had robbed her. As Davy sat astride the wall and dragged Mickey up he saw the man moving faster and faster. He was going after Lar, the smallest, the slowest, the most frightened and vulnerable of the three. Lar had already thrown the bag over the wall, so Davy dropped, picked it up and headed for the wire. Once on the other side, he waited for Mickey who was already climbing. Somehow, maybe Mickey had dragged him up, Lar had gotten over the wall. But so too had the man. He had a hold of a passive Lar by the hair and was dragging him back towards the bushes. Mickey was screaming, "For fucksake." He had caught his shirt, where the wire was nailed to a concrete post. In his haste, he ripped it from the trap and jumped. Davy was still waiting, holding the bag, and what happened to Mickey delayed them long enough for him to see what happened next.

Mickey was already running hard when Davy went after him. He didn't catch up until Mickey ran into the flats on Sandyhill Avenue. They sat on the stairs while they caught their breath and Davy asked him, "Did yeh see wha' happened?"

"It wasn't my fault," said Mickey, "I got him up on the wall. It was up to him after tha'. We probably should've fucked the bag back, he might rat on us now."

"No, I mean did yeh see wha' the oul' fella done?"

"Wha'?"

"He pulled Lar's trousers down and started to ride him."

Mickey laughed, in disbelief.

The next time they saw Lar, all he would say was that he got away, "And anyways, if youse had of given back the bag he wouldn't have tried an'thin'." He asked them not to tell anyone, in case it got back to his da. They promised they wouldn't .

They kept their secret, for a couple of years. Until they started drinking Special Brew and popping sodium amytal, and sitting around fires in fields. Then Davy would taunt him. Nobody else who sat around the fires paid much attention to what was going on. They got bored with it. Lar always denied it, until one night he jumped up and shouted, "If you're so sure wha' happened, then the same thing must've happened to you."

Poor Lar. He died a couple of years ago. A stolen car he was joyriding collided with a wall and burst into flames. A rumour went round at the time that he crashed it on purpose, because he made Elvis Ruddell get out of the car just before it happened.

Davy went back into the living room. No matter how long, or how short a time he spent in prison, he always felt the same effect. It was the tension; it strained him, exhausted him. He sat in an armchair and dozed. The combination of the tiredness and the Diconal encouraged a narcosis, and this he welcomed by struggling against it, by resisting it. It made the experience all the more pleasurable. The final surrender was graced by a childlike glee. For a while. And then he resisted its desertion. So soon? He struggled to hold on to it, to keep it, dreamland. He was losing it, and he needed more.

When his ma returned from work, her tired, bony hands tightened into a knot when she saw Davy dozing on the chair. She tried not to wake him, but as if he had read her thoughts he opened his eyes and rubbed them aggressively. "How a'yeh, Ma? Listen, I'm in a hurry, have yeh got me money?"

"When did yeh get out, Davy?"

"Today, Ma. Where's me money?" He asked again, suspicious.

"I don't know, Davy, it's gone," she told him, and raising her hands to her ears she began to walk away.

"Wha' d'yeh mean, it's gone? Seven hundred fuckin' pounds? Gone?" He followed her to the kitchen. "Wha' happened? If tha' bastard's after drinkin' it or losin' it on the horses, I'll fuckin' kill him."

"Don't go near him, Davy, he's not well. And anyway, it wasn't him."

"Then who was it?"

"I don't know, Davy, but I'd know if your da had £700 or an'thin' like it."

"It had to be tha' Jojo, then. That's why he legged it when I came in," said Davy, more to himself than his ma. He snatched his jacket and left, slamming the door.

His ma went to the landing and screamed after him, "Tha's all I need now, one of me sons murderin' another one. Jaysis! Wha' did I do to deserve a life like this?"

Davy didn't hear her. She had been asking the same question for as long as he could remember and he had stopped trying to answer her a long time ago. All he could think of was the money. Seven hundred quid and the bastard wasn't even stoned when he saw him. This meant there was none left. Jaysis. Breen charged seven and a half quid for each dike so he would need another £22.50, just to get the three he had asked him to hold. He didn't want to think about the £30 he already owed him.

His anger began to engulf him, when someone on a motorbike stopped beside Davy and asked if he was only out. With his rage edging ever closer to violence, it was with a mixture of regret and jittery relief that Davy realised who it was.

"How a'yeh, Mickey? I got out this mornin'. Have yeh seen Jojo?"

"No," said Mickey, "I haven't, why?"

"The bastard robbed £700 on me, when I was locked up," Davy said, like he was close to tears.

Mickey Hughes started to laugh. He was the only person who could do this with Davy and not suffer a consequence. They had thieved together since childhood, progressing from petty shoplifting to violent robberies. There wasn't much about the other that either of them took personally, though when he realised that Davy wasn't finding anything funny, Mickey said to him, "C'mon, if it's a bit of gear yeh want, I'll get yeh some."

Davy explained the situation with Breen to Mickey.

"That's strange," said Mickey, "I've just scored off him and he told me it was his last seven."

"He oney says tha' in case you're thinkin' of robbin' him. How much money have yeh?"

"Abou' £270," said Mickey. "Why, how much d'yeh want?"

"Jaysis, I hope it wasn't you who robbed me," Davy joked. "Gimme a ton."

Mickey laughed again, took a bundle from his pocket, and peeling off ten notes he handed them to Davy. "I'll run yeh over to Breen's if yeh want."

"Where can we go for a turn on?"

"I have a gaff over in Balcurris."

"Things are lookin' up," said Davy, grinning. He hopped on to the back of the Enduro and they sped off.

At Breen's, Mickey waited at the bottom of the flats with the bike, while Davy ran up the stairs again and successfully negotiated another ten dike.

"That's seventeen between us," said Mickey, when Davy told him the news.

"Yeah," said Davy, "nine for me and eigh' for you," before throwing his leg over the motorbike.

When Mickey parked the bike, he told Davy that the flat was on the seventh floor.

"Aw fuck tha', I'm not walkin' up any more stairs."

"It's okay," said Mickey. "The caretaker in this block is sound, he cleans the lift every day."

It wasn't Davy's idea of clean, but at least they didn't retch from the stench of stale piss. That smell had been disguised by a daily saturation of cheap disinfectant. It hadn't been scrubbed out, just poured over the top, functioning the way a deodorant might on an unwashed armpit. Both exhaled eagerly, inhaled deeply, and spat over the balcony as they left the lift.

Davy was impressed with the flat. The only furniture inside was a double bed with a spare mattress and a fridge. Because of the emptiness, it looked clean. After he had shown Davy around, Mickey got everything they would need for their fix. They decided to use five dike each and to try to keep the rest for the following day.

They went through the same routine Davy had gone through that morning. He went first again, but this time he got so stoned, Mickey had to take the syringe from his groin and stop the bleeding as best he could, before having his own fix. Both then goofed, drifted, each to his own separate, secret world, sometimes opening their eyes, and constantly scratching and rubbing their noses. It was a while before they could talk and make reasonable sense.

"I was sure yeh made a statement, Mickey, when yeh got bail and I didn't."

"For fucksake, Davy, yeh know I haven't made a statement since I was abou' twelve."

"It was easier to believe tha' when I got out. But yeh know wha' it's like when you're locked up. The longer I was in there, the worse I began to think. It didn't help that the only appearance we made together was the first one."

"Tha' was just tha' O'Toole bastard bein' smart. He was tryin' to freak yeh out into makin' a statement, or even worse, pleadin' guilty."

"I know tha' now," said Davy, "but I didn't know it then, especially when yeh didn't visit."

"Did yeh get the gear I sent up."

"Yeah, every week. I'd've been fucked without it," said Davy, and the memory shifted his attention from how bad it was, to how bad it might have been.

"D'yeh want to use the rest of them dike now?"

"No, leave them till in the mornin'. We'll go for a pint instead."

"Alrigh'," said Mickey, "I'm nearly finished rollin' this joint anyway, so we can smoke it on the way over. I'm leavin' the bike here though. I goofed off on it the other nigh', and nearly went up the arse of a parked bleedin' truck."

Davy laughed as he stood to put on his jacket. As they walked and shared the joint, Mickey gave Davy some of the local gossip:

who was riding who and who was robbing who. Davy completely forgot about Jojo.

They went to the upstairs lounge, because it was only ever busy at weekends and childrens allowance day, they knew it should be quiet enough to have a chat. As soon as they sat down, a young waitress came over and took their order.

"A pint of Harp?" Mickey asked. Davy nodded. "Two pints of Harp."

When she went off to get them Davy, continuing the gossip, asked casually, "Is Tony Nolan still doin' the smack from his gaff in Coultry?"

"No, I forgot to tell yeh, he fucked off to London abou' a week ago."

"Why? I thought he was doin' well."

"He was. But he kept gettin' robbed. He got really fucked off with it the last time, when he got fourteen stitches across the chest. The bloke he was gettin' it from in Raheny was fucked off with it too."

"Why didn't he give him any back up?"

"Because he heard it was one of the Sheringham's."

"Which one?"

"Johnny Dazzler."

"The little bastard! I would've fuckin' slaughtered him."

"Yeah, I know, but it's his brother, Georgie, the bloke from Raheny is afraid of. I think he's afraid of his shite of anyone from town."

The waitress came back with their drinks and although she was a local, they both stopped talking, while Mickey paid her. She beamed at him when he gave her a fifty pence tip. As soon as she turned and walked away, Davy impatiently asked, "So, who's doin' the gear now?"

Mickey, smiling after the waitress, said, "Wha'? Oh there's a bloke doin' it in the next block to Tony Nolan's. Mick Murtagh. Do yeh know him? He's from Cabra."

"I never heard of him," said Davy. "D'yeh fancy robbin' him in the mornin'?" he smiled.

"Bollix! He's doin' it for Georgie Sheringham," Mickey grinned back.

"Fuck me! So Georgie sent Johnny Dazzler out to give Nolan a few digs, just to see wha' the bloke from Raheny would do?"

"I haven't a clue, but that's the way it is now, and tha' Murtagh bloke is cleanin' up," said Mickey.

"Jaysis," Davy sighed. "And every week we risk five fuckin' year just to give it to wankers like tha'. We're in the wrong game, Mickey."

"Yeah, I know. But wha' the fuck can yeh do?"

"Start sellin' the bleedin' gear," Davy told him.

"Yeah," said Mickey, "that's a fuckin' great idea. We wouldn't last a couple of days without Sheringham and a firm from town comin' out here and lashin' us out of it."

"I done eighteen months with Sheringham, and he's only a wanker," said Davy, tasting the opportunity.

"And who's goin' to lay gear on us to get us started?"

"Wha' abou' your man from Raheny?"

"Are yeh mad? He's your man from Raheny, not your man from Del Monte. And even if he did, tha' would oney be a couple of grams. We'd use tha' in a couple of days, without sellin' any."

"I suppose so," said Davy, and sensing that Mickey was beginning to think he was talking like this because he was stoned, Davy decided to entertain the idea of selling heroin, privately. He knew however that he could explore how to finance it by approaching it from a different route. "D'yeh have any work lined up?"

"Yeah," said Mickey, "Skinnier Martin reckons he has a snatch lined up from the bank in Whitehall. We're goin' to do it Tursda'."

"Skinnier Martin?" Davy laughed, but before Mickey could explain, Davy asked him how much it was for, and how they were going to do it.

Mickey hesitated. He wondered if he had been a fool to believe Skinnier. "He reckons there's about six grand in it." When Davy didn't laugh, he went on. "An oul' fella comes from a pub near the bank twice a week, Monda's and Tursda's, and does a drop. He always changes his times on the Monda's, probably because he has the weekend takin's. But he goes at the same time every Tursda'." When Davy still didn't laugh, Mickey went on, "The fuckin' eejit goes into the back of the bank too, so we can take him there, without anyone seein' us from the main road. All we have to do is follow him from the pub."

"Tell Skinnier you're doin' it with me," said Davy.

"Jaysis, Davy, it's his stroke, and you'll get a whack from it anyway. He migh' set us up, if we cut him out."

"D'yeh see wha' I mean, Mickey? Yeh think he migh' set us up and yet you're goin' to go out robbin' with him. All he's ever snatched in his poxy life is a few handbags."

"Alrigh', alrigh'. I'll ask him."

"Lookit, Mickey, just tell him. Tell him yeh can't fit three on a bike. Tell him yeh oney stroke with me. Tell him I got out today. Tell him we'll give him a third of the money. By the way, wha' time does the oul' fella make the drop at?"

"I don't know," said Mickey. "Skinnier told me he would tell me Tursda' mornin'. He's cute enough for tha'."

"We better find out tomorrow, in case he goes into one and decides to do it with someone else," said Davy.

Mickey, resigned to the new arrangements, nodded his consent.

Davy needed a break, needed time to think, to absorb the information he had just heard, so they played some pool. Mickey was high spirited and fooled about. Davy was intense and preoccupied. He soon bored with the game and asked Mickey if he wanted to return to the flat in Balcurris.

"D'yeh not want to hang on and get a couple of birds, first nigh' out and all tha'?" Mickey smiled.

"No, I don't feel up to it," said Davy.

"Don't feel up to it? Sure you'd be goin' all nigh' on them dike."

"That's wha' I mean," said Davy, "and anyway, the only fanny in this place is those two oul' wans over there and I don't fancy them."

Mickey glanced over at two women in their early fifties. Both wore a slash of bright red lipstick and a layer of thick deep face powder, and sat in black-brown imitation mahogony chairs with deep red seating beneath framed posters of big-breasted models holding Martinis, sucking bright red cherries through brighter red lips and with expressions of either orgasmic anticipation or satisfaction. "Well I'm hangin' on. You're a model to get a couple in the chipper, when the pub closes. D'yeh want me to bring one back to yeh?" he offered.

"Wha' you'd pick up? Fuck off! Gimme me your key though and I'll wait up and let yeh in."

"There's no need to, I have another one. Take the spare mattress and sleep in another room," said Mickey, handing the key to Davy.

"Okay, if yeh wake before me in the mornin', call me, and we can use them dike then."

"Three and a half each?" Mickey asked.

"Fuck it then, three and a half each," smiled Davy, and he swallowed the end of his drink before leaving the pub.

When Davy got back to the flat he was tired and stoned, but he didn't want to sleep just yet. There were too many things to sort out. He knew his luck wasn't going to last, not doing desperate snatches and jump overs for drug money. This one on Thursday was going to have to be the last time. Whatever money they got then, they were going to have to use to sell gear. There was no point in trying to buy gear from Sheringham. He would charge them £160 a gram, even if they bought a kilo from him. That left was the bloke from Raheny, who he didn't even know. If he could get him to sell at two grand an ounce, or less, Davy knew he could make money on it. A lot of money. To lessen the risk, he could cut Skinnier Martin in with the money they would owe him from the snatch. And if he wasn't into it, then fuck it, they would rip him off and give him nothing. His plan was full of ifs, yet if they got six grand on Thursday, that would be the biggest If out of the way. He only had to persuade Mickey.

HE KNEW, BEFORE he opened his eyes, and as he felt the spring sun that shone through on to his face. Frowning playfully, he turned on the mattress away from the light, but it didn't really matter if he slept or if he woke. It wouldn't affect the deep warmth he felt, the preciousness of knowing that he wasn't in prison. The feeling grew, it exalted him, it rolled him on to his back again, where he lit a cigarette and switched on an old clock-alarm radio. It was plugged into a socket that hung precariously from its fitting, evidence perhaps that desperate policemen had been here before and had unscrewed the plate from the wall to search behind it.

When the nine-thirty news announced itself, it surprised him. He had slept longer than he expected. But so what.

Still a little hazy from the opiates, he smiled at the memory of the previous day. Until he remembered Deirdre. He remembered he had three and a half dike. He hadn't actually forgotten them, but to acknowledge them helped. To remind himself of the little surprise he had, which wasn't really a surprise at all.

He hadn't heard a sound throughout the night and he began to wonder if Mickey had come back at all. To find out, he stood from the mattress and stepped into his jeans. In the bedroom, Mickey was lying naked on the bed, asleep. Davy noticed the limp, satisfied penis resting on his groin. Beside him, a girl was half covered by a cool sheet which lay on her like a lazy lover, hanging from soft full breasts and gathering between her legs, which had arched and opened to accommodate the crumpled cotton. Davy thought she looked familiar and then remembered who she was. It was the waitress who had served them in the pub the night before. He looked at her hungrily, stared at her. Something appealed to him, gave him an appetite that excited him, the thought of screwing the living bejaysis daylights out of her, without waking her. For her to suspect having had the most wonderful sexual experience she was ever likely to have. To believe it, but not remember. For her to open her eyes, to see him smiling a smile, a self-satisfied smile, that said he would never forget.

He decided he would have his fix before waking Mickey. He would have it in the bedroom where they slept and the idea of this thrilled him too. When he had it prepared and was pulling down his jeans, he noticed the girl had opened her eyes and was focusing on him with increasing bewilderment. He signalled to her not to wake Mickey, by placing his index finger to his lips and shushing. This seemed to terrify her. Having an idea of what she might be thinking, he pulled his jeans back up, picked up his syringe and left the room.

His fix was as pleasurable as those from the previous day. Again it left him crouched forward for a few minutes, tasting the bitter, chugging finale at the back of his throat. The enjoyment was whole, consummate, but never for ever. An experience which bequeathed an overwhelming desire to recreate itself. When he regained some self-control, he went to the bathroom, tidied himself up and cleaned the syringe for Mickey. Washing it was part of the experience and he gave it the kind of reverence a priest might give to the chalice from which he has just served holy communion. By the time Davy returned to the bedroom, the girl was fully dressed and sitting nervously on the edge of the bed. He ignored her and bent down to shake Mickey from his sleep.

"Wake up, Mickey. Wake up."

Mickey opened his eyes and needed a moment to gather his senses. He saw Davy was stoned but before he had time to ask, Davy said, "Here's your pinkies. Listen, I want to go over to me oul' wan's and catch tha' Jojo bastard. When yeh have your turn on and get rid of tha' thing," he said, pausing to nod at the waitress, "give us a shout and we'll go and see Skinnier."

Mickey reddened a little but just said, "Okay, I'll be over in abou' an hour."

"See yeh then," said Davy and he stopped on the way out to pick up his jacket, sniffing it reluctantly, carefully, to make sure it didn't smell of piss.

He left, as he normally did when he was walking, by the front, the quiet side. The rear of the flats were served by access roads, but the front was peaceful and road free. Here, a wide path ran the length of all the four and eight storey blocks, giving the estate its own peculiar privacy. The blocks, Balcurris, Sillogue, Coultry and Shanghan, seemed to ramble and meander at their ease, like the tenants who strolled them, on a morning like this, usually young mothers walking towards the shopping centre with children too young to attend school. These women frequently walked in pairs, if not groups. Their children, who had no tolerance for buggies, would stumble haphazardly and slowly in the same direction. Mothers who walked alone were gossiped about as they passed, as were single men. The conversations, greetings and observations were good humoured and often sounded like songs.

It was this fine, dry morning scene that Davy barged through, barking at brats who wandered into his path. To get to Sillogue from Balcurris took ten minutes. On the way, he passed between the shopping centre and Joseph Plunkett Tower. The seven tower blocks stood like sentinels guarding the central roundabout and shopping centre. These rambled nowhere but skywards. Each had been named after a signatory of the 1916 Republican Declaration of Independence. Davy loved the Irishness of this. He could have been picked up off the floor in hysterics every time he thought of it. Seven, fifteen storey, ninety flat tower blocks, standing as commemorative monuments, in honour of those brave Irish martyrs who died so we all might be free. Free? He wondered what they might think of it. James Connolly, executed in a chair because he was too ill to stand:

"Well, Mr Connolly, no, you don't have to stand up to thank us, we know how proud you must feel, but it is important to us that you know how grateful we all are. What's that, Mr Connolly? You would like to get the bastard by the bollix who. . .?"

At night, Davy thought, to give them credit, the flats had a certain charm, their greyness either darkened sufficiently in shadow, or flattered by internal and external electrical light. Each of the seven tower blocks had an aerial crowned by a sharp red, ever-lit bulb. Local intelligentsia said that these, because of the proximity of the flats to Dublin airport, were there to act as a beacon and warn pilots of the danger. Local comedians said they gave any kamikazes who might be in the area something to aim at.

At night the estate had a certain kind of charm, from a distance, because from a distance was the safest way to be enthralled. If you wanted a closer look, well, strangers needed to be taken by the hand and guided gently, by someone with authority, someone in the know. Someone who could laugh when a television came crashing through a fifth storey window and find it all the more hilarious the closer it came to hitting a passer-by. Someone who could respond with indignant righteousness to the isolated, ascending cries of infants. Someone who could walk through the doors of the pub, with the noise of those cries still ringing in their ears and drink with the infant's owners. Someone who could leave in unison with the rest at closing time and sing out of tune and hear the fear up there, hear clearly the terror that waits in agony for the shouting and the screaming and the punching to begin, because what else could they do? It takes a special kind of love that can be enchanted by this charm and not fuck itself, with a sigh of relief, happily, from the top of the nearest tower block.

When he reached his ma's flat, he used his key to get in and went straight to the bedroom he shared with Jojo. He was lying back flat on his bed, snoring. He stood over him for a moment and felt a rising, surging shame that what lay before him was his brother. Struggling to contain his rage, Davy raised a clenched fist above his head and smashed it straight into Jojo's sheeted stomach. The forcefulness, the shock of the punch, almost jolted him straight to a sitting position, which allowed Davy to grab him by the back of the hair.

"Where's me money, Jojo?" Davy struck him a second time, before he got an answer, stepping back to slap him across the face. "Where's me fuckin' money, Jojo?"

When Jojo could answer he began, "Wha' money. . .?" but when he saw Davy raising his hand again, he quickly said, "Jaysis, Davy, I didn't know it was yours. Well, not until yesterday. And anyway, I oney meant to take £40, but it just kept pilin' up, 'cos I couldn't get a shillin' anywhere, but I'll. . ."

Davy squeezed a tighter grip on the fistful of hair he held. "Listen, yeh hungry cunt, I want all tha' money back by Frida'. If yeh haven't got it by then, well, keep out of me sight and out of this gaff until yeh do get it."

"I'm doin' a stroke tonigh'. . ." Jojo began.

"Just get me me fuckin' money," said Davy, and he flung Jojo's head towards a wall on the other side of the bed. Davy felt uneasy as he walked away, but ever a master of self-persuasion, through the medium of blame, he thought, Fuck it. He shouldn't have robbed it on me in the first place and he'll only do it again if I let him get away with it.

Davy's father and younger brothers were still in bed, but his mother had gone to work. This agitated him too, as it meant he would have to make his own cup of tea.

Not long after he finished his first cup, Mickey arrived. They boiled another pot and with the others still in bed, sat down to talk in some peace.

"Did yeh see Jojo?" Mickey asked. "Or have I just missed him leavin' in an ambulance?"

Davy frowned with mock disapproval and said, "He's still in bed. I just gave him a few slaps."

"Wha' did he do with your £700?"

"Wha' do yeh think he done with it? It all went up his poxy arm."
Just to mention it sent Davy back into a spin. "C'mere," he said to
Mickey, "did yeh get a bike yet for this snatch?"

"No. We were goin' to get one tomorrow."

"Righ', then. Me and you'll get one in town and leave it in
Chuckles' shed for the nigh'. We can give him a score."

"Fair enough," said Mickey. "Do yeh want to go and see Skinnier
now or d'yeh want to get a bit of smack for a turn on?"

"Wha' d'yeh want a bit of smack for? Yeh oney had a turn on an
hour ago."

"I still have a few bob left and yeh know wha' them fuckin' dike
are like when you're comin' down off them."

"We have to take things easy for a while," said Davy. "I have a
few ideas yeh migh' like, if this thing comes off on Tursda'."

"Aw, for fucksake! You're not still goin' on abou' bein' a drugs
baron, are yeh?"

"Wait until after Tursda' and we'll talk abou' it then. C'mon and
we go over and see if we can get hold of this Skinnier."

A sideways glance showed Mickey a self-assurance on Davy's pale,
chiselled face, and a purpose in his green-blue eyes. His manner
carried the confidence of someone who has backed the winner in a
race, but still pretends he awaits the result.

As they walked towards Skinnier's, Davy talked about the crude
and lewd time he had with the waitress that morning, while Mickey
was still sleeping.

"Yeh did alrigh'," smiled Mickey. "She told me yeh were just
abou' to get in beside us when she woke up."

Davy tried to explain through his own laughter, but it was
Mickey's turn to tease. He talked about the possible effects on Davy
of having spent the last two months in Mountjoy prison. They were
still laughing and joking when they got to Skinnier's. His ma
answered their knock. When she realised who they were, she asked
them abruptly what they wanted.

"Is Skinnier there, Mrs Martin?" Davy asked her.

"James has gone into town today, to sign on," she replied.

Davy and Mickey looked at each other, before Davy said, "Well,
can yeh tell James to come over and see me in the snooker hall when

he gets back. Me oul' fella migh' have a job for him."

Mickey began to giggle. Mrs Martin muttered something. She knew as well as Davy, his da had never done a day's work in his life. When Davy hinted he wasn't quite sure what she said, by pointing his ear to her, she stated firmly, "Tha's righ'," and slammed the door in their faces.

Davy and Mickey preferred playing pool in the long wide snooker hall, dark from the neck up and the waist down, because it wasn't too hard to be good at it. They usually played for small stakes and whoever lost never seemed to get round to paying the other their debt. They were in the middle of a "doubles or quits" game when Skinnier arrived, swaggering with a fragile cockiness.

"For fucksake! Wha' did yeh say to me ma?"

"Listen, James, we oney asked were yeh in," said Mickey.

Skinnier cringed and quickly asked Mickey, "Did yeh want to see me abou' tha' other thing?"

"Yeah," said Mickey.

"Well listen, I met a bloke I know in town today and he said he'd rob a bike for us."

Davy threw a knowing glance to Mickey which said, "See wha' I mean." He butted in and asked Skinnier, "How many people have yeh told abou' this?"

"None, well oney Mickey."

"Yeh won't be doin' the stroke on Tursda'," Davy told him, as he turned, bent and slam-potted a shot.

When Skinnier began to complain, Mickey explained to him that he would still receive a third of whatever money they got.

"Don't worry, lads," he said. "I know wha' yeh mean. I suppose three's a crowd and all tha', but don't forget, if there's an'thin' yeh can think of tha' yeh want me to do, just say the word."

"Wha' time does the oul' fella go to the bank at?" Davy asked, between shots.

"Oh, between ten to and five to eleven," said Skinnier, and getting excited he told them how he had sussed the stroke. "Me aunty works there."

"Wha' kind of fuckin' aunty would go round sayin' things like tha'?" Mickey asked.

"I was at a weddin' with her a little while ago and she was pissed. She told me her boss was a stingy bastard. Then she told me abou' the drops and tha' she hoped he got robbed one day. I've checked it out for the last couple of Tursda's and she's righ'."

"There's one thing I want yeh to know, Skinnier," said Davy, after he had missed a shot. "If you get a pull when we do this and then we get reefed, I'll hurt yeh."

"Jaysis, Davy! Tell him wha' I'm like, will yeh, Mickey?"

"He knows wha' you're like."

"Once yeh understand me," said Davy, with a disturbingly casual shrug, "then it's not a problem."

"Aw I know wha' yeh mean," said Skinnier. "I'd be the same. D'yeh want me to sort out the bike with your man?"

"No, it doesn't matter, we have one," said Mickey.

"Nice one then, nice one. Will yeh gimme a shout when yeh get back?"

"Sure," said Mickey.

Skinnier had left a prescription for his mother's leg ulcer at the chemist shop and had been told it would take fifteen minutes to prepare. He couldn't tell them about the prescription because he knew how funny they would find it, how funny they would find him. So he left saying, "Well, places to go, people to see, yeh know wha' it's like, lads." He didn't like staying in the presence of Davy Byrne for any longer than he had to. There was something about him, about the way he could look at you and make you feel like it was only a matter of time.

Mickey and Davy left shortly after Skinnier and went round to the local cafe for something to eat. Both ordered sausage and chips. They disguised the quality of the food with excessive ketchup. As they were eating, a solidly built man walked in and came over to them.

"How is it goin', Mickey? How is it goin', Davy? Did yeh just get out?"

"I got out yesterday," said Davy. "Wha' a'yeh up to yourself? Collectin' the rent?"

Tony Freeny laughed. He was a criminal past active robberies, who now lived on a pension of money he hustled from younger thieves. "No. Not today. I spotted the two of yis through the window, so I just thought I'd say hello." He noticed Davy's bloodshot eyes, the pinned pupils. "Jaysis, look at yeh. I thought yeh would have given tha' shit up when yeh were in the Joy."

Annoyed that the effects had worn off while the evidence was still apparent, Davy said, "Just a bit to celebrate, yeh know how it is."

"Not really, but it's your life. Listen, I have to fuck off now. If yeh want to drop up to the pub later on, I'll buy yeh a couple of pints and I might even have a bit of work lined up for yeh," Freeny told Davy.

"I have a couple of things to do meself," said Davy, "but if I get a chance, I'll drop up."

Freeny wished them both good luck and Mickey and Davy looked at him enviously as he left. "A bit of work!" said Davy. "He probably wants me to murder someone for a tenner."

"I'm not lookin' forward to him puttin' the hammer on us after the stroke."

"The only hammer that'll come between him and us," said Davy, putting his fork across Mickey's plate to stop him eating, "is the hammer I'll give him across the bleedin' head."

Mickey tried to whistle, to mock how impressed he was, but only succeeded in spitting a few potato crumbs on to Davy's food.

"Aw, for fucksake, mind me dinner will yeh?"

Mickey blushed, embarrassed, but then found it hysterically funny. The laughter, infectious, soon had Davy laughing uncontrollably too and the flushed plump woman behind the counter was convinced they were mad druggies who were laughing at images no one else could see.

When they finished eating, they decided to wash down the food with a pint. After they had been served, they sat away from the counter and began discussing Thursday's stroke again.

"Wha' kind of bike will we get this time?" Mickey asked.

"A fuckin' fast one," joked Davy.

"You never stopped moanin' about the last one I got, so you pick this time."

"I dunno, somethin' ligh' and quick. We'll see wha' we can pick up in town."

"A'yeh goin' to pump the ignition?"

"No! Just fuck someone off and make sure we get the keys. If it cuts out on me, I'll be able to start it straigh' away."

Almost as an afterthought, Mickey said, "I'm not mad abou' small ligh' bikes. If we get a chase we could come off it in an act. Do yeh not think we should use somethin' like an Enduro?"

"Lookit, Mickey, we'll have to get from Whitehall to Ballymun pronto, like before your man starts screamin', do yeh know wha' I mean? And somethin' small and zippy will do it quicker."

Mickey wasn't driving so he didn't argue. They discussed which route to take back to Ballymun. They also decided they would go to the flat in Balcurris. Davy could drop him there with the money and then use the back roads at St Margaret's to drive to Finglas and dump the bike. They didn't dwell on the possibility of being caught, believing it bad luck.

Although they spent the rest of the day together, Davy wasn't good company. Mickey wondered, though didn't quite believe, that he may have been having doubts about the stroke. Worst of all, he insisted that they didn't take any more drugs that day. And there were no doubts. Had there been, it wouldn't have mattered. Nothing was going to stop him doing the stroke now. This was one of those occasions when it was too late to change his mind. One of those times where a right or wrong move didn't apply. One of those moments that would irrevocably determine the direction his life was about to take. It thrilled him, the pivotal tension that separated something he was convinced of from the unknown.

He could think of nothing else. It would be the Last Time. Once he had the money, he would use it properly. He knew what to do with it. This was what had been niggling him for the past two months. No wonder he hadn't sussed it. How could he? He didn't know about Tony Nolan. He didn't know about Georgie Sheringham. The penny hadn't dropped. He couldn't see the opportunity that was waiting, patiently, staring him in the face. Jaysis! He just needed the fucking money. Then . . . then? Then he would shout check . . . *CHECK CHECK CHECK, MISTER. I've hit the fucking jackpot.* Then he could buy the gear. And sell the gear. And make so much fucking money. At 21. Hmm, laugh all the way to, well you never know these days, could live to be a hundred. And no more tearing around the city on motorbikes for poxy peanuts. But no mistakes. One mistake and he was fucked. Risks? Yeah, risks would make him his fortune. It would pay for his ticket out. And Jaysis help anyone that got in his way.

IT WAS NEVER a serene affair, when they went robbing. There was nothing professional about it. The usual drama occurred; the robbery couldn't have taken place without it.

They had ridden into the city centre on Mickey's motorbike and parked it just off Parnell Street. The reckless part of their performance had been agreed already: to take a bike at the traffic lights on the corner of Upper Abbey Street and O'Connell Street. Davy would then drop Mickey back at Parnell Street, before racing out to Chuckles. If they had to hang around any longer than a couple of minutes, they would move to a different set of lights.

"Jaysis, Davy, we should have got a bit of gear this mornin', or at least last nigh'."

"Wha'? And come in stoned? For fucksake, Mickey, I told yeh we're goin' to have to cut down on the gear. It's time to box clever now, try and see a bit further than the end of your nose, d'yeh know? A hit this mornin' might cost yeh the money we're goin' to get tomorrow. That's an expensive fuckin' turn on."

"Well I'm dyin' bleedin' sick now. The last poxy turn on I had was them three and a half dike yesterday mornin'."

"It was the last one I had as well and I'm not moanin'."

"You haven't got the same habit."

"Lookit, we'll get a quarter each when we get back to the Mun, but that's all, until after the snatch tomorrow."

"That's all I wanted before we came in to get the bike."

"For the love of fuck, Mickey, will yeh shut up? Yeh oney have to wait until we get back, maybe another hour?"

The sparring continued as they walked and it was a captivating sight, Mickey walking with the enthusiasm of someone who knew he was heading in the wrong direction, Davy like he was being restrained by an inadequate leash. Both of them side by side. It took them down Marlborough Street. If you had been sitting on the steps of the Pro-Cathedral you might, without hearing what it was they said, have seen it was the exchanges which moved them. Davy would have moved nowhere, had he no one to drag. Mickey the same, had he no one to drag him.

At the Pro-Cathedral they turned right and walked towards O'Connell Street. There they crossed to the opposite side and went on to Abbey Street. As they approached Easons, Davy couldn't believe his luck. "Quick, Mickey, look, look." A bike like the type they wanted had just braked at the front of the traffic lights. It was an RD-350.

The change was beautiful, frightening. It was like witnessing two forces intent on collision suddenly converge and swoop rapidly, knowingly and with an arrogance to leave you breathless. They ran, as if to cross the road before the lights changed. Both had enough sense to delay at the corner and look down Abbey Street to make sure there were no uniformed police, or anyone resembling a plainclothes officer, in sight. Mickey shoulder-charged the motor-cyclist, who landed on the bonnet of a car that had pulled up beside him. By then, Davy had his helmet on and was picking up the bike, as Mickey was putting on his helmet and at the same time screaming at both drivers, "Stay where yeh are. Stay where yeh fuckin' are. Stay there."

The lights dropped to green, but with Mickey on the back and nothing to obstruct him, Davy would have taken them anyway. It was never a Secure Time, the precise moment of the offence. As he turned left, back into O'Connell Street, he hoped there were no bravery-badge seekers about. Once he passed Henry Street, the traffic he had weaved through would obscure the view from the scene of the crime and the only help a witness might be in a position to offer the investigating Gardaí would be a scratch of the back of a baldy, scabby head and the comment, "Yeh wouldn't be up to them, would yeh? Wha?"

Davy had the bike in third gear when they reached the turning for Cathal Brugha Street. Again the lights were green and, certain no one was following him, he sped around to where Mickey's bike was parked, braked for a moment and took off again with Mickey's leg still hip high in the air. All he wanted to do was get to Ballymun as quickly as possible. On the last couple of minutes of the journey, with the adrenaline deserting him and nerves taking over, he kept expecting to hear the call of sirens. There were none and when he reached Chuckles', he half hoped that Mickey was right behind him. But he wasn't.

Davy put the bike in the shed at the bottom of the back garden and walked up the path to knock at the garden door. When Chuckles opened the door, Davy told him, "I've left a bike in the shed and I'll need it in the mornin'. Is a score alrigh'?"

"Sure, no problem," Chuckles replied.

Davy handed him £20 and said, "Listen, Mickey's followin' me on his own bike but he must have got stopped at a ligh'. Do yeh mind if I wait in your gaff for him?"

"No, not at all. Come in. Do yeh want a cup of tea or somethin'?" Chuckles asked.

"No," said Davy, looking at the can of Pils in Chuckles' hand. "He should be here in a minute."

When he was a boy, Chuckles wanted to be a dustbin man when he grew up, because he thought they only worked one day a week. Now he did the next best thing: he didn't work at all, but he made enough to get by.

Five minutes later, when Mickey hadn't arrived, Davy asked for a cup of coffee. Before the kettle had boiled, Davy heard the comforting sound of Mickey's bike pulling up and spluttering at the end of the garden.

"It's okay, don't worry about the coffee," Davy told Chuckles, before walking out.

"Jaysis, I thought yeh were reefed."

"Reefed? I was nearly fuckin' crippled. When we said I was gettin' dropped at the bike, I didn't think it meant from a heigh'. Yeh left me two feet in the fuckin' air and I landed on me arse. I hope yeh don't drive like tha' tomorrow," said Mickey, to Davy's laughter.

"Yeh never know," said Davy, "yeh migh' end up hopin' I do. C'mon, let's get a bit of gear."

MICKEY GRIPPED THE blackjack familiarly and with each push used it to slap the palm of his left hand. It was a prized possession, his pride and joy, and although three years old, it still fit his hand like a glove. Arthur, the ex-mercenary (so he said) and saxophonist with The Sinking Dublin Blues Band, who Mickey had met in The Meeting Place, had crafted it for him, in exchange for a quarter ounce of dope. Arthur had measured Mickey's grip on an old chair leg and returned a week later with a quarter pound of lead, cased with rubber, that pouched comfortably in a wrist-strapped, smooth-finished jacket of leather. It was small, sleek and discreet and he loved the surprise it carried when a victim braced themselves for a punch to the head; the look on their face, just before the lights went out; the shock and nowhereness in the eyes, before the slow inevitable slump.

Pressing his forearms down on to his thighs, he pushed again. This achieved nothing, apart from an acidic bubble. It was his second visit to the toilet that morning and the only thing left to excrete was the fear. Gently, he picked up and moved back his scrotum before peering down into the obscure pool, where a few empty pea shells floated close together. With an air of acceptance, he dropped his scrotum back into space, rolled the blackjack on to the floor and tore a few sheets from the toilet roll, which sat patiently at his feet. Having folded them neatly, he hunched upwards slightly and ran his hand along the crack of his arse. The paper scuffed, ooh, the inside tip of his hole, which because of his exertions had failed to recede properly. Grinding his teeth, he raised his hand and examined the pathetic, cigarillo thin stain with a one drop pinhead splash of blood. Pessimistically, he carried the paper to his face and sniffed. Nah! There wasn't enough for this connoisseur's nose to determine the state of his health. Years of practice, with a suitable sample, had enabled him to distinguish fear from food poisoning, withdrawal from maintenance, and malnourishment from a good old-fashioned, roughage-packed shite.

That day was a fear day, although Mickey wanted to believe that the drug-free periods, which Davy began to impose, had contributed to the frequent bowel movement. Both had been up long enough to chain-smoke their way through twenty Major before they left to go over to Chuckles' to collect the bike. But once they began to move, the fear changed features. There is nothing quite like the power of intent, especially as it gathers momentum, and to these young intenders this meant with a manner of intolerant confidence.

First stop was a garage in Santry, where they bought some petrol. With enough in the tank, they moved on to the garage in Whitehall, which gave them a view of the pub. Because they were a few minutes early, Davy got off the bike at the garage air pumps and bent down to examine the back wheel. Mickey stood beside him, glancing across at a purple Volvo estate parked in the car park of the public house. After a minute or so, Mickey noticed a garage employee, dressed in mechanics overalls, walking towards them. He prodded Davy's foot with the toe of his boot. They both still wore helmets, a cause for suspicion.

"Are yis alrigh', lads?" the mechanic asked.

"Yeah," said Davy, "me back wheel was a bit flat. I've put some air in it and I'm waitin' to see if it's punctured."

"Wouldn't yeh be better off drivin' it to find tha' out?"

"I suppose you're righ'," said Davy, and to Mickey's surprise, he got back on the bike and switched on the ignition. He circled the forecourt a couple of times and then came back. "I think it's alrigh' now. C'mon, Pat," he said to Mickey.

The purple Volvo was pulling out of the car park and on to the road. Neither acknowledged the mechanic before driving off. It was a short journey to the bank, so they stayed a couple of cars back, almost stopping when the Volvo indicated to turn left to give the driver time to park. When they drove around, he had just got out from his car and was carrying a briefcase.

Oliver Hanratty looked nervously at them, but only for a moment, because they drove on the opposite side to where he had parked. He seemed the last thing in the world they were interested in. Perhaps they worked in one of the . . . oh it didn't matter anyway. He was always this nervous when banking the takings and nothing ever happened. Jesus, he thought, as walked around the back of his car towards the bank, all this worrying would be the death of him. He tried to make up his mind if Dawn Run would win the Gold Cup and how much to have on.

As Hanratty passed the boot of his car, Davy was just about to pass him on the bike, which he had slowed considerably and noiselessly. Mickey dropped off while it was still moving and ran, raising the blackjack, with one eye on the crown of Hanratty's head and the other on the briefcase. As he was bringing the weapon down, Hanratty began to turn and crouch in the same movement and, raising his arm that carried the money, he instinctively tried to protect himself. He didn't quite manage to, but neither did Mickey succeed in hitting him as hard and as accurately as he had hoped. Hanratty went down, but not out, and he managed to pull half of his body beneath the boot of the car. All that remained visible were his legs and his right arm, which still held the briefcase. It lay frozen across the edge of the kerb, his knuckles whitened by the vice like grip he had on the handle.

Mickey took a deep breath, adjusted slightly the helmet on his head and set about with invective and relish the task of relieving Hanratty of the money. He controlled the volume of his voice but not the tone, and with each kick and stamp, cursed and abused the two legs and one arm which hadn't made it beneath the car. For some reason, Hanratty didn't seem interested in pulling the briefcase to cover, but neither would he let go of it. With another deep breath, Mickey decided he would have to get to Hanratty's head.

"Righ', yeh oul' bastard, I'm goin' to fuckin' kill yeh now." He clasped Hanratty's ankles and pulled, spreading his legs as he lifted them towards the air. With each violent attempt to drag him out he kicked viciously into the open groin, but in a see-saw movement Hanratty, clinging to a metal bar beneath the car, managed to pull himself back under. Thwarted in his efforts to get to the head, Mickey hurled the legs to the side and aimed a boot at Hanratty's ribs, but he only succeeded in catching his shin on the bumper.

"Bollix! . . . Okay. That's it. I have a hatchet. D'yeh hear me? I'm goin' to chop the fuckin' hand off yeh."

Still the fist closed firm on the handle of the briefcase.

Removing his helmet, Mickey glanced at Davy, dropped to his knees, and sank his teeth into Hanratty's hand.

Davy sat with the bike revving, a couple of yards from Mickey. Listening for sirens, he began to keep an increasingly alert ear to the main road. By the time Mickey began shouting something about a hatchet, Davy, using his eyes more than his ears, was watching the exit to the cul-de-sac with a growing terror that a flashing blue light would arrive in silence and block their escape. He knew they were almost at desperation point, where madness infects reason, when they know they should leave but don't and that they had reached this point with a scream that he heard behind them. He looked back and saw a hysterical middle-aged woman, leaning from a window above the rear of a shop.

"Leave tha' chap alone. Leave him alone, yis dirty bowsies. I've rang the police yeh know, and they're on their way. They'll be here any minute now. . ."

Davy looked back to Mickey who was still kneeling with his jaw wrapped around the fist. Instantly, frantically, he turned the bike, trundled over the lolling legs and down on to the forearm which lay pressed against the firm leverage of the kerb. The noise from the engine blanketed the sound of the bone snapping, but not the piercing howl, as short as it was loud, which shrieked from beneath the car. When the hand opened on the handle Mickey, who had jumped back like a Jack Russell at the sight of the bike, leapt back in for fear the fingers might close again, and he snatched the case lightningly. Davy had to take the bike out of gear and roll it back over the legs because there wasn't room to turn. As he did so, he noticed the distorted angle of the arm. Mickey was already clambering on to the bike, putting the briefcase between Davy and himself, and when he was on, they drove off.

Soon they were speeding westwards down Collin's Avenue. Davy had the bike travelling at seventy m.p.h., when he spotted a large blue saloon coming on to the avenue from a small link road, blocking his side of the road as it did so. The driver of the car braked when he saw them. Davy was going too fast to brake hard so he attempted to slow the bike, swerving at the final moment to miss the car. A light van coming from the opposite direction had to swerve also, but in doing so mounted the pavement and demolished a garden wall before it sprang back out on to the road. Davy had stopped the bike just in time to avoid being crushed but what he then saw caused him to cry, "Jaysis fuckin' Christ!" The road was blocked. They couldn't pass on the right because the path was covered with the debris from the garden wall. On the left side,

Telecom Eireann had dug a crater in the path and part of the road, and the car and the van, bumper to bumper, blocked the road completely. From somewhere in the distance behind them came the heart-wrenching wail of sirens. To turn and go back looking for an alternative route was impossible, and if he turned into Larkhill they would find themselves cornered.

"Tell the oul' fella in the car to reverse it," Davy shouted at Mickey.

Mickey stepped off the bike and, clinging the briefcase to his chest, had already dropped the blackjack down smoothly from beneath his sleeve into the palm of his hand. He tapped it against his hips to the rhythm of his thoughts. I knew we should have got an Enduro. I just knew it. This poxy piece of piss! Jaysis.

The driver of the saloon had got out and was asking, "Is tha' man alrigh'?" pointing to the driver of the van, who was sitting, traumatised, back in his seat with blood trickling from multiple cuts in his face which had shattered the windscreen.

"Go back and reverse tha' car," Mickey told him.

"We'll have to call an ambulance, son. Tha' man needs an ambulance."

Mickey hit him across the head with the blackjack and helped him crumple by pushing at his chest, before walking to the car and slipping into the driver's side. A woman in her sixties was sitting in the front passenger seat, her decoratively scarfed head and black-gloved hands shaking uncontrollably. Mickey placed the briefcase on her lap, changed the gears to reverse and screeched the car back a few yards. Retrieving the case, he muttered a thanks and got out of the car. It wasn't until then that she began to plead, rising from a whisper to a scream, "Oh Jesus help us, Jesus help us."

Davy couldn't now risk the dual carriageway to Ballymun. Halfway towards it, he took a right turn on to Shanowen Avenue and drove into Santry. At the top of the Avenue, as they reached Shanard Road, they heard a police car wailing towards them from the left, which had been the turn Davy had wanted to take. Their view of the turn to the right was short, obscure, silent and because of these, dangerous and unappealing. Behind them they heard an unmarked Task Force car. The peculiar call of its siren, because of its threat, was particularly familiar. Ahead of them, a group of shops were split by a narrow lane. Davy drove up on the path, sped down the lane and turned right on Shanliss Road. It would help if they had to dump the bike and run through the back gardens. At Shanliss Avenue he turned left and sped to Shanliss Walk, a cul-de-sac with a gap at its walled end, wide enough to allow a bike through. As soon as they got to the other side, they felt some relief, standing on home soil. Although their circumstances were just as dangerous, for a few seconds it felt a like place to resuscitate intent.

Davy continued on for a couple of hundred yards from the gap, across a grass space, and braked. Both were white, almost repentant, with fear.

"Listen, I'm goin' to have to drop yeh here with the money and then I can get rid of the bike," Davy said quickly.

"Ask me arse," said Mickey. "You take the money, and I'll get rid of the bike."

"We haven't time to argue about this. Yeh know I'm better on a bike."

"There isn't tha' much of a difference. And anyway, why do I have to do all the poxy bits?"

"For fucksake! I can see us in court yeh know, and a copper sayin' how he arrested the defendants at the back of Shanghan Gardens, kickin' the shite out of each other."

"Okay. But I'm not walkin' all the way over to Balcurris. Not from here."

"Where are yeh goin' then?"

"I'll go to me sister's instead. Tha' way I'll only have to cross one road."

"Which fuckin' sister?"

"Anne. She got a flat last week in Pearse Tower. I can cut through Shanghan Road and once I get behind the flats I'll be alrigh'." He gave Davy the address. Inside the briefcase, they found three night-safe pouches. Mickey stuffed these into his jacket and dumped the case in some bushes near by before handing his helmet to Davy.

"Wha' the fuck are yeh waitin' for?"

Davy smiled. "Make sure yeh have tha' money counted be the time I get back."

"Go on, yeh gobshite. Fuck off, will yeh?"

Davy slipped his arm through the spare helmet and roared off towards a new housing estate and a short cut to Santry Lane.

Mickey cut through the first block of flats, anxious not to waste time walking around them. From the ground floor balcony, he noticed two Gardaí on motorbikes speeding down Shanghan Road towards where he had just left Davy. Deep down his bowels rumbled heavily, painfully, causing him to clutch at his abdomen in an attempt at restraint. A fucking gee hair was all he missed those coppers by. Still, he had made it to the front of the flats which gave him good cover from the road.

He trotted on and the closer he got to safety, the more his body had begun to shake, his teeth to rattle. Although Anne lived on the eleventh floor, he couldn't wait on the lift. Instead he ran up every flight and was snatching at the steps by the time he reached her landing. His knock was a desperate rap-tap-tatting, much softer and much longer than normal. When it opened he almost fell in the door asking, "Is there anyone with yeh?"

"No, just the baby. Why?"

"Nice one," he said, without answering her. "Lock the door, will yeh," and he went to her kitchen and sat down.

"What's bleedin' happenin', Mickey?"

After lighting and sucking hard on a cigarette he began to mutter and mumble, revealing just enough for her to understand he had been robbing again, and they had almost caught him. He sucked deep, quick successive drags on the cigarette and the smoke his nostrils exhaled enveloped his head as his mind flashed images and memories alike. Click click, one after the other. The heroic, stubbornly clenched fist on the briefcase. Crashed vehicles. Shouts and other sounds, sirens. Panic. That can be heard too and seen, in the space between the mouth and the eyes. It is drilled there, like the pain from eating ice cream too quickly, though it never knows whether to look or to scream and quite often ends up doing neither.

TIME SOMETIMES COMFORTS and always resolves, one way or the other. It arrives at a wry acceptance with a breath of surrender or an irrefutable shrug of the shoulders. This is all there is left to say when the greatest threat has been imagined, the most frightening fear shamelessly exposed. When the question, "Why did I do it?" answers itself with, "Well, it's done now anyway." When the panic moves from the front of the face, to the back of the head and sits there waiting to heckle the trickery of conscience, the illusory explanations that roll from a tongue on the slippery descent to disaster. And what a treacherous journey!

It was past seven that evening by the time Davy arrived at the flat. He had called in briefly to Skinnier Martin on his way and explained that because of the chase, because things hadn't gone according to plan, they were forced to stash the money they got from the stroke and hadn't had time to count it.

"Don't worry abou' it, Davy. Yeh can give us a shout in a couple of days when everythin' cools down. And don't worry abou' me, I'll keep me gob shut, d'yeh know wha' I mean?"

Davy reached Anne's flat, praying everything was all right. She answered his knock. Habitually, like the smooth dash of a Dublin Corporation decorator's paint stroke, he brushed past her, asking, "Is Mickey here?"

As she locked the door, and before she had time to reply, Davy arrived in the living room where Mickey was sprawled across a sofa. He was stoned. All Davy could ask was, "Where's the pouches, Mickey," kicking him gently on the sole of his bare foot which hung over the side of the bottom cushion.

Mickey opened his eyes and looked up. "Jaysis, Davy, I thought yeh were reefed."

"Where's the fuckin' pouches?"

"Don't worry! I took the money out and got Anne to dump them."

"How much was there? How much, for fucksake?"

"Five thousand two hundred . . . in cash. I got Anne to dump the cheques too," said Mickey, smiling.

Davy sat back into a chair. "Jaysis! We done it. Can yeh believe it? We fuckin' done it." He pressed down on the arms of the chair and breathed deeply, in and out, trying to control and direct his elation into one whoosh of feeling, one whistle of success. "Where is it?"

"Here," said Mickey. He pulled out a plastic Superquinn bag from under the cushion beneath his head and flung it to Davy, who dropped six bundles down on to his lap. He picked up two and kissed them, softly. There was one awkward bundle of £200, composed mainly of one and five pound notes. Davy tossed this to Anne. "Here, here's the bill," he said, and he cackled a laugh that carried on the arrogance of pound-note power. A laugh strengthened by the fact that until recently, the money had belonged to someone else.

Mickey, with a deliberate casualness, threw him a small paper packet. "Here's a quarter for yeh. I got Anne to get me a half a gram earlier. I really thought yeh were reefed. Did yeh not see the news on the telly?"

"No, why? Are we famous? The oney thing I've ever been on before is Garda Patrol."

"I wouldn't say we're famous, but we bleedin' will be if we ever get reefed for this."

"There's nobody dead, is there?"

"No, nothin' like tha'."

"Well hang on for a minute until I get this together."

Anne had already torn a strip of foil for Davy. He burned the shiny side with a naked flame and poured the heroin on to the opposite side, the dull side. Again, he ran a flame below the foil, more carefully this time, melting the little hill of powder into a small pool of oil. When he took the flame away, the oil hardened to a sticky substance, which stuck to the foil. Mickey, watching everything with avidity, had a pen-thin tube of foil ready to pass to Davy. He took it from Mickey and repeated the procedure, but this time sucked lightly through the tube the smoke from the simmering oil which flowed along an angled tilt. Lung-full, he sat back in the chair and swallowed the inhalation. When he finally exhaled back through the tube he asked Mickey, "So, wha' was on the news?"

Mickey headlined his reply. "The oul' fella from the van is in a stable but critical condition in hospital. The oul' fella from the pub is in a serious condition in hospital. The oul' fella from the car is bein' kept in overnight for observation. And so is his wife, because she has a bad heart. The Gardaí believe they have recovered the stolen motorbike used in the robbery. They found it in

Finglas . . . ON FIRE. And they have arrested a man from north Dublin, who was helpin' them with their enquiries. That's how I thought yeh were reefed! How come it took yeh so long to get here?"

Davy sucked another deep smoke, as much as his lungs would hold and swallowed it for as long as he could, before exhaling reluctantly. "Well I got to Finglas alrigh'," he told Mickey, as he pushed his nose from side to side. "I torched the bike in a ditch in a field beside the Cappagh. And the helmets, just in case the Filth got them. Then I walked down to the village."

"But tha' must've been before twelve this mornin'."

"Yeah, it was. But I bumped into Carmel Walsh near H. Williams'."

"Aw, so that's it then. Yeh still have a soft spot for her, haven't yeh?"

"Don't be stupid. She's not like tha'. She's gettin' married soon. No, we just went over to the Shamrock for a pint."

"Wha'? Until now?"

"Well, we had a plate of chips durin' the holy hour and then went back to the pub. It was the best thing to do, keep me fuckin' head down. I could oney stomach a few pints anyway, wonderin' whether you had got back or not. And she had to pay for them! I hadn't a shillin' on me, had I? Though I persuaded her to put a tenner on Dawn Run. It won at 15/8. It was a bleedin' model with Jonjo on board. Did yeh see it?"

"No, but it wouldn't have been the most urgent thing on me mind, would it? Anyway, I forgot all abou' it, until I saw the news."

"He was bleedin' deadly he was. Anyway, you got back alrigh' then?"

"Yeah, just abou'. I'd only got to the flats on Shanghan when I seen a couple of speedies pissin' down to the gap. They didn't see me," said Mickey, shivering.

"I called in on Skinnier on the way here too," said Davy. "I told him we'd sort him out in a few days."

"Wha' was he like abou' it?"

"Yeh can imagine! When I knocked on the door he came out with his hands up. I think we should crash out here for a couple of days, yeh know? Stay in. Wha' d'yeh reckon?"

"I suppose so," said Mickey. "Out of sigh' is out of mind and all tha'."

"Yeah, tha' kind of thing. I think we should stay off the gear for a couple of days too."

"Bollix, Davy. I mean it. I don't mind cuttin' down on the gear, but I'm not givin' it up."

"Yeh make me laugh, d'yeh know tha'? It's oney for a couple of days, until we sort things out, yeh know? I can't believe yeh sometimes. This is the quickest way to get reefed."

"How is it? And why? What poxy difference does it make?"

"Well, if yeh have a big habit when we start sellin' the gear, you'll only fuck yourself up."

"*When we start sellin' it?*"

"For fucksake, Mickey. How long is tha' money goin' to last if we use it on gear? Well? How long?"

"I dunno. A few months I suppose."

"A few fuckin' months? You're jestin', aren't yeh? But even if it did, well let's say tha' it did, we could still get five year for it."

"Yeah, and five year would be like a fuckin' holiday compared to the amount of time we would have to do if we were caught with the amounts of smack you're talkin' abou'."

"Jaysis, Mickey, are yeh bleedin' blind or wha'? Look at me. We've had a run, a good fuckin' run, at the snatches, but it's time to do somethin' else. And if yeh don't see tha' after today, you'll never fuckin' see it. Anyway, if yeh want to leave it at tha', well fair enough, but I'm goin' to start knockin' it out."

"Righ' then, tell me how we're goin' to become two big drug barons?"

"It's easy," said Davy. "Buy an ounce off tha' bloke in Raheny and sell it in quarter grams. Then buy another ounce and do the same thing. After tha' we'll be able to buy two ounces, yeah? If we start with an ounce and an'thin' goes wrong we'll still have three grand to fall back on."

"How do yeh work tha' one out?"

"An ounce should cost us no more than two grand," said Davy, "And two from five leaves three, doesn't it?"

"Yeah. But wha' abou' Skinnier?"

"I'm goin' to tell him he's comin' into business with us. If he doesn't like it, I'll give him fuck all—we can owe it to him," said Davy. After thinking about it for a moment he went on, "We can pay him back in smack. Tha' way he'll use wha' we owe him in abou' a month."

"Jaysis. We're stoopin' a bit now, aren't we. Wha'ever yeh think of him, we wouldn't have got this stroke without him."

"Skinnier's only a cunt, Mickey. And all we'll ever get out of him is a cunt's worth."

Anne, who had been in the bedroom with her baby, walked back in to catch the gist of the conversation. She knew Skinnier, and nodded complicitly.

"We'll have to work a lot of things out before Monda', and the rest as we go along," said Davy.

"Why Monda'?"

"That's when I'm hopin' we can pick up the smack."

"Righ'," said Mickey, and he stretched out his hand and asked, "Give us a chase off wha' yeh have left there. Mine's all gone."

What a Time it was. What a Time they had. A Time for Thursday morning to mirror itself. To reflect images, some obscure, some clear. Sometimes in private. Thoughts. Memories. The angle of the arm. Sometimes a slagging: "When yeh were down on your hands and knees with his hand in your mouth, yeh looked like the fuckin' pope kissin' the ground when he got off the plane. 'Yunga people of Ierland, from my knees, I beheg of you.'"

"Tha' was your fuckin' fault, yeh bollix. I had to drop off when he was between the two cars. How was I suppose to hit him properly, ha ha. I felt like cryin', I'm tellin' you. Ha ha ha. I was even thinkin' of askin' him nicely, please Mister. . ."

"Wha', by tellin' him abou' your hatchet. Ha ha ha."

It was a Time for refreshments. For tins of Holsten Pils and fish and chips and smelly heroin. They couldn't complain about the service. Anne was an excellent hostess, running out at least three times a day to meet their needs, following the do's and don'ts of their instructions to the letter.

A Time for resurgence too. At least for Davy. Of old ideas, well new ideas, ideas they could afford now. Still, plenty of hard work ahead. Had to think. Figure things out, though not aloud.

A Silent Time.

By Saturday night, Mickey had had enough. "Fuck this, I'm goin' for a pint!" To his surprise, Davy not only agreed, but seemed relieved. They told Anne she was to stay in until they returned, which might mean the following day. The possibility that someone might burgle the flat and steal their money was a temptation they didn't want to taunt fate with. On their way to the pub, they stopped at the snooker hall. They were looking for Skinnier Martin. When they asked him to accompany them for a pint, he thought it was pay time, a night to cha cha cha. He had to wait until they reached the pub before they would tell him anything. By the time they arrived, his gait was contorted by anticipation, almost giddied towards caricature. The transition from expectation to desolation was barely noticeable, the effects being very much the same. Joy and grief often terminate at the same stop, tears, and he was close to these when, with a ring of permanence, Davy told him,"We've no money for yeh."

For just a moment a quietness, so heavy it ached, hung between them. And the twisting features on Skinnier's face made an attempt to force his mouth around the words he wanted to say. "But why, Davy? Yeh said yeh got the money."

"Yeah, but you said there'd be six grand in it," Davy answered.

"It said five and a half grand in the papers. Surely to Jaysis that's near enough."

"Don't mind the papers. The oul' fella just said tha' for the insurance."

Mickey sat cross-legged on a stool glancing casually around the bar. His arms were folded, clenched rather, and gripped at the biceps. Skinnier saw the underbelly and plunged. "Jaysis, Mickey. Yeh promised. Yeh swore I'd get two grand and I done everything yeh said."

"Are yeh fuckin' deaf, Skinnier?" Davy asked, closing that route. "We didn't get six grand."

"I don't believe yeh. It was even on the news and they said. . ."

"Skinnier, shut it," said Mickey. "Just shut it. Or I'll shut it for yeh."

"Listen," said Davy. "We're goin' to start sellin' a bit a gear and the money we got on Tursda' will go towards tha'. If yeh want to come in with us you'll make a few bob, but if yeh don't, then fair enough. It's up to you."

The subtlety of the move wasn't lost on Skinnier. A big part of him knew he should have expected it. Shit, he had expected it. But he had also ignored it. Even the day they did the stroke. Unlucky for some, the 13th. Unlucky for them, he had thought, if they got caught. And now it was so obviously unlucky for him. He should have warned them something would happen if they let him down. Warned them? Jaysis! To threaten Davy Byrne was suicidal. He'd heard enough rumours. "Wha'll I have to do?"

"Sell it," said Davy. "I'll give yeh five quarters at a time and you give me back a hundred and sixty quid. Tha' way yeh can either keep a quarter for yourself, or sell it and make forty quid."

"Where, in the name of fuck, am I goin' to sell it? If more than two people knock at me ma's door, she'll call the police."

"We're goin' to sell it from the snooker hall. One of us'll be there most of the time, so yeh won't be on your own. It'll be like a little team. Don't worry, you'll be looked after."

Skinnier wasn't in the least impressed. " I'll give it a go for a while, see how it goes. I suppose it'll be no prob' if we're all in it together."

"Yeah, suck on it for a while and see if yeh like the taste," said Davy.

After a pause, Skinnier asked, "Listen, can yeh give us a few bob out of the money tha' yeh did get? I'm dyin' sick and I haven't a shillin'."

Davy had expected the request, passed the money under the table. "Here's a couple of hundred quid for yeh. That'll keep yeh goin' until we start doin' the gear."

"Aw nice one. Thanks. When are yeh goin' to start knockin' it out?"

"Soon," said Davy, before Mickey could say Monday.

Skinnier swirled the remains of his pint, then finished it. Licking the dregs from the sparse black hairs above his lip, he rubbed his hands together and said, "Well, better do wha' the banana did to the ice cream."

They both looked at him, confused.

"Split?" Skinnier offered. "Good, isn't it?" said Skinnier. Winking at Mickey he said, "I can't remember where I heard it though." He hurried off when Davy scowled at him.

After he had pushed his way out past the plate-glass door, Davy turned to Mickey and asked, "Wha' are yeh laughin' at, for fucksake. Yeh oney encourage him."

Mickey couldn't answer. Tears were streaming down the side of his face.

"I swear I don't know who the bigger gobshite is, you or him."

When Mickey managed to control himself, he said to Davy, "I wasn't laughin' at him, I was laughin' at you, when yeh got the joke, the look on your face, I swear, Jaysis, it was the funniest thing I've seen in ages."

"Shut up, will yeh? You'll get us fucked out of here. Yeh know wha' they're like. If you're happy, they think you're on somethin' and they come over and clean out the ashtrays twice a minute. I told yeh tha' was goin' to be easy, didn't I?"

"Yeah, but yeh wouldn't like it if someone done it on us."

"Nobody would do tha' to us."

"Yeah? Well, I still didn't like it."

"D'yeh fancy goin' out to Harmonstown tomorrow? I want yeh to call in on tha' fuckin' hippy, what's his name. . .?"

"Eamo Thompson?" ventured Mickey.

"Yeah, him. I want yeh to find out wha' yeh can abou' the bloke from Raheny. Thompson'll know. He's sellin' gear for him."

"Why? Are yeh not comin' with us?"

"No. Thompson ripped me off once for twenty quid and I gave him a hidin', so he probably won't even open the door to me."

"Yeh could always wait in a pub or somethin'."

"Jaysis. It won't kill yeh to go on your own. You'll only be half an hour on the bike.

"Okay," said Mickey, stung by Davy's remark. "Righ', I'll go on me own."

"Are yeh stayin' here until closin' time?" Davy asked him.

"Yeah, well I'm stayin' for a few pints."

"I'm not. I'm goin' when I finish this. I want to go and get a bit of gear and then go to the gaff in Balcurris and use the gismo." He missed the syringe.

"Typical," said Mickey. "And you're the one that's bein' goin' on abou' only usin' so much and havin' to be careful."

"I'm only talkin' abou' havin' a proper hit. Me teeth are goin' bleedin' brown smokin' tha' gear. Still, if you're not into it, I'll just get some for meself."

"No, hang on, wait for me, I'll go with yeh."

They wondered would they bump into a stoned Skinnier, a satisfied Skinnier. But they didn't bump into him. And if they had, they would have seen that he was stoned, but nothing more. And even that wasn't working very well, wasn't hiding the wrangled, nagging thoughts that sought to torment him.

Maybe they didn't know what it was like? Didn't know that he had already asked Whacker Cleary (who had laughed and asked was he going to tap up the money outside the post office) how much he was selling his Yammy 125 for. Had already told Dodie Stevens that he would buy 500 Difs from him for £150, and sell them at 50p each. Make his own money. They thought he was like the other gobshites. Would be honoured to walk around with five bags that belonged to Davy bastardin' Byrne, plugged up his arse. But this was Mickey Hughes' fault. See what he got for trusting him? Robbed!

But not to worry. Little apples grow. The money's gone. The last few days had been a nightmare, had dragged in, had kept him awake at night and in a spin during the day. And what had he got to show for it? Fuck all! Had paid Mick Murtagh the money he owed him for a bag, and bought two more. The gear was lousy, so he would probably use before tomorrow the gear he said he would keep until then. He would be lucky if he had anything left to buy a few dike from Breen on Monday.

The waiting had only brought its own trouble. But now he had something. Something nobody else knew he had. Now he had all the time in the world.

"HE's A LAZY bastard tha' Eamo Thompson. I had to get his ma to get him out of bed and then I had to wait on him to get a turn on."

Mickey dropped his helmet and gloves on to the armchair, silencing the baby who had been chattering on a quilt laid out to accommodate her and her toys. She looked up at him with a mouth open, quiet, expectant.

Davy had been roused by the noise from Mickey's knock, but only opened his eyes at the sound of his voice. Lying full on the sofa, his arm had pillowed his head during a dreamy doze while the light from the sun blazed through his closed eyes, its heat magnified by the window. Stretching with a taut rigour, he sat up and rubbed his eyes. "Hur . . . I see . . . hur . . . you had . . . haah, one with him," he said as he yawned, and bent to pluck a cigarette from a packet on the floor.

"Yeah, well I wanted to see wha' it was like. Hello, Áine. Are yeh glad to see your Uncle Mickey? Gis a kiss. Hmm. Jaysis! If yeh keep those big blue eyes till yeh grow up, you'll break a few hearts. D'yeh know tha'? Wha's tha' you're playin' with?"

"Are yeh tryin' to tell me yeh can't remember wha' fixin' smack is like? Yeh only had a turn on last nigh'."

"Yeh know wha' I mean," Mickey sighed. "If we're goin' to start sellin' it, I wanted to test it, tha's all."

"Yeh didn't use his gismo, did yeh?"

"No. He has loads of new ones."

"Yeah? Well, at least tha' was handy."

Mickey tutted his tongue between his teeth and shook his head.

"So wha' did he say abou' this bloke?" Davy asked.

"Aw, yeah. He's meetin' him in the Concorde, in Edenmore, at one."

"Wha'? Today? For fucksake, why didn't yeh tell me tha' when yeh came in?"

"Yeh never gave me a chance, did yeh? And anyway, Thompson said he'd be havin' a few pints with him, so they'll be there for a while."

"C'mon then. Let's go."

THOMPSON WAS SITTING at a table with four older men. He was dressed in his usual dark, dirt-hardened jeans, which tightened around the bottom of his skinny legs before dropping into a baldy pair of boot trainers. The sleeves on his red-checked shirt had been folded twice and hung between his wrists and his elbows, casually screening the needle tracks on his arms. Unkempt, his stained, fair hair wisped away from a sick-coloured, spotty face. Davy recognised the pathetic slouch, but the other four were strangers to him. Two looked like they might have just finished playing a round for Cadbury's Pitch and Putt Club. One had the blank gaze of a moron who, Davy suspected, would be ordered to the front in times of danger. The final member of the group reminded him of a solicitor he once had, though dressed perhaps the way a solicitor might dress on a bank holiday weekend. Thompson had looked down at the floor as soon as they had walked in.

Davy dispatched Mickey to the bar and sat at a table where it was possible to catch Thompson's attention. As soon as he had, he nodded him over. "How a'yeh, Eamo?"

"Alrigh'," Thompson answered. "Mickey called out to me this mornin'. He was tellin' me you're oney out."

"Yeah, that's righ'."

"Are yis lookin' for gear?"

"Yeah."

"I never do any from the pub, so I haven't got it on me."

Davy smiled. "Oh we're not lookin' for quarters."

"Well tha's a pity," said Thompson; "tha's all I do."

"I know, Eamo, I know," said Davy, and then his expression changed instantly, from a gaze to a stare. A taunt full of purpose, which reminded Thompson what happened the last time he didn't give Davy what he wanted. "Wha's the bloke's name tha' yeh get the gear off?"

"I can't tell yeh, Davy. He asked me, told me, not to tell anyone. You'd do the same," said Thompson. His voice changed tone, lost its confidence and was replaced by a plea for empathy.

Mickey returned with the drinks.

"Yeah?" said Davy. "Just go over and tell him tha' I want him for a minute."

Indecisive, Thompson began to say one thing, then changed his mind and said that his dealer had left.

"If yeh don't tell him, Eamo, then I'm goin' to have to go over there," he said, tipping his head towards Thompson's drinking companions, "and find out who he is meself."

Thompson returned to his table.

"Jaysis, Davy," said Mickey, "don't get cheeky with them or they might all come over and lash us out of it."

"Don't be so ridiculous," said Davy. A couple of moments later, he saw Thompson stand and leave his table, accompanied by one other member of the group, the one who reminded Davy of the solicitor. They both went out to the toilet. When they returned, Thompson sat down and his companion said something to the moron, before walking over to Davy and Mickey. Sliding in beside them, he stuck his hand out and said, "Hello, my name is Robin. Eamon tells me yeh want to have a chat. I hope it's important because I like a quiet pint on a Sunday mornin'."

Mickey shook his hand without saying who he was. Davy introduced them both and looked at Robin for a moment before asking, "Can I get yeh one?"

"Well, I'm in company at the minute . . ."

"That's okay," said Davy. "Mickey, get the man a drink. See wha' his friends want and have a cha' with Eamo abou' tha' other thing we were talkin' about."

The command stung Mickey, but Davy just lowered his brow to him.

"A Guinness, is it?" Mickey asked, before going over to Eamo's table.

Davy rested his arm on the back of his chair and turned to face Robin. "I know the way I went abou' this was a bit awkward, but it was the oney way I was goin' to get a chance to have a word with yeh, abou' a bit of business."

"Well, like I said, I hope it's important."

"Tha' depends on one thing."

"On what?"

"On if yeh can get me an ounce of smack for the righ' price."

"What makes yeh think I can do that?"

"Listen, Robin, I'm not tryin' to be smart, but I'm sure Eamo's already told yeh somethin' abou' me. I know nothin' abou' you. Yeh could be anyone really, so I'm the one that's takin' all the fuckin' chances. D'yeh know?"

He smiled while he scrutinised Davy. There was nothing remarkable about him, nothing extraordinary or memorable. Except perhaps the eyes, the moments when, with a deranged switch, the intent flashed with a peculiar inexorability.

"Well, can yeh do it?"

"I can, but I'm not sure I want to."

"Why? Are yeh afraid I migh' be someone like Georgie Sheringham?" Davy asked. "I'm not! But I heard abou' Tony Nolan and the hassle he had."

Robin was impressed by the calmness and irritated by the conceit. "Why do yeh want the ounce?"

"I have a few bob and I don't want to blow it. I want to let the spondulicks swell in a way I can handle. D'yeh know wha' I mean?"

"When do yeh want it?" Robin asked, as Mickey delivered his pint of Guinness.

"Today, if yeh can get it for less than two grand."

"Two grand's the bottom line and I think yeh knew that before yeh asked."

"Okay," said Davy. "Two grand, then."

Arrangements were made for Davy to pick up the gear that evening. When Robin returned to the table, Mickey stood and said to him, "See yeh later, huh?"

"Yeah, Mickey, see yeh later."

He walked back to Davy, who stood too and indicated that they were leaving. When they got outside Mickey asked him, "Wha's happenin' then?"

"He's gettin' it for us," said Davy, ecstatically. "C'mon, I'll tell yeh the story when we get back to the Mun. Go to Anne's gaff first."

Mickey jerked his head to shift his hair and pulled his helmet on. He kicked the bike stand impatiently and on the journey the throttle was squeezed hastily, the gear changes kicked violently. He drove the bike hard at the kerb where he planned to park and, braking fast before he hit it, he caused the bike to bump on to the grass verge.

"Jaysis! Wha' the fuck's goin' on," Davy asked, almost falling off.

"I've had enough, tha's wha's goin' on. I'm takin' me share of the money," said Mickey, walking towards the tower.

Davy followed him and removing his helmet asked, "Wha' the fuck are yeh on abou'?"

"Yeh can keep the rest and do wha' yeh fuckin' like, tha's wha' I'm on abou'."

Davy waited until they were in the lift before asking, "Have I annoyed yeh abou' somethin'?"

"Annoyed? Is tha' wha' yeh call it? Well I'll tell yeh wha' I'm annoyed abou'. All I ever hear from yeh is drive me here, drive me there, do this, do tha', kiss me fuckin' arse! Yeh haven't talked to me abou' an'thin' since yeh got out of the Joy. Well I've had it up to here," said Mickey, supporting his chin with the back of his hand.

"I've told yeh wha' I can, Mickey, and there just isn't tha' much more to say. A lot of this we just have to take as it comes. I'm not even sure wha's happenin' meself."

"Yeah? Well you're just treatin' me like a skivvy."

The lift stammered to a halt. "Tha's a load of bollix, Mickey. If yeh have any better ideas, tell me wha' they are."

"I have. Forget this shite abou' sellin' the gear, because it's goin' to be nothin' but poxy trouble."

"Trouble? Hang on and I'll tell yeh wha' trouble is," and they continued talking after they had walked into the flat. "We nearly killed a couple of oul' fellas the other day, and for wha'? For the price of a turn on? Jaysis, Mickey, we'll be made this way. I have it all worked out. We get an ounce and make eigh' quarters from each gram. From one ounce we can make nearly nine fuckin' grand. Even if we lose a couple gettin' people like Skinnier to sell it, tha' still leaves us with seven."

"You're talkin' wonders now, Davy, while yeh try and shite a miracle. How are yeh goin' to get eigh' quarters from one gram?"

"Yeh know as well as I do, they're only £40 bags now. You've seen the state of the ones tha' we're buyin', they're cut to fuckin' bits."

"When are we meant to pick up the ounce?"

"Do yeh know the Boot Inn? Well, I've arranged to meet him at the turn off at six this evenin'."

"Wha'? Do a deal like tha' in the middle of the road?"

"Yeah. We wait there on the bike, he'll come along in the car. We hand the money in, he hands the smack out."

"Are yeh mad? Without weighin' it, or even seein' it? Say if he rips us off? Say if the gear's crap?" ·

"He said it's the same gear tha' Eamo has, only it hasn't been cut as much."

"Of course he fuckin' would. What else would he say? I don't believe this, Davy, I just don't believe it."

"Don't worry, I told him if he ripped me off, I'd kill him."

"Yeh hardly know his fuckin' name."

"If he rips me off, you keep the rest of the money and we call it quits. If he doesn't, then we're partners, okay?"

"Okay! Okay then, I will."

"Right then," said Davy grinning. "All we have to do now is work out where to bag it up."

"We could use the gaff in Balcurris."

"No, it's no use. I don't want anyone to see which flat we walk into, especially the Filth. Ask Anne can we use this gaff for the time bein'. Tell her we'll give her a few bob."

It was one of those things he loved about the towers. From the outside, it was practically impossible to discover which of the ninety flats you might enter. From the inside, it took an experienced ear to tell from the clinks which floor the lift had stopped at. Or from the bottom of the stairs, to tell from the sound of footsteps running and doors slamming, which floor was being used. And even if that was possible, if an outsider had those skills, with four on one side of the landing and two on the other, no flat was sufficiently isolated to betray them.

Mickey called Anne into the bedroom, where Davy and himself had been talking, and explained to her what they wanted to do. Although he was vague about how much they would pay her, anything that would supplement her Unmarried Mother's Allowance was enough to persuade her to agree.

When she had left the room, Davy turned to Mickey and said, "Wha' I think we should do is cut the ounce into four quarters." He realised they would need a set of scales, a decent set, by that afternoon. Mickey volunteered to go and find them. A half an hour hadn't passed when he returned.

"Guess where I got them? Tony Nolan's bird! I heard she was sellin' everything before she legs it after him to London. I just tried her, on the off chance. Twenty quid! I called up to Billy Murtagh too and got a couple of quarters, just to check tha' they work."

ARROGANCE WAS SOMETHING that sometimes made them nervous. It was sometimes something they were superstitious about and came accompanied by touch wood rituals and angelic glances towards heaven. But it was sometimes too a true arrogance, more than a belief based on conceit, more than an assumption without foundation. It was often an arrogance that bordered on madness, where a willingness was required to skip gaily through minefields and not always with the conviction of reaching safety, because Mickey was often convinced of the exact opposite. Yes! Theirs was an admirable, an irresistibly gorgeous arrogance, because, selflessly reckless, they would do anything anyway. When witnessed, this had that tickling, almost piss yourself appeal, a charming, hypnotic allure of breath catching force. I've sometimes wondered if it takes a special quality just to recognise it. I mean, can you?

Davy nurtured his, internally. It was a quiet, determined arrogance and he valued it like his life depended on it. Behind the growls it sometimes smiled, it sometimes laughed out loud with the surety of experience, with knowledge. It wasn't that he knew a lot, but what he needed to know, he knew in depth. Like the application of initiative, of enterprise, that this was a sure fire recipe for success, it was the formula, the compound his age prescribed. In a sense it was something that he had no choice about. It was the Time he lived in.

Mickey's was less certain, was less secure, and because of this, because he doubted it, he had a tendency to display it flamboyantly. But only in spasms, only in involuntary outbursts.

Sunday at six was a Safe Time to be arrogant. With people's money tucked away behind locked doors and their property secure until the pubs closed, the Gardaí were as rare as sin. As they neared the Boot Inn Mickey, riding pillion, stopped playing "Name That

Tune" on the back of Davy's helmet. They were only a minute at the meeting point when a silver BMW pulled alongside and the window opened electronically. An arm reached out, palm open. Davy stuck his hand inside his jacket, took out a wrapped bundle of cash and passed it over. The arm went back in to the car and reappeared with a small polythene package.

"See yeh later, Davy."

"Are yeh not goin' to check the cash, Robin?"

"No, I trust yeh," said a voice from the car, and with the window sliding up, the car pulled away.

As soon as it was out of sight, Mickey said, "Give us a look, tha' doesn't look an'thin' like an ounce."

"Did yeh ever see an ounce before?" Davy asked.

"No."

"Well neither did I, so let's go home and weigh it."

At Anne's, they gave the impression that they had just returned from an ordinary Sunday spin and had a little job to do, a chore so lacking in necessity, the first thing Mickey did was switch on the TV. Anne automatically walked to the kitchen and began to fill a dented dirty grey aluminium kettle. Even Áine only stopped drinking her bottle to glance from the baby bouncer and was more concerned her mother had moved away.

They smoked a small amount each and agreed that it was good gear. When they weighed it, it was a gram too heavy. The weight of the packing they thought. Davy poured the heroin on to a mirror and with a flat sharp knife cut the ounce into four quarters. He carefully packed three of these into polythene coin bags which were then waterproofed with cling film, before being tightly wrapped with sellotape. The last quarter was cut into as close to seven equal grams as he could get and each of these were cut into eight equal amounts. As Davy was doing this, Mickey was using a pair of scissors to cut from a child's jotter the paper wraps required to pack the £40 bags.

By the time they had finished, on the table before them lay three quarter ounces and fifty-six £40 bags. Almost ready for business, all that remained was to stash the quarter ounces.

"I don't want to stash it in Balcurris," said Davy in reply to a suggestion from Mickey. "Especially in the first few lifts. Someone, either goin' over to the Club, or comin' back from it, migh' spot us and they're bound to suss wha' we're up to."

"The same thing is goin' to happen in Coultry. Over there, we're just as likely to bump into any junkies comin' and goin' from Murtagh's gaff."

"Hmm, I know. I don't think we should stash any of them in the flats at all. We can stick one in the back of Pappin's, like we said, and bury two in the forest."

"Okay then, " said Mickey. It seemed simple, but out in the open, crossing Shanghan Road to McDonagh Tower, he shuffled along nervously. "We probably should've plugged these."

"I don't know wha' you're worried abou', I'm carryin' two. If we get a pull, just swally it."

"Swally it? It's the size of a potato, for fucksake. If I see any coppers, I'm off," said Mickey. "I know there's enough wrappin' on these, but do yeh think they'll stay dry? I mean, if the gear gets wet, it'll rot."

"Mickey, these are as safe as a camel's arse in a sandstorm."

"Wha' abou' here?" Mickey asked, after they had passed McDermott Tower and reached the side of the power station.

"No, keep goin'. Here, gimme yours. Run up to the church and make sure nobody's around."

Mickey ran ahead and checked the quiet grounds of St Pappin's Church. A security light hanging from a wall of the chapel illuminated the path that ran from back to front, which only served to shadow in deeper darkness the many hedges and bushes that adorned the gardens. When Davy arrived, he moved with a capricious busyness towards the nearest bush and dug furtively, using a kitchen fork which he had taken from Anne's. After he'd buried a quarter they left by the front of the church for Santry Woods.

"This is the worse bit," said Mickey, exchanging between hands the quarter ounce Davy had returned to him.

"Wha' is?"

"Goin' by the knackers."

"Wha's wrong with them?"

"There's nothin' wrong with them, it's the traffic tha' comes flyin' around from Santry Lane. Yeh can't see the cars until they're on top of yeh and at this hour all yeh can see is the headlights."

"Well yeh can always leg it through the camp if an'thin' happens."

"Wha'? And get savaged be the dogs? Fuck tha'! I'd rather get reefed."

Davy giggled, though Mickey was right. If an unmarked police car drove by and recognised them, they would have very little warning. "C'mon, it's alrigh', we're nearly there."

They hurried by the itinerant camp and the smell of burning timber, past the sound of hushed conversations and across Santry Lane through a gap in the hedge that led them into a field beside Santry Woods. Mickey reached for his cigarettes.

"C'mon" said Davy. "We'll stash them on the edge of the wood, beside the fields the magic mushrooms used to grow in."

The grass they walked across was soft and soggy.

"Look at the ligh'," said Davy.

"Wha'? Where?" Mickey said, startled, and he searched for the beam of a torch.

"The ligh' from the moon and the stars."

"It's pitch fuckin' black, yeh gobshite."

"You'd know wha' pitch black was alrigh', if we didn't have this ligh'."

"Davy, it's so fuckin' dark…" Mickey's next step forward felt his foot rest on a deeper, softer cushion of grass. The squelch at the bottom of his weight came too late to warn him to pull his foot away. Water rushed over the edge of his trainer and past his ankle. It spread instantly along the sole of his sock, towards toes that curled down to try and keep the wet away. "Bollix!" he cried, as the coldness slippered his foot and rested, pooled between his toes. For a couple of minutes, every second step was a grimaced limp.

"Righ', we'll bury them separately, at the bottom of these two posts," said Davy, as they stood at a barbed wire fence that bordered the woods. "Fair is fair, it's hard to see if there's any stingers here, so we'll bury one each."

"Yeh can't see? Why don't yeh step back then and use the ligh', from the stars and the silvery fuckin' moon."

"C'mon, yeh know wha' I'm talkin' abou'."

"No, I don't. And anyway, we oney have one fork and you're used to doin' it already. I want to have a smoke and warm me hands. Me feet are fuckin' freezin'."

"Your feet are freezin', so yeh want to warm your hands?"

"Yeh don't expect me to have a smoke with me foot, do yeh? Who do yeh think I am? Christy Brown?"

"Wha' have your hands got to do with your feet?"

"Nothin'! The thing is, I'm fuckin' freezin' and I want to warm somethin'."

When the second and third quarters were safely interred and the fork flung wildly into the blacker darkness of the woods, they turned and went back the way they came. At St Pappin's they didn't cut through the church, but instead sneaked a glance in its yard, as they passed with pretended solemnity and eye twinkling mischief. At the mobile chip van, they bought some chips and returned to the flat.

Anne smelt, when she opened the door, the nasal gaping choke of vinegar. Then she saw their feet.

"Mother of Jaysis, did yis have to go and pick the badaydas for those chips? Take them shoes off yis, I mean it, and don't come any further than the end of the hall until yis do."

After they had eaten, they cling-filmed tightly, into five separate bundles, fifty of the £40 bags. "Sunda'," said Davy, "is an unlucky day to start workin', so we'll use a bag each from these six and start first thing in the mornin'."

Mickey nodded his head in agreement and said, "Yeah, tha's the best thing to do. Are yeh sure we'll sell all these? I don't think they're as big as Murtagh's."

"They must be about the same size and it's definitely better gear," said Davy. "Why? Are yeh thinkin' tha' by the time we sell them, we'll have used the gear we stashed?"

"Somethin' like tha'. But I don't give a fuck anyway, because this lot will nearly get us back the two grand. How long do yeh reckon it'll take to get rid of it?"

"I don't know. The best thing to do is make sure there's somebody in the snooker hall from the time it opens, until the time it closes."

"Who? Me, you and Skinnier?"

"Fuck tha'! Me and you won't be knockin' it out. No, it'll be Skinnier and Jojo."

"Jojo? After him robbin' yeh?"

ON MONDAY MORNING Mickey went to get Skinnier. Davy brought some of the heroin with him and went to his ma's flat. He found Jojo asleep, in the same position he had seen him the last time.

He woke, terrified, with Davy standing over him saying, "C'mon, I want to talk to yeh."

"Jaysis, Davy, I got three scream ups durin' the week. I nearly got reefed twice. I don't know how I got away, if it wasn't for..."

"So, how much money have yeh got for me?"

"Thirty quid. Yeh can have tha' if yeh want it."

"Which means you're oney short £670."

"I'll get it for yeh, honest, Davy."

"Do yeh want to do a bit of work for me ?"

Jojo blinked cautiously. Davy in a generous mood could be just as frightening as Davy pissed off and he recognised that grin on Davy's face. It would be just like him to offer a brother something extremely dangerous and badly paid, and find it funny into the bargain. "Have yeh got a stroke lined up?"

"I want yeh to sell a bit of gear for me, a bit of smack, up in the snooker hall. I'll give yeh ten quarters and you give me back £320. Tha' way yeh keep two for yourself, but I also want yeh to start payin' me back the money yeh owe me."

"Is tha' all yeh have?" Jojo asked. "Ten quarters?"

"No. When yeh sell those, I'll give yeh another batch. Skinnier Martin will be doin' it for me as well, so yeh can work somethin' out between the two of yeh."

Jojo couldn't believe what he was hearing and he tried to remember if it was something he might have gone to bed dreaming about. Better try and get one off him now, he thought, in case he changes his mind. Could sell at least twenty a day, use two, sell two and keep the money. Soon have enough for a bike, or a fuckin' car. Sell them where? Twenty?

"I'm oney lettin' yeh do this because I trust yeh. If yeh let me down once, you're finished."

"I won't let yeh down, Davy, honestly."

"I hope so, Jojo. Now c'mon, get ready. I'll give yeh a chase before we go down to the shoppin' centre."

AFTER THEIR FIRST four days in business, all concerned were more than satisfied: they were delighted. The first day, St Patrick's Day, had been a bit shaky, uncertain and they only sold ten bags. Davy and Mickey wondered that night, as they watched *The Playboy of the Western World* on Channel 4, if they had made a mistake. But the next three days saw a much improved performance. Their timing (the decision to begin selling on Monday) coincided with a change in conditions that favoured them greatly. Murtagh's gear declined sharply in quality, as did the reliability of his supply. There is nothing quite like the fickle loyalty of junkies.

Thursday evening saw almost eighty bags sold and it was becoming all so apparently easy. Jojo and Skinnier strutted about with a new status. Heads normally directed downwards were carried high and they often indulged, eagerly, in deriding most of those who looked for credit. Particularly those who, when the boot had been on the other foot, had taken nothing but pleasure in refusing Jojo and Skinnier the same service.

Davy was satisfied too, though only with the rate of sales. Mickey was beginning to drive him around the twist. Already, he was using more than half a gram a day and had begun to stay away from the snooker hall for longer periods than they had agreed. He even whinged about the daily £20 snooker hall bill. That evening Davy decided it might be best to go and have a few pints with him, have a chat and work things out. They arranged to meet at half seven, but Mickey didn't turn up until almost nine.

"Wha' kept yeh?"

"I had to do somethin'. And anyway, I didn't want to go round to the pub too early. I'm not into drinkin' any more, it makes me fall asleep when I'm stoned."

"C'mon," said Davy, taking his jacket from a peg beside the pool table where he had been playing with Yako, "we might pull a couple of birds."

"No, I've a pain in me arse with all tha' too."

"A pain in your arse? Wha' the fuck's wrong with you?"

"There's nothin' the matter with me!"

"Do yeh not like things goin' well? I mean, does it do your head in tha' we're makin' a few bob, no prob' like, without any of the disasters yeh said we were goin' to have?"

Mickey tried to ignore him and gave himself the few minutes walk to the pub to think of a clever answer. Once inside though, there was something else that caught their attention: four strangers were sitting huddled at the bar.

"Do yeh know them? They're not the Filth, are they?" Mickey asked.

"No, I don't think so. Not unless they're on the Garda boxin' team. Did yeh see the state of the faces on them?"

"No. I can't really see them properly. Are they knackers?"

"Are yeh jokin' me? There's no bleedin' way tha' Hoppy would let one in here, let alone a crew."

"Yeah, I suppose so. I hope they're not vigo's."

After paying for the drink at the bar, they sat at a table, putting two pints of lager on to wet, dirty beer mats, and got back on to the subject that brought them to the pub in the first place.

"Yeh know we're goin' to have to sort somethin' out, Mickey, don't yeh?"

"Abou' wha'?"

"Yeh know abou' wha'! Abou' the fuckin' gear! Abou' you using it and us sellin' it. It's not workin' out, is it? We're not stickin' to doin' the things we said we'd do."

"We're makin' a fortune, aren't we? So how are things not workin' out?"

"Because, if your poxy habit gets much bigger, we're not goin' to see much of it. Like I told yeh, one of us would have to stay in the snooker hall, if the two of us couldn't be there together, but as soon as I go anywhere, you fuck off for most of the day!"

"C'mon, Davy, if that's so fuckin' important, how come the two of us are sittin' in the pub now?"

"Do yeh know somethin'? Me oul' fella used an expression one time, he said tha' I gave him a heartburn on the arse and that's how I feel now. If yeh were anyone else, Mickey, I'd swear yeh were doin' it on purpose."

"Yeh know wha' it is. But every time I open me mouth abou' it, yeh take a bluie."

"Jaysis! Are yeh goin' on abou' knockin' the gear out again?"

"See?"

"Mickey, yeh know wha' you're like. Yeh won't do an'thin' unless yeh can have a fuckin' whinge abou' it first."

"This isn't like tha'. It isn't somethin' I'm nervous about. It's not like if we do a stroke or somethin' and we get caught… touch wood tha' doesn't happen for a while," he said, tapping his head. "Then yeh just think, well, fair enough, tha's the way it goes sometimes. But this is different, it's wrong, it's bad luck wrong."

"There is no righ' or wrong to this."

"See? Yeh never listen to a word!"

"I do. To get caught, tha's the only wrong. And from where we're sittin', we won't have to worry abou' tha' any more."

"Here's something to worry about. Have a look at who's comin' over."

Davy turned as Georgie Sheringham arrived at their table.

"How a'yeh, Davy? Mickey? Mind if I sit here?"

"No, go ahead," said Davy. Mickey began to tap the table with his fingers.

"I'm oney here for a minute," said Sheringham. "I just want to find out for meself why you've moved in on me pitch, without even askin' me."

"We don't sell gear from Coultry," said Davy.

"Tha's not very funny. Yeh know wha' I mean. And I'm talkin' to the two of yeh by the way," he said, nodding to Mickey. "You're takin' all me punters and you're goin' to have to stop."

"Is tha' righ'?" said Davy. "Well I'm not stoppin' an'thin'. Tha' snooker hall was nobody's pitch when I moved in, so I'm stayin' there."

"Because I was locked up with yeh, Davy, and because I've always liked the two of yis, I'm goin' to give yeh a choice. Yeh can either stop altogether, or yeh can give me a grand a week. Whichever yeh prefer."

Davy was silent for a moment, and he took a breath to give him time, to give him a chance to summon the strength required to deal with Sheringham. He had glanced to Mickey, in search of inspiration, but he was leaving the decision up to Davy. "Warn me? Listen, yeh little bollix, if yeh ever threaten me again I'll hurt yeh, I mean it."

Mickey glanced to heaven and measured the distance between himself and his pint glass. Sheringham stood and raised his hands, making a gesture that said fair enough, lads, but he didn't say a word. Instead he spent a second straightening his padded leather jacket, put one of his hands into a side pocket and took out a cigarette packet. By the time he lit up, he had already begun to leave the pub, stopping briefly on the way to talk to some people and point back. A self-satisfied smile lit up his face when the four strangers at the bar nodded that they knew what they had to do.

"Oh no, no," said Mickey. "I don't fuckin' believe it! See? Why couldn't yeh just talk to him properly? Christ!"

Their only exit was blocked by the advancing bruisers, even more menacing now their intentions were clear. Turning to Mickey Davy said, "Don't think abou' it. C'mon, we'll just run through them." He lifted the table they were drinking at and ran towards the men, screaming, "Righ', yis cunts…"

Mickey ran behind him and sneaking a peep at the disbelief on the barman's face, thought, that's it, we'll definitely be barred now.

The men stopped and looked at each other. Sheringham had told them to just give the little bastards a few slaps. Now there were two madmen running at them with a table that still seated two half full pints of lager. As Davy reached them he threw the table and they jumped aside, allowing him to run through for the door. As he pushed it open, he looked back and saw that Mickey had been almost dragged, by the scruff of the neck, to the floor. Punches and kicks were being lashed wildly at him. Still cursing, Davy ran back, picking up a bar stool on the way. Gripping it tightly by the legs, he smashed it sideways into the nearest head. The man crumpled and desperately tried to crawl away in an attempt to avoid another blow.

Davy quickly spun the stool round, held it by the seat and jabbed it towards the face of Mickey's nearest attacker. When one of the legs from the stool entered the man's mouth, Davy pushed violently and felt the tear, felt something travel through the leg of the stool up his arm and it made him shudder, it made him gasp. The man jumped back, spitting the debris of tissue and teeth, blood and spit on to the carpet, trying to see from behind the tears in his eyes if it was the last of his few good teeth.

The barman, Cassidy, was shouting from behind the bar that he had called the police, as he looked on with dismay at the furniture and glass being damaged and broken. Two bouncers, summoned upstairs from the front door, were standing clear, but they shouted too, "Take it easy, lads, for Jaysis sake. Aw now, there's no need for tha'! Yis'll all be reefed in a minute!"

Mickey had lost all sense of balance and co-ordination, but could hear Davy screaming at him, "Leg it, for fucksake, leg it." He stumbled forward, managing to get his legs to carry his weight and soon realised that Davy was dragging him out of the pub and into the shopping centre. Three of the men followed shortly afterwards, half dragging and carrying the other, more seriously hurt. They saw which way Mickey and Davy went, but they left in the opposite direction.

Mickey and Davy walked towards Balcurris, and headed for the safe side of the flats. When he felt able to walk without help Mickey turned to Davy and asked, "Is me face bad?"

"No, it's alrigh'!"

"Well it doesn't fuckin' feel alrigh'," said Mickey and he tried to stop the blood dripping down into his mouth. "I think me nose is broken. Jaysis! I hope they didn't break me nose."

"Give us another look," said Davy and he smiled at Mickey's vanity. "No, I told yeh, it's alrigh'. You'll probably have a black eye and a thick lip in the mornin', that's all. Anyway, you're an ugly fucker, so it can oney improve yeh."

"It isn't fuckin' funny."

When they arrived at the block, Davy told Mickey, "Listen, go on up to the flat on your own. I want to go over to the snooker hall and get whatever money Jojo and Skinnier have. I'll oney be a few minutes so wait until I come back and then we can have a turn on."

"Alrigh'," said Mickey, "but you be careful; yeh don't want to bump into those saps again."

"Yeah, I will be."

And he was careful. As he walked, he left some space between himself and the flats in case he was attacked again, and between himself and the road, because he was sure the fight had been reported, along with his name. When he ghosted into the snooker hall there was no sign of Jojo or Skinnier. Davy wondered had they sold out. He didn't want to walk back through the shopping centre searching for them. Nor did he want to hang around the snooker hall waiting. A scratch of the back of his head helped him decide to walk back to Balcurris.

Nothing ever awoke in Davy an awareness of his Irishness more than those moments when he completely missed the obvious. When what he clearly should have expected, should have been able to bet his life on, was at the most inappropriate times the least expected thing of all. When he got up to the flat, Mickey was lying on the mattress holding toilet paper to his nose and Jojo and Skinnier were sitting anxious on the floor.

"Jojo, when I told yeh oney to come up here in an emergency, I meant it." He nodded towards Skinnier and added, "And I told yeh never to show anyone where it was."

"I know," said Jojo, "but we're after gettin' robbed! Well, I got robbed because I had the gear. They didn't know tha' Skinnier had the money."

"Robbed? Who fuckin' robbed yeh?"

"Johnny Sheringham and some other bloke," said Jojo, his mouth drying fast in case Davy wouldn't believe him.

"Yeh let him rob yeh? Why didn't yeh give him a fuckin' slap?"

"I'm goin' to kill one of those Sheringhams," Mickey muttered.

"I didn't get a chance to," said Jojo. "He asked me had I any gear and when I said yeah, he said he wanted to look at it in the jacks. When I went in with him, he took a blade out, stuck it to me throat and said he wanted the lot!"

"How many bags did he get?" Davy asked.

"Eigh'. There was nothin' I could do."

"Here," said Skinnier, "here's £160. We sold four."

"I hope you're tellin' me the truth, Jojo, because I'm goin' to get tha' bastard back. Are yeh sure that's wha' he got, eigh' bags?"

"I swear on me ma's life! That's wha' he took, eigh' bags," and he relished the thought of his brother unleashed on Johnny Sheringham.

Davy wasn't convinced his ma's life was worth that much to Jojo. When Jojo asked for a bag between himself and Skinnier, he asked in a manner which suggested he intended to persist until he got either the heroin or the £40 they would need to buy some. Davy only had six bags on him, but he gave them one.

"Can we use it here?" Jojo asked.

"No, yeh fuckin' can't," said Davy. "Go over to me ma's or somethin'. I want to talk to Mickey."

"We'll oney be a minute."

"Are yeh fuckin' deaf or somethin'?"

Jojo didn't answer. Instead he turned to Skinnier and said, "C'mon, let's go."

After bolting the door behind them, Davy poured some gear on a spoon and cooked it over a candle. Mickey fixed first, "To get rid of the pain," he explained. When they had both used, they talked for a short time, until Davy noticed that Mickey was dozing off.

Davy felt alone. There was, just at that moment and just for that moment, a silence between himself and the world, a pause that separated him too from Mickey. Sitting on the mattress with his back to the wall, he looked down on to Mickey's face. A bubble of blood had hardened at the entrance to the right side of his nose. The same side of his face was red sore and unevenly swollen. It would be worse tomorrow. Across Mickey's closed left eye, a fallen lock of hair bridged awkwardly. Davy brushed it backwards. As a gesture, it touched something deep in him, something he didn't understand and didn't feel compelled to. He stood and gently pulled a blanket to Mickey's sleeping shoulders and dropped it kindly. One hand ran through and in passing softly stroked an unintended glance, gliding finely across the sleeping skin on Mickey's bruised young face.

LATE AT NIGHT is a Kind Time to manoeuvre safely. When the pubs have closed and the singing has stopped. When the lights still shine in the flats that belong to those tortured souls who march backwards and forwards. And the hashish heads who grin blankly at videos they're so familiar with they know the lines off by heart. "Are you talking to me?" And they begin to think about eating the dog food. It isn't that bad with a bit of Bisto! And those few who need to have the lights on anyway, just in case. Nothing as bad as waking in fear and the pitch dark, especially if you have a need to march. It is an In-between Time. When Gardaí rest. Those manning checkpoints, watching for drunken drivers, go back to the barracks for a cup of tea. The mandatory one or two detectives on night duty have no need to cruise the streets, because the night-time robbers won't have gone out yet. And anyway, they are only interested in them when they are on their way back.

He tried to knock without making a noise and thought it was like trying to punch someone without offending them. But he soon heard Anne whisper softly from behind the door, "Who is it?"

"It's me! Davy. Hurry up and open the door." As he walked in, he could see she had that sleepy look, that intrusion of comfort look. That harsh, must wrap something round me look. "Sorry for wakin' yeh."

"It's alrigh'. I didn't think yeh'd be back. Tha's why I went to bed. Where's Mickey?"

"He's in the gaff in Balcurris. I just came over to cut up a bit of gear."

"D'yeh want a cup of tea or somethin'?"

"No," said Davy. "You go on back to bed."

"I'm makin' one for meself anyway," she told him, and then asked easily, "D'yeh want a hand with the gear?"

It surprised him. She didn't use heroin. "Fuck it, why not, hey?" While he measured out the heroin, she cut out the paper wraps for him and they were soon into the swing of it.

"Don't tell Mickey I let yeh do this."

"Don't worry," Anne smiled, "I won't say an'thin'." Then she asked, "D'yeh know wha' I do be wonderin'?"

"Wha'?" said Davy. He was attracted by the look in her face that suggested she was about to say something naive, the look of a child about to utter to a parent, in the form of a question, a wisdom that belonged to Another Time. A sweet question. And he was right.

"Why you and Mickey never think of gettin' a proper job."

"That's funny, we were just talkin' abou' tha' earlier on."

"Abou' gettin' a job?"

"No, abou' gettin' ripped off. But it's the same fuckin' thing, isn't it?" said Davy, and he forced a laugh. He listened to her talk of her little dreams for him and Mickey which were all about them not getting caught. He listened as she tucked some hair behind her ear and looked past him, over his shoulder and he wondered could she see what she talked about. He couldn't.

"Tha's it," said Davy, leaning back in his chair and stretching himself after they had finished. "Yeh migh' as well go into bed. I'll kip on the sofa."

"Okay," Anne said, carrying the cups they had used to drink tea back into the kitchen. She looked for other things to delay her, the child's toys, chores she hadn't bothered to do before she went to bed. She felt him watch her, knew he wasn't missing even the slightest swish of her long dressing gown, nor the sight it revealed: the slow lazy form of her legs. He said nothing. Was he patient or shy? As she left the living room she stopped and, partially sheltering her own shyness with the door, she turned her face back over her shoulder and said, "Yeh can sleep beside me tonigh', if yeh want to."

Davy looked down to the floor, though it was only a glance to give him enough time to think. Time that the situation demanded of human relationship. He had seen her move tonight, felt her laugh and heard her thoughts. Really, there was simply never any question that he wouldn't.

Anne moved, shifting her weight from one foot to the other, and this made him look at her again. He saw her discomfort while she waited for an answer, saw the hint of hurt in her pale thin face, half hidden by the loose black hair resting on her shoulder.

"Wha' abou' Mickey?" Although he couldn't see it, he sensed her grip lighten on the handle on the other side of the door, saw the relief in the smile that opened her lips.

"Mickey's me brother, Davy, not me husband."

"Yeah, I suppose so, " he said casually. "This can only be for tonigh' though, so don't say an'thin' to him."

"Don't worry," she smiled. "I won't say an'thin' and make sure you don't either."

"Sure, okay then," said Davy, "I'll be in in a minute," and he shooed her towards the bedroom with his eyes. When the door had rolled gently shut behind her, he stood and rubbed his hands together, and thought . . . no, he didn't think at all! It was a time to get prepared, so he twisted a hand down the front of his jeans, down as far as the crotch, and he rubbed and lifted his fingers to his nose and sniffed. It was all right. And he knew Mickey had a toothbrush there, somewhere!

Teeth were scrubbed so vigorously the gums bled, and he cursed his luck for what seemed like a haemorrhage, but that soon stopped. Finally, he smoked some smack on the foil, left some handy in the kitchen cupboard and walked to the bedroom and pushed open the door.

"Will I turn on the ligh'?"

"No, no, you'll wake the baby."

Davy stripped at the door and stepped carefully towards the bed. Crouching, he crept rigidly beneath the covers where Anne lay waiting, stiffly. "Okay?" he said. "Yeah," she said, and he crawled and she stretched and they met, heads colliding, and it was hard and it wasn't right and he prayed and she regretted and they both got angry, but pretended it was cool.

"Sorry," he said. "It must be the gear," so he rolled away and he lay with his arm across his eyes.

"It's okay," she said, and after a pause asked, "Just hold me, will yeh?" She turned and slipped her head on to his chest and felt his soft hairless skin on her cheek, felt his strong arm drop across her shoulder and his fingers rest around the side of her breast. Face full, she let her lips cling to his skin, his hard breasts, firm nippled and speckled, and then let fingers run, just the tips, through the gorge of his chest, across the flats of his stomach and felt his shudder tremble through her hand.

"Easy," she said. "Easy."

"Hey," he said. "Hey, hah," as she stroked his private hair and held his sex and he heard her giggle.

"It's nothin' to do with the bleedin' gear at all, is it?" And he blushed. With one swift movement she swept above him and sank, sank gorgeously, saying, "Davy Byrne, Davy bleedin' Byrne!"

"Yeah?" he asked in the darkness.

"Oh shut up, yeh fool—Jaysis! You're a bleedin' ride, d'yeh know tha'?"

"Kiss me," he asked.

"Oh Davy, of course!" So she kissed him, she kissed him like a child, like a little boy, on the cheeks and the brow and the eyes, while her hands caressed his neck.

HE WASN'T SURE what it was that woke him the following morning. With his eyes closed, he tried to concentrate. Tried to recall had he heard a noise, or was it just the dull daylight sneaking through a gap in the curtain? He didn't care and went to pull the duvet to his face, but then remembered he didn't want to be there if Mickey called. He felt the warmth of Anne's back just a few inches from his own, could sense the curve of her spine and felt her hot, full arse sleeping tight against his. He found her toes and touched them with the heel of his foot, but she grunted, or was it groaned? She pulled her feet away. He felt himself go hard, sore hard, aching hard. But what was it that had woken him?

He opened his eyes and saw just a yard away, between the bars of the cot, Áine gazing across to him. She sucked on a blue soother that bobbled between her chubby cheeks and her fingers squeezed the teat of an empty bottle. Her expression hadn't changed when she saw that he had seen her, except perhaps to blink lazily. She seemed, sitting in her stained cotton sleeping suit, to be waiting for him to get up and go.

A couple of hours later, from the sofa in the living room, he heard Mickey's knock and was aware of the chill he felt. He heard Anne shriek at Mickey's call, "I'm comin', yeh stupid bastard," and knew then why no one would sleep with her regularly. And he remembered the commotion Áine had made earlier that morning, just after he had left the bedroom. Jaysis! She was even bad humoured with the child, screaming at her at that hour, when all she probably wanted was a bottle.

"Did yeh feel sorry for me last nigh'?" Mickey asked, pressing the sofa with the sole of his boot.

"Why?" Davy asked, opening his eyes.

"Because yeh came all the way over here and did all the work, without wakin' me."

"How d'yeh know wha' I did?"

"I just woke Anne up by batin' down the door, and she said when she went to bed last nigh', yeh were cuttin' up the gear. So c'mon, get up and give us a turn on."

"Yeh never think of an'thin' else, sure yeh don't? By the way," said Davy grinning, "I told yeh tha' yeh'd only have a black eye and a thick lip this mornin'! Is your nose alrigh'?"

"I don't think it's broken, but it's far from alrigh'. Look at the state of it! It's so sore, I could hardly wash it this mornin' and it looks like I've been hit in the face with a beetroot. I'll tell yeh, I want to get that Sheringham sap, I swear."

"I know wha' yeh mean. I've been lyin' awake half the nigh' thinkin' abou' the same thing meself."

"Really?"

"Yeah, really."

Never again. So far, they had only agreed that something would have to be done about it. As to what, well, the answer is always the same. But in what form? Just never again, because if you let people walk all over you, you get walked on.

Fight back. It was something they were better able to manage, something they knew about. It was an attitude they shared, though with a distance between them in how they believed it might best be expressed. Although he could throw a punch and swing a kick with the best of them, Mickey liked peace and quiet. But it was never a peace worth any price. It lost its value if he had to pay with a thick lip or a black eye. Then he believed at least the same should be returned. Davy, with a more extravagant sense of his own worth, didn't quite view the subject with the same kind of equanimity. No, for him a tooth in his hand meant six from the head of whoever put it there.

Davy liked to satisfy a grievance. Real or imagined, they both met with the same summary response: a calm, determined decision to get the culprit back. And it was a calm, determined Davy who said, "I think it's abou' time we got ourselves a couple of pieces."

"A couple of pieces of wha'?" Mickey asked.

"Guns, for fucksake!"

"But sure we didn't even think abou' gettin' into them when we were robbin'."

"This is different. We're goin' to need them, if Sheringham gets heavy again."

A delicious thrill surged through Mickey, with a flurry of images. All of himself looking cool. Like him in a black Italian silk suit, with turned up trousers and French pleats and the double breasted jacket buttoned casually. Where a hand could easily reach inside and lift out . . .

"Wha' are yeh gettin'? I mean, where are we goin' to get them."

"When I was in the Joy I shared a cell with Jamesie Riordain and he told me he can get his hands on a couple of pistols. He got bail the same day tha' I got out, so I'm goin' to go over to Edenmore today and see if he can still get them."

"Wha' kind?"

"Well, he said tha' they're the business, like they're not a couple of relics from the Civil War or an'thin'. One's a Charter Arms .38, and don't ask me wha' tha' means. I just know tha' they're the ones that yeh see in the films all the time, the ones with the snub-nosed barrels? The other's a Brownin' 9mm, semi-automatic with a twelve-round clip."

"Jaysis, yeh sound very technical all of a sudden."

"I didn't know an'thin' about them," said Davy, "but Jamesie wouldn't shut up abou' the fuckin' things, when we were locked up. Two hours is all yeh need with him and he'd make anyone an expert. He reckons that the Brownin' is bleedin' deadly. All yeh have to do is point it in the righ' direction and yeh can't miss."

"How much can he get them for?"

"It's £400 for the .38, that's with six rounds, and £700 for the Brownin', with the clip."

"It's a bit bleedin' steep isn't it?"

"Not really, not with the two of them fully loaded, and he says he can get more rounds for both of them."

"I'd love Sheringham to walk up to me then. I'd love to have the chance to tell him I'd kill him if he didn't fuck off. And when he asked me was I threatenin' him I'd say, 'No, I'm just goin' to blow your fuckin' head off,' and I'd take the Brownin' out and . . ."

"And wha'? Waste him in the pub?"

"Yeah, well . . ." said Mickey, "yeh never know."

"Somethin' else," said Davy, solemnly, "tha' we're goin' to have to sort out, is the money."

"Wha' do yeh mean?"

"Well, we're goin' to get reefed at some stage and it's different with the gear. While we only carry small amounts, we can swallow it or dump it durin' a chase, but we can't do tha' with the money. If the Filth get their hands on it, they'll seize it and we'll lose out one way or the other. They'll either say tha' they found traces on it, or else they'll rob it. Wha' we need is a place to stash it. A flat we don't stay at, just until we figure somethin' out."

"Do yeh know Kathleen Burke?" Anne asked Mickey. She had been dressing Áine in the bedroom and returned in time to catch the end of their conversation.

"No," he answered. "Why?"

"Yeh do know her," said Anne.

This was a habit which infuriated Mickey, like she needed to make him out to be either a liar or a gobshite.

"She used to go out for a drink with me, every Tursda' when we got our money."

He was curious and perhaps it was this that annoyed him. "Yeah? Well, wha' about her?"

"She's gone to live in England for a few months," said Anne.

Mickey snapped, "Wha' the fuck has tha' got to do with an'thin'?"

"Well I have the keys to her flat," she said, and in case it was important added, "All her furniture is still there."

"Jaysis," said Davy, "she must trust her neighbours." The significance hadn't been lost on him.

"Yeah," said Anne. "The people tha' live in the three flats beside her are alrigh' and they know tha' I'm lookin' after it for her. Every couple of weeks, she sends me over a couple of quid. All I have to do is open the windows for a while every few days and turn the ligh's on now and again, yeh know, check the letters and tha'."

"Where's her gaff? "

"Three floors up, on the fourteenth. It's a three bedroom flat."

"Give us the keys," said Davy.

They got the keys from Anne and went up to the flat, Mickey talking excitedly on the way. "This migh' be just wha' we want."

"Yeah, so long as nobody finds out abou' it."

"How will they? Oney me, you and Anne know abou' it."

"I suppose so. But we'll just use it for cuttin' up gear. We'll still have to do somethin' abou' the money. Can yeh imagine some little bastard creepin' it and comin' across five grand?"

They had a quick look around the flat. When they told Anne what they planned to do and that it would mean less risk to her, Davy suspected it was for the same reason she had told them about it in the first place.

SKINNIER AND JOJO were waiting for them at the snooker hall. Davy was secretly pleased with their punctuality, though he had warned them if they were late for work they would both be sacked. He knew many who were willing to take the same risks for the £100 a day Skinnier and Jojo currently earned. That they chose to draw this in heroin wasn't something that bothered him.

Jojo told him that Tony Freeny had been looking for him.

"Wha' does he want?" Davy asked.

"Wha' do yeh think? Though he just said tha' when I seen yeh, to tell yeh tha' he'd be up at half eigh'."

"Wha' are yeh goin' to do?" Mickey asked Davy.

"Does it ever fuckin' occur to yeh tha' it's wha' are we goin' to do?"

"Are *we* goin' to give Freeny a few bob?"

"We can't," said Davy. "Like we can't give it to Sheringham. If we give it to one, then every stroker in the bleedin' town'll be out puttin' the hammer on us."

"Wha' are we goin' to do then?"

"I don't know yet. I'll have to think about it."

Mickey flipped a coin in the air, caught it at the bottom of its fall, and called, "Heads or Harps?"

"Harps," said Davy.

"Your break then."

"Okay." He preferred playing pool like this, where you paid for the light rather than the game. He chalked his cue while he looked at the balls. A habit he had, and he only glanced at his work when it was time to lean and phew the dust from the tip. After edging the white ball to its spot, his left hand palmed the table and he bent to prepare to shoot, practising his cue stroke first with piston like precision. With proper aim, the cue struck the white ball below centre. Firm, controlled, it moved forward and smacked the yellow at the bottom of the pack. Both balls clung together, only for a moment, while the white spun, reversed direction and then rolled back towards Davy. He rose and watched. The pack clacked open, vulnerably, and the white continued to roll gently towards his cushion, where on impact, it rolled back a few inches on to the table.

"Fuck it anyway!"

"Ha ha ha, I don't know why yeh play tha' shot, when more often than not yeh make a bollix of it."

"No, neither do I." He waited until Mickey potted three balls, before putting his cue down and saying, "Get Jojo or someone to finish the game. I'm goin' to go over to Edenmore and find out wha' the score is with Jamesie."

"Do yeh want me to go with yeh?"

"No. I better go on me own."

"I wouldn't mind goin' meself."

"For fucksake, one of us has to stay here."

"Alrigh'" said Mickey. "But don't be long. Remember, it's your turn to get a hidin' if any of Sheringham's saps come back."

Davy left the snooker hall and walked to Patrick Pearse Tower, using the subway that tunnelled the dual carriageway. He collected £1,100 from Kathleen Burke's flat and two £40 bags, before walking back to Balcurris to pick up a helmet and the motorbike. He loved motorbikes and not for the usual reasons, like sitting astride a warm engine, while hands gripped control of both accelerator and clutch. Nor the kicking of gears, or the pose that's a consequence of speed and swerve. Rather, they offered him a space where he could think and make decisions encouraged and shaped by the speed and agility of the bike. It was a space he couldn't find when driving a car. A car could never flush out the trivial, like the way the wind that passed a bike could sweep the insignificant from the mind. Yet as he sped that day towards Coolock Lane, none of his thoughts seemed unimportant. Instead, as he rode towards Edenmore, his thoughts only seemed to circle around his head. Was Sheringham going to do anything else, before he had time to get him back? What was he going to say to Freeny? Would Jamesie be in? Could he still get the guns? He'd have to see Robin soon. Would he be able to get him two ounces this time? And all the while the thought which frightened him more than any other, the one that seemed to recur with more frequency: did the police know anything? He wouldn't have put it past Sheringham to tell them!

With all of this came the biggest doubt. While not always nagging, it was nevertheless constant. Would he be able for all this? He longed for the Time when the only problem of any significance was money, a Safe Time.

THERE IS A tradition in Dublin, a kind of cultural ritual which occurs with the birth of a son and concerns the chopping of the umbilical chord. Upon being severed at both ends, one end of the chord is noosed around the throat of the infant son and the other wrapped tightly around the fist of the mother. There is nothing sinister in this. It is a survival technique. While it might be argued that it traps the boy and stops the man wandering too far, benefit of the doubt should be given to what motivated the ceremony in the first place: a desire to create for the male a notion of home. A place that's always there. Somewhere to head for, whatever the reason. So even when we get the chance to get the fuck out of there, when the desire is to get as far away as possible, once we keep moving we're going to head for home anyway. The world is round!

As with anything, the whole process can lead to misconceptions. Chief among these, in relation to our little union, is the problem that it is often mistaken for a kind of pact, an unholy matrimonial alliance. Incestuous? Incestu-Shush!

Jamesie's mother, an aproned women in her early forties, answered Davy's knock. She recognised him as one of her son's friends and, after inviting him in, led him to the kitchen.

"He's oney out of bed yeh know and eatin' his breakfast, at this hour of the day. It's a bloody disgrace it is. The kids'll be home from school for their dinner in a minute."

In the kitchen, he saw that Jamesie was just about to start eating a fried breakfast. Two stiff eggs, two burnt sausages, two rashers of bacon, two sliced tomatoes, black and white pudding and any space left on the plate was filled with baked beans. He had a side plate with two chunks of salted, fried bread and a large mug of tea.

"How a'yeh, Davy? Wha's the story? Do yeh want a cup of tea?"

Before Davy could reply, Jamesie's mother interrupted, "I have a coddle ready for the kids and there's loads. Do yeh want some?"

Davy hesitated, but when he realised he would have to wait for Jamesie he said, "Why not! Go on then, I'll have a little bit."

Mrs Riordain served Davy a steaming bowl of boiled, split skin Keirns sausages and shrivelled rashers of bacon. Piping hot potatoes and strands of onion cushioned the meat and oily stew juice seeped around the rest of the bowl. He sprinkled the meal with salt and pepper and spiced it generously with brown YR sauce. Mrs Riordain cut and buttered a couple of thick slices of bread from a fresh turnover and presented these with the offer, "If yeh want any more, just help yourself." She knew Jamesie would probably go to his bedroom to talk to his friend when he finished his breakfast, so she slipped upstairs and made her son's bed.

Jamesie, being the eldest child and an only son, was an apple of innocence in his mother's jaundiced eye. Unwaveringly loyal, her defence of him was simple, if double barrelled: a complete denial that he ever did anything wrong, and if that was incapable of hitting its target, then the blame for his behaviour was laid firmly at the feet of anyone or anything else. It was never, ever, Jamesie's fault. Even, remarkably, after three prison sentences. These, for some reason, rather than diminish her fidelity, only hardened it still further.

When Mrs Riordain had slipped upstairs, Davy turned to Jamesie and asked him, "A'yeh still on the gear?"

"Of course I am. Wha' did yeh think?"

"Well how in the name of Jaysis do yeh eat all tha'?"

"Me ma says I have to look after meself. Mind you, I have to pay her for the food because the oul' fella isn't workin'."

"Does she feed him like tha'?"

"Are yeh jokin' me? She used to, but the doctor told him he'd have a heart attack within six months if he wasn't careful. Yeh wouldn't believe wha' he's doin' now."

"What's tha'?"

"He's goin' around tellin' everyone tha' me oul' wan has been tryin' to murder him for years. I'm bleedin' serious. Wha' made it worse was, me oul' wan also told him not to worry too much, tha' it was just a mid-life crisis, tha' all oul' fellas get them when they get to his age."

"I'll tell yeh, I don't know abou' your oul' fella, but if yeh keep eatin' breakfasts' like tha', they'll kill yeh before the gear does."

Jamesie leaned across the table and said, "I doub' tha', Davy, I doub' tha' very much. Wha' brings yeh out here anyway?"

"I was wonderin' if yeh could still get those guns?"

"Why?"

"Because I want to buy the things off yeh."

"Hang on, here's me oul' wan back. We'll talk abou' it in me room."

When she walked into the kitchen Davy said, "Jaysis, Missus Riordain, this coddle's lovely. If yeh had any to spare I'd take it home with me."

"Go on out of tha'," she said, but enjoying the flattery she turned to Jamesie and told him, "It's a pity the rest of your friends aren't like tha'."

As Mrs Riordain predicted, Jamesie told her that he would get out of her way and talk to Davy in his bedroom. There, Davy asked him had he any foil and when Jamesie said he had, Davy locked the door behind them.

"Here, here's a quarter for yeh."

"You'll have to pay for these rods."

Davy took the money out from inside his jacket and said, "I've eleven hundred quid here. That's wha' yeh said yeh could get them for, wasn't it?"

"Holy fuck! You've made a few bob quick enough, haven't yeh?" said Jamesie, staring at the bundle.

"Yeah, but listen, I need the guns today. I need them as quick as yeh can get them."

"Well it'll take me at least an hour."

"That's alrigh'. But I'll need a spare bullet for each one."

"Why?" Jamesie asked.

"Because I'll have to test them before I pay yeh for them."

"Where in the name of fuck are yeh goin' to test them?"

"In Santry Woods," said Davy. "I need to be certain they're workin' properly."

Jamesie sighed. "Nothin's ever simple with you, is it?"

KILLING TIME, DAVY decided to call to the garage on the Howth Road where Robin told him he worked. After taking the keys from the ignition and stepping off the bike, he mooched around until he found Robin in an office around the back. He went in without knocking. "How a'yeh, Robin? Wha's the story, hey?"

Robin was surprised and he wondered had Davy mistakenly believed he could call on a casual basis. The Borstal mark below his left eye, even though Davy had put it there himself, was a fashion accessory Robin didn't want strolling about in his father's garage.

"Hello, Davy. What can I do for yeh?"

"I need two ounces for tomorrow," said Davy, smiling.

"Two? What's wrong? Did yeh lose the last one?"

"No," said Davy smugly, "but I'll oney have a quarter ounce left by tomorrow nigh' and I don't want to leave it until the last minute."

"That's okay," said Robin, impressed. "I'll meet yeh tomorrow at the same place as the last time and at six o'clock too."

"How abou' a reduction in the price?"

"Sorry. I can't afford it. Have yeh had any other problems yet?"

"What kind of problems?"

"I dunno. Drug squad? Georgie Sheringham maybe?"

"Well, I've had a bit of hassle, but just from Sheringham so far."

"How much does he want?"

"A grand a week, or else I've to stop."

"He's a bit of a pain in the arse like that, oul' Georgie. Still, if yeh keep knockin' it out as fast as yeh are, then a grand a week shouldn't be too much of a problem."

"I'm not givin' him a fuckin' penny."

"What are yeh goin' to do then?"

"I don't know yet. I mean, I haven't made up me mind. I just know what I'm not goin' to do."

Robin nodded, admiring the confidence. "Any other problems?"

"Money!" said Davy. "I don't know wha' I'm goin' to do with it, I mean, where to put it and tha'. The last thing I want is for it to be confiscated or checked for traces."

"Yeah, I know what yeh mean. I might be able to help yeh with that, but it's goin' to cost yeh a few bob."

"This is the fuckin' thing abou' it," said Davy. "It seems to me tha' if I start payin' money out, it won't stop and I'll end up makin' nothin'. It's amazin', isn't it?"

Robin smiled tolerantly. "I'll tell yeh what, I'll see yeh tomorrow with the gear. Then if yeh want to meet me here on Tuesday, at about six, we can go for a pint. I have a few ideas that might interest yeh, about how to protect your cash."

"Fair enough," said Davy. "I'll do tha'."

Robin could sense the hesitance in Davy, could see the kind of suspiciousness his gesture had aroused.

"You're right, Davy, if you're wonderin' why the generosity, or why the friendliness? You're right because it has nothin' to do with either. I want yeh to make a few bob because then I'll make an extra pound or two as well."

"So do I," said Davy, and he smiled at any doubt that Robin might have had. "So do I."

DAVY DECIDED TO cruise out to the harbour at Howth, where he walked along the west side of the pier. With each step he bounced the helmet he held off his thigh. Some of his problems were starting to sort themselves out. Robin was going to have the gear for him. Robin? He still didn't know his surname. And Jamesie was going to get him the guns. This helped dilute some of the doubt, protect some of the rawness and sheltered his susceptibility.

As he walked the length of the pier, he passed the harbour master's office and a fresh fish shop which window displayed iced trays of chilled surprise-eyed fish. To his right, long lines of idle trawlers sat steady on the water. Were there no fish to be caught?

He climbed some large granite steps at the end of the pier which staired the inside of the harbour wall and sat down on the summit, letting his legs hang seaside. The friendly breeze that brushed his face encouraged him to breathe deeply, to let the sea-salt air rush in, up past flared nostrils. This, aah, he exhaled with a slight cough, ahem, and spat, flop, a gollier of phlegm, casually on to the green-brown sea below him. He watched it drop and hit the water and sway on the slight swell of the sea. It was time to think, to concentrate unconsciously in a way that blurred everything else, like the beach that ran along the left of him and the harbour and its trawlers in residence behind. Even Ireland's Eye, which sat in the sea ahead. Everything but the sea itself. The sea was reassuring, comforting, friendly. As he sat staring at the water softly wet-slapping the sea stones below, he lit a cigarette and pulled deeply, like he might be trying to protect his lungs from too much fresh sea air.

Moments like these were used to strengthen himself and to attempt to determine a sense of assurance. He knew it was an opportunity to dump the doubts of that morning. Doubts that could make him feel like he carried the weight of the sea across his shoulders. Mickey's doubts were different, something he could smile at. The rights and wrongs of things. Only with a wistful heart could he entertain that kind of simplicity, the ideas of someone else's Time. Consensus Ireland was dead and gone and Davy wasn't going to lose out.

Wasn't there only one way into this life? Only one way out. And you only got one go. The only fucking problem was, his kind always seemed to run out of Time before they got a go. The words rang loud in his ears: "Work hard! Tighten your belt!" But his oul' wan had been working her fingers to the bone all her life, and her oul' wan before her. All right, so his oul' fella was a bit of an exception. But on the whole . . . no, he was right. He knew what to do. If you can't beat them, join them. And he would work hard, he would tighten his belt. And it was every man for himself. Yet something still lingered to haunt him and he couldn't figure out what it was. Was the obvious sitting at the end of his nose and mocking him? Or was all that a paranoia, a fear that kept him sharp?

When he finished his cigarette and tossed the butt into the sea, he climbed back down the steps and hurriedly walked the length of the pier again. On the stretch of the Howth Road that he used on the way back to Jamesie's, he drove as fast as the bike would allow. He drove like all he had was the Time.

JAMESIE WAS WAITING for him.

"Did yeh get them?"

"Yeah," said Jamesie. "Here, d'yeh want to have a look at them?" He offered Davy two polythene parcels.

"No, hang on until we get to the woods. Have yeh got a helmet? You'll need one for the bike."

"I'll go and get it."

On the Airport Road, at the bottom of the rise to the Furry Park Pitch and Putt Club, Davy parked the bike behind a bus shelter and both lads leapt over a low wall into the woods. They had a look and, seeing no one around, walked to their left, circling a neglected pond which was being slowly suffocated by young saplings, rotten logs, greedy water reeds and lilies and a screen of wild hedgerow.

Davy and Jamesie explored the area thoroughly to make certain no one was there. They finally settled somewhere near the centre. From there, the noise of the traffic from the Airport Road was only a hum, a soft wall of sound that offered them privacy.

Jamesie opened one of the parcels and took out the .38. He showed an impatient Davy how to examine and handle the gun. Opening the chamber revealed it contained six rounds, and when Jamesie flick closed it, he handed it over. Davy smiled, big-eyed. It was heavier than he anticipated, but smaller too. He was almost deliriously giddy when he raised his arm, aimed and fired at the trunk of a tree. The fucking noise! Christ!

He looked at Jamesie and tried to shoo the noise, tried to wave it away. He tried to shush it, even after it had passed. Cowering slightly, he glanced round, sure that any animal or bird within earshot had scattered. He heard Jamesie laugh and say, "It's alrigh', for fucksake." Davy laughed with him and blew a breath that was like a nod and a wink at the power of something new.

He handed the .38 back to Jamesie, who replaced the spent round and rewrapped the pistol in polythene. He followed the same procedure with the Browning, showing Davy how to fit the clip and where the spent shell would pop from. He showed him the safety catch, how to slide back the barrel and let the first round slip in front of the firing pin. Davy wasn't so impatient this time and when he held it he realised why Jamesie had been so exuberant in the Joy. This time, when he aimed and fired the pistol, he felt the power jump back into his wrist. The noise wasn't so harsh, more of a sharp crack, and the action smoother. As the bullet thudded into the trunk of the tree, the gun flung its head back nonchalantly, like it had just plipped a spit that might take the head off you. This thing was full of itself.

Jamesie stood with his hand held out, waiting to receive the gun to rewrap it, but Davy held it longer this time. He felt it sit in his hand and saw how it looked there. Then, turning to face him, he raised his arm again and pointing the pistol at Jamesie's head he asked, "Did yeh really believe I was goin' to give yeh £1,100 for these?"

Jamesie said nothing as the colour sank from his face, but he began to step backwards. All he could see was the blood-beat pulsing on the side of Davy's neck and the horribly obvious nowhere to go, no space, no cover, no time, no . . .

Davy, dropping his arm to his side, said, "I'm only jokin', for fucksake."

"You're a cunt, Davy, a poxy fuckin' cunt! Jaysis!"

"Did yeh really think I'd do somethin' like tha'?" Davy asked, chuckling.

"Of course I thought yeh'd fuckin' do it. I wouldn't put an'thin' past yeh, yeh fuckin' mental case. Like wha' a'yeh buyin' them for anyway? I've a good mind not to sell them to yeh now."

"Hey," said Davy, like Robert De Niro. "Don't tempt me." Smiling, he looked at him for a moment and said, "Sorry 'bou' tha'. Here, here's your money."

They replaced the spent round from the clip and wrapped the Browning in polythene before walking back to the bike. Jamesie agreed with the suggestion that he pick up a taxi on the main road. Davy didn't want to be driving around any longer than he had to. He certainly didn't want to have to stop near Santry police station, where Jamesie could catch the 17A. They parted with a wave. With a broad grin from Davy and a rueful shake of the head from Jamesie.

At Pearse Tower, Davy went to the spare flat first to stash the guns and then down the few flights to Anne's. He felt important, safe, and he chuckled every time he remembered pointing the Browning at Jamesie. Life had a habit of looking after him. It really had. It had a habit of pointing things out to him, of pointing him towards the right direction.

Davy allowed Anne to persuade him, after she had promised not to tell Mickey, to let her chase a line from the smack. He saw the colour drain from her face too, saw the look that said her sense of balance was being rattled. He could see she was feeling the inside of her head fall to her stomach and her stomach drop to the soles of her feet. He hid his smile on the other side of his face when she lurched to the toilet to vomit. He didn't know that it wasn't her first, that she had already had a couple from Mickey.

At Balcurris, he parked the bike and left the helmet in the flat before hurrying off to Mickey to let him know how things had gone. It amazed him how easy it was sometimes. Retrospect made it easy. To get it. To see what the point was. When he was going forward, looking back was a great way to see with certainty. It was a great way to see with clarity the things he was meant to see. As Davy reached the car park, at the rear of the north-west side of the shopping centre, life decided to remind him how hard it could get.

As he walked towards the shops, he heard a car drive behind and then alongside of him. He kept walking until a voice with a rural accent called out, "Whoa, slow down, Mr Byrne. What's your hurry?"

Davy turned and watched the driver step out from an unmarked police car, a navy-blue Allegro.

Detective Noel Maskey spoke as he walked towards him. "Well, where are you off to this fine day?"

"Tha' way," said Davy, pointing towards the shopping centre.

"Don't be so fuckin' cute with me, boy," Maskey told him. "Turn round and put your hands behind your back."

"Why? Wha' are yeh arrestin' me for?"

"Why? Is that important?"

Davy, relieved he wasn't carrying anything, answered, "Well, it gets a bit borin' gettin' arrested for the same fuckin' thing all the time, either the Drugs Act or the Offences Against the State Act, yeh know? And it isn't right either. There's a certain breed of bastard that offends me all the fuckin' time and there isn't an act to arrest them with, is there?"

Detective Garda Joseph Langley, who had slunk from his side of the car, was strolling lazily with his hands in his pockets. "Maybe we should get them to amend the act, especially for you."

"Yeah? Well, while I'm waitin', why don't yeh arrest me for somethin' different, like murder? Or maybe a bank robbery?"

"Nothin' in this world would give me greater pleasure," said Maskey. "Do you think you could help me with it?"

"Why don't yeh make one up? You're usually good at tha' kind of thing, aren't yeh?" said Davy, and even Langley had to smile.

"You're a barrel of fuckin' laughs, Byrne, but that suits me fine. Now put your hands behind your back like a good little boy and laugh all the way to the barracks."

It was time for Davy to comply. He could sense it, so he joined his hands behind him and his wrists were handcuffed tightly. A small group of women had gathered a few yards from the police car and watched what was happening. Davy didn't recognise any of them, but this didn't stop him shouting, "Mrs Reilly? Will yeh go and tell me ma I'm after gettin' arrested again? For nothin'. Tell her to get a doctor for me and let her know tha' when yeh seen me there wasn't a mark on me. Can yeh see?"

The women, having rested bags of shopping at their feet, chattered excitedly amongst themselves.

"Shut your mouth, Byrne, and get into the car, otherwise it'll be an ambulance you require," Maskey told him and he aggressively bundled Davy into the back seat.

As the car pulled off, Davy asked again, "Well, wha' are yeh reefin' me for?"

"I'll tell you after I search you," said Maskey.

"You're getting very fond of seein' me with no clothes on, aren't yeh?"

Although stung by the remark, Maskey didn't answer him. This was about the fifth time since Christmas that he had arrested

Byrne to search him for drugs, but he had yet to find anything. It might have been illegal had he used the Drugs Act formally, but hadn't used anything. He had just pulled him in and would have used whatever act he needed had he found the means to charge him.

It was Langley who responded first saying to Davy, "We've been hearin' a few stories about you recently."

"I'm sure yeh fuckin' have," Davy replied, "especially if you're givin' tuppeny junkies the price of a bottle for the privilege."

"By Jesus, you're like lightnin' with them smart answers, Byrne. What did you do, spend the last two months in Mountjoy thinkin' them up?"

"D'yeh really think I'd nothin' better to do? Anyway, I know yeh oney send the likes of me there to keep your culchie cousins wealthy with overtime."

Davy leaned forward to emphasise his point and this enabled Maskey to catch him with a backhanded slap. He grinned like a retard at his own accuracy. Davy, smarting from a burning left ear, sat back in relative safety and continued. "I just had a rest for a couple of months. It's a nice place to use a bit of gear because yeh have a lot of peace and quiet. Of course, I had to pay some of your cousins to bring it in for me, but then nothin' in life is free, is it?"

At the rear of Ballymun Garda station they removed Davy from the car. As they were taking him through the building, they passed a uniformed sergeant. "Ah, Mr Byrne, back with us already I see?" Two more uniformed Gardaí, rookies, who had been standing beside him, began to laugh.

"Well, I can't stay long," Davy said. "It's just a flyin' visit."

The rookies made some loud remarks about how long it would be before Davy saw the light of day again. The sergeant didn't waste his breath.

Maskey and Langley brought Davy into an empty interrogation room, removed his handcuffs and told him to strip. As he removed his clothes, Maskey searched each item thoroughly. He picked up Davy's underpants using a pen, held his nose and taunted him. Spinning the pants on the pen, he asked Davy, "Are you sure you haven't got anything buried in here?"

Langley sat and with his hands behind his head and watched the procedure.

Davy complained, "I'm sure youse get off on this."

"Well," Maskey said, with mock sincerity, "if you weren't the dirty little junkie that you are, we wouldn't have to."

"Okay," said Davy. "So I'm a junkie, but you're a copper and what's the difference?"

Maskey looked puzzled, Langley uninterested.

"I think about drugs all day and take them whenever I can. I go to sleep dreamin' about them. Now, I bet yeh tha' you do the same thing with criminal offences. I bet when yeh haven't got any real ones, yeh begin make some up. Personal ones, like the crimes your wife commits against yeh, or your sons or daughters, yeah?"

He only had Maskey's attention, so Davy concentrated on him. "D'yeh worry tha' someone like me will give your daughter a ride up the arse? Give her the germ? And maybe take a photo while I'm at it, of her arse full up to the brim with my prick, hey?"

"By Christ, you're one sick whore, Byrne. Do you know that? But your filthy disgusting gob won't work on me. I haven't got a daughter."

"Sorry," said Davy, "I meant your son. It's just tha' he looks like a daughter when he's dressed up like that."

Langley smiled. Maskey, feeling threatened, rushed confidently, "I haven't got a son either."

Davy smiled. "So that's it then. All yeh have is a couple of empty shells for those things tha' yeh call balls. And yeh like to look. Is tha' it? Yeh like to look at a couple of real ones like these," said Davy, cupping his in his hands, "and wonder wha' life migh' be like if yeh had any yourself."

Maskey couldn't help but strike Davy across the side of the head with an open hand, a hand he had only managed to open from a full fist at the last moment.

Trying to stay both out of reach and on his feet, Davy asked, "What's wrong? Am I cuttin' a bit close to the bone?"

Maskey raised his arm to strike again but before he could do so, Davy warned, "If yeh do tha' again, I'm goin' to smack me face against the side of tha' wall and then start screamin'. You can explain it to the doctor. Those oul' wans saw me gettin' into the car without a scratch on me."

Maskey hesitated, before restraining himself. Byrne's threat hadn't deflected him. Instead, a discernible eye encouraged him to wait. It invited him to add another year to the sentence he was sure he would see Byrne get one day.

Langley had similar ideas. When he had first been stationed at Ballymun, Byrne had just been released from St Patrick's Institute for Young Offenders. On that occasion, Byrne had returned to prison for breaking his probation order by mixing with known and older criminals. He had also faced more serious robbery charges at the time, but still escaped conviction due to a lack of evidence. The thought that Byrne, by twenty-one, had established a reputation of almost mythical proportions, stretching back to the time he had thrown a dog someone had threatened him with on to the roof of the school, bothered Langley. When informers on the estate were reduced to guessing who was responsible for a crime, Byrne's name was often first on their lips. He too wanted a reputation, and to establish it he would have to send someone like Byrne to prison for a very long time. But how? While the sleeveen hadn't a good bone in his body, he also had nothing but the cunning to go with it.

Davy noticed that Langley's gaze had rested on his groin. "A'yeh enjoyin' this, too?"

"Put your clothes back on." When Davy had dressed, a rookie was called to the room and told, "Fuck him out."

YES, LIFE REALLY had a habit of looking after Davy, reminding him why important things he had to do should be done soon. A self-satisfied smile spread across his face. It was nice of those Garda bleedin' Síochána to warn him. And then he smiled a bitter smile, a twisted, frightened smile. That poxy fuckin' Maskey! Why did he always take things so personally?

At the snooker hall, he told Mickey what had happened and asked him, "What's me face like? The fucker caught me there, just there over the eye. Is it red? Can yeh see it?"

"There isn't a mark on it, for fucksake," said Mickey. "It just looks a bit dirty."

"Tha' must be a bruise," said Davy, looking for a bump between his eye and the side of his head.

"It's been all go here on the Western Front, while yeh were away in the East. Jojo and Skinnier oney have a few packs left, so I'm goin' to go over and get another twenty. I've got £500 on me, so I'll leave tha' in the flat while I'm there. Where did yeh stash the guns? I want to have a look at them."

Davy said where they were hidden and told Mickey, "Now be careful. The two of them are loaded. Don't be long. I don't want those two runnin' out of gear."

Mickey promised he wouldn't be longer than half an hour. After he left, Davy went over and tried to see his reflection in the windows of the slot machines, but the image was too hazy. When he tried to do the same with the chrome panelling his features were distorted, so he cursed the absence of mirrors in the toilet. There had been three the day the snooker hall opened, but one had been smashed in a fight and the other two were robbed in the commotion. He sought the opinion of Jojo and Skinnier. When they too said that they couldn't see anything, he accused them of being too stoned to see properly and snarled at Jojo, "I fuckin' warned yeh abou' usin' too much gear, didn't I?"

He then told them to tell every junkie who bought a bag to put the gear in their mouths until they left the shopping centre. Each bag was well wrapped in cling film to keep them dry. He explained the necessity for this, that the police knew something. So Jojo and Skinnier were to stay away from any strangers who came in. They were both standing beside him when he explained this, but he could tell they weren't listening. Both were stoned and that was probably all that mattered. It irritated him. Oh, how it fucking irritated him. The bastards! It was all that concerned them. Did they think there was nothing else to worry about?

"Hey, Jojo, c'mere. Wha' a'yeh doin' near the fuckin' door? Didn't I tell yeh to stay down tha' end? If yeh don't want to knock out the gear, then just tell me, yeah? I'll get someone else to do it. Well?"

"I do want to do it."

"Then do wha' I fuckin' tell yeh. I mean it."

While waiting on Mickey to return, Davy played pool with Yako, who had started to lodge in and around the snooker hall, running errands for Davy and Mickey whenever they needed him. He was earning more than he had been when bumming with the 20p brigade. So much so, he had almost stopped abusing his favourite cough mixture, Phensedyl, and had progressed to Dyhydrocodeine, or Difs as the kids in the shops called them. These cost Yako 50p each and he took a dozen at a time. When Mickey came in, Yako was dispatched for a Chinese takeaway.

At sixteen, he felt important too. Davy liked him, and nobody else was better than Yako at getting the things Davy wanted. Like the food. He knew to go to the mobile van at the back of the snooker hall and not the takeaway in the shopping centre. And to ask for extra onion in the chicken curry. And not to be too long about anything, or to lie about anything. That was all Davy ever really asked. "Don't tell me lies now," or "Don't be long now."

This job was ten times fucking better than that milk round. Half past four in the morning! Dragging screeching crates around the alleyways and lanes of Poppintree. And the metal cage on the cart that stuck to your hand with the cold. And Mick the milkman talking about sex all the time. The only thing they ever got out of the oul' wans on their round was abuse if they woke them, or a sob story every Friday when they were collecting the bill money. That was when Mick the Slick came into his own. It was a laugh that day, when he tried it on with Mrs O'Malley. She told Mick she was waiting on Mr O'Malley to come back from the labour with her money. Mick told her she could forget about it if . . . he next thing was Mr O'Malley coming out from the kitchen and chasing Mick down the road and fucking milk bottles at him. He even started fucking them at Yako, just because he was laughing. Yako couldn't stop laughing.

After the round, Yako, too tired to go back to bed, would fall asleep on the sofa. His oul' wan would wake him with his dinner, mashed potatoes and fried eggs. All he seemed to have time to do was to run round getting a cough bottle and then kill a few hours before it all started again. He only lasted three weeks at it. Not that it mattered. He didn't have to tap up the price of a bottle every day any more. Especially now he knew Davy, who was capable of dropping into his sweaty palm what Yako used to earn in a week, without so much as a how's your father. Yako hadn't got a father. Well he had. Everybody had. But his ma and da got divorced when he was two and his da stayed in England and his ma came back to live in Dublin, where she knew she should have stayed in the first place because you couldn't get divorced here. And that was that really. But now his ma was sick. And she was very thin. And she was too ashamed to tell him. But he knew. He knew that they wanted to cut off her diddy and she wouldn't let them. And now she hurt. And when the pain got bad she blamed it on men, and said that there was only ever one thing on their filthy minds. Of course, she knew Yako wasn't like that.

When he came back with the food, they stopped playing pool. They sat on the floor to eat, as it was more comfortable then eating from the small stools that scattered the hall and the manager moaned when they ate from the tables.

Davy picked at his food. "Look at this fuckin' thing! He never gets enough fuckin' onions."

"I don't give a bollix. I'm starvin'. Aren't yeh?" Mickey asked.

"Well, I had a coddle out in Jamesie's today. It was fuckin' gorgeous, full of onions too."

"I migh' go over to me ma's tomorrow and see will she make one for me."

"Yeah," said Davy, "yeh should bring her up a few bob too. I'm goin' to give me oul' wan a ton tomorrow."

"Wha' for?"

"Because she probably hasn't a shillin', tha's wha' for."

"Righ'," said Mickey, a little guiltily, because he hadn't thought the same way. "I'll tell her I won a few bob on the horses or somethin'. I haven't seen her in ages." He smiled at the thought, of her giving out because he was staying at Anne's and getting her to collect clean clothes for him.

"Have yeh thought of wha' you're going to say to Freeny?"

"No," said Davy. "I'll wait and see what he says and then take it as it goes."

He knew exactly what he was going to say! But there is nothing quite like the danger of intent, especially when there's just time for another breath and a que sera sera, whatever will be, will be.

They finished eating and were smoking cigarettes, when Yako came over and began cleaning up. "Wha' are yeh doin' later?" Davy asked him.

"Nothin' much. Why?"

"I want yeh to be here at half seven. There's somethin' I need yeh for, okay?"

"Sure, yeah."

"Don't be late now, alrigh'?"

"Yeah, okay."

Davy then turned to Mickey and said, "C'mon and I'll show yeh how to play pool."

"Show me how to play pool? How much do yeh owe me now? It must be a grand."

"A grand?" said Davy, with mock surprise. "Alrigh' then, doubles or quits on the first game." When he played, he left Mickey with five reds on the table and he teased provocatively, mischievously, "See? Any time I want, I just change gear, and that's it, bang! The game's over."

They played another game to prove his point, then began all over again at a fiver.

At half seven, Davy stopped playing and walked over to Yako. He explained to him what he had to do. "In about ten minutes, meet me on the stairs at the tenth floor in Pearse Tower. I don't want yeh to go straigh' there. Walk down Shanghan Road first and cut back through the flats."

Yako, nodding, concentrated on what Davy was saying.

"If yeh come across any Filth in the Tower, still walk to the tenth, but when yeh get there, fall down a few of the stairs and start screamin'. Yeh know, make out that you've had an accident." Yako began to giggle. "I'm fuckin' serious. Go on now, and don't tell anyone where you're goin'."

Yako left and repeated Davy's instructions to himself. Tenth floor in ten minutes in Pearse Tower. Seemed simple enough. Just walk there in a direction that was the shape of a horseshoe.

Davy called over to Mickey, "I'm just goin' over to the flat for a minute, okay?"

"Yeah. Just make sure you're back for eigh'. I don't want to be here on me own when Freeny gets here."

"I won't be any longer than fifteen minutes," Davy told him, and he was casually saluted by Mickey as he left. Outside, he guessed that Yako would just be leaving the opposite side of the subway. When he reached Pearse Tower, he walked to the thirteenth floor, to Burke's flat, where he took out the Browning and kissed it. Or rather, he carried it to his lips and touched it softly. It was a way of stressing the importance, a way of asking not to be let down, and he was sure he had seen someone doing this in a film, so it was probably a lucky thing to do. Having rewrapped it in the polythene and shoved it down the front of his jeans, he waited for one minute.

In the circumstances, a minute was a difficult time to calculate, an Edgy Time, but when he was sure it had passed, he left the flat, closing the door quietly and turning the key for the mortise lock smoothly. He had the knack of it now, knew to just slip his fingers in the letter box, pull the door and turn the key in the same movement, clunk. He crept to the stairway, trying to walk lightly, silently. He could hear nothing except the eerie wind that whistled from the bottom of the tower. When the lift chugged into movement, it hurried him. At the stairs, the temptation was to call down to Yako, but he was afraid Yako might fuck himself down a flight of stairs and start screaming his back was broken. Descending, Davy gripped the grey painted rail with one hand and fingertipped the smooth-pebble wall with the other. The only way he could call to Yako was to breathe loudly and cough familiarly, in the hope that Yako might recognise it. From the eleventh floor he heard Yako do the same and soon saw him bending midway through a flight while pretending to tie a lace. "What's the story, Yako? Is everything alrigh'?"

Yako stood and said, "Yeah, Davy, why?"

"Nothin'." Davy listened carefully again and said, "Here, stick tha' down your trousers."

Yako took the parcel. He had seen Davy remove it from his jeans, so he hid it the same way, then holding his cheap bomber jacket up, he childishly asked, "Is tha' alrigh'?"

Davy tugged at the waistband on Yako's jeans and tucked the

package in tighter. As he dropped the front of the jacket over the bump, he told him, "For fucksake, Yako, you'll have to get a better jacket." When Yako blushed, Davy smiled benevolently. "The next time yeh see Maree Whelan scorin' off Skinnier or Jojo, give her your measurements and tell her to get yeh a decent leather jacket. Tell her I'll fix her up and don't take an'thin' off her that's out of Dunnes or Pennys. Make sure tha' she gets yeh somethin' that's the business, okay?"

"Really, Davy? Really? Are yeh serious?"

"Of course I am. Now go on, go over to the snooker hall. Go straigh' to the toilet and wait for me in the last cubicle. If there's any strangers there, just have a piss, come back out and stay somewhere tha' I can see yeh."

Yako nodded, but didn't say anything. He was in a hurry. Maree Whelan was up nearly every night and everybody knew that she could get anything you wanted. Everybody knew what she couldn't get on the kites, her sister could get shoplifting. "Make sure it's the business." He would! And he wondered what colour he would get and how long he would have to wait.

"Go on," said Davy. "Wha' are yeh waitin' for? I'll be righ' behind yeh."

Yako skipped down the stairs, and when Davy guessed that there was a safe distance between them, he followed. At the snooker hall, he went straight over to Mickey and asked, "Has Freeny been in?"

"No, not yet."

"Is everything alrigh'?"

"Yeah, sure."

Muttering something about having a piss, Davy went out to the toilet and walked slowly to the last cubicle. The sound of the permanent trickle of water from the overflow was accompanied by Yako's soft breaths. Davy banged on the door. "It's me, Yako, hurry up."

Startled, Yako opened the door clumsily and let him in.

"Quick, give it to me," Davy demanded. He took the parcel from Yako, removed the Browning from the polythene and shoved the naked pistol down his jeans. He wanted Yako to see what he had been carrying, wanted to see the look on his face. After he folded the wrapping into a neat square, he handed it back. "Here, mind that for me. Now listen, I might have to leave here in a hurry . . ." Yako looked a little confused, unsure, so Davy told him, "I mean the snooker hall, not the toilet. If I do, then don't worry about an'thin'. But if yeh see Tony Freeny comin' and goin', then come back in here and wait on me. Have yeh got all tha'?"

Yako, wide eyed, nodded.

"Don't tell a soul abou' this, I'm warnin' yeh. I'll hear it if yeh do."

"I won't open me mouth, Davy, honest I won't."

Davy peeled a twenty pound note from a small bundle of money he had pulled from his pocket and handed it to Yako. "Here, that's in case I don't need yeh later."

Yako took the money and bowed with gratitude. Davy left the toilet and walked over to Mickey, where he waited nervously for Freeny to arrive. Smoking heavily was something Davy did in order to control his fear. He would smoke until it sickened him.

Mickey recognised the symptoms. "Don't worry, Davy. If the sap starts any hassle, just give us a shout. The two of us can give him a half dozen swift digs to the head, that'll soon shut him up."

Davy carefully slid his jumper up to reveal the butt of the pistol.

"For fucksake, Davy! Wha' a'yeh up to?"

"Don't worry. I've no intentions of shootin' him . . . well, not really."

"Is tha' thing loaded?"

"Yeah."

He glanced at a clock on the wall, five minutes to eight, and as he looked down Freeny walked in. Davy watched him from the shadows around his pool table thinking Freeny, in his Burtons overcoat, looked bigger than usual. He watched him greet people, smile smugly and stroll towards their table. Davy looked to make sure that Yako was waiting.

"How a'yeh, Davy?

"Not bad, Tony." He lounged as far back as he could from Freeny while he tried to assess his mood. "Wha's the story?"

"Well, I heard tha' yeh migh' have a little message for me, tha' you've been havin' a nice bit of luck lately."

Davy grinned. "C'mon and we talk abou' it in the jacks."

Freeny grinned too and his swagger swayed a little more distinctly as Davy led him towards the toilet. He even took his hands from his overcoat pocket and began to rub them in anticipation.

Davy opened the toilet door and guided them in. Facing Freeny's back he told him, "Yeh know you're not gettin' a fuckin' penny off me, don't yeh?"

Freeny hunched a little as he turned defensively and asked, "Wha' do yeh mean? Wha' the fuck's got into yeh?"

"I'm knockin' a bit of gear out now, from up here?"

"Well that's no fuckin' secret. Everybody knows tha'."

"Yeah well, wha's mine is me own. I owe yeh nothin'."

"I always thought tha' yeh had a bit of sense, Davy, but I'm goin' to have to . . ."

Davy had slipped the Browning from his jeans and raised it with apprehension. When his arm stopped, the gun was aimed at Freeny's face. "You're goin' to have to do wha'?"

Freeny heard the fear rattle in Davy's voice and saw the effort it took to control the shake in his arm. Memory reminded him of that Time when his own voice had been full of fear and the effort it had taken when his own arm shook.

"This is my fuckin' pitch, Tony. I don't want to cause any aggro abou' it and I don't want any trouble. But I don't want anybody interfering either. D'yeh understand tha'? This is mine. I mean mine and Mickey's."

"Yeah, yeah, sure I do. Jaysis, Davy, put the gun away, will yeh? There's no need for all tha'. All yeh had to do was have a chat with me, tell me how serious yeh were. Yeh know me, we could always come to some arrangement."

Davy raised his voice and spoke clearly when he said, "There's goin' to be no fuckin' arrangements. That's wha' I'm tellin' yeh. Can yeh hear me?" When Freeny nodded, Davy let his arm drop to his side, though he was reluctant to put the gun away. "I'm not tryin' to embarrass yeh over this, Tony, I'm not tryin' to get one up on yeh. If yeh don't want anyone to know abou' it, then don't say an'thin', because neither will I. But remember this. If yeh want to do an'thin' abou' it, then anyone yeh send after me better make sure if they put me down, I don't get back up. Otherwise, I'll come after yeh and I'll hurt yeh."

"Don't worry" said Freeny. "I wouldn't even think abou' it. Don't forget, I could always help you out."

Mickey saw Freeny leaving and noted he didn't seem too concerned, but when he waved to him and didn't get a response, he thought there goes another one, but at least he wouldn't be getting the blame this time. He saw Davy leave the toilet with a grin so wide, it looked like he might soon break into a laugh and when he got to the table, Mickey asked, "Is everything cool, yeah?"

"Yeah, everything's cool."

THAT SATURDAY MORNING, at about ten, they hired a taxi from a rank between Ceannt and Connolly Towers and asked the driver to take them to O'Connell Street.

Although he had a fix that morning, Mickey was bad humoured. "I don't know why we had to get up this early." Tormented by a tiredness that made his head heavy, he had a weariness that sneaked up on him and lulled his eyelids, lowering them shut. It was irresistible.

"I told yeh, I had to meet the other pair to give them the gear."

Mickey's eyes snapped open at the sound of Davy's voice. "Well yeh could have met them first and then come back and called me. Jaysis, Davy! Half eigh' on a Saturda' mornin'! Nobody gets up at tha' time." He lay across the seat and dozed in the back of the taxi. Early was a bad way to start Saturday, and it didn't seem like such a good time to go shopping either. Another of Davy's ideas. Town would be packed.

Davy sat in the front passenger seat and talked with the driver. "Where do'yeh reckon's the best place in town to get a haircut?"

"Is tha' wha' you're lookin' for?" the taxi man asked, shoving his fingers beneath his peaked cap to scratch his head. "Well there's a barber in Drumcondra tha' I always use and he oney charges thirty bob."

"Thirty bob?" said Davy, glancing sideways. "It's not a short back and sides I'm lookin' for. Where's the best place in town?"

"I don't know an'thin' abou' them unisex ones. If it's an expensive shop tha' you're lookin' for, then there's a place on Dawson Street. I forget wha' it's called. It wouldn't surprise me though if it was full of queers. They all are these days."

"Bring us there anyway," said Davy. "We can check it out."

"Wha' line of work are yeh in yerself?"

"A bit of this and a bit of tha'."

"Yeah? I wouldn't encourage anyone to get into this game, that's for sure." When Davy threw him a look of doubt, the taxi man told him, "Incurable haemorrhoids I have, from havin' to work from one end of the day to the other. People are more likely to query the fare now than they are to give you a tip. Some even have the cheek to suggest I rig the mileometer. Who'd believe it, hey? Do yeh know tha' the only day of the year tha' I can earn wha' can justifiably be described as a fair day's pay is Christmas Day? And even then, well yeh wouldn't believe it. People have threatened to report me to the police for robbin' them! Robbin' them? Now tell me, who else would do it? Who else would give up the one day of the year yeh should spend with the family and go out and provide a service tha' people need? Like, yeh wouldn't want to have a heart attack on Christmas Day, because yeh won't get an ambulance. In fact, your oney chance in gettin' to a hospital, if yeh were unfortunate enough to find yourself needin' one, would be be taxi. And even then, yeh wouldn't have a hope of gettin' seen be a doctor. Speakin' of heart attacks, me own ticker hasn't been great lately. Yeh can sense it when yeh get to my age. I've been to the doctor, but he says tha' it's oney stress, tha' I've the constitution of a horse and there's no reason why I shouldn't live to a hundred. Still, I made sure he sent me to a specialist in the Mater. Thank God we don't give those bastarden GPs the kind of power over us tha' we use to give to priests. Me own brother, me own brother mind, went to his one day, complaining of chest pains. Let me see? Yeah, it's nearly five years ago now. Well his doctor told him not to worry, tha' it was oney indigestion or somethin', like a bit of wind. Without a word of a lie, without a word of a lie now, he dropped dead on the way out of the surgery. Wha' are yeh laughin' for?"

"It's just the way yeh said it."

"This is one of the most dangerous jobs tha' yeh can get, did yeh know tha'? And the proof's there. The Irish Taxi Federation commissioned a survey, informally like, yeh know. Wha' they did was ask taxi drivers to ring in and tell of their experiences. It turns out, and this isn't a word of a lie either, tha' to be a taxi man in Dublin is one of the most dangerous professions in the world. I've been sayin' the same thing meself for years, but no one would believe yeh. Only stress? I can feel it! I can feel me heart tighten every time I pick up a fare tha' asks to go to Finglas South. Jaysis! I'd rather take an Arab to Beirut. Of course you've no choice. Yeh have to take them. If yeh pick up a fare yeh can't refuse to take them anywhere within a five mile radius. Otherwise, they can report yeh to the Carriage Office and then, well yeh can start kissin' good-bye to your livelihood. Well then, here we are now. Is he alrigh' in the back?"

"Yeah, he's just shattered. He's a rent boy and he's been suckin' cocks all nigh' on the Quays, for a fiver a go."

"Holy Mother of God! Really?"

"Yeah, really; well, so he says. I used to go to school with him, but I haven't seen him in years. Not until he turned up at me door first thing this mornin' and told me all abou' it. He's startin' to get depressed abou' it now, so I'm goin' to help him change his life. Ssshh. He's wakin' up. What's the damage?"

"Oh that's eh, £5.65 will do yeh. I won't charge yeh for the extra passenger."

"£5.65? From Ballymun to town?"

"Did yeh not notice the traffic in Westland Row?"

"I'm only jokin' yeh," said Davy. "Yeh know? Because of wha' yeh were sayin' earlier on."

"Oh I see, very good, very good. Yeh were very convincin'. Were yeh jokin' abou' the other thing be any chance?"

"Oh no, no. I wasn't jokin' abou' tha'. Here, here's £5.70. Keep the change."

Mickey woke as Davy paid for the fare outside the hairdressers. "Where are we? I thought we were goin' to O'Connell Street."

"It's Dawson Street. We're gettin' our haircuts first," said Davy. "C'mon."

As the taxi pulled off, Mickey read a detailed price list in the window of the hairdressers. "Eighteen fuckin' pounds for a haircut?

Are yeh mental or somethin'?" he asked Davy and he turned to walk away.

"C'mon, for fucksake," Davy laughed. "If we're goin' to be makin' a few bob, we might as well enjoy spendin' it," and he pulled Mickey back by the arm.

When they entered, a male receptionist asked if they had an appointment. When Davy told him no, he asked would they like anyone in particular to cut their hair.

"Who's tha' with the pink hair?" Davy asked .

"That's Joan, sir. She's a stylist and our top colourist. I think she'll be available soon."

"Okay then," said Davy, "she'll do."

"And you, sir?" the receptionist asked Mickey.

"Wha' abou' tha' one?" Mickey asked, pointing to a girl who was sitting drinking coffee.

"I'm afraid she's a client."

"Oh," said Mickey, disappointed. "Well wha' abou' tha' one that's talkin' to the one that's goin' to do his hair."

"That's Jake, sir."

"What's she? A fuckin' cowboy or somethin'?"

"No sir. She's another of our top stylists."

"Well, can I have her then?"

"I'd imagine she might object to that," the receptionist said, as he studied the fingernails on one of his hands, "but I'm sure she'll style your hair."

"Oh, you're a fuckin' riot."

They had to sit and wait for a while in the warm air of the salon, air stifled by the sweet scents of hair sprays, and watch the receptionist having an adulterous relationship with a full length mirror. It wasn't long before two junior staff came over and accompanied both of them to basins. "Take your time," Mickey told the girl who had aproned him with a waterproof smock. "Give me scalp a good scrub. Not with your nails though. Give us a look, have yeh got long ones? No, don't use them, use your fingertips. D'yeh know wha' I mean? Just massage me head, like this," and he demonstrated by opening and closing his fingers. While the girl nodded, he told her, "Make sure yeh don't get any shampoo in me eyes either, because I'll go mad. Actually, get me a flannel or somethin', because I don't even like water in them. And make sure the water is lukewarm."

Davy's hair was washed by the time the girl had started on Mickey's and he was led to a chair where the stylist he had chosen was waiting. When she asked what he wanted, he asked, what did she suggest. After thinking about it, she told him, "I think yeh should have it cut to just above the ears," and she finger marked her idea. "Here at the sides, and leave some length at the back, but tighten it in. I think some highlights would suit yeh too, if yeh had the nerve to get them."

"What's tha'? Streaks?"

"No. It's almost the same process, though we bleach a lot less hair. It's just somethin' to brighten it up a bit."

"Okay then," said Davy. "I'll leave it up to you."

"Are yeh sure?" she asked.

"Yeah, just don't make a mess of it."

As she set to work, Davy watched her in the mirror in front of him. He watched her tug his head when her comb tangled in a knot of hair. Watched how she palmed his forehead as she combed back and how she too used the mirror.

Snip snip snip. The scissors had appeared from nowhere. He watched how she positioned his head by putting her soft thin fingers under his chin and by pushing above his ear and was patient when she pointed him down, before she lifted his head again with a touch that said relax, and she sighed. The scissors disappeared and were replaced by a plastic bottle, which she used to water-spray the parts of his hair which were already beginning to dry. This motion too was checked in the mirror. And it was there that she looked at him, from below the pink fringe of hair that fell from her forehead. As the scissors reappeared, she asked him, "Where do yeh normally get your haircut?"

"He usually does it," Davy said, nodding towards Mickey.

"What?"

"I'm only jokin'. I don't go anywhere in particular really. Just wherever's handy."

"Where did yeh last get it cut?"

"Why? Is there somethin' wrong with it?"

"No, it's all right. It's just a kind of professional curiosity," she reassured him. "I ask everybody that question."

"Well I got it cut in a barbers the last time. A barbers in Drumcondra." He couldn't bring himself to tell her that Angie Pearson did nixers in her flat in Balbutcher, that she only charged three quid a go.

"Do yeh live in Drumcondra?" she asked.

"No, I live in Santry. What side of the bridge are you from?"

"The south side," she said proudly.

Before Davy could ask what part, the stylist who had been cutting Mickey's hair came over to them. "Your friend has gone to wait in reception for yeh. He says that you're payin'. Is that right?"

"Are yeh finished already?"

"Yeah, he just wanted a trim."

"Alrigh' then," said Davy. "D'yeh want the money now?"

Davy took a twenty pound note from his pocket and handed it to her.

About five minutes later, Mickey walked up the salon to Davy, "I'm gettin' the fuck out of here."

"Why?" Davy asked. "What's wrong?"

"Tha' arse bandit's givin' me a downer. How long are yeh goin' to be?"

Davy looked at the reflection of the stylist in the mirror and she informed him, "About an hour and a half."

"An hour and a fuckin' half? Wha' are yeh havin', an operation or somethin'?"

"No," Davy smiled, "I'm gettin' highligh's put in."

"Highligh's? I'm goin' for a pint. I'll be back at abou' twelve," said Mickey, and he left the salon, scowling at the receptionist on his way.

It was an ordeal having the highlights done, and Davy had to suffer the indignity in silence while the stylist worked on another client's head. He had to sit and wait while strands of his hair, poking from holes in a plastic cap, stewed in peroxide paste. A corrosive smell wore at his nose. It stung his eyes, so he closed them, which saved him studying his foolishly capped head in the mirror.

Mickey returned when he said he would and indicated, by waving a newspaper, that he would wait for Davy at that end.

After the stylist had checked his hair for the final time, a junior took Davy away and showered the peroxide down a sink. The tight cap was pulled from his hot head and his hair washed again. The same stylist blow dried it. As she did, he asked her, "Are there any good nightclubs around here?"

She switched off the hairdryer to speak. "There's a good one around the corner from here, the Pink Elephant, do yeh know it?"

"I've heard of it. Do you go there?"

"Sometimes. Sometimes we all go from work, at the weekend."

"A'yeh goin' there tonigh'?"

"I'm not sure. Why?"

"Well, I'll be goin' out meself later on, but I haven't made up me mind where to go yet," he told her, cautiously.

"It's very hard to get in."

Davy paused for a moment before asking, "Is it?"

She could tell by the look in his eye that the duplicity was intentional. A look that had changed from apathy to appetite and the intensity dazzled her. It made her look around to make sure no one else had seen it and when she was able, she told him, "Yeh won't get into the nightclub wearin' jeans and trainers. And the bouncers have to know yeh."

"Maybe I'd get in if I was with yeh."

"Maybe you would," she said, "but I'm not even sure if we're goin' tonight. We usually go over to Davey Byrne's for a drink after work and decide then."

"That's me name."

"What? Davey Byrne? You're joking."

"Really," said Davy. "If yeh don't believe me ask him," and he nodded towards Mickey.

"That's a bit of a coincidence, isn't it?"

"There's no such thing," he told her.

"What do yeh mean?"

"Nothin'," he said, and then asked, "Your name's Joan, isn't it?"

She knew the receptionist would have told him, so it didn't impress her. "Yeah, that's right."

"Well listen, Joan, d'yeh mind if I come in and meet yeh later in Davey Byrne's? Yeh can let me know then if you're goin' and if you're not, don't worry, it doesn't matter. Okay?"

"All right then, I'll be there until about ten. How does that sound?"

"Brilliant," said Davy. "I'll see yeh then. "

Mickey and Davy spent an hour or so shopping around Grafton Street. Although Davy was looking forward to the night, Mickey was already making excuses about not wanting to go. When they got back, they left the clothes they had bought in Anne's and went straight to the snooker hall, to check that everything was all right with Jojo and Skinnier.

When Jojo saw Davy's hair, he cackled with laughter. "Wha' happened to your head?" he asked. "Did a seagull shite on it?"

"It isn't half the state tha' your face is goin' to be in if yeh don't shut up. By the way, have yeh got any of the money yeh owe me?"

The rest of the day went as they had planned, though by the time they had finished cutting and bagging the heroin, Mickey was insistent that he wasn't going out. "Go on your own, Davy. Sure tha' bird's goin' to be waitin' on yeh. I'm bollixed and anyway, one of us should stay here and get the money from the other pair. If both of us go out, they'll have to keep it overnigh'."

DAVY STASHED THE heroin with Mickey and then headed for his mother's flat. When Anne saw the clothes they bought and heard that Davy had planned to meet a girl in town, she looked at him bitterly. She looked at him in a way that made him want to grab her by the throat and demand, "Why are yeh fuckin' starin' at me like tha'? Well? Do yeh remember? It was you who asked!" Instead, he told Mickey he should take his sister out for a drink. "Maybe she's in her rags or somethin', but she looks like she's on the verge of crackin' up."

"Why don't you take her out then? I'm not sittin' beside a face like tha' all nigh'."

Davy smiled. "I would if I could, brud, but I can't," and he left, carrying a bag of clothes across his shoulder.

At his ma's, Davy met his da pacing the hallway, rattling a few coppers in his pocket to his march. It was a sure sign that he hadn't a shilling. "How a'yeh, Davy? Are yeh not courtin' tonigh'?"

Fuckin' courtin'! "Where's me ma?"

"She's in the sittin' room, I think, havin' forty winks."

Beneath a dull lamp, Davy saw his ma dozing in an armchair. She slept with her bleached head resting reluctantly back, her small mouth open and with her top and bottom teeth in her hand. She was always ready.

"Ma! . . . Ma!"

She woke with a jump. "Jaysis, Davy! Don't wake me like tha'. Amn't I always telling yis? Are yeh alrigh'? What's wrong?"

"Nothin'! Will yeh iron a shirt for me? I bought a shirt today and I need to get rid of the creases."

"Okay, plug the iron in for me then, will yeh?"

"Jaysis, Ma, I want to have a bath as well!"

"Go on then, I'll do it. Hang on, wha' have yeh done to your head? Jaysis, Mary and Holy Saint Joseph! Willy? Willy? C'mere and have a look at wha' he's done to his head." She covered her mouth with her hand in mock surprise and slipped her teeth in.

Davy blushed. "Do yeh not like it?"

"Oh, it's lovely! It's nicer than me own! But I don't know wha' the world's comin' to, fellas gettin' colours in their hair. I heard Sonny Knowles does it with his, to make his grey look silver. Are yeh not afraid someone migh' think you're a bit funny?"

"Our Davy would soon know wha' to do with anyone who thought he was queer, wouldn't yeh, son?" said his da, who had arrived from the other end of the hall. "Anyway, Kathleen, it's all the rage now. Did yeh not know tha'?"

Davy left them discussing fashion and went and locked himself in the bathroom. His ma ironed his shirt as he washed, and when she was finished, she hung it with a loving pat on a door of a wardrobe in his bedroom. He didn't talk to them again until he was ready to leave. He went to where they sat in the gloom and pretended to look for something. He went to see the look in their eyes, the pride and the envy.

"Jaysis!" said his ma. "If I didn't know better, I'd swear the ghost of me own father had walked into the room. Isn't he the image of me daddy, Lord have mercy on his soul, isn't he?" Davy's da nodded. His ma went on. "You're the spittin' image of your Granda Bonney, d'yeh know tha'? He wouldn't go anywhere if he wasn't dressed up to the nines. Though he couldn't go anywhere durin' the week because me poor mother, God rest her soul, used to pawn his suit in Jack Rafters on a Monda' mornin' and she wouldn't have the money to get it out until a Frida'. One mornin', this isn't a word of a lie, the bad weather came in and he was havin' a bit of breakfast before he went out. 'Have yeh seen me overcoat?' he asks her. 'You're eatin' it,' she says to him. And he was a handsome man too. That's probably where yeh get your looks from. Yeh must be goin' out with a girl, are yeh? I hope yeh haven't wasted tha' money on one of those brassers from the shoppin' centre, have yeh?"

"No," Davy assured her, "I'm meetin' someone in town."

"Who is she? Do we know her?"

"I only met her today meself. She's from the south side."

"Do yeh see, Willie? That's his granda all over. Said it was the ruination of the family when he and me poor mother got married and had to leave Townsend Street to take a room in Summerhill. Jaysis, David! You're every bar of him. It must be the blood. That's wha' it is. I've passed it down through me blood. But mind them ones too! Them girls is all the same these days, they know more than their prayers. Know more than wha's good for them. Buy and sell yeh before yeh had time to blink, let alone think. So don't go spendin' your money foolishly on her, whoever she is. Make sure she goes dutch with yeh. That's all the rage now too, since equal righ's came in, isn't it, Willy?"

Davy interrupted her. "Righ', Ma, I have to go, otherwise she'll be gone before I get in there." He saw the envy in his da's eye and dwelt to savour it. He saw the shame. Before he left, Davy called his ma out into the hall. "Here, Ma, here's a few bob for yeh. Give the oul' fella a tenner out of it."

"Jaysis, Davy, I hope yeh didn't hurt anyone for it, because it'll oney bring me bad luck."

"No, don't worry, Ma. I got a bit of a touch durin' the week, tha's all. Why don't you and the oul' fella go over to the Penthouse for a drink?"

"Your da will probably go, but I want to have an early nigh'. I have to be up early in the mornin'."

"You're not workin' tomorrow? Sunda'?"

"Well, Mrs Fitzpatrick asked me would I do a couple of hours. Her son's comin' home from Canada and she wants the place lookin' lovely for him."

"Why doesn't she do it her fuckin' self then, or get those lazy arsed daughters of hers to do it?"

"She hasn't been well lately and her daughters are studyin' for their exams at university."

"She hasn't been well, Ma, since yeh started workin' for her ten bleedin' years ago and her daughters have been at university nearly as long."

"Don't be like tha', Davy. Yeh know she's been very good to us over the years, especially when yis were children."

"Aw yeah, that's righ'. She used to bring us out those oul' jigsaw puzzles at Christmas, with half a dozen pieces missin'. The fat cunt wouldn't even get out of the car. She use to beep the horn and the oul' fella would go runnin' down the stairs like the fuckin' things were for him."

"Aw here," said his mother, lifting her hands to her head, "take your money back. It's not worth havin' to listen to tha' language in me own home."

"I've a good fuckin' mind to," said Davy. "But don't worry, I'm goin' out now anyway," and he left slamming the door behind him.

It was almost twenty to ten when he reached the pub. He was surprised she was there. By the way she greeted him, he could tell that she'd already had a few drinks. Standing up, she threw her hands around him, smack-kissed the air close to his cheek and said, "Oh I'm so glad yeh got here."

Joan had been sitting at a table with four people from the salon. He was introduced to two who he didn't know (who then ignored him for the rest of the night), and reintroduced to two he had already met that morning. Jake, the stylist who had cut Mickey's hair, said, "Oh hi," with an insincerity he had expected. The receptionist greeted Davy flatteringly. "My my, what a transformation," he said, looking up and down at Davy's clothes.

"This is Stephanie," said Joan.

"Yeah, we met this mornin'," said Davy.

Davy offered to buy a round and swallowed a large rum and blackcurrant at the bar. It only wet his regret at a time when he was looking to drench it. As the barman prepared the drinks for the order, Davy looked over to the table. From a distance, he watched the pretence like he might have watched a bad film. They weren't good at it, smiling half smiles when their eyes never smiled at all. Even Joan, the reason he was there, looked like she was going to annoy him. It was her exaggeration. The pouted lips, the gesturing hands, how she blew her pink fringe away from her eyes and fanned her face. How she could snatch his attention for a moment and pretend that she didn't know he was looking. That's what annoyed him. When he was certain she knew that he hadn't missed so much as a breath.

Joan was curious. When he settled at their table, the alertness that had walked through the door disappeared. She watched him scowl at Stephanie, by moving no more than an eyebrow. It was the same when he frowned at Jake's shrieky laughter, though on those occasions he lowered both. Jake had told her that Davy's friend had said both of them were from Ballymun. She warned Joan, in the way that girls do with each other, not to let herself like him. Joan managed to get her to admit that there was something about Davy, you could see it, how he sat there and seemed to simmer. How, if he wanted to turn himself down, he rested his chin on his thumb and kept his jaw straight with a finger. Or how, when he wanted to turn himself up, he dropped his head back and tugged at an ear while taking a deep breath and did that thing with his eyebrows. It was all that he did, just lowered them, and it disturbed everyone. Jesus! But she liked someone who could laugh and he didn't laugh. Well, she liked someone with a sense of humour and she supposed he had been cheeky in the salon that morning.

In the Pink Elephant, Davy sat on his own at the bar all night. At one point, she suspected he was falling asleep, but most of the time he just looked bored. Why did he stay, if he wasn't enjoying himself? What was he trying to prove? She tried him one more time. "I don't normally ask a fella to get up and dance but we're goin' to be headin' off soon. So c'mon, why don't yeh come out on to the floor and have a bit of a jive."

He smiled at her sheepishly, disarmingly, and she wondered later did he know what he was doing.

"What's wrong? Can yeh not dance or something? If that's all you're worrying about, don't be bothered, neither can anyone else, so they won't be mindin' yeh."

Still smiling, he told her, "I can dance alrigh'," making sure he pronounced his words clearly, "but I like to save tha' stuff for between the sheets."

She believed him. "We're all goin' back to Stephanie's place for a bit of a party. Would yeh like to come?"

"Jaysis! I've had enough of Stephanie for one nigh'. Do yeh fancy gettin' the fuck out of here?"

"Where do yeh want to go?" she asked.

"I don't mind."

"I've a flat in Sandymount. We could go there?"

"Tha'd be great," Davy told her, keeping his mouth tight to disguise his delight. "C'mon then, we migh' as well leave now."

All of Joan's friends kissed them, including Stephanie, which Davy pretended didn't bother him.

He was surprised to find that Joan's flat was in a private block. Though a bigger shock came when inside the flat, Joan pulled her pink hair off and flung it towards a sofa.

"Jaysis! I don't believe it! Tha's a wig?" He picked it up and examined it. He stroked it, carried it to his nose and sniffed.

Davy woke before her the following morning and remembered. He remembered waking sometime in the early hours, curled face down and fully clothed, though shoeless, on the bed. The hair from the wig had annoyed him awake, and the cold. It was fucking freezing and he ached for a piss. His eyes would hardly open when he went in search of a toilet, or a sink. He found the toilet first and though he was shivering, he stripped as he pissed. It would save time, might soothe the desperation he had to get under the covers of a bed, where he could hold his hand to his face to comfort his teeth. They ached too, like cold hollow bones. Like he could count them in his mind. And when he got back to the bed and out of his clothes, she still slept, looking like nothing more than a crease in the linen.

When he woke again, she was looking at him. Her little, tight-hair head had popped out from under the duvet, her big brown eyes blinking. He tried to remember again. "Did I fall asleep?"

"Yeah, yeh did, yeh fucker!" She managed to sound polite and even betrayed signs of a smile.

"I drank too much rum, I think."

"You drank too much."

"I need to get up for a minute."

"Okay."

"Do yeh keep any foil here? Tin foil?"

"For what?"

"I need some."

"It's in the kitchen press, below the sink."

Davy got up and searched for the foil. When he found it, he took the roll and gathered his clothes on the way back to bed. As he walked in, Joan, who had wrapped herself in a purple robe, was on her way out. "I'm goin' to make some coffee. Would yeh like some?"

"I could murder one."

When Joan returned with a coffee pot and cups on a tray, Davy had finished smoking the heroin, but he still held the foil and the tube. She noticed the difference in his mood as she slipped into the bed and poured them both some coffee. "Sugar?"

"Yeah, two, and milk," he told her and soon the room smelled like Bewley's. It was all luxuriously new to Davy.

"What was that?" Joan asked him, nodding towards the foil.

"Just some opium."

"Isn't that addictive?"

"No. But it's good for a hangover."

"Can I have some?"

"No."

"Why not?"

"Ask me for somethin' else."

"What have yeh got?"

"Wha' do yeh want?"

"A dance."

"Wha'?"

"Yeh promised me a dance last night."

"Me? I never dance!"

"Yeh don't remember, do yeh?" she asked and she leaned over and pulled a hair from his leg. He yelped and almost spilled the coffee, but realised that her malice was suggested rather than intended. "Yeh can't even remember!"

"Remember wha'?"

"You and your Ballymun charm."

Christ! He must have been fluthered if he told her where he was from.

"Ballymun bullshit more like," she mocked.

Davy grinned and swallowed some coffee. "Wha' a'yeh goin' on abou'?"

"When I asked yeh do yeh dance," she curled her lips and pulled another hair from his leg, "yeh said that yeh only danced between the sheets."

"Aargh, stop tha'," he told her through clenched teeth. "So?" He put both their cups on the floor.

"What are yeh doin'?"

"Let's dance." He turned to her and knelt, pulling a sheet up round his shoulders. This exposed them both and she closed and curled her thighs upwards at the unexpectedness. It enabled Davy to pull her towards him, to push her between his own legs. He separated her thighs, lowered his head and rolled his tongue around her naval. "Do yeh like to jive like this?" He moved on and found her breasts, small and hard. To play with them, he used his hands and lips and all the while he probed and searched and when he found a way in, he tightened the cheeks of his arse and pushed. She grimaced, for a moment, licked her lips in anticipation and then leaned over to snatch a pack of Marlboro and a lighter from the bedside table.

"Wha' are yeh doin'?" he asked her, as she lit one and lay back with her head on her hand.

"You owe me a dance," she said, after exhaling a drag from the cigarette. "So just dance," she ordered, in a way he had never heard before. A way that was like a breath of fresh air.

So Davy danced, sometimes leaning forward and resting his weight on his arms. Sometimes kneeling back to watch the secrets on her face, so secret he could not even begin to guess what they might mean. She saw him looking, those times when she opened her eyes to tap the ash off her cigarette. Those times after she had taken a drag to delay things. Davy kept moving, but he was delayed too. She fascinated him, with her shyless, shameless delight in pleasure.

After she stubbed out the butt of the cigarette, she opened her eyes and showed him. She showed him that she had been in control down there all along. Reaching up, she curled her light thin arms around his neck and she kissed him, frantically, managing to wrestle him down on top of her and to wrap her little legs around his arse. "Ride me then! Ride me, ride me!"

Heroically, magnificently, Davy responded. Heroic and magnificent because, when she had dragged him down, his calf muscle had cramped. She took his muted screams to be his insatiable appetite for nothing but her. He knew this, but couldn't tell her. It was a secret he kept for ever, because he didn't want to disappoint her. When she was happy and wet and only tingled slightly, he rolled her on to her side and lay behind her, and made himself happy too.

He didn't wake until he heard her leave the bed and when she returned he asked her the time.

"It's just past two o'clock."

"Jaysis! It's a Sunda', yeah? I have to go."

"Yeh can have a shower if yeh want."

"I think I will."

Joan made more coffee which they drank as he dressed. He smoked some more heroin and they both smoked cigarettes and chatted politely, awkwardly.

"This is a nice gaff yeh have. I was goin' to say tha' it must cost yeh a few bob, but with the money they charge for a haircut in tha' hairdressers of yours, I suppose yeh can easily afford it."

She smiled. It was the inaccuracy. "Actually, my father bought it for me, for me twenty-first birthday present."

"Bought yeh a fuckin' flat? Wha' is he?"

"He has his own business. Do you work?"

"Not really."

"Are yeh on the dole?" she asked him excitedly, like she hoped he might be.

"Oh no, I've never signed on in me life." When she looked a little disappointed he told her, "I suppose I'm a bit of a businessman meself."

"Really? What business?"

"Well, I mind me own business for a start."

DAVY CAUGHT A number 3 off Sandymount Green and enjoyed the ride down past the Star of the Sea into silent Irishtown. A Quiet Time, when publicans relaxed between periods of excessive thirst. A good oul' Dublin Sunday afternoon. The bus rolled effortlessly and pulled itself with just a cough up over Ringsend Bridge, past the Bottle House to its right and Shelbourne Park to its left. He'd gone dipping there once and he smiled at the memory, at the madness. Ringo had persuaded him there was nothing to it and had given him an impromptu lesson on the bus on the way. He had told him not to worry, he could just block if he wanted to. It was all right for Ringo. He had been picking pockets since he was eight. Davy was just as frightened by the memory of it as he had been when he put his hand into the oul' wan's bag. He had done it because he was impatient. Because Ringo hadn't got a dip. Because he wanted to get back into town to score. He'd managed to get his hand beneath the leather flap and he hesitated when he felt two zipped pockets. Which one? Ringo couldn't believe it. Although he had shown Davy the mechanics, he didn't believe that he would have the nerve to try it. Having hesitated first, Ringo moved in front of the woman to distract her. By ignoring her and pointing to something else, he hoped he might keep her attention away from what Davy was trying to do. But she ignored him and began to walk away. She began to move towards the window for the Tote with Davy's hand still in her bag. He tried to follow her, still intent on robbing her, but because of the angle he had to walk like a crab. She sensed him. He panicked and whipped his hand free. She saw, shocked, his empty hungry fingers and knew where they had been. And he saw her eyes, how she looked at him, almost with pity, and he witnessed her decision. She forgave him. She forgave him with a look of disgust, by closing her surprise-opened mouth and by marching away in anger.

The incident had frightened Davy because the oul' wan might have decided to do the opposite. She might have begun to scream. Then he and Ringo would have been battered and thown in the Dodder and left to swim home with the mullet. The bus rolled past Boland's Bakery and the Cats and Dogs Home. Ringo! Davy laughed out loud. A young couple a few seats in front, turned and looked back at him. He wanted to explain. He always thought Ringo had got his name after the drummer in the Beatles, but Mickey told him it was because he got caught riding a mongrel in a derelict in Sean McDermott Street.

At Ballymun, Davy went to the snooker hall to check how things were. Mickey wasn't there, but he had given Jojo and Skinnier the gear that morning and they were knocking it out. Reassured, he headed towards his ma's flat.

"I've a lovely leg of lamb here, son, are yeh stayin' for some? There's plenty for everyone and I can stick a few extra roast potatoes for yeh into the oven."

"I'm not hungry, Ma, and I want to go to bed for a while. Call me at six on the dot, if I'm not up before then," Davy told her, as she scraped carrots into an empty plastic bag.

As soon as he stripped and lay down on his bed, he fell into a deep sleep. He hadn't waited to hear her finish asking what she could do for him and it seemed like he had only closed his eyes when he heard her calling his name.

"Davy? Davy? It's six o'clock. Have yeh to go anywhere? D'yeh want me to leave yeh asleep?"

"It's alrigh', Ma, don't worry, I'm awake." He got up before he had time to drift off again and went to wash himself. After he splashed his face a few times, he watched beads of cold water roll and fall from his chin and noticed the new colour of his hair. He wasn't sure he liked it, but he was sure he liked Joan.

On his way out, he asked his ma to leave his suit in to be cleaned and pressed.

"I'll drop it in first thing in the mornin', on me way to work," she told him. "I kep' yeh a bit of dinner. Do yeh want me to heat it up in the oven for yeh?"

"Yeh know tha' I don't eat an'thin' tha's been reheated." He saw the pain his remark caused, how she twisted the fingers she held close to her chest around each other.

Davy called to Anne's flat first, on the off chance Mickey might be there. He wasn't, but Anne was, with her bitter looks and her sharp tongue, which Davy soothed by letting her chase some heroin. He was careful not to give her too much, in case she goofed off when he left and something happened to the baby.

That was what she wanted. Not for something to happen to the baby. She could stick her in the cot. She wanted to goof off. Though, God forgive her, because sometimes too she did want something to happen. She just wished the baby wasn't there. Davy fixed his. The difficulty he had with the barbed needle reminded him they needed new syringes.

When he got to the snooker hall, Mickey was playing snooker with Yako.

"So it's finally dawned on yeh, tha' I'm too good for yeh at pool."

"This is a man's game. It's wha' I play when you're not around," said Mickey, laughing. "Yeh must have had a good time last night."

"It wasn't bad," said Davy and he told Mickey where he had ended up. Mickey was impressed. "A nice one-bedroom gaff, not far from the strand, with a bed the size of the box rooms in the three-bedroom gaffs in the Mun." It sounded like somewhere Mickey might like to go for a break.

Davy took the cue from Yako and sent him, armed with a fiver, to go and get ten new syringes, from a diabetic he knew who sold them for 50p each. "And I don't want to find out later they're oney 30p or somethin'"

After playing for half an hour, he was almost ready to leave. Yako had returned with the syringes, and while Mickey wanted to go for a hit, Davy wanted to go for a pint first. He got a better whack that way.

"Holy mother of fuck, are yeh wide? Would yeh look at who's just walked in."

Davy had his back to the entrance, but he sensed the urgency from the way Mickey gripped his cue too tightly. It caused him to turn quickly, too quickly. He felt the pain strike his neck where he tweaked the muscle, felt it stiffen, then lock immediately and he saw Johnny Sheringham swagger towards them, alone. Shit! He wanted to stroke his neck, to massage the side of his tongue that had numbed. To blame Mickey for causing him to turn too quickly. While he gripped his neck to hold it straight, he almost giggled at the audacity of Sheringham, and he heard Mickey say, "I'm goin' to fuckin' lash him out of it."

"No, Mickey, don't touch him, don't say an'thin'. Just wait."

There is nothing quite like the power of enlightenment, especially when the penny drops.

"How a'yis, lads, wha's the story?" Sheringham asked when he reached their table.

"Wha' do you want?" Davy asked him.

"Georgie said that you'd fix me up with a bit of gear." He addressed Davy, while Mickey played a shot at the table.

"Yeh already had a bit of fuckin' gear off us durin' the week!"

"Yeh know how it goes. I was dyin' sick and hadn't a shillin' and anyway, this one is for Georgie." Johnny thought this would make things less dangerous for him. He could see that Hughes was ready to explode and, well, you could never tell with Davy Byrne.

"Yeah?" Davy said. "Well you'll have to hang on for a few minutes. Here, pot a few balls with Mickey while you're waitin'," and he handed Sheringham the snooker cue.

Sheringham accepted it and asked Mickey, "Wha', are we just havin' a knock abou', like just play a shot until yeh miss?"

Mickey shrugged his shoulders. "Yeah, why not?" He played the first shot.

Davy walked down the hall towards the manager's office, rubbing his neck as he went. It looked like some kind of code to Sheringham and after glancing around nervously he asked Mickey, "Where's he goin'?"

"Probably to get yeh a bit of gear, I'm not sure. But if I'd an'thin' to do with it, it wouldn't be a bit of gear you'd be gettin', do yeh know wha' I mean, Johnny?"

"Jaysis, Mickey, don't be like tha'. It's just been a bit of a mix up, tha's all. And there's no need to worry, Georgie said he'd sort everything out."

Davy came back before Mickey had time to tell Sheringham what he thought of that. "You'll have to hang on another couple of minutes," said Davy, and he gestured to Sheringham to continue playing snooker. Sheringham played nervously, but he complimented Mickey on some of the shots he was playing. To show him he was capable of better, Mickey tried some trick shots, but before he could make a fool of himself, Jojo walked down the hall and handed Davy something.

"Here's your turn on," Davy told Sheringham. "There's five bags there."

"Is tha' all? I think Georgie was expectin' a bit more."

"Where is Georgie?" Davy asked.

"He's in town, but there's a couple of blokes waitin' for me in the car park."

"Well, Johnny, I'm oney givin' yeh these, how is tha' you'll take a message back to Georgie for me."

"Yeah? What's tha' then?"

"Tell him I want to have another chat with him soon, to sort all this out, yeh know?"

"Alrigh', I'll tell him, but I don't think this is goin' to make him very happy," said Sheringham, holding his hands open to show Davy the five bags.

"I know tha'," said Davy. "It's not goin' to make him happy at all, but that's wha' I want to talk to him abou'."

Sheringham took a couple of steps backward and then turned and walked out.

"Was tha' really five quarters yeh gave him?" Mickey asked.

"Yeah," said Davy. "It was."

"Wha' the fuck did yeh give him them for?"

"I just got one of the blokes behind the counter to ring the Filth. He's given them a description of someone he's been watchin' selling drugs in the snooker hall and who he was sure was just abou' to leave. Maskey's waitin' outside to reef him."

"Holy Jaysis! Yeh know he's not a gobshite and as soon as he realises it, he'll tell Maskey tha' you've set him up."

"Yeah and tha's probably the first excuse Maskey'll be waitin' to hear. I bet yeh he gives Johnny a slap, for tryin' it on."

DAVY MET ROBIN on the Tuesday at the Raheny Inn. They talked about money.

"Righ' then, Robin, wha's the story? Wha' do yeh reckon's the best way to stash the oul' spondulicks?"

"There's lots of ways, Davy. Some people just stick it in the bank. Others buy things like property, or a little business."

"A business?"

"Yeah, like a video shop, or a cafe. Somethin' small, though big enough to pass the money through the books."

"Jaysis! I wouldn't mind doin' somethin' like tha'."

"It's not worth the risk, mark my words. They'll bring a law out soon that'll allow them to seize it."

"Seize the business?"

"Well, put it this way, the days when yeh can rent out a half a dozen videos a week and make five or even ten grand profit are comin' to an end."

"Wha' are yeh supposed to do then?"

"Take it out of the country," said Robin. "Those priests have the right idea when they're goin' to Cheltenham." He fixed his moustache after a sip from his Guinness. It was habit. Instead of wiping the cream from the head of his pint from his whiskers, he shampooed it in and groomed them.

"Take it where?"

"To London."

"And wha'? Stick it in a bank there?"

"No. Not straight in. Soon they'll bring out tougher laws there too."

"Wha' then?"

"Well, I know a way, but it'll cost yeh ten per cent."

"Aw, for fucksake . . ."

"Before yeh get your knickers in a twist, just remember, I won't be gettin' a penny from this. It's the price anyone has to pay."

"Wha' do I have to do?"

"It's watertight this one, but you'd better bear one thing in mind. If yeh use it, the people you'll be dealin' with are much heavier than the likes of Georgie Sheringham. If yeh fuck up with them in any way, you'll be in trouble."

Davy lit a cigarette and dragged deeply. Robin paused to lick and massage the tips of his fingers. Davy paused too when Robin asked was he interested. "Yeah, I am, but I can't give yeh a deffo until yeh tell me a bit more abou' wha' the story is."

"All right. What yeh have to do is open an account with a bookie."

"Wha'? And gamble me bleedin' money?"

"Yeh don't gamble anything for fucksake. Will yeh listen? That's the beauty of it. He's a track bookie, with no shops. Any bets he accepts off course are private accounts."

"So? Wha' does tha' mean?"

"It's simple, Davy. If yeh want to pass ten grand through him, yeh give him the money and he gives yeh a cheque for nine. In his books, he has yeh down as a client. He covers himself by makin' sure that any winners he selects for yeh all come from the same stable. If it's ever investigated, it looks like yeh know someone in the yard. He'll also stick some losers into his books for yeh, but he pays your account himself."

"Wha' do yeh do with the cheque then?"

"Yeh bank it, or spend it, or do whatever yeh want with it. The point is, it's legal then, and no one can seize it. Anyway, have a think about it and if yeh want to go ahead with it, let me know."

Davy nodded. At that moment it was all he could do about it.

They bought another couple of pints and Davy began to wonder if Robin just liked to keep his moustache wet.

"By the way," said Robin, "I hear Georgie Sheringham isn't too pleased about his brother," and he smiled a smug smile that told Davy he had heard what had happened.

Davy wondered if he had also heard that Johnny Dazzler had been slapped all the way from the snooker hall to the cop shop, with Maskey asking him on the way, "What do you take me for? Do you think I came up on the last bus? You might get away with this in Beaver Street, but byjaysis, ye won't be comin' out here again in a hurry to sell your dirty rotten filth. It's not yours? Is it not? Well, I'll tell you what will be. The toe of me boot. Because that's what you're goin' to feel in the nether regions of your arse as soon as I get ye into the barracks."

One of the 20p brigade, who witnessed the incident, had repeated verbatim the scene for Davy and Mickey and had earned himself a fiver by doing so. He had to tell the story twice, because they laughed so hard the first time they missed some of the details.

Davy smiled at the memory and he told Robin, "I wasn't delighted with his attitude meself."

They chuckled together, but Robin more at the twinkle in Davy's eye. "Do yeh know what Georgie's goin' to do about it?"

Davy could tell by the confident tone that Robin knew, so he shrugged his shoulders and waited.

"I hear he's got a team together and they're goin' to pay you and Mickey a visit tomorrow night and go over yis with pickaxe handles."

Davy tutted. He sighed. "Yeh hear a lot, Robin, don't yeh?"

"Dublin's a small place. Yeh can't do much here without people findin' out about it. Includin' the police," he added, almost as an afterthought. "There's a way to avoid what he's intent on doin' tomorrow night, if yeh want to."

"Yeah, I know. Go into town, kiss his arse and give him a grand."

"I was thinkin' of somethin' different," said Robin, widening his eyes.

"Like wha'?" Davy encouraged.

"Georgie Sheringham and his old man sign on at the labour exchange in Gardiner Street every Wednesday at eleven o'clock. After that, the two of them go to Madigan's in North Earl Street for a couple of pints and stay there until about half two," said Robin, and he waited for a response from Davy.

It took a moment, before Davy said, "You've just as much reason as me for wantin' somethin' done about Sheringham."

"Well, if you're talkin' about Tony Nolan I can see what you're gettin' at, but all that business didn't make a blind bit of difference to me."

"Wha' part of Madigan's do they drink in?"

DAVY RETURNED TO Ballymun and stayed in the snooker hall until closing time. It was a great place to wait for bedtime, watching the lights at the tables click off one by one and hearing the noise of people's voices go softer and softer, until only a couple of tables remained occupied and the manager would shout, "Will yis ever fuck off out of here, yis bastards. C'mon! Finish up or I'll turn the lights off."

At the post box at the bottom of the stairs, a gang was beginning to form. Jojo and Skinnier had girlfriends, who carried gear for them, and they had hangers on who Skinnier loved, because they asked could they use his spoon. Even Yako had a girlfriend. A young girlfriend. A fifteen year old, eager for him to leave his ma and move into a squat with her which she would keep clean and feed him from. And most of all, she told him, she promised, he wouldn't have to answer to her, the way that he had to answer to his ma. She loved him. She really did!

Yako was leaning against the post box with his hands resting around her tiny waist. He touched her lips with his, because that was more important than squats, that was proof of whom he loved the most, and he showed her this with the look in his Dyhydrocodeine-glazed eyes. Jude stood close, keeping her hands warm under his new, lined leather jacket. When he stopped kissing her to take a drag from his cigarette, she turned her face sideways and rested it on his chest. She felt him stroke her hair, felt their hearts beating and the violent jump when the command, "Yako?" left Davy Byrne's lips as he descended the stairs from the snooker hall. She felt him push her sideways and reply, "Yeah, Davy?"

"Did yeh check the car park?"

"No, I was waitin' for yeh to come down."

"Well, go and do it now."

Jude trotted behind him and watched him scour the car park on the Thomas Clarke side of the shopping centre. Davy had been joined by Mickey, Skinnier and Jojo when they returned and reported that everything was okay. She saw Davy leer, heard him snigger and say to Yako without caring if she heard, "D'yeh know yeh can get reefed for givin' someone tha' young a dart?"

Yako tried to protect her, "We're nearly the same age, Davy."

This made Mickey Hughes laugh and he said, "Maybe yis'll both get reefed."

Davy told Yako where he would see him the next day and he went off with Mickey, towards Balcurris. Jojo and Skinnier, along with their troupe, headed for a squat in McDermott Tower. Yako walked Jude down to Shanghan Avenue where they stood in one of the basements for another hour or so and kissed, and he pressed against her in private and listened to her say, "Not until we're livin' together."

IT WAS JUST after twelve when Davy walked into Madigan's long public bar. He spotted Sheringham, in company with a middle-aged man, sitting on a high stool at the counter. Sheringham saw Davy at the same time. He saw him strolling through the door, but he didn't move. Not immediately. Instead, he took a moment to suss the situation and this wasn't because he was slow to react. No, Sheringham had a motto. *Unless it's obvious yeh should do somethin', do nothin'.* There didn't seem to be a need to do anything. Davy Byrne was on his own, and Georgie's oul' fella wasn't called Shoulders for nothing. There didn't seem to be a need to do anything until Davy dropped his hand into the motorcycle helmet, which sat like a baby on his left arm. Then, Sheringham couldn't get off his stool fast enough. Knocking it over in his haste, he left it to clatter to the wooden floor behind him, as he ran clumsily in the opposite direction.

"Mother of Jaysis . . .," his father began, his pint halfway to his lips, as Davy stepped over the stool and followed Sheringham towards the toilets.

Georgie swung left first and ran down an alleyway storing empty beer kegs and bottle crates. When Davy caught up with him, Georgie was standing in the middle with nowhere to go, because Mickey was walking towards him from Cathedral Street, holding a pistol to his chest. The visor from his motorcycle helmet hid the hunger which spread clean across his face. Davy carried his pistol openly too, but the most obvious thing about him was the grin, like a dash, a cut between his chin and his nose. It wasn't a cruel grin. If anything, it looked like it was just about to fall into a friendly laugh.

Slightly stooped and with his back to the alley wall, Sheringham began to speak. "Please, no please, don't do it, lads, Jaysis, please don't do it. Oh, Christ?"

When Davy opened his mouth it wasn't to laugh, but to tell Sheringham, "Get down on the ground."

Sheringham fell heavily to his knees, with hope, thanking whoever it was that was looking after him. They would have shot him by now if they were going to, surely. Even Byrne couldn't be that bad.

"I want yeh to know somethin' . . .," Davy started.

"For fucksake!" Mickey interrupted. "Hurry up and shoot him. We haven't got all fuckin' day." At the same time he caught sight of Sheringham's father standing hunched in the doorway, his shoulders threatening to collapse under the burden of an unimaginable weight. "That's it, mister. Stay where yeh are. We don't want to shoot you too."

Sheringham senior stood frozen and felt compelled to watch, as if it was some kind of penance. His son knelt terrified at the feet of men who later, all he could recall of them, was their anonymity. With Mickey this was understandable. He had kept his helmet on at all times. But of Davy, the only thing he remembered was the back of his head and his intent.

"Please, Davy, I'm sorry. Jaysis, I'm sorry. Don't shoot me, not in front of me da, for fucksake. There'll be no more trouble, I promise, this'll be the end of everything."

"Oh no, Georgie. This isn't the end of everything. Johnny Dazzler robbed eigh' quarters on me last week and I laid five on him on Sunda'. Do yeh know wha' tha' is? That's £520. I want it tonigh'. If I don't get it and I get tha' team of yours comin' out to me instead . . . Yeah, I heard all abou' tha', then yeh won't even see me comin' the next time. Have yeh got all tha'?"

Sheringham nodded and some of the colour began to come back into his face. Some of the grey began to leave.

"Yeh better not annoy us again," Davy told him.

Just as Davy opened his jacket and dropped his gun inside, Mickey smashed his into the side of Sheringham's head. The blood, which trickled first and then ran past his ear was warm and comforting around the sharp pain he felt, and he fell back from relief rather than the force of the blow. For the same reason he held his hands to his head, though they drew away when the next blow came crashing into his kidney. It was a pain that took his breath and exposed his face, mouth gasping, in a way that Mickey hoped it would, a way that allowed him to stamp the heel of his boot down hard on Sheringham's nose.

"D'yeh think I broke it?" Mickey asked, when they got back to Ballymun.

CRADLING A CAN of beer in his arms, Davy rested the sole of one foot and his back against the tower wall. Mickey stood with legs apart and kept one hand warm in the front pocket of his jeans. With the other, he held a cold can of Pils, reluctantly. It was dark at seven. From the bottom of Thomas McDonagh Tower, they had a clear view of the snooker hall, the car park behind it, the Garda station, the Towers pub, and they could see people entering and leaving the shopping centre. Both were confident enough to believe they would smell even the hint of trouble. Mickey changed hands with the can of Pils. It didn't take them long to get cold. It didn't take long because the can was full, so he swallowed as much as he could and then held it tenderly.

"Hangin' around here for ages is goin' to put the eye on us. D'yeh know tha'?"

"Wha' a'yeh talkin' abou'? You've spent half your life hangin' around these flats and has anyone ever given a shite?"

Mickey laughed. "Yeah, well, yeh know wha' I mean. We're not fourteen any more."

Davy laughed after him. "I know wha's wrong with yeh! It's because tha' kid called yeh "mister" the other day. The one tha' said, "Sorry, mister" when he ran into yeh. It's gone to your head, hasn't it? Yeh gobshite! Ligh' tha' joint up, will yeh? Me hands are fuckin' freezin'."

"It didn't go to me head."

"Well somethin' went to it. Ligh' the joint up, will yeh?"

"You'll have a rush of blood from your head in a minute, if yeh don't mind your lip."

"Ho, ho, ho," said Davy. "Touchy, aren't we? It was tha' then, 'Sorry, mister.' Wha' do yeh think yeh are, an oul' fella? Come on then," he said to Mickey and he put his can down on the ground before playfully skipping, boxing style, around in a circle. "C'mon then, I'll give yeh a rush of the back of me hand across your fuckin' ear."

Mickey smiled. "Okay then, but don't say tha' I didn't warn yeh. This is goin' to end the way it always does, with you in tears," and he too bent to put his can on the ground. Davy took his chance and kicked him accurately up the arse.

"Yeh poxy sleeveen bastard! You've caught me right on the bone on the top of me hole." He paused to let the pain pass and rushed Davy, whose laughter was contained by a jolt of fear.

Davy ran and tried to turn the corner of the block, but he stopped suddenly. He stopped in time to allow Mickey to swing and catch him with the toe of his boot.

"Aargh! For fucksake! Tha' was a deadener. You've given me a fuckin' deadener at the bottom of me arse." Davy had run into Yako and almost knocked him over. "Wha' do you want?"

"Yeh told me to meet yeh here. Is everything alrigh'?" he asked, concerned.

"Of course it is, for fucksake," said Davy, rubbing the top of his leg.

Mickey greeted him. "Wha's the story, Yako? Don't worry, I'm just givin' this cheeky cur the good kick up the hole he deserves."

"Did yeh ligh' tha' joint yet?" Davy asked.

"Gimme a chance, will yeh?"

"Righ' then, Yako," said Davy, putting an arm around Yako's shoulders. "I want yeh to scout around the car parks at the shops and if yeh suss an'thin' out of the ordinary come back and tell me."

"An'thin' like wha'?"

"Use your noggin, Yako. If yeh see anyone yeh don't know hangin' around then come over and tell us."

"Come over abou' every twenty minutes anyway," Mickey told Yako.

"For wha'?" Davy asked.

"Well, we could be hangin' around here for abou' an hour and we migh' need somethin'."

Davy thought for a moment and said, "Yeah, come over every twenty minutes. Don't bring anyone with yeh and don't tell them wha' you're doin'."

"Okay," said Yako, and before he left he asked Mickey, "Can I have a blow of the joint?"

"Go on out of tha', for fucksake," said Davy. "I've been waitin' a half an hour for him to ligh' it."

"Don't worry, Yako. I'll roll another one for when yeh come back," Mickey told him.

Jojo had already received specific instructions from Davy. "If anyone is lookin' for me, take a message. If they tell yeh tha' Georgie Sheringham sent them and tha' they need to talk to me, still take a message. Okay?"

"Yeah, I know wha' to say," Jojo had told him.

They waited nervously at the bottom of the tower block. Nervous for Jojo. He was too much of a gobshite to realise what was happening.

Neither did Yako. He came back every twenty minutes and tried to find out more about what he was supposed to be looking for. Mickey didn't skin a joint either, until the second time he returned. Even then, he didn't leave him much more than the roach, but Yako didn't mind. He didn't mind because he was able to do what Davy had asked him, with Jude. Well, from the far side of the health clinic to the Penthouse he could, because no one could see him from there. He was able to show her how important he was. He showed her the three-inch lock knife he carried, just in case. She showed her concern. She showed it by linking him tightly and trotting alongside on her loud, hollow stiletto heels. After his final reconnaissance, he was told to pick Jojo up from the snooker hall and take him to the tower block.

"Wha's wrong?" Jojo asked Davy. "Why aren't yeh comin' over?"

Davy answered him by asking, "Was anyone lookin' for me?"

"Yeah. Mick Murtagh. He said he wanted to sell gear for yeh."

"Is tha' all?" Mickey asked.

"No. He gave me this for Davy," said Jojo, handing Davy an envelope.

The corner was torn and Davy glanced at Jojo in disbelief. "You've been fuckin' moochin' at this, haven't yeh?"

"That's the way it was when I got it, I swear on me ma's life. Ask Skinnier if yeh don't believe me. He was there when Murtagh gave it to me."

Davy ripped the envelope open. Inside he could see that there was probably £520.

"Is Murtagh payin' yeh for the gear up front? Is he not doin' it for Sheringham any more?" Jojo asked.

"Why? Wha's it got to do with you?"

"Nothin'. I just wondered, tha's all."

"Yeah? Well, if I was you, I'd be wonderin' how you're goin' to pay me back the money yeh owe me. That's why I gave yeh the chance to earn a few bob. In fact, if yeh don't start payin' me back soon, if I was you, I'd be wonderin' if I was goin' to get Murtagh to knock out the gear I give you. Now go back over to the snooker hall and wait for me there. You go too, Yako. I'll be over later."

When Yako and Jojo were out of earshot, Davy turned to Mickey and said, "Yeh mustn't have broke his nose yeh know."

"Of course I broke his fuckin' nose. Why else do yeh think he sent the money out."

Davy chuckled. "I suppose you're righ'. C'mon and we'll go down to the Swiss Cottage for a pint."

"The Swiss?"

"Yeah, it's only half eigh' and I don't want to hang around here tonigh'. We won't know anyone down there either, so we can go over this money thing again and wha' we're goin' to do with it."

"Alrigh' then, c'mon."

The pub was comfortably quiet, the noise from the customers no more than a drone. Two sweaty barmen kept everyone happy from a oval shaped bar. While Davy admired the barman pulling two pints of Harp in one hand, Mickey looked round and glanced at the girls.

"Jaysis! Look who's over the far side?"

"Who?" Davy asked as he counted out change to pay.

"It's Johnny Trolan. You said yeh wanted him for somethin', didn't yeh?"

"Johnny? Where?"

"Over there, in the alcove."

"Who's tha' he's with?"

"I don't know who the birds are, but that's yer man Gerry tha' he hangs around with from Sherriffer."

"Is he into the gear?"

"Who, Johnny?"

"No for fucksake, the other one."

"I don't think so. As far as I know, they just work together. They used to work in Cadbury's, until they were laid off. Now they're packin' lorries with boxes of nappies, so Johnny was tellin' me anyway."

"I wonder wha' he's doin' down here?"

"He probably won on the horses. Any time I see them two together, that's wha' they're up to. Wha' d'yeh want him for anyway?"

"I want to fix him up with a bit of gear. He gave me a fiver tha' day when I got out of the Joy and I hadn't a ligh'."

"He's off the gear."

"No! Johnny's never off the gear. He just goes through stages when he can't afford it. Here, get these pints. I want to go out to the jacks and put a few bags together for him."

"A few bags? You'll kill him, for fucksake! Yeh know wha' he's like these days. When he does have a hit, he has to call an ambulance first and put them on standby."

Davy laughed as he headed towards the toilet. When he came out, he went straight over to Johnny. With his back to him, he didn't see Davy coming, but his face lit up when he arrived. "Davy? Wha's the story? Still out then?"

"Yeah, Johnny. How's tricks?"

"Not bad, Davy, yeh know? I'm just out for a few pints with a few people from work. We won a few bob on the horses today. This is Gerry and Carmel and Harriet and Mary." Davy nodded to them and Johnny asked, "D'yeh want to sit with us?"

"No," said Davy, "I'm with Mickey, but I just thought I'd come over and say hello." He turned to leave and as he did he blocked the view of the company Johnny was keeping, bent slightly and pressed, discreetly, the gear into the palm of Johnny's hand, saying quietly, "I told yeh I wouldn't forget yeh." Davy winked, grinned and walked away, before Johnny even had time to thank him.

"Wha' did he say?" Mickey asked Davy when he returned. "Is he still off the gear?"

"Not any more he's not. He was deligh'ed."

They stayed in the Swiss Cottage for a couple of pints and then left for Ballymun in time to catch the off licence. Davy gave Yako £30 to spend on cans of Pils and told him to take them to the squat in McDermott Tower. It was time to have a hooley. Time to buy the boys a drink, and the girls. Time to share out some smack, though no one was sure why. But Davy knew. Davy knew how to motivate people, knew how to reward them, knew how to get the best out of them and the worst. Davy knew all about incentive.

A FLOCK OF voices, strange ones, were soaring down the hall with the voice of his ma swooping in behind them. When the bedroom door opened he kept his eyes shut until he heard someone calling, "Wakey, wakey, Davy."

When his eyes opened they focused quickly on the barrel of the pistol, which pointed determinedly towards his face. "Good mornin', Sleeping Beauty. I want you to stay where you are and don't move an inch. Don't move a fuckin' inch."

He didn't recognise the voice, nor the person holding the gun. Drifting upwards, his glance moved from the pistol to the eyes of the stranger, who looked like a doctor. A doctor? What would a doctor be doin' with a gun? Think! Get it together, for fucksake! What had he done the previous night? Nothing! Sheringham? It was the Filth. What took him so long? The pistol was used to push the bedclothes down along Davy's body cautiously, and when Detective O'Toole strolled into the bedroom, a truth dawned on Davy.

"Where are the guns, Davy? Are they somewhere in the flat?" O'Toole asked.

Davy looked from his bed and saw Jojo behind O'Toole, leaning with his hands pressed against the wall and his legs spread apart. So he must have come back last night too. Had he remembered to stash the gear in the electric meter box on the outside landing? He had warned him, "Never bring it into the flat." These detectives weren't looking for gear, but the Drug Squad would soon be here if they found any.

"How long am I supposed to fuckin' stand like this?" Jojo asked.

No one answered him. O'Toole hadn't got a reply either, so he told Davy, "Get out of bed and get dressed."

Davy threw his legs over the edge of the bed and sat rubbing his eyes.

A detective wearing surgical gloves searched the chest of drawers beside his bed. "Have you got AIDS or hepatitis?" he asked Davy.

"Yeah, I have them both. Do yeh want a cup of tea?"

The detective laughed, a hearty rural laugh. "Byjaysis! I think we'd have to be early to catch you, boy."

"I told you to get fuckin' dressed," said O'Toole.

The clothes Davy had worn the previous day were lying in a heaped pile beside the bed. He turned the pile upside down, rested it at his feet and began to dress, beginning with his socks. When he was finished, O'Toole ordered him to stand and place his hands behind his back.

"For wha'?" Davy asked. "Have yeh got an arrest warrant or a search warrant?"

"Just put your hands behind your back."

"Wha' am I gettin' reefed for?"

"What fuckin' difference does it make?"

"I want to know."

"Well, if it's goin' to make you more co-operative, this is a Section 30, relating to the illegal possession of firearms."

"Wha' fuckin' firearms?" Davy asked O'Toole, as his wrists were handcuffed behind his back. "The usual, Ma, a solicitor and a doctor," he said, as a firm hand pushed into the top of his back and propelled him towards the door.

"Where are yeh takin' him?" his ma asked O'Toole, as Davy walked to the stairs on his way to the unmarked police cars that waited at the bottom of the flats.

"Ballymun Garda station. Don't worry, Mrs Byrne, we'll look after him," O'Toole told her.

"Yis are a dirty shower of bastards, always pickin' on him. It isn't lost on me tha' you lot have come lookin' for him the day before Good Friday," his mother shouted as they all left the flat. "Is it any wonder any of them ever turned out other than the way they are, when yeh never leave any of them be? Yis are nothin' but a shower of bitter culchies!"

At Ballymun Garda station, Davy was taken before a

superintendent where it was explained to him that he was being transferred to the Bridewell for "further questioning". O'Toole and two other detectives travelled with him in the same car. It was a fifteen minute journey down past Phibsboro and Broadstone. Davy sat in the back, handcuffed to the larger of the detectives. The other two sat in the front and it was a Time for him to ignore their singsong.

"Still on the gear, Davy?"

"Becomin' a big boy now, aren't we?"

"Where's the guns, Davy?"

"We're only doin' you a favour you know."

"It might be the Murder Squad next time, not us."

"Where's the guns, Davy?"

"Have you got them buried somewhere?"

"Hughes'll show his face soon, he'll tell us. Why do you think he got bail the last time?"

"Is your habit big?"

"Oh, Davy. Forty-eight hour lock up, at least! You'll be in fuckin' bits you know."

"You don't like doin' time, do you? Well, you know what they say, if you can't do time, you shouldn't commit the crime!"

Davy wondered what the words meant. Doin' Time! Doin' fuckin' Time? They meant more than bein' locked up. Screwin' Time! It was a bleedin' laugh, that's what it was. A lousy poxy laugh, because it was Time doin' you, Time screwin' you. The coppers knew it, because that was all that they had, your Time. But Time did them too. Time was the price they paid and that was the biggest fuckin' laugh of all.

And what Time now? Forty-eight hours! That's what Time. He was goin' to miss Robin. He was goin' to miss the gear. He was goin' to be fuckin' sick. Forty-eight hours.

At the Bridewell, Davy was taken to a room and interrogated unsuccessfully. He told them his name, address and date of birth, but wouldn't reply to any other questions. After they gave up, he was removed to a cell. The bed was a concrete step a foot high, six foot long and three foot wide. The Garda who escorted Davy told him he couldn't have blankets until the evening, so Davy folded a thick jumper he had been wearing into the shape of a pillow and lay down. Soon he was freezing. He hadn't requested a doctor, not from the police, because he didn't want them to know when the withdrawals began, but waited instead for the one he asked his ma to get, along with his solicitor. And where the fuck was he?

Joe Morgan was a socialist, he insisted, before he was a solicitor, and this told Davy all he needed to know. Because of a weakness for backhanders, he was popular with criminals who used the Free Legal Aid scheme and for his ability to get these clients bail. Davy doubted if any of this money found its way to the Workers' Party, but he both smiled and scowled at the thought that it might be used to buy his oul' fella a pint when Morgan was canvassing for votes.

At five that evening a uniformed Garda, responsible for suspects in custody, opened Davy's cell door, called him out and accompanied him to a room where Morgan was waiting.

"How are you, David?"

"How d'yeh think?"

"Listen to what I have to say first. There's very little I can do in this situation. You have been arrested under Section 30 of the Offences Against the State Act. As you probably know, access to legal representation is given at the discretion of the investigating Garda."

"I know why I was fuckin' arrested," said Davy, "and I probably know the workin's of the Offences Against the State Act better than you. Wha' I really want to know is, when am I gettin' out?"

"I have to be honest and tell you, I don't expect them to release you until the two days that they are entitled to hold you have passed. Detective O'Toole has informed me that information has been made available to him, disturbing allegations have been made, which is serious enough to merit an investigation. For this investigation to be carried out thoroughly, he will need to detain you until he has completed his enquiries, or for so long as the law allows him."

Morgan was beginning to irritate Davy because he was beginning to sound like O'Toole's solicitor.

"As I'm sure you're aware, there's very little I can do now. Have you made any statements?"

Davy looked at Morgan and didn't answer, but swallowed his contempt at the bottom of a deep breath.

"Of course you haven't! But you know they can question you until early on Saturday morning."

"Can yeh not go and fuckin' protest or somethin'?" Davy asked. He only heard Morgan insist that of course he would, before shutting his hearing off. It was time to detach again. He knew he was going to be there for the full detention period.

Because it was a single cell, Davy knew it was a dangerous cell. He wasn't sure how long he had been in there when O'Toole walked in and said, "Where the fuck do you think you are, Byrne?" and then laughed loudly before walking back out again.

Ten minutes later, another detective entered Davy's cell. He spoke to him gently, "Jaysis, yeh get yourself into some scrapes, don't yeh."

He was young, thin for a policeman, a runt in the litter, thought Davy.

"I realise you're a stroker, Davy, that's not goin' to change. You're goin' to get away with some things and you're goin' to get caught for others. But Jaysis, do yeh not think that this is a bad move, this gun business? Yeh can be straight up with me. I know yeh probably think that I'm a bollix because I'm from Dublin and I'm a copper, but I'm goin' to put yeh wide anyway. Yeh don't want to upset O'Toole. He's not even really interested in yeh. He just wants the guns. C'mon, I'll take yeh down to the interrogation room, it's fuckin' freezin' in here."

Davy was told to sit at a table by the same thin detective who took a packet of cigarettes, twenty Major, from the pocket of his red checked thermal jacket and offered one. Davy accepted, pinching one free from the full packet. He accepted a light too, without ever looking the policeman in the eye. Because he sat with his back to the door, he didn't see O'Toole come in, and by the time he was aware of a hand swerving towards the side of his head, it was too late to avoid it. He felt his ear swell, felt it tingle and then sting inconsolably.

"I've better things to be doin' Easter week, Byrne, so hurry up and tell someone where them guns are or byjaysis, I'm warnin' you, I won't let up until I put yeh away for a long time," said O'Toole, and he walked straight from the room again.

Davy caught a look in the eye of the thin detective, a look that betrayed the pleasure he took from Davy's glowing ear. The detective hid it well though and pretended that the chuckle which followed was really a cough. He replaced the cigarette that had broken between Davy's fingers and still speaking softly he said, "Do yeh see what I mean, Davy? Yeh migh' as well tell us where the guns are. Sheringham has made a statement against yeh, so you're goin' to be charged anyway. If yeh just tell us where the guns are, as soon as we pick them up, we'll give yeh bail. By the way, wha' kind of guns are they?"

After dragging deeply on the cigarette, Davy exhaled and said, "I've nothin' to say."

"Do yeh know that Mickey Hughes has made a statement already and he's back out?"

Davy didn't even try to disguise the relief he felt at the detective's remark. He smiled so wide he bared his dull, creamy teeth, because he knew if it were true then they wouldn't be asking him what and where the guns were. He laughed, a short, shrill cackle.

"I've already told yeh, I've nothin' to say."

Picking up the packet of Major from the table, the detective told Davy, "I think this was your last chance, so don't say I didn't warn yeh." He called a uniformed Garda to accompany Davy back to his cell.

Davy's next visitor was a doctor, a stand in for his GP. He told Davy that he looked fine and that he couldn't really do anything to relieve his withdrawals, because he would need some time to establish his tolerance. What he could do was leave some Paracetamol with the custody sergeant who could dispense two every four hours for the two days that Davy expected to be detained. Also, the Gardaí had informed him that they knew a local doctor who was much more experienced in this area and they would be willing to contact him if Davy made the request himself.

"Do yeh not see wha' they're up to, yeh gobshite? Tha's their way of offerin' me drugs if I make a statement."

"I don't know anything about that, son, but would you not consider the fact that you might be over-reacting?"

"Over-reactin'? No I'm not over-reactin'. Neither am I over-reactin' when I say tha' if an'thin' happens to me, because you refused to treat me, then I'm goin' to fuckin' sue yeh. In fact, I'm not just goin' to sue yeh. Yeh wouldn't believe what I'm goin' to do to yeh. Where are yeh goin'? Go on, fuck off then and shove your Hippocratic oath up your arse." As the cell door slammed shut, Davy was still shouting after him, "You're a fucking hypocrite alrigh' . . . I suppose you'll still get paid for this too."

Time has a sharp edge to it when passed in custody. For the forty-eight hours, Davy didn't eat and he didn't sleep. He was familiar with the tactics of the police. They were more likely to irritate him than terrify him into telling them anything. And he had time to figure things out, work things through in his mind. When he needed a break, he would browse through the graffiti that decorated the cell door and walls: "19 years for a fucking ride".

Sheringham must have told people what happened. O'Toole must have picked it up when it got on to the streets. But it didn't really matter how O'Toole found out. All Davy had to do was wait. He wondered where Mickey was. Ballymun Garda station? Store Street? He might even be in another part of the Bridewell. And that made it easier, that they might be doing this together. But it was hard, as hard and uncomfortable as the concrete bed. As lonely as the empty space of the cell. And it hurt in other places. His joints ached. His arse burned between shites, between blowing bubbles, and this made him smile a demented smile. Bursting bubbles and the drop of cooling liquid, soothing the red raw entrance to his hole, dowsing for a second, like inflammable fuel on a flame, before burning more fiercely, without respite, until the next bubble. The memory, an infant memory, helped him smile a while through the torment of muscle spasms that twitched without warning, up and down the length of his legs and arms, the most intolerable of torments, that almost drove him out of his mind at times. A torment that drove him towards that question, "Why?"

If you don't risk your arm, you won't break your neck.

That was why.

On the Saturday morning, at precisely 7.30am, a uniformed Garda opened Davy's cell door and informed him he was being released.

"Wha's it like then? . . . huh?" Davy asked. "Havin' a junkie yeh don't have to give a hidin' to just to shut him up?"

The Garda casually informed him that someone was waiting for him outside. A silent prayer swept through Davy's mind which hoped the remark wasn't the Garda's sense of humour and which begged, "Jaysis, please don't let it be O'Toole, with an extension to the Section 30."

Jojo stood leaning against a Blue Cab taxi. "Wha' the fuck are you doin' here?"

"Mickey sent me in," Jojo answered, apologetically. Davy looked rough, so Jojo was unsure of his mood.

"Wha'? How come he wasn't reefed? Where is he?"

Not knowing which to answer first, Jojo tried to answer both at the same time. "The mornin' tha' yeh were tore out of it, I legged it over to Balcurris and told Mickey wha' the story was. He stayed in most of the time and just told us to come over to him to get the gear. Then we sold it and brough' back the money."

"How does tha' jammy bastard never get reefed?"

As the taxi passed through Phibsboro, Jojo turned to Davy and said, "Here, Mickey told me to bring these in to yeh." He handed Davy two £40 packs and continued, "I told him there'd be nowhere open for yeh to go and use them, but he said tha' you'd be dyin' sick."

Davy took the two packs and opened one. Shaking loose some of the heroin that had stuck lightly to the side of the wrap, he bent his face to the bag. With his mouth closed, he inhaled through his nose and almost cleared the paper with the one snort. The membrane of his nose, raw from the running cold of withdrawals, burned as the heroin ran along its tender wall. Jojo told him that some of the heroin had caught on top of his lip, so Davy brushed it away, carelessly and what clung to his fingers, he snorted too, sucking clean the speckles that wouldn't budge. He did the same with the second bag, even before the first had time to take effect, and sat back in the taxi. O'Toole would be goin' bleedin' mad. And the gear! His throat was beginning to go numb. Everything was okay again. Even Jojo had shut up, at least until they reached Ballymun.

"Where d'yeh want to go?"

"To me oul' wan's," said Davy. "I need a kip."

"THE SOONER THE better then," said Mickey, shifting the weight on the cheeks of his arse from one side to the other.

"I want to talk to Robin first, before we get the tickets," said Davy, opening with one hand a can of Holsten Pils that sat at his side. "And Monda's a bank holiday, so we'll go Tuesda'."

"Why do yeh think it's warmer in here than it is in the bedroom?" Mickey asked.

"It's the central heatin', isn't it. It isn't on as long in there as it is in here. Why d'yeh ask?"

"Me arse is gettin' numb from sittin' on this floor," said Mickey, shifting again and taking a swig from his can, like it might comfort him.

"Why don't yeh bring the mattress in here?"

"This is the livin' room."

"Says who, for fucksake? There's only a fridge and a poxy mattress in the whole kip."

"Yeah, well fuck it, we won't be stayin' long tonigh', will we?"

"I shiver every time I think of it, d'yeh know tha'?"

"Wha'? The cold?"

"No, the fuckin' money. Jaysis!" said Davy, looking towards the ceiling. "I could have been reefed with it. Can yeh imagine it? Apart from the fact tha' I don't know when I would have seen the ligh' of bleedin' day again, it would have been good-bye to the spondulicks, finito Benito, do yeh know wha' I mean? You could have been reefed with it too, though it's tha' long since you've been bleedin' reefed, you've probably forgotten wha' it's like, huh?"

Mickey chuckled. "Yeh have to be wide to the tide in Malahide, Davy. I'm tellin' yeh, the Filth'd have to be up early to catch *mise*."

"Yeah? Well it amazes me how often they do fuckin' miss yeh."

Mickey swallowed some more lager. "Talkin' of tits, I hear those English birds love a bit of Irish mickey."

"Where did yeh hear tha'?"

"Padser Kiely told me. He said he knows wha' turns them on, tha' it's the soft Irish voice and the rough Irish arse."

"Wha' the fuck would he know abou' it, when his are the other way round."

"Well, I'm goin' to have a bit of crack when I'm there."

"We have to be careful. If some bastard robs us, findin' them won't be like walkin' into Madigan's and chasin' them out the back."

"Are yeh sure this is the best way to do it?"

"Well it's not just the Filth, is it? Them fuckin' vigo's and Concerned Parents are all over the place now."

Mickey tapped the side of his head twice and said, "Yeah, touch wood. We don't want them puttin' the fuckin' eye on us."

"Well, think abou' it. They've been everywhere. Dun Laoghaire, Rialto, Fatima, Crumlin, Ballyfermot, Theresa's Gardens, O'Devany Gardens."

"Yeah, I know, and the junkies know too. There's only two places left where they can score for certain. Either here or O'Connell Bridge."

"And that's full of mavericks; which reminds me, I think we should send Jojo into the bridge with some decent quarters. He can show everyone tha's wha' ours are like. Yeah, I think we will, but we'll leave it until we come back from London."

"Wha' do yeh think we should do when they get goin' out here?"

"Who?"

"The vigo's. Do yeh think we could just set someone up, like we did with Johnny Sheringham."

"I was wonderin' abou' tha' meself," said Davy. "But this isn't the Filth we're talkin' abou'. These are the families of junkies we're sellin' the gear to and they're not tha' stupid. I suppose one thing might be to get more people to sell the gear. Tha' migh' confuse the vigo's."

"Who'll we get to do tha'?"

"I don't know yet, but we can think abou' it over in London. In the meantime, we better stay out of the snooker hall as much as possible, at least for the next few days. Me oul' wan was tellin' me yesterday tha' the Concerned Parents were collectin' a petition in the shoppin' centre."

"Yeah, they were there this mornin' as well. I signed it meself."

"Wha'? Were yeh havin' a laugh? It's a wonder nobody said an'thin' to yeh."

"Well, they probably would have done if I'd walked by them. Yeh have to be wary of them bleedin' vigo's," Mickey said, and he giggled before telling Davy, "I was up in Theresa's Gardens when all this started first. D'yeh know how there's only one way in there and one way out, if you're drivin'?"

"Yeah," said Davy.

"Well, I drove over with Smiley Coughlan one day to get a bit of gear and when we turned into the flats there was abou' thirty oul' fellas with pickaxe handles and hurlin' sticks blockin' the road. I hadn't a bleedin' clue wha' was goin' on, but Littler Flood was standin' with them, so I called him over and asked him wha' the story was. He told me they were stoppin' all junkies from goin' into the flats and givin' them one chance to fuck off. If they came back again, they were goin' to get a hidin'." Mickey smiled before adding, "Littler was stoned out of his head and not only tha', but he bends down into the car and tells us tha' his brother was doin' some lovely gear over in Fatima. Can yeh believe it?"

Davy laughed. "I wouldn't have put an'thin' past tha' Littler. How long is he dead now?"

"I dunno, a couple of years I suppose. He had a turn on with a couple of Palf' after a couple of pints and tha', as they say in China, was tha'."

"D'yeh know how those vigo's started?"

"It's obvious isn't it, they were findin' dirty syringes all over the stairs in the flats. The fuckin' kids were pickin' them up and squirtin' them at each other. Some of them were even stabbin' each other in the arse with them."

Davy tutted and said, "Jaysis, Mickey, you're so gullible, aren't yeh? They only started because all the robbers in the flats who weren't into gear couldn't rob. They kept gettin' reefed by coppers doin' surveillance work on dealers and it was all the junkies who led the coppers there in the first place."

"Whatever the reason, it's got an awful lot bigger since those vigo's in the Gardens. These Concerned Parents are the business. They had a meetin' in Finglas last week and someone stood up and named Cha Cha. Can yeh believe it? He only sells poxy Valium. Anyway, as soon as the meetin' is over, about fifty of them march down to Cha Cha's oul' wan's and tell her that if her son wasn't out of the area by the mornin', they were goin' to come back and fuck her, her family and her furniture out on to the street."

"Concerned Parents me arse! I heard that the person who stood up at that meetin' was someone who Cha Cha had ripped off. And anyway, it's tha' poxy Sinn Féin who are organisin' it all. They come down from the North and because they've nothin' better to do, they get involved in this. And all the while they're just lookin' for a scam."

"Yeah? Well I don't know abou' tha'," said Mickey, "but if anybody from the Provos comes near me, I'm just goin' to say, 'Yes sir, no sir, can I kiss your arse sir?' and do whatever they ask."

"Jaysis, Mickey, d'yeh ever think abou' an'thin'?"

"Wha' do yeh mean?"

"D'yeh think tha' the Provos give a fuck abou' junkies, dead or alive?"

"What difference does it make wha' they think abou' an'thin'? If they're goin' to shoot yeh for sellin' gear, you're hardly goin' to start wonderin' why. You're just goin' to stop, aren't yeh?"

"Yeah," said Davy, "you're just goin' to stop. But the reason why they're goin' to shoot yeh is not because a few oul' fellas and oul' wans are worried abou' their kids gettin' strung out. It's not because some poor fucker is in a heap because one of his kids has overdosed. The Provos just use them as an excuse."

"Wha' do yeh mean, like, when they're lookin' for votes and tha'?"

"Votes? When yeh add up the few gobshites stupid enough to vote for them, how many do yeh think tha' makes?"

"So, wha' a'yeh gettin' at? The point is, they hate drugs, don't they?"

"They might hate drugs," said Davy "but they wouldn't mind gettin' their greasy Republican fingers on the few bob they could make from them."

"No, they wouldn't sell gear, for Jaysis sake," said Mickey.

"Oh you're righ', they wouldn't sell it. But when they get the likes of us out of the way, they'd have some gobshite knockin' out a few ounces a week for a few hundred quid."

"I think yeh're wrong abou' this one, Davy. Sure tha' would go against everything they believe in."

"Believe in? What's sacred, Mickey? Wha', in the name of fuck, do they believe in?"

Mickey paused for a moment, took time to find and swallow the dregs from his beer can before saying, "Well, they believe in, yeh know, everythin' that's righ' and tha'. And a united Ireland."

"Are yeh tryin' to tell me, now listen, tha' they can walk up to two coppers escortin' a Post Office van and blow their brains out, all for a few poxy grand? They're able to do tha', no swea' like, but they'd turn their noses up to the hundreds of thousands they'd be able to make if they knocked out all the gear and all because it's not righ'."

"Yeah, well robbin' money and tha', it's all for the cause, isn't it?"

"Wha' have two coppers mindin' money down the bog got to do with the cause? Wha' have they even got to do with the fuckin' North come to think of it? And wha' abou' your man who was caught with a forty foot container full of hash on the Naas dual carriageway? Do yeh remember tha'?"

"Well he was left the IRA by then, wasn't he?"

"Left the IRA me bollix! When d'yeh ever leave tha'? But even if he was left, why didn't they shoot him for gettin' them a bad name?"

"Look, I really couldn't give a fuck, Davy. I don't see wha' it has to do with an'thin' anyway. But I'm tellin' yeh now, if they ever ask me to stop sellin' gear, then they're only goin' to have to ask me once. I don't mind tryin' to be smarter than a few coppers, or Georgie Sheringham, or anybody else for that matter. Anyone, apart from them," said Mickey.

"What's the difference between them and us? We can be just as smart."

Mickey smiled, a weary smile. "I wondered wha' yeh were gettin' around to, Davy, and yeh must be fuckin' mad. But I'll tell yeh, yeh can be mad on your own if it ever comes to it."

"Well it migh' come to it, Mickey. It just migh' and if I haven't set meself up in somethin' else by then, well, I'm not stoppin' for anyone."

"It's real powder power this, isn't it?"

"Wha' d'yeh mean?"

"Yeh know wha' I mean, but I'll put it to yeh this way. When me oul' fella found out, years ago, tha' I wasn't goin' to mass any more, he said to me, 'Son, if you've given up believin' in God, then that's alrigh'. But just be careful yeh don't grow up thinkin' tha' yeh are him.'

"Don't worry, Mickey, for fucksake, you're always worryin'. How did we end up talkin' about the Provos anyway?"

"You started it."

"Well, let's get back to wha' we were meant to be sortin' out. We're off to London on Tuesda' with fifteen grand. Fifteen fuckin' grand."

"Yeah, and that's April Fools Day!"

"So who's a fool then, hey? Tha' money we got from the stroke would have been gone by now, or nearly, if we hadn't done wha' we done."

"I know," said Mickey. "I suppose you're righ'. I suppose the only thing we really have to worry about is gettin' reefed."

"Yeah, I don't know why I'm goin' on about the Provos for either, when they're not a problem yet."

"Yet? I swear, Davy, if I ever hear those three letters IRA bein' used against me as a threat, then I'm off."

"Can we wind up now?"

"I'm tellin' yeh. I don't mind doin' a few year. If we'd enough money stashed away, then I'd do it on me back. I don't mind gettin' me legs broken, but I'm not goin' to die for this. And tha', as they say in China, is tha'."

"Fair enough. So can we give it a rest now?"

"I wouldn't mind givin' me arse a rest, away from this bleedin' floor."

"Go and get the mattress then."

"Fuck it! We'll be goin' in a minute."

"There's one other thing we need to sort out."

"Wha'?"

"The gear. We're goin' to have to work somethin' out for Jojo and Skinnier, for when we're away. Don't forget, we're goin' to be in London for a few days."

"How much gear do yeh want to leave them?" Mickey asked, too uninterested to try and calculate it for himself.

"I reckon abou' three quarters of an ounce will do them. Wha' d'yeh think? That's about a hundred and fifty £40 bags. We can take the eighteen bags left over to London with us."

"Fuck! That's a lot to leave them with. I know they won't rob us, but say if they get reefed with it? And anyway, eighteen bags won't be enough for us for three days," said Mickey, having effortlessly calculated that they were using almost as much between them every day.

"It'll have to be enough. We can't afford to get stoned over there, not while we're carryin' tha' much money."

"But we can afford to leave Jojo and Skinnier tha' much gear?"

"I know wha' we can do. We won't tell them tha' we're goin' to London."

"For fucksake, wha' are we goin' to do? Tell them from now on, we'll be givin' them a hundred and fifty quarters every three days?"

"Listen, we can give them fifty on Tuesda' mornin', righ'? Then, I'll collect whatever cash I can, as late as I can, on Tuesda' evenin'. And then wha' I'll do is get Yako to collect the rest for me."

"Yako? Are yeh off your fuckin' head, Davy? He'd be worse than the other two with the gear."

"No, it'll work, watch. I'll tell Jojo on Tuesda' evenin' tha' I won't see him until Wednesda' mornin' and tha' he has to give Yako whatever money he has for me on Tuesda' nigh'. Then Yako can just keep turnin' up as if I've been sendin' him over. Once they get the gear, they won't give a fuck, and we won't be back any later than Thursda' nigh'."

"Just in case I'm hearin' things, let me go through this again. Yako, who, apart from the gear, has probably never seen more than ten bob at any one time, is goin' to end up holdin' nearly five grand for us?"

Davy laughed. "Don't make it out to be like tha'."

"There's somethin' weird abou' tha' Yako fella, Davy. I'm tellin' you. I noticed it before. I even asked him once. I said to him, 'Yako, d'yeh sometimes think tha' yeh've come from another planet?' And do yeh know wha' he said to me?"

"Wha'?"

"He turns around and says to me, 'No, but I sometimes think tha' everybody else has.'"

"I trust him a lot more than I do those other two fuckers." Davy laughed and part-repeated what Mickey had said, "'No, but I sometimes think that everybody else has.' Ha ha ha, fair play to yeh, Yako. Fair fuckin' play to yeh."

"HEY, GORGEOUS?"

Joan glanced in the bevelled mirror on the wall to her left. It was him. She saw him smile. It was her reflection he spoke to when he said, "Here, happy Easter," and he offered her a package in a Switzer's bag. "C'mon. You'll like it. It's a dear one."

Jake could see Davy over Joan's shoulder. Joan looked to her for empathy, because she wasn't going to say all the things that she had promised to say, but Jake wasn't going to give up that easy. "Tell him," her hot eyes urged and her folded arms demanded. "Don't let him swagger in here and charm all over you," said her tight closed lips.

"You said that yeh'd ring me on Thursday," Joan told the mirror. "It's now Saturday." It was as angry as she could get.

Davy knew this. Davy also knew he should get her away from Jake, because it wasn't as angry as Jake could get. "C'mere for a minute. C'mon, down here, I want to talk to yeh." He walked to the front of the salon and Joan followed. She walked behind his soft, full black leather jacket that hung just above the arse of his tight, faded 501s, and her footsteps echoed the silence of his white Reebok trainers, until he turned and touched the bare flesh at the top of her arm and said, "Hey, c'mon, listen to me. I really couldn't ring yeh when I said I would."

"Why didn't yeh ring me on Friday then." When he shrugged his shoulders in reply, Joan told him, "Don't piss me about, Davy. I haven't the time for it, yeh know? And I don't like bein' made to look a fool in front of me friends."

"Alrigh'. But have a look at this egg. I was nearly tempted to start eatin' it meself on the way up here." Davy handed her the Switzer's bag.

She breathed easily, smiled slightly and told him, "Don't think I'm goin' to let yeh get away with this."

"Have yeh nearly finished here?"

"Yeah, we're just about to close. The boss is finishin' off out the back and he's goin' to take us out for a drink."

"Are yeh out for the nigh'?"

"No. I hadn't made up me mind. If we do go for a drink, I'm only goin' for one. I need to go home for a bath."

"Why don't I come for a drink with yeh and I'll walk yeh home after."

"Walk me home? Are yeh jokin' me? I've been on my feet all day."

"Hmm . . . righ'. So we could get a taxi back to your place and let yeh spend some time on your back."

She hit him playfully across the shoulder with the Easter egg. "Shit. I think I've broken it."

"That's okay. We can eat it in bed. Wet sex and broken chocolate. There's nothin' like it."

Joan blushed and looked around to make sure no one heard him.

"C'mon," he said, "let's skip the drink. Tell the others you'll meet them later."

Joan hesitated. She looked towards Jake, who was still standing in the same place, leaning against a counter at the bottom of a mirror.

Davy called Joan back. "Here," he offered, and his eyes directed her gaze towards his groin.

Joan saw his hardness swell a lump in his jeans. She saw it was time to get her own back. "That's not enough," she giggled.

He could tell she didn't mean it. She could tell he could tell this. She could tell he could tell that she wanted wet sex too. And broken chocolate. But she wanted to know when she felt warm afterwards, warmer than she was now, that he would ring her when he said he would. She wanted some attention, before and after. To be able to laugh when she told Jake about it, about him. She knew all she wanted and more, but didn't know if he would give it to her. "You're lucky that I'm tired at the moment and not in the humour of goin' out. Hang on, until I go and get my jacket."

She told him in the taxi, "Yeh know what Jake thinks? She thinks you're married or somethin'."

"Don't be stupid," Davy told her, and he tried to slip his hand inside the back of her denim jacket and up under a loose blouse, around towards her breasts.

Joan leaned in towards him. "Don't fuckin' molest me in front of the taxi driver," she whispered, before biting his ear lobe sharply.

Davy pulled his hand down and pinched his ear free of the pain. "Don't be savage," he told her. "Not yet anyway. Hey, driver? Is the Beach Road not quicker at this time of the evenin'?"

"Not so much as to make a difference, son. Yeh get a lot of traffic goin' down the new road to the Pidgeon House durin' the rush hour. I think it's all them new houses they built."

"Righ'," said Davy and he leaned into Joan and told her, "Christ. Look at me. I'm so horny, I'm startin' to hurt."

"Well yeh better cool down. I don't want two minutes of wet sex and two hours of broken chocolate. And anyway, I'm goin' to have a bath first."

"I'll have one with yeh."

"No, yeh won't. I've been workin' all day. I'm sweaty and I need to wash."

"Jaysis. Stop. You're makin' me worse. I'll wash yeh."

Davy ran the wet flannel across the short space of her back, from shoulder to shoulder and then down the length of her spine, until he reached below the waterline. Sloppily wet, he pulled it up again and squeezed a rinse which ran the few remaining suds away. Kneeling outside the bath and naked from the waist up, he asked her to kneel too. Relaxed, with her legs stretched out in front of her, she groaned her reluctance, but he insisted. "Just for a minute." When she did, he worked a lather into her pubic hair and began to spread the suds up her soft flat stomach, around and over the button nipples on her breasts, down the length of her arms, and he wouldn't let her sit again until he had sudsed the cheeks of her arse, until he ran the side of his hand between them and she had giggled, embarrassed. She sat again and some suds floated up, gathering together around the hint of a fold in her waist. The soap bubbles on her chest and breasts remained a creamy, sudsy wet. Softly, with his eyes closed, he massaged them in and up, towards her small round pixie face, around her neck and up behind her ears. The higher he worked, the lower she sank in the bath until only her head remained above water and her hands, which came out to rest on the side. When Davy stood and tipped off his trainers, she giggled again.

"I wondered how long it would take yeh. Is this what yeh meant by wet sex?" she asked, as he pushed off jeans, shorts and socks in one movement.

As the soles of Davy's feet splashed into the bath, he told her,

"No, it wasn't . . . isn't . . . but c'mon, I can't wait," and he knelt and carried her head towards him.

"Yeh better be clean, and warn me when you're comin'."

"It won't be long, for fucksake," and he kissed the top of her head, still holding it gently by the side.

She leaned in and kissed him too. She kissed him slowly and licked the length of his sex, while prodding with the middle finger of her right hand.

He'd liked that too the last time.

"Don't shove it into my mouth." She scolded him and held the base of his penis with the fist of her left hand, to help her measure a safe size. He gasped, infrequently at first, but not for long, and he listened. Instead of pushing out, he squatted down and slid deeper down her finger. His grip on her head clamped when her mouth and his arse were full and she splashed him, twice, for not telling her and spat down the toilet bowl.

"Have yeh ever had this with anyone else?" she asked him later, after wetter sex and as they ate the chocolate.

"Not chocolate this dear."

"I'm not talkin' about chocolate."

"Wha' a'yeh talkin' abou' then."

"I'm talkin' about us two. I think I've really fallen for yeh, but I'm probably just another slut to you."

"For fucksake, Joan, we've only known each other a week."

"I knew you'd say that," she told him, and she moved away a little in the bed. "So what about today then?"

"Today was great." He took a bite from the last piece of Easter egg and handed what remained to her.

"How do yeh feel about me then?"

"I think you're gorgeous, Joan. I've already told yeh tha'."

"But I didn't ask what yeh thought?"

"What's the difference?"

"Oh, what's the point."

"Jaysis! Wha' d'yeh want me to say?"

"I shouldn't have to want yeh to say anything."

"Well you were the one tha' started askin' . . ."

"Sometimes you're pathetic, do yeh know that?"

"D'yeh really think so?" he asked her.

She had time to stop herself. He had asked her calmly, but with a menace that frightened her so much, it chilled her. Pulling her duvet as close around her as possible, she answered, "No, of course I don't, Davy, but sometimes . . ."

He laughed, threw an arm around her waist and pulled her under him saying, "Sometimes, sometimes."

DAVY ARRIVED AT Heathrow feeling a new excitement, new in the sense that it was different from the usual excitements, which were really just old monotonous fears. The fear of getting caught; the fear of not getting any money; the fear of not scoring. It was a new excitement in that it encouraged a friendliness in him, rather than the old hostility. He smiled, in a Mickey Hughes kind of way, at stewardesses. He helped an old lady put her luggage on a trolley. He even joked with custom officers who had beckoned him through the red light zone, asking them what kind of contraband they were expecting a young Irish innocent like himself to be carrying, "A few bottles of stout?"

On the way to the Underground he caught himself clicking his fingers, discreetly, as he bounced along the automatic walkway. It was enough to make him smile, a self-satisfied smile, while the clicking fingers said "Hey, hey, hey". It was too late to stop anything now. Once Mickey arrived with the money and they banked it, then tha', as Mickey said they say in China, was fuckin' tha'. "Hey, hey, hey." Although it all seemed so certain, a peculiar disbelief still accompanied him, a too good to be true feeling.

The queue for tickets at the entrance to the Underground was long and patient. The politeness of people didn't prepare him for the crush of the crowd at the bottom of the escalator, the kind of crush that Ringo would have loved, which reminded him to look for anyone dipping at the doors leading on and off the train.

He emerged at Kings Cross, one stop away from Euston, but on a different line. Davy presumed it would be easier to leave the Underground and walk to meet Mickey, who was arriving on the boat train. Under the outside roof of the station, he asked a newspaper vendor where he might find a cheap hotel. The man, wrapped warm with a grey scarf and a polluted cap, pointed across the road. "They're the cheapest you'll get in London, mate."

Davy found a room in the first hotel he tried.

"Thirty-six quid for this?" said Mickey, when he saw it. "I don't know how they got two fuckin' beds into it. They must have made one in here."

The two fragile single beds had a narrow passage between them. At the end of one, a wardrobe fitted so tightly it couldn't afford doors. At the end of the other, a hand basin was fixed to the wall.

"Did yeh bring the works with yeh?"

"Don't be fuckin' stupid."

Mickey didn't bother to ask why it was a stupid question. He still had plenty of foil left, but he did get two packs from Davy and began to smoke them immediately.

"Don't forget this oney works out at three quarters a day, so if yeh fuck up it's your own fault, okay?"

When Mickey told him not to worry about it, Davy got annoyed, but he almost smiled when he realised that he was going to smoke two packs too.

"We need a map."

"Wha' do yeh want a map for? Sure yeh can hardly read, for fucksake."

"So wha'? You can, can't yeh?"

"I know I can, but wha' do I want a map for?"

"So as we'll know where we're goin'. This place is fuckin' huge yeh know."

"Jaysis, look! There's a telly," said Mickey. A television screwed to brackets had been fixed into the wall in the top right hand corner of the room. He used a remote to switch it on and search for channels.

"Righ'. I didn't come here just to watch telly. I'm goin' for a walk. Whatever yeh do, don't go out and leave tha' money here."

"Yeah, righ'," said Mickey, without turning to look. "See yeh later."

From the hotel, Davy walked down the Euston Road. Its busyness, the onslaught of fast traffic, impressed him. He turned left on to Tottenham Court Road, with no idea where he was. The thought of buying a map deserted him, while he got lost in the novelty and seduction. No one noticed the glee he felt as Porches, BMWs, Rolls Royces roared past, one after the other, or so it seemed to Davy. He was also impressed that the crowds who hurried past didn't seem to notice. He couldn't think of a road like it in Dublin and wondered why the fuck they had riots. Maybe it was London's answer to Grafton Street. And hadn't Kings Cross hinted at what was just around any corner. He wondered too where would Tottenham Court Road end. Hadn't he read somewhere that O'Connell Street was the longest street in the world? Another lie. Maybe it was the widest? Oh yeah, it was a street, not a road, so it didn't matter. Just another trick. Always catching you out.

At Tottenham Court Road tube station, he crossed Oxford Street, walked down Charing Cross Road and spotted something else which made him look around to see if anyone else had noticed. This place was fucking amazing, and because Mickey wasn't with him to ask, "D'yeh see tha'?" Davy had another look at the two youths standing at the entrance to a subway. As one captured a customer, another took him down the steps. He knew well the look on each customer's face when they surfaced. To watch a little longer, Davy stood on the piss-stained steps of the Astoria Theatre. They noticed him almost as quicly as he noticed them, but didn't seem concerned. Could they tell too? Probably. But the barefaced cheek of them impressed him anyway. During a slack time, and after speaking to his companion, one of the youths skipped through the traffic.

"Are yeh lookin', mate?"

"Am I wha'?" Davy asked him.

"Do yeh wanna score?"

"What've yeh got?" Davy asked, looking for policemen.

"Smack. Are you Irish?"

"Why?"

"Oh, it's just that my dad is from Ireland, from County Cork."

"I'm from Dublin," Davy told him.

"Is that in the North or the South?"

"It's in the South."

"So is County Cork."

"Yeah, I know."

"Is it near Dublin?"

"No. It's nowhere near Dublin. Which way a'yeh doin' the smack?"

"They're score bags, quarters."

"Weighed quarters?"

"Yeah, and it's kosher gear."

"Cosha? Is there somethin' wrong with it?"

The youth smiled and scratched the back of his head. "No, it's sweet, man. It's sweet, honest."

Davy looked at the smiling white teeth in the brown face and asked, "How could your oul' fella be from County Cork?"

"Sorry, man, what do yeh mean?"

"I'll tell yeh wha' I mean. Yeh better not be thinkin' abou' rippin' me off, with your fuckin' cosha gear."

"Listen, if yeh don't want any, it's cool. And the gear is kosher."

"Well wha' the fuck is tha', when it's not sweet?"

"Kosher, man! It's Jewish for sacred. Yeh can check it if yeh want."

Davy accompanied the youth over to the subway and bought a bag. As he walked back along the Tottenham Court Road, he couldn't resist the temptation to peep another look. He opened the bag carefully. Fuck me! The size of it, he thought. He was so surprised, he checked it twice during the half hour it took him to walk back to Kings Cross and on each occasion dipped his finger into the bag and tasted the speckles of dust that clung to his fingertips.

At the hotel, Davy found Mickey asleep with the television still on. When he woke him, Mickey asked, "Did yeh get the map?"

"No," said Davy, "but have a look at wha' I did get."

"Wha's tha'?"

Davy threw him the £20 bag. When Mickey opened it, he asked, "How much is there?"

"Abou' a quarter," said Davy. "And it only cost £20."

"Twenty fuckin' quid? Is tha' all?"

"I swear to Jaysis. And wait until yeh hear this, this is the best part. A bloke just walked up to me on the street and asked was I lookin' for gear."

"Wha'? Out of the blue?"

"Well, not really out of the blue, cos I was lookin' at them for a while. I spotted them as soon as I saw them. I swear to Jaysis, I don't know how they're not reefed. I mean, there's no way they'd get away with it in Dublin . . ."

"What's it like?"

"I don't know yet, do I?"

"What'll we do, smoke it now?"

"Yeah, here give us it." Davy poured the bag on to some foil and chased a line before passing it to Mickey.

"It runs clear enough, doesn't it?"

"Yeah," said Davy, "and it tastes strong as well."

"It is strong. Jaysis. This is the fuckin' business. It's bleedin' lovely," said Mickey, as he passed the foil back.

"Isn't it?" said Davy, before he chased some more. After he exhaled he went on, "If they're able to sell near enough a weighed quarter on the street, for £20, we'd easily get an ounce for a grand, d'yeh know tha'? Probably even less if we're buyin' a few."

"Buyin' a few? A'yeh mad? Yeh'd be ripped off like a ligh', especially when yeh don't know anyone."

"I know we'd be ripped off, if we didn't do it properly," Davy said, and he knew he wouldn't be doing it that day, but it was food for thought. The least he would do for the moment, would be tell Robin that he had been offered an ounce in London for a grand. He was sure to lower the price.

"I'm fuckin' starvin'", said Mickey. "D'yeh want somethin' to eat?"

Davy said he would try a kebab and Mickey left to get the food. Davy couldn't stop thinking about London. He had seen a Jaguar pull up outside a discreet club in the West End. There was nothing discreet about the doormen who wore top hats and tails, nothing discreet about their enthusiasm. When the Jaguar pulled up, it had hardly rolled to a stop and the windows hadn't opened, when one of the doormen instructed the other, "Get Mr Simpson's papers." The one who received the command held on to his hat and sprinted to the door of the club and back again with a bundle of broadsheets. The window of the Jaguar opened electronically and the papers were handed in, accompanied by a, "Here you are, sir. Have a nice day, sir." The same doorman then walked out into the middle of the road and stopped the traffic with an authoritative arm, allowing the Jaguar to pull out and off without, Davy noticed, so much as a nod of appreciation.

London was like Dublin, in some respects. Here, the "haves" had a lot more because there were a lot more "have nots" to rip off. But something else appealed to Davy, something more attractive than the opportunities, and that was the size. Dublin was small. It was impossible to disappear in. But here! Fuck! You could get lost in London, for ever. The time was going to come when he would have to get out of Dublin, within a year if he wanted to be safe about it. Where better to come to than London? Where else? Mickey would come too. A year? How much money would they have then? Too much to count now. Enough.

Fuckin' loads, ha ha ha. "Get Mr Byrne's papers." I could run over the gobshite in the top hat and if he could still speak, he'd still say, "Thank you very much, sir. Have a nice day, sir."

Mickey returned with the food and before he opened it he threw Davy, who was lying stretched on the bed, a pornographic magazine.

"Is it any good?"

"It's alrigh'. I was able to buy it off the bloke selling the papers but Freeny gets better ones. He had one in the pub one nigh' and there was a mot in it lettin' a dog get up her. A big bleedin' Aller."

"Shut up, for fucksake," said Davy. "I'm tryin' to eat me kebab."

"Another one was shovin' a bit of a Hoover up herself, a huge bit. Yeh know the part that sucks up the dirt?"

"Really? Were they English."

"No, I think they were German, or somethin' like tha'."

"Well, I bet yeh tha' they weren't Irish, wha'ever they were," said Davy, as he threw his half eaten kebab into a bin beneath the hand basin.

"Fucksake," Mickey told him, "I would've finished tha'."

Davy lay back on his bed and dozed as he listened to Mickey snarl and slurp his way through his food. When he woke again, the fazed screen of the television was buzzing. Mickey was lying in a contorted sleep on top of the covers of his bed. Davy hauled himself up and switched off the television and the light, before stripping and climbing beneath the bed covers. He could hear London outside and it reminded him that he had seen hundreds of thousands of people that day. People who didn't dare to look at anyone else, certainly not eye to eye. Everybody was in a hurry somewhere. Even on the tube, where people couldn't hurry, they wished it faster. And they hardly glanced at each other. Some seemed to prefer to stare at their own reflections in the windows opposite. If these were dangerously close, they pretended to study advertisements or gazed at the floor. Some read newspapers. Nobody wanted to know anything, or see anything, apart from the stop on the line they were waiting for. But there were some who liked to look at others who weren't looking at them. They managed this by looking at the reflections of faces on windows and glass partitions. It was a game he would like to get used to, especially when he realised many were looking at him. Why, he wondered, as the hum from Kings Cross traffic drifted into the room, had any eyes rested on him?

The manager, as requested, woke them the following morning. Neither Davy or Mickey, who woke freezing, had an appetite for breakfast, but Davy insisted they both have a shower. It annoyed him how Mickey, before he got off his bed, prepared to have a chase. Instead of complaining, Davy went and showered in an adjoining bathroom and stayed under the water for twenty minutes. A good scrub always made him feel better, even when he was suffering from withdrawals. That morning he was neither sick nor stoned, so the water had only to wash away the doziness he woke with. The shave he had made him feel reinvigorated and when he rubbed his smooth face he looked at his reflection in a mirror he had rubbed clear of condensation. He looked good. He looked to his eyes. He looked determined!

He was going blind. He just couldn't see how thin his face had become in the past few weeks. The saucer of shadow deepening round his eyes was something else he couldn't see either. Determination? Desperation was a word the deceitful peepers on the tube might have used, had they been asked to recall what it was they remembered about him.

When he went back to the bedroom, he saw two empty packs beside Mickey. "D'yeh know that's all tha' yeh have for the day?"

"I know," said Mickey. "Sure we're goin' in the mornin'. And anyway, if we get stuck, we can always get some of the gear yeh got yesterday."

Davy didn't argue, because Mickey didn't look that stoned. Neither, Davy thought, would he look that stoned if he used three. So he did.

DEPOSITING THEIR MONEY into a safe account kept them busy until late in the evening and involved, as Mickey said, "Runnin' around half of fuckin' England." It brought them to a hotel, the Runnymede, halfway between Egham and Staines. A lunchtime pint with a young looking bookie, and then into Staines to open a bank account which Davy made sure gave them instant access to their cash. Mickey didn't believe the bookie was what he said he was and told Davy so, as they travelled back to London on a train.

"He's too fuckin' young."

"Is it written in stone somewhere tha' yeh have to be a certain age, before yeh can be a bookie?"

"No," said Mickey, "but it isn't a three year fuckin' apprenticeship either."

"Well yeh seen the draft and yeh heard your man in the bank sayin' tha' I was the oney one tha' could get the money out."

"How come then, he wasn't able to give us a tip for a winner?"

"Because he's a bookie, not a gambler."

"Tha's another thing," said Mickey. "The next time we bring a few bob over, open an account tha' I can get the money from. Otherwise, it'd be just my luck tha' you'd go and get shot or somethin' and I wouldn't be able to get a fuckin' penny."

"They're goin' to give us a card, aren't they? Yeh can get as much as yeh like out then."

"I still think he should have been able to give us a tip, yeh know."

"Wha' d'yeh need a tip for? We still have £400 in cash to have a laugh with, before we go back. Wha' we can do is use the gear we have left and buy some more."

"That's the best idea you've had since we got to London," said Mickey. "D'yeh know, I can't wait to get out of this bleedin' kip."

"Why? What's wrong with it?"

"What's bleedin' righ' with it? It's too fuckin' big for a start."

"You're talkin' like the place frightens you."

"The place is a fuckin' dive. Yeh oney have to look at it."

"For fucksake, Mickey, look at how much yeh can do here. Yeh can walk around without havin' to think you're goin' to get tore out of it any minute. Nobody knows us here. Yeh can have an'thin' yeh want. And the place is full of fuckin' money."

"I'm not surprised. With saps like tha' so called bookie chargin' ten per cent just to open a fuckin' account, it isn't any wonder, is it? He wouldn't get away with tha' at home yeh know."

"Just because we don't know any bookies doesn't mean there isn't any at it. And think abou' it, he's oney tryin' to make a few bob."

Davy didn't want to tell Mickey about the plans he had for them both to come and live in London, even if those plans were still young enough to be no more than little thoughts. So, after they got back to the hotel and grabbed something to eat on the way down to Charing Cross Road, he took Mickey down Tottenham Court Road and hoped that he would be impressed too. He pointed out the flashy cars, the pretty women and the big shops.

"Yeh'd swear yeh weren't goin' back, the way yeh're talkin'," he told Davy.

"Oh I'm goin' back alrigh'. Fifteen thousand quid wouldn't last pissin' time in this place. But remember wha' yeh were sayin' abou' the IRA and all tha'? Well we could always come over here then. That's all they do anyway, as Ireland's new landlords, is fuckin' evict yeh."

"Come over here? For wha'? To get battered every time a bomb goes off? To get killed in a Zulu charge in Brixton? I bet yeh tha's oney around the corner from here."

Davy laughed and told Mickey not to be stupid, but he knew it wasn't a good time to try and convince him. He didn't need to persuade him, not yet.

At Charing Cross Road the two youths who had been selling the smack were there again. The youth who had spoken to Davy recognised him and came over. "Alrigh', mate? Are yeh lookin'?"

'Yeah," said Davy, "I'm lookin'. By the way, what's your name?"

"Suleman, but call me Sully. Was the gear sweet then?" the youth asked, smiling.

When Davy answered, "Yeah, the gear was cosha," the youth laughed. When Mickey looked puzzled, Davy said to him, "Cosha. It's Jewish for sacred."

"I don't give a fuck if the Pope's blessed it," said Mickey, "once it's as good as it was last nigh'."

They all laughed then, before Davy asked, "Can yeh get us a weighed gram?"

"Sure."

"How much will it be?"

"C'mon, I'll get you one for £75." Sully led them towards the heart of Soho and Wardour Street, via Soho Square. He still asked Davy questions about County Cork, telling him he had been there once, when he was a kid. Davy had told he was never there. Mickey had been once, on a school tour, when he kissed the Blarney Stone. He hadn't the inclination to explain what that was, because he was too dazzled by the strip clubs they passed, particularly the thin girls who stood in the entrances and who called to him in Cockney accents. At one club the youth took them inside, telling a hefty doorman they passed that it was sweet, they were with him, and they followed him to a small room at the back of the club. Mickey wasn't sure if they were going to be fucked, served or robbed.

In the small room, a fat, dark haired man sat at a rickety, cafe-type table, topped with claret coloured Formica. After talking with Sully in Turkish, he handed him a small package. Sully handed Davy the gear and asked him for the money. Davy checked it before paying.

Mickey tried to engage the dealer sitting at the table in conversation by asking, "Alrigh', mate? Wha's the story. "

When the dealer snapped something back in Turkish, Sully seemed anxious that they should leave. "Don't worry," he told Davy. "It's kosher."

Davy smiled and said, "It better be."

Davy and Mickey separated from Sully as soon as they left the club and went for a wander round Soho.

"C'mon, let's try one of the peep shows."

"Ask me bollix. I'm not payin' a fortune just to see some skinny thing dancin' round in the nip."

"Yeh must have some hang ups."

"Yeah, and all you have is stick ups. Let's get somethin' to eat where we can have a chase in the jacks."

They ate small and smoked big in MacDonalds on Shaftsbury Avenue, before walking back through Soho again. Davy was curious about the characters who loitered along the streets, the pimps, brassers, queers and junkies. He was saddened by the rent boys who stood in the entrances to amusement arcades, saddened by their age, saddened by the look which was familiar to him, the look which said they had it all worked out. He was particularly saddened by the thin shape and grey shade of the faces, which still found space to accommodate the saddest thing of all, the smiles they smiled when plying what they had to sell.

Mickey noticed none of this, enchanted by the neon lights flashing "Nude Girls, Nude Girls" and he was saddened too, passing signs which promised the best girls in Soho. Sad that he couldn't find out if the signs which promised the biggest girls in Soho were telling the truth. Not that he was concerned with the truth. It was true he was horny for the hour they spent circling. Well, it was true that he was horny in the head. He had a horny curiosity, but a limp prick, because they'd been chasing the gear. But that didn't worry him. His limp prick was only sleeping. It wasn't dead, he was sure of that. Hadn't he felt, now and again, during the first ten minutes of their wander, that little warm glow in the heart of his balls? Ha ha ha. There was no doubting that. So, although they had covered Soho in ten minutes flat, or at least the parts of it Mickey wanted to see, he had demanded, like a little boy, to do it again and again and again. And when, with his thin grey face, he smiled a smile that Davy had seen in the entrance to the amusement arcade on Old Compton Street, Davy insisted they leave Soho.

They left by returning to the Charing Cross Road and walking down to Shaftsbury Avenue via Cambridge Circus. This time dazzled by the theatre neons of carnival reds and fizz bag yellows. Smiling faces on theatre billboards and a smiling face on Mickey for the pretty girls who passed. Girls lit up by the neon seemed even prettier. They drifted by him, around him, not noticing him, or pretending not to, he wasn't sure. He didn't mind. He tried to imagine them all in the one big beautiful bed. Different colours, different breeds. Jaysis.

At Piccadilly Circus, traffic headlights, flashing advertising neons and many more people. Around to Leicester Square, past the Empire Cinema, Japanese tourists, hundreds seemingly, and flash lights. Immaculate streets, contented tramps, polite policemen. Lovely London.

Even Mickey, irritated by Davy's intoxication, had to smile, bewildered almost, at more polite policemen moving on a few punks who were drinking cider near the fountains in Trafalgar Square. Spot lights from the National Gallery fell down on the fountains, still shimmering, still dazzling, and song, chants, enthusiastic chants, hopeful chants, confident chants, from demonstrators outside South Africa house.

Davy asked a policemen was Big Ben far from where they were and was directed down Whitehall where, he was told, he wouldn't be able to miss it.

"Did yeh hear tha'?" he asked Mickey. "He called me sir. Can yeh believe it? When was the last time a copper called yeh an'thin' nicer than a little bollix? And did yeh hear where he said we had to go? Down Whitehall? I'm tellin' yeh, Mickey, it's more than a coincidence yeh know, doin' tha' stroke in Whitehall and look at us now."

"D'yeh know who lives over there?" Mickey asked, nodding towards a street guarded by a couple of policemen.

"Who?"

"Maggie Thatcher."

"Really? Seriously? You're fuckin' jokin' me. How d'yeh know?"

"It says it on the wall."

"Wha'? Tha' she lives there?"

"No, for fucksake. It says 'Downin' Street'."

"Jaysis, it's amazin' isn't it. Yeh can just walk by it like tha'. It's a wonder they don't shoot her from one of those buildin' sites across the road, isn't it?"

"Shoot her? They should kidnap the bitch and starve her to death."

"For wha'?"

"Because of the hunger strikers."

"Oh, yeah, I forgot abou' tha'. Here, tell us wha' those signs say. Read them out for us."

Mickey listed the names for Davy: "Trafalgar Square, Parliament Square, Pall Mall, Buckingham Palace, Hyde Park and James Park."

The majesty of the names impressed Davy, in a similar way that the size of Big Ben had. He gazed up at the clock from both sides, from Parliament Square and from Westminster Bridge. The Thames too, its width, its swell, pushing, heaving upstream, announced with hanging bulbs from river boats cruising against it, lamplights on riverside walks and headlights from traffic coming up the embankment. Davy hadn't bothered to consider that it might be wider than the Liffey. It hadn't occurred to him that it wouldn't smell, that there wouldn't be knackers sitting on Westminster Bridge sniffing glue. He looked down river from the east side of the bridge, before crossing and looking upriver from the west side. The Houses of Parliament lit up the river too, standing confidently, authoritatively.

Mickey was bored and wanted to go back to the hotel. There he got stoned and fell asleep. Davy got stoned and stayed awake, wandering out on a couple of occasions to buy coffee from one of the burger bars across from the station. Why didn't Mickey like London? He couldn't work it out. "No soul," Mickey said. No soul? Where did he get that from? The fucking place was more alive than anything Davy had ever seen. Okay, so people kept themselves to themselves. But what was wrong with that? Didn't Mickey notice the vibrancy, the variety? "No character." Something like that, Mickey had said when he'd been complaining. No fucking character? And here they were, back to Dublin the following day. Dear dirty Dublin, with its smelly fucking river, its Ballymun bleeding tower blocks and their poxy prison cell flats, its cheeky poxy policemen.

Davy didn't realise that for the same reasons he wanted to stay, Mickey couldn't wait to get out of it. What neither of them realised was how soon one of them would have to return.

Before they left London, they retraced the tourist steps they had taken the day before. Davy really wanted to. Mickey didn't mind, because it was the day that they were to leave. At Horseguards Parade, two ceremonial soldiers sat astride passive horses and had photographs taken beside tourists, who stroked the beasts and fed them mints.

"D'yeh think they're real?" Mickey asked.

"Well, they're not dummies."

"I mean real soldiers, for fucksake."

"Of course they're real. But if you're not sure, why don't yeh ask one?"

Before Mickey had time to, a motorcade swept on to Whitehall from Horseguards Avenue, comprised mainly of police motorbikes, but two unmarked police cars escorted from the front and the rear a sleek black Rolls Royce. "Jaysis," said Mickey, "would you look at who it is? It's the Queen's oul' wan." He jumped up and down as the motorcade passed, singing a Smiths song, something about dropping his trousers to the Queen.

Davy wanted to burst into a round of applause, he was so impressed with the Guard's response. While Mickey had insisted on making a gobshite of himself, the soldier hadn't moved so much as an eyelid. Yet Davy wouldn't have been surprised if he had unsheathed his ceremonial sword and removed Mickey's head at the neck. He might not even have been disappointed. The only official reaction to Mickey's antics came from the horse, who had taken two steps forward, dropped a few balls of warm moist shite and stepped back to let the steam rise and heat his underbelly.

THEY ARRIVED IN Dublin late afternoon. It was easy. Both were able to travel together, because they weren't carrying anything illegal, though both were surprised, disappointed even, that they hadn't been stopped by customs. From the airport, they caught a taxi straight to the snooker hall. Yako had their money and Skinnier and Jojo had enough smack to last them the rest of the day.

"See? I told you everythin'd be okay," said Davy, and he took Mickey off to celebrate with a fix. There is nothing quite like the power of a syringe, especially when it hasn't graced inside of flesh for a few days.

They fixed in Kathleen Burke's flat. They fixed to celebrate the success of the visit to London. They fixed enough to send them to sleep standing up. They didn't mind. Everything was easy. Everything was sweet, ha ha ha. After the rush, they had another hit, because everything was "bleedin' cosha". Everything was "alrigh', mate".

When they could get it together, they went downstairs to Anne's. The emptiness of Burke's flat was curiously apparent to two so stoned and they wanted the company, the reassurance, of familiar faces and familiar voices. Anne did what she always did and made them tea. Áine gave her Uncle Mickey a smile and a kiss and to Davy, the same impassioned look he was used to. He didn't notice. When he lay on the sofa, he was unable to keep his eyes open.

Mickey lay flat on his stomach and tried to read a paper, but he too couldn't keep his eyes open long enough. It was a favourite game, trying to finish newspaper articles while he was stoned. Davy liked to light a cigarette just before the lure of oblivion proved irresistible. Setting fire to himself or something near was an occupational hazard. The shriek Anne let at Davy for almost doing just that roused Mickey and persuaded him to have another go. He decided to cheat. Instead of starting on page one, he turned to his favourite page, the page that carried the court reports. The heading of one column, "Drug Baron Arrested", leapt out at him. "Fucksake, Davy! Davy? Listen to this."

"Listen to wha'?" Davy asked irritably and he opened his eyes. He suspected he was about to hear something Mickey found funny, but which he wouldn't tell very well.

Mickey read straight from the paper: "A man from the Raheny area of Dublin was arrested in the early hours of this mornin'. Robin Tumble (38) was charged by Detective Thomas Judd of possessin', with intent to supply, a large quantity of heroin. Detective Judd told District Justice O'Dálaigh, of the Dublin District Court, the heroin had a street value of over £50,000. Tumble was remanded in custody for a week. No further details were given in court this mornin', but sources close to the Garda Drug Squad unit responsible for the seizure say they believe they have smashed one of the biggest suppliers in the city and that more arrests are imminent."

Even though Davy heard Mickey ask what were they going to do now, he was too shocked to answer. It was bad enough trying to get his body to do what he had just been trying to avoid. Even worse, he had just been fantasising about London. He had imagined nodding a polite head towards the Queen's oul' wan as she swept past in motorcades, but now Robin had gone and got reefed. Why, in the name of fuck, did things always go wrong?

"Well, tha's tha' then," said Mickey, "we're fucked now. We'll have to go back over to London and get the money back."

"For wha'?" Davy asked.

"Well, where are we goin' to get gear now tha' he's locked up?"

Davy thought for a moment. "I'm goin' to go up and see Robin in the mornin'."

"What's the point of tha'?"

"We have to find out where he was gettin' the gear."

"Sure yeh migh' not get a visit and even if yeh do, you're bound to be puttin' the eye on yourself straigh' away."

"I should get a visit alrigh'," said Davy, lifting himself to his feet to help him concentrate. "He's oney on remand, isn't he? He'll be allowed a visit every day. It doesn't matter either, not now anyway, if it does put the eye on us. He's reefed, isn't he?"

"Well I wouldn't put it past the fucker to set you up, just to get a couple of years off his sentence. He looks the type to, yeh know?" Mickey wasn't sure what way Davy was thinking. "D'yeh think it's goin' to be easy findin' someone like Robin to score from?"

"I'm not lookin' for someone like Robin. I want to score it from whoever he was scorin' from."

"For fucksake, Davy. You're mad! The DS'll be on to us straigh' away." Mickey knew it. Davy was going to make a bad situation worse.

"Think abou' it, Mickey. All we need is a name. Yeh know Robin must've been makin' a grand on every ounce he was sellin' us. If we can make the same, just get it for the same price he was gettin' it, all we'll have to do is organise it. All we'll have to do is pay for it. Then we can get someone to carry it, someone to cut it, someone to bag it, someone to sell it. All we'll have to do is sit back and get stoned, while the money fuckin' rolls in. Wha' more could yeh want?"

"Who's goin' to do all the donkey work? Jojo, Skinnier and Yako?"

"Why d'yeh have to moan all the time, Mickey? I swear, it oney puts the mockers on us. Yeh know we've done all the hard work already. We have a pitch tha' half of fuckin' Dublin comes to. We're knockin' out fifty quarters a day just in the snooker hall. With a couple more knockin' out bags, we could double tha'. Do yeh know wha' tha' is? That's three grand a fuckin' day. Listen, just wait till I see Robin. See does he tell me an'thin', yeah?"

"Okay then, I'll wait," said Mickey. "But I hope he tells yeh nothin', Davy. I know tha' if we start bringin' our own gear into the country, the DS'll be down on us in an act."

"If Robin gives me a name, Mickey, I'll work out somethin'. Don't worry abou' it. I'll work out a way tha' we can't get caugh'."

"I think yeh ought to remember somethin', Davy. There's no such thin' as can't get caught. What's wrong with yeh? Have yeh forgotten tha'? Yeh used to know it. I bet yeh tha's wha' Robin thought and look wha' happened. Do yeh know wha' I mean?"

Davy could only nod to Mickey. He was already trying to work something out, but it all depended on him getting a name from Robin. He needed to be alone for a while, so he went to the flat in Balcurris. It angered him. When he was in London, if he wanted time to think, all he had to do was walk beautiful streets, full to the edge with crowds of people. Here, he had to go and lock himself in an empty flat, another cell, and only better than a cell because there were no screws to disturb him.

On the mattress, Davy knew there was fuck all he could do until he saw Robin. He knew what he wanted to do, but it was a pain in the bollix that all Mickey could do was get ready to give everything up. He really did just get in the fucking way sometimes. It didn't stop Davy wondering when Jojo was going to pay him back the money he owed him. It didn't stop him determining that if things started to go wrong, it was bound to have something to do with Skinnier, because that sap was just pure bad fucking luck. It didn't stop him looking forward to seeing Joan and wondering how she was. He had arranged to see her the following day, Friday. Tight arse Joan. His hand reached down and gripped his hardening penis.

He gripped it tight, before stroking it softly and tugging open his 501s. Tight arse Joan with the little tits, hard little horny tits. Tight arse Joan with the big little mouth. Davy lifted his balls and crossed his legs beneath them. Tight arse Joan who went red when they had sex and who had the nicest kiss he ever tasted. Deep wet kiss . . . If Tumble just gave him a name, everything would be all right. Give him a dealer the way he had given him a bookie to look after the money, there wouldn't be a problem. Davy went soft. He had forgotten, fuck, to keep thinking about tight arse Joan, fuck, start again.

Mickey called to the flat at midnight and told Davy that they would have to cut another quarter ounce. The money had been stashed in the spare flat and he had brought six packs for them to use. "We only have an ounce left, Davy, and that's not goin' to last very long." He seemed more pleased than concerned.

"How much money have we got in the flat?" Davy asked.

"There's six and a half grand over there."

"I'm goin' to stay in me ma's tonigh'. I want to get up early in the mornin'. Will yeh bag up the gear on your own?"

"I don't mind."

"Well, don't have a turn on now. Wait until yeh finish. We'll have to give Jojo and Skinnier twenty-five each, every day now."

When Mickey muttered something about being able to handle a turn on, Davy snapped at him, "For fucksake. Will yeh just wait until yeh bag the gear?"

"Alrigh', I'll wait, if it's such a big fuckin' deal to yeh."

DAVY RESENTED HAVING to visit Robin, because walking in left him with a fear that he might not walk back out. When the time came, after his request had been processed in an adjoining portacabin, he was escorted with a collection of mothers and wives to the main prison building and the visiting room, where Tumble sat on the far side of a long row of wooden cubicles. An apathetic prison officer sat in a high chair from where he tried to ensure that no suspicious contact took place between prisoners and visitors.

"How a'yeh, Robin?" Davy asked, sympathetically.

"I'm fucked," said Robin, "but apart from that, I'm fine."

"I left a couple of papers in for yeh. D'yeh need an'thin' else?"

"A ticket out of here."

Davy smiled, "I was just wonderin' if yeh wanted any gear brought into yeh."

"I thought yeh realised, I never touch that shit."

"I did," said Davy, "but the Joy isn't a bad place to start. Especially if you're goin' to be here for a while."

"I'll only be here until next Tuesday, Davy. After that, it'll be a long time before yeh see me again."

Davy nodded his head and shrugged his anxious shoulders. "I thought yeh might plead not guilty, just to get bail. That's why I came up to see yeh."

"Why? To offer me a hidin' place in Ballymun?" Robin's lips twisted wryly.

Davy forgave him. He knew Robin was pissed off because he was locked up. Davy forgave him, because he had no choice. "No. The reason I came up to see yeh is because I'm goin' to run out of gear in a few days."

Robin laughed loudly. "Did yeh not read in the papers why I'm in here? I haven't any fuckin' gear left."

"I thought yeh mightn't," Davy said, "but that's not goin' to stop me runnin' out, is it? If you're goin' to leg it next Tuesda', I need yeh to tell me how to get it."

"Why should I do that?"

"Well, wha' difference is it goin' to make to yeh now."

"Exactly."

"Wha's the story, Robin? For fucksake. It had fuckall to do with me, you gettin' reefed, d'yeh know wha' I mean?"

"You're not a thick, Davy. It won't take yeh long to find out where to score."

"Did yeh score in London?"

"Where else?"

"For how much?"

"Seven hundred and fifty quid an ounce."

"Seven fuckin' fifty?"

Robin smiled. "That's the goin' rate."

Davy smiled then too. "I was goin' to tell yeh when I got back from London tha' I'd been offered the gear for a grand an ounce. Would yeh have dropped the price?"

"Are yeh jokin' me?"

"No, I suppose yeh wouldn't. Listen, can yeh point us in the righ' direction, and if I can do an'thin' for yeh, I will."

"I don't think there's much you have that I haven't."

Robin's mood swings were unpredictable. It made it hard for Davy to talk to him and harder to get what he wanted. "Okay. So I haven't got much, but I could owe yeh one. Yeh never know when the offers of favours come in handy, and I bet yeh haven't had too many of them recently."

Robin brushed his moustache and thought hard before saying, "If yeh keep usin' the smack, Davy, you'll be caught within the month. So, I don't think I'd be doin' yeh any favours settin' yeh up in this."

"There's a difference between me and you, Robin. Yeh see, I've been here before," said Davy, sweeping Robin's side of the room with his eyes. "I've no intention of comin' back. I'd rather die first, which reminds me of somethin' I've been meanin' to ask, who set yeh up for this?"

"There's a difference between me and you, Davy. I'll bet yeh every time you're reefed, yeh think someone set yeh up, that someone grassed."

Davy didn't say anything. He didn't need to, because Robin could tell by the look on his face that he was thinking, how else could he get reefed?

"I realised," Robin went on, "and always have done, that the police were smart enough to catch me. Smart enough to stop me, anyway. You've inherited your mentality by surroundin' yourself with shite-bags, with hundreds of schemin' little rats who come crawlin' out of fifteen-storey tower blocks, in your precious Ballymun."

Davy chewed on the inside of his gum. He didn't mind slagging the Mun off, but he didn't particularly like anyone else doing it, especially the likes of Tumble. He remembered what Mickey had said the day before, and thought yeah, the ruthless bastard probably would set them up. "That's why I want to know where to get the gear, Robin. It's me oney way out, the oney fuckin' hope I have."

Robin looked across the table and straight into the eyes of Davy Byrne. He looked with the eyes of one who has nothing left to lose, at one who had nothing to lose to begin with. It wouldn't matter whether he helped Byrne or not, because Byrne would help himself. He was a capable animal. What he lacked in style, he made up for with instinct. You only had to look at him to see that, to witness his face being moulded by insincerity, while his eyes held firm with intent. All Byrne ever needed to be sure of was what it was he was looking for, and then anything went. There were no rules.

ALL THAT WORRYING for nothing. Always the same. Things always work out. What was it? Luck? Or Fate? Things always worked out, if you worked them. That's all it was. So, it was neither luck nor fate. It was about taking things by the bollix. Amazing how it makes you feel afterwards too. Makes you feel like you can have anything in this world, if you go after it. You can have fucking anything. True. There were many who took nothing but pleasure in putting things in your way. There were many who felt nothing but jealousy. There were some, Davy smiled, like Mickey, who were always full of doubt. It was amazing he could be that way when all he had was evidence of the opposite. There was something in that. Davy smiled again. Maybe Mickey was no more than Davy's carefulness.

With the optimism of a drunk and the confidence to go with it, Davy called over to Joan's salon to see if she'd be free to go for a pint at lunchtime. She couldn't take a break until two.

Joan was surprised. He hadn't arranged to meet her until that evening. She liked the attention though and smiled a loose smile when he said he would call back and take her for a cheese sandwich and a glass of wine.

He hadn't wanted to go back to Ballymun, but with nothing better to do, he caught a taxi to the snooker hall. There he found Jojo, Skinnier and half a dozen addicts waiting on heroin.

"Wha's the story, Davy?" Jojo asked nervously. "Have yeh any gear?"

"Any gear? Where's Mickey? Has he not been in yet?"

"No, I haven't seen him since last nigh'. And I've checked the flat in Balcurris. He's not there."

"Hang on here, I'll be back shortly."

Davy bumped into Yako as he left the snooker hall. "C'mon with me, Yako."

"Where, Davy?"

"Don't fuckin' worry where, just hurry," said Davy, marching off.

Yako had to trot alongside Davy to keep up. At Pearse Tower, Davy sent him up to Burke's flat and told him to have a look and see if the gaff had been raided. If it didn't look like the door had been kicked in, he was to knock and call inside.

Davy waited on him in the draughty entrance to the first block on Shanghan Road. From there, he could see what traffic came into the tower. He didn't see Yako, baffled, scratch his head in the lift as it went towards the floor for Burke's flat. When the lift jerked to a halt and the doors opened, Yako didn't step out straight away. Instead, he waited until they began to close again, before he leapt on to an empty landing. There didn't seem to be anything wrong. He could see the door of the flat and there wasn't a scratch on it.

Davy moved constantly in the confined space of the hall while he waited for Yako and interrogated him when he returned. "Wha' d'yeh think, Yako?"

"I dunno, Davy. There doesn't seem to be anyone up there. There isn't a sound."

Davy dismissed him and went up to the flat himself. After he had called and knocked, he unlocked the door with a key, silently. Inside, he held his breath and listened. It was just as quiet. He walked the length of the hall looking into the rooms he passed. He found Mickey when he reached the kitchen. A deathly white Mickey had slumped hunched against a cupboard. A syringe hung from his groin and blood seeped from the punctured wound which dried and hardened in a trail that seeped down his thigh, past his knee and almost to the jeans he had pushed down to his ankles. His grey white face was peaceful, his thin lips dark.

Davy lost his breath in one quick snatch and with it all co-ordination between his brain and his body. Mickey had overdosed and Davy couldn't move. "Mickey? Mickey? For fucksake." Davy's breath returned with his cry and he rushed forward and began shaking Mickey by the shoulders. He lifted Mickey's chin and began slapping his face, as he continued to call, "Mickey? Mickey?"

The eyes opened first, just for a couple of seconds, and then closed again.

Davy slapped him harder. "Yeh fuckin' gobshite! Get it together, will yeh? Jaysis."

Mickey opened his eyes again. "Wha's the story? Wha's wrong?"

"Wha's the fuckin' story?" Davy asked, pushing Mickey violently from his arms. "I thought yeh were fuckin' dead, that's wha' the bleedin' story is. And it's after twelve o'clock, there's a gang of junkies hangin' around the snooker hall waitin' on gear, because you haven't sorted out Jojo and Skinnier."

Mickey took a couple of moments to lift himself up and remove the syringe from his groin. He dried the small trickle of blood that followed and scratched off the hard blood, before pulling his jeans up. He could feel Davy looking at him, standing with his hands on his hips in judgement. He could sense Davy waiting on an explanation and Mickey hadn't got one. He tried something else. "So tha's it. Yeh thought I was dead, but there's a few poxy junkies waitin' on gear in the snooker hall? Well tha's bleedin' great."

"Look at the fuckin' state of yeh, Mickey. You're a fuckin' glutton, d'yeh know tha'? You're worse than a bleedin' child sometimes. I can't believe yeh. Wha' were yeh tryin' to do? Kill yourself? Go ahead if yeh want to, but don't get me reefed while you're at it." Davy kicked the kitchen door closed.

"I didn't think I put tha' much gear on the spoon," he told Davy, as he cleaned his syringe at the sink.

"Don't give me tha' bollix," Davy told him. "I don't know why enough is never enough with you. We're supposed to be partners, Mickey. I don't want yeh to croak it. Wha' would I do if tha' happened?"

"Yeh'd do exactly as yeh do now. It wouldn't make a blind bit of difference to yeh, or an'thin' yeh want to do. And anyway, I just like gettin' stoned. Tha's all. I love gettin' stoned. Wha's the problem with tha'?"

"I like gettin' stoned too," said Davy. "There's nothin' the matter with tha'. It's one of the reasons we started knockin' out the gear in the first place."

"But you want to be the big man too, the hard man. Fuck off

here, fuck off there. Don't cod yourself, Davy. Well don't try to cod me, because I know why yeh like to get stoned. It's for the same reason as me. You're a junkie too."

"Am I hearin' things here, Mickey? I mean, is tha' all yeh expect to do? Go from the Mun to the Joy and then back again? Do yeh think tha' because you're a junkie, tha's all yeh can do? Everyone's strung out on somethin' and I mean fuckin' everyone."

"The gear is a different thing to be strung out on, Davy, yeh know tha'. It kills people."

"Jaysis Christ! What's goin' on here?" Davy asked the wall. "I really do, I really believe tha' I'm startin' to go off me bleedin' head, because tha's a laugh comin' from you, especially after the state I just found yeh in."

Mickey turned his back to Davy and looked into the sink. Tears began to roll down his cheek. Davy saw them and wasn't sure what to say. He could see Mickey was hurting and he wanted to make it all right. So he did what he always did. He pretended Mickey wasn't hurting at all, that he hadn't noticed anything. "Did yeh bag all the quarters?" he asked casually.

"Yeah," Mickey answered, sniffling away any tears that were left. "There's fifty under the carpet in the sittin' room."

"Why don't yeh go down to Anne's and get somethin' to eat. Or d'yeh fancy baggin' up that last ounce?"

"Why? Won't fifty do them today?"

"Yeah, they will, but it's something to do, isn't it? And we're goin' to be busy over the next few days, so it'll be better to have everything ready." Davy told Mickey that Robin had given him a name and what he planned to do about it. Mickey, with a false enthusiasm, agreed to bag the last ounce, even though it would take him the rest of the day. He watched Davy have a fix and knew that Davy using two bags was just an attempt to impress him. He knew the restraint was a sham.

Before he left with the bagged gear for Jojo and Skinnier and to meet Joan, Davy told Mickey to get ten bags from each gram. "With Robin locked up, there's goin' to be nothin' but junkies out here lookin' for gear. I'll be back at about four, okay? I'll see yeh then."

"Yeah, okay. I'll see yeh later."

Mickey knew he needed to cut down on the gear and he promised himself he would try. It was easier said than done. Even what he had to do now didn't help. They had their last ounce cut into quarters and stashed all over the place. Getting the quarters one at a time and bagging them up, well, it was the most natural thing in the fucking world to do, to throw some on to a piece of foil and have a chase as he worked. He knew it never really got him stoned. He knew it was just habitual. He knew it just gave him a bigger tolerance. But what could he do? Asking himself not to have a chase while he was bagging the gear was like asking himself not to have a piss when he was having a shite.

He tried with the first quarter, which he picked up from the back of the Virgin Mary Church. While he tried, he lied and he lied and he lied and he lied. As he worked, he told himself he wouldn't use any, unless there was some left over, some which wouldn't be quite enough to fill a bag. Right from the very start, he planned how much he would like left. It was just a little less than enough!

He thought back the couple of hours to when Davy had found him with his heavy head resting chin first upon his chest. Maybe some day he would laugh at it. He wondered where the tears had come from. They were unexpected, embarrassing, though Davy wouldn't hold them against him. He wouldn't slag him off. It's not as if he was Lar Dempsey, or someone like that. It's not as if he was Skinnier. Though it was just as well. Things were starting to get bad enough without having to put up with all that. Taking the gear was beginning to stop being a laugh.

DAVY RETURNED AS Mickey was just about to leave the flat and pick up the second quarter. "I got me ticket for tonigh'," Davy told him. "The boat leaves at a quarter past nine. A'yeh sure yeh know wha' to do now, when I'm gone?"

"Yeah, I know wha' to do. A'yeh still bringin' one of the guns with yeh?"

"Yeah, otherwise I'd get the plane. I'm goin' to bring the Brownin' with me, though oney because I'll be takin' most of the money. The most important thing is to sort a bleedin' flat out over there. We're goin' to need one."

There was a silence between them for a moment, before Mickey said, "Yeh better come back, Davy. Don't leave me here on me own, sure yeh won't?"

"Jaysis, Mickey, you're beginnin' to make me think tha' you're goin' crazy or somethin'. I'm not jokin' yeh. Half of all this is yours, so wha' the fuck have yeh got goin' on in tha' mad head of yours?"

"Wha' abou' your woman? You're gettin' very fond of her recently, aren't yeh?"

"Who? Joan?"

Mickey nodded.

"For fucksake, she's just a dart."

"Yeah, well don't let her fuck your head up."

"And how is she goin' to do tha'?"

"Well, just don't think abou' goin' and buyin' her a flat, or an'thin' like tha'." Mickey laughed and tried to convince Davy he was joking.

Davy didn't believe him and heard something else, something altogether different. "You're fuckin' jealous, aren't yeh?"

"Wha'? Of a skinny little cunt like tha'. Yeh must be jokin' me."

Davy was about to laugh when he realised something that wiped the smile right off his face. Mickey wasn't jealous of Davy. Mickey was jealous of Joan.

They went over the plans. "So have yeh got it? Give your man tha' was doin' the gear for Sheringham ten quarters a day. Get hold of Eamo Thompson and give him the same. Go out and see Jamesie Riordain and see if he wants to do a bit of work for us. Don't mention money to him. Just tell him wha' it is we want him to do and see how much he's lookin' for. Now, whatever happens with all of tha', yeh have to make sure tha' yeh get the keys for three legal flats in three different towers, okay?"

"I'm not sure abou' this three flats business. How the fuck am I goin' to manage tha'?" Mickey was also beginning to suspect that he would forget half of the rest of it too. Still, it was better than having to go back to London.

Davy read Mickey's thoughts. "Listen, I'll run through most of this with Yako and get him to give yeh a hand, especially with the flats. He's abou' the only one I'd trust out of the other lot put together, so make sure tha' none of them have an'thin' to do with the gear. Actually, make sure none of them have an'thin' to do with an'thin', especially, are yeh listenin'? Especially tha' fuckin' Skinnier."

"I'm listenin', don't worry, I know wha' to do. But I'm still not sure abou' the flats."

"Jaysis, Mickey. We're goin' to pay fifty quid a week for them. It shouldn't be a problem, should it?"

Yeah, you're righ'. A'yeh sure yeh want Yako to know abou' them?"

"Yako's sound. I'll make sure and tell him tha' he isn't to tell anyone else and you can keep remindin' him."

They bagged another two quarter ounces together before it was time for Davy to leave. He told Mickey he would be back by Saturday night, or Sunday morning.

The threat from chaos was immediate. All Davy had really given him was a day to sort things out, so Mickey guessed that the best thing to do was send for Yako, close his eyes and hope when he opened them, Yako had fixed everything up. He still had one quarter left to bag, which he collected from the grounds of St Pappin's, but not before going over to the snooker hall and instructing Yako to call up early the following morning. Yako told Mickey that he had spoken to Davy and he had some ideas.

Some ideas, Mickey thought, and he wasn't sure if Yako was getting too big for his boots.

The first night, Friday, Mickey didn't use as much as he would normally and he worried that things might go wrong in London. He stayed with Anne for the company, rather than on his own in Balcurris. Anne was glad because it gave her access to the gear, though Mickey told her she was goin' to have to cut down, after he caught her goofing off with a cigarette in her hand.

"For fucksake, Anne, yeh have to think of the babby."

"Do I ever think of an'thin' else?"

When Yako called, Mickey took him over to Balcurris, when Anne started screaming that her flat wasn't the fucking Meeting Place. The first errand he sent him on was out to Eamo Thompson with ten quarters. He told him to call into Jamesie Riordain on his way back and to give him the message that he wanted to see him.

"Here's twenty quid for the taxi. Make sure yeh bring back the change and don't be any longer than an hour. When Davy gets back, I'm goin' to teach yeh how to ride the bike. But wha' you'll have to do is get Jojo to rob one for yeh and I'll bring yeh over to the fields to get some practice on it."

"Really, Mickey? Are yeh serious?"

"Of course I'm fuckin' serious. At this rate, with wha' it's costin' on taxi fares, it'd be cheaper to buy yeh a bike. Yeh'd be gettin' the bleedin' 17A, if I wasn't in such a hurry. So go on, don't be long."

Mickey, after he'd sorted out Jojo and Skinnier, then called over to Mick Murtagh, who had been knocking the gear out for Georgie Sheringham, and asked him did he want to knock out a bit of gear, "For Davy and meself."

"I don't mind. Wha's the score though?"

"Well, I'll give yeh ten £40 bags, you give me back £320. Okay?"

"Yeah, tha' sounds okay. Have yeh got them on yeh?"

"Yeah, here. The next time, yeh can get them off Jojo, Davy's brother, after yeh give him the money of course, ha ha ha."

"Yeah, righ'."

"And no messin' with the money. Yeh know wha' Davy's like."

Mickey couldn't believe it. It wasn't eleven o'clock yet and all he had left to sort out was the flats. When he got back to Balcurris, Yako was waiting outside the flat for him.

"Wha'? A'yeh back already?"

"Yeah, I did wha' yeh said. Jamesie Riordain said he'd meet yeh in the Towers at half one, for a pint and chat abou' whatever it was yeh wanted him for."

"Jaysis, Yako, me and you work well as a team. C'mon in and I have hit and yeh can tell me about these ideas of yours."

This was the first day that Yako had a fix. He knew, as he clung to the toilet bowl and threw his guts up, that his days as a milk boy were long behind him. Mickey had got the hit plum in the middle of his arm and left an inauspicious needle mark that Yako was more proud of than anything else he had ever had.

Between them, by Saturday evening, Mickey and Yako managed to rent three flats. By Saturday night, Mickey had just one hundred £40 bags left and everything done that Davy had asked. He'd sorted out the gear, the flats, even Jamesie was just waiting on a shout, to do whatever it was that Davy and Mickey wanted him to. But Davy didn't come back on Saturday night.

On Sunday, Mickey went through the same routine. Jojo and Skinnier got twenty-five bags each. Mick Murtagh got ten. Eamo Thompson got ten and Yako got a hit, when he came back with Thompson's money. During a Quiet Time, as Sunday night came into Monday, Mickey counted the gear that was left. He had twenty-three bags and Davy still wasn't back.

On Monday morning, before Mickey would even contemplate the idea of giving Jojo and Skinnier twenty bags between them, he called over to Breen's.

"Did yeh get your dike yet?"

"Yeah, I just got back. A'yeh lookin' for a couple?"

"Here's £300, give me forty."

"Holy fuck! I can oney do yeh twenty, because I oney got thirty meself."

"Don't gimme me tha' bollix. I know yeh get sixty every week, so gimme me the forty or I'll take the bleedin' lot off yeh, for free."

Breen didn't argue.

Mickey was relieved to have the dike in his hand. He gave Jojo and Skinnier twenty bags between them, sent Yako out to Eamo and over to Murtagh and had him explain to them that they would have to wait. When he returned, Mickey gave him two dike and began to tear into the rest himself. Davy would have to be back by that night. "Sunda' mornin' at the latest," he had said and it was now Monday.

Davy didn't get back on Monday night, so on Tuesday Mickey began to panic. He had a few bags, a few dike and £8,000. When Jojo and Skinnier complained, Mickey asked what did they think they were on, sick pay? He told them they weren't on a pension either, so they would just have to wait, like everyone else. From the balcony of Anne's flat, he watched junkies come and go from the snooker hall, but he had to give her a bag for the privilege. Even she was missing the gear. On Tuesday night, there was still no sign of Davy and the only news Mickey heard was how everyone was looking for gear. The only news anyone wanted to hear was that there would be some soon.

ON TUESDAY NIGHT, when Jojo realised that Mickey intended to stay barricaded in Anne's until Davy returned, he thought the best thing to do might be get hold of Yako. He seemed to know more than anyone else these days. Jojo found him, along with everyone else, hanging around the snooker hall. Jude was with Yako, but Jojo called him aside and asked him how he was. "A'yeh sick?"

"Not really," said Yako, "but I wouldn't mind a livener."

"A livener? Is a deadener any good to yeh?"

"Wha's tha'?"

"Here, there's a couple of Valium for yeh."

"Nice one, Jojo. Thanks."

"Listen, Yako, every time Davy goes away, if he's goin' to be gone for a while, he leaves a bit of gear for me, do yeh know wha' I mean?"

Yako nodded and wondered if Jojo was about to be uncharacteristically generous and if so, he wondered why.

"I forgot to ask him where he left it this time. I don't suppose he mentioned it to yeh?"

Yako realised Jojo was being characteristically cunning. He shook his head and waited.

"D'yeh know where his stash is? Because if yeh do, we can take a bit out, I'll give yeh a hit out of it and I'll sort it out with Davy when he comes back."

"Wha' stash?"

"He hasn't said an'thin' to yeh abou' it?"

Yako shook his head again.

"D'yeh know where he left his money?"

"Wha' money?"

"It doesn't matter. Don't bother mentionin' to Davy wha' we've just been talkin' abou'. He gets annoyed, yeh know, if yeh tell someone else somethin' tha' they're not supposed to know."

"Yeah, I know wha' yeh mean."

Jojo looked at Yako and wondered if he knew more than he meant. He had another idea.

"A'yeh into makin' a few bob, Yako, and we can go over to Crumlin and score. I hear Whacker Larkin has some lovely gear."

"Say if Davy comes back?"

"Wha'? Has he asked yeh to wait here or somethin'?"

"No, but yeh know . . ."

"C'mon, for fucksake, I've a lovely little stroke lined up. We're a model to get a few bob out of it, I swear. The last time I done it, I got £180."

"Wha' is it?"

"We just have to hit the 36A at the terminus."

"Rob a bus?'

"No, not the fuckin' bus. The busman!"

"How are we goin' to do tha'?"

"Well, this is the thing, I can't do it. I've done it so often now, if they see me comin', they pull off. I'm not jokin', Yako."

"And wha'? Yeh want me to do it on me own?"

"No. I have a rep'."

"Yeh have a wha'?"

"A replica gun. It's metal, so as soon as they feel it on their head or their neck, they hand over the money, because they think the gun is real."

"Really?"

"On me ma's life, Yako, I'm not jokin' yeh."

"When d'yeh want to do it?"

"We can do it now, if you like. I have the rep' stashed down in the darkers in Shanghan Ave. We can go down and get it and just hit the next 36A that comes along. Wha' d'yeh think?"

"Wha' are you goin' to do?"

"I'll keep sketch from the last block in Shanghan Road. If an'thin' comes on top, I'll whistle or somethin'. There's nothin' to worry abou', Yako, I swear. I usually do it on me own. All you'll have to do, when yeh get the money, is leg it back over to me. I'll take the rep' and the money off yeh and meet yeh up in the squat. Tha' way, if yeh get a pull, yeh won't have an'thin' on yeh."

"But the busman'd be able to identify me, wouldn't he?"

"Don't worry about tha'. I'll make yeh a bali'."

"Out of wha'?"

"We'll rob a jumper from one of the washin' lines on the ground floors along Shanghan. All yeh have to do is pull one of the sleeves off and burn a couple of holes for the eyes."

"Okay then," Yako said. Jojo seemed to know what he was on

about and it sounded like it was easy enough. Yako told Jude that he had to go and do something with Jojo. He told her the same way he did when he had something important to do for Davy.

Jojo could hardly contain his surprise when Yako agreed and he worked on sustaining his enthusiasm as they walked along Shanghan Road. Near the end of the flats, they spotted a full washing line. Jojo gave Yako a lift up on to the balcony and let him have a look. He reappeared and hopped down with something stuffed inside his shiny leather jacket.

"Did yeh get a jumper?"

"No, there wasn't any."

"Wha' did yeh get then?"

"I got a pair of leggin's."

"A pair of leggin's?"

"Yeah, well, we can cut one of the legs off, instead of one of the sleeves. That'll do just as well, won't it?"

"Yeah, I suppose so. Gimme a look."

Yako pulled out a pair of pink leggings and handed them to Jojo.

"Was there nothin' black?"

"Why? Does it matter wha' colour they are?"

"No, it's just tha' yeh want to give him a fright, not a bleedin' laugh."

"D'yeh think he's goin' to laugh at me?"

"No, he won't. I'm oney jokin'. Just make sure tha' yeh sound like yeh mean the business, and if he does laugh, give him the fuckin' gun across the head. That'll stop him."

"Yeah, righ'."

They got ready in the last block in Shanghan. Jojo prepared the bali' for Yako and rolled it up to look like a hat. After Yako had rehearsed rolling it down his face a couple of times, Jojo went and got the rep' from where it was stashed. All they had to do was wait for a 36A to arrive.

One came, eventually, and the final passengers got off at the last stop. Yako leaned against the stop where the bus picked up passengers for the return journey and waited. His collar was pulled up around his face and while he was starting to feel ridiculous with the bali' on his head, he was grateful there was no one else to notice.

The bus driver had parked off a mini-roundabout, where he smoked a slow cigarette. Finally, he moved forward and let Yako on.

"Where to?" the driver asked, before he looked up.

"I'm not goin' anywhere and neither will you be if yeh don't hand over the fuckin' money. This is a stick-up."

"In the name of Jaysis . . . this is a bus, son, not a bleedin' stagecoach."

"Listen, Head the Ball, just give me the fuckin' money. Yeh wouldn't be givin' me any of tha' lip if yeh knew wha' me nickname was."

SCARCE WERE THE moments of peace for Davy, as he travelled to London through Friday night. Nothing happened on the journey to distract him, but the reality of Tumble getting reefed had time to dawn on him. There was no going back and he would have to be more careful than ever. Especially with the way Mickey was going on. And what was going on? Jaysis! There were times when Mickey was attacking the gear, attacking it the way a parched man drinks water. But what could he do? Talking to him didn't seem to make a blind bit of difference. Maybe he could try to get him just to chase for a while? He could hear, clear as anything, Mickey's response, "Why don't yeh stop fixin' and just chase it for a while?" And what could he say to that. Well for a start, it was Mickey who was fucking up all the time. It was him, who for whatever reason, probably his poxy rights and wrongs, who seemed intent, like he was doing it on purpose. Yes, that's it: it really seemed that Mickey just wanted to fuck everything up. Well fuck him.

And fuck her too. Moaning because he wasn't going to be around before Sunday. She was probably secretly delighted that he wouldn't be there. It would give the slag the chance to ride whoever she wanted. "Well, you do what yeh have to do and so will I." There's a fucking thing to say, just because he told her he was going to be busy until Sunday. The way they went on, you'd swear he was doing something to the two of them on purpose. Fuck them both.

And fuck sleep too, because he couldn't get any. Not on the boat, or the train. At Euston, he walked to Kings Cross and checked into a different hotel, another cheap one, and found a few hours sleep there.

It took the Italian manageress a few knocks, each one louder than the last. "Meester Byrne, Meester Byrne?"

Davy called back that he was awake and almost told her to fuck off too. He still felt tired, a tiredness no amount of sleep was going to soothe. What he needed was rest, not sleep, but there was no rest for the weary, hey? Or was it the wicked? He could never remember. Davy phoned the bookie from a coin box which smelled of urine, outside the post office. He told Davy he couldn't see him until Sunday, because Saturday was his busiest day of the week. It meant Davy, because he would need access to a bank, wouldn't be able to leave London before Monday night. It meant he wouldn't get back to Dublin before Tuesday morning, at the earliest. After he had a minute to think about it, he thanked Jaysis for the chance of the rest, ha ha. Fuck the lot of them so. There was nothing he could do about it. He went back to the hotel and rescheduled his weekend. There was nothing to stop him trying to make contact with the name that Tumble had given, other than the dilemma concerning what to do with the Browning and the money. It would be less risky to leave them in the hotel, though only just.

What concerned him wasn't the thought that both might be robbed, but rather, a nosy cleaner might come across them. The idea of English policemen discovering an Irishman with a gun concerned him, because English policemen tended to take these things the wrong way. They tended to take them personally. If this happened, he would have all the time in the fucking world to rest.

None of his belongings seemed like they had been disturbed while he had been away to make the phone call, so he hid them in the obvious place, beneath the stained dead mattress, not because people often look in the most obvious places last, but because he could at least deny that they were his if they were found. Mind you, he thought, when English policemen found Irishmen with guns, the bastards tended to find all kinds of other things too, like plastic explosives and a bomber's guide to blowing up London in ten easy steps: "Step one: Load transit . . ." Fuck it.

There is nothing quite like the power of confidence. He knew this, but recklessness was something else, just a sigh of reluctant faith.

Davy hailed a taxi outside Kings Cross station. He gave the driver the address he required, before getting into the cab. The driver tipped a peaked cap and pulled off. From the back of the taxi, Davy asked him would he read out the names of the roads they passed.

"Wha' do yeh fink this is, mate? A bleedin' tour bus?"

Davy pushed a tenner through a glass partition and told the driver, "I'll give yeh the fare when we get there. I don't know me way around London, do yeh know wha' I mean?"

"Cheers, mate. I'll give yeh the bleedin' history too if yeh want," the driver said, grinning.

Davy smiled too when he saw the stained teeth crack the driver's insincere smile and thought, "Fuck him."

He sat back and listened. Although he wasn't always sure what the driver was talking about, he found the accent a novelty. The humour he enjoyed too, though not the way it was intended. The dry sardonic comments, the bitter undertones. He loved it. The fear of being overrun by Pakis and arse-banditing Arabs. "Got a fare to Gatwick last week and saw thousands, arrivin' in waves they were."

In between, the driver bellowed out names: Blackfriars Road, London Road, Elephant and Castle, New Kent Road, Old Kent Road and finally Peckham.

"There yeh go, mate. Gloucester Court estate. Yeh want to watch yourself here, bleedin' bandit country."

He paid the driver without tipping him and as the taxi spluttered away, Davy had a look around. Mickey was right, there was another side to London, not that Davy had ever doubted it. Maybe it hadn't been such a good idea to leave the Browning in the hotel.

Two coloured women walked towards him and he wondered if he should ask them for directions. The taxi driver had led him to believe that most coloureds were just off the banana boat, but Davy could imagine him talking to his next customer: "Just had a Paddy in the back of the cab. Only off the ferry he was. Yeh wouldn't believe wha' he asked me to do. Read him out the names of all the roads we passed. Lookin' for a bleedin' geography lesson, he was."

"S'cuse me? Do you know where Sharpness Court is?"

"There, look," one of the women answered. "It has a sign above it."

"Aw yeah, thanks," said Davy, and he sauntered into the block of flats. It didn't bother him that he couldn't read. He could count, and this, he believed, was much more important. He could read numbers.

The flat he was looking for was on the first floor of a landing which shocked him. Narrow, with doors to flats on both sides, it was longer and more claustrophobic than any prison wing he'd been on. There were no windows on the landing either and both walls and ceiling were full with bad graffiti. It was quiet too and he didn't see another soul before he found and knocked at the door he wanted. A scared voice called out asking who it was.

He called back, "Is Cyrus there?"

The door was opened by a black girl about the same age as Davy.

"Cyrus ain't here at the moment." She looked him up and down and sounded more confident when she asked, "Wha' yeh want?"

"I want to know wha' time he'll be back at."

"I ain't sure," the girl said casually, though she still looked at him suspiciously.

Davy had another look up and down the balcony and asked, "Wha' time did he go out at?"

"'Bou' one," the girl told him. She looked like she was starting to get bored.

"It's not even twelve yet," Davy told her and he wondered was she stoned. Her eyes were dark, it was hard to tell in the false light of the landing. Maybe it was hash?

"He went out on Wednesday."

"On fuckin' Wednesda'? It's Saturda' now."

"Yeah, I know wha' day it is."

"D'yeh know where he went?"

"Out to play a game of pool." The girl glanced at a Donald Duck watch she was wearing.

"Listen, for fucksake, I'm after comin' all the way over from Ireland, just to see him. So will yeh tell me where I can get hold of him."

The door opened another couple of feet to reveal a tall black youth who had been standing behind it. "Are you Cyrus?" Davy asked.

"Hasn't the girl just told ya da man ain't here?"

Davy, when he considered the size of him, was more polite. "A'yeh a friend of his?"

"Why?" the youth asked, moving forward to fill the doorframe.

"I need to talk to him. A friend of mine, Robin Tumble, gave me this address and told me I'd be able to get hold of Cyrus here. It's abou' a bit of business, d'yeh know wha' I mean?"

"Are ya ol' bill?"

"Am I wha'? A copper?"

The youth nodded.

"I'm Irish, for fucksake."

"So wha' ya say? There ain't no such thing as Irish policeman?"

"Well, there couldn't be tha' many in England, could there?"

"C'mon in," the youth told Davy, and he led him up a set of stairs to a bedroom, bare apart from a meagre bed and a clothes rack peppered with an assortment of underwear. This partially covered the only window in the room.

Davy stuck his hand out and said, "How a'yeh? I'm Davy, Davy Byrne."

The youth slapped Davy's hand and said, "Yeah, sweet, man."

"Are yeh Cyrus?"

The youth smiled and said, "Jesus," like it was inconceivable that Davy could ask that question again. "No, Cyrus is gone away for a couple of days."

"Bollix," said Davy. He quickly added, "I don't mean wha' you're sayin', I just mean, yeh know, tha' he's not here like. D'yeh know when he'll be back?"

"A couple of days," the youth repeated.

"Listen, em . . . What's your name, by the way?"

"Junior. Junior Brown."

"Listen, Junior, d'yeh know Robin?"

"I might do."

"Oh for fucksake, wha's the point?"

"Wha'?"

"I thought yeh people were supposed to be friendly and all tha'?"

"What people's dat?"

"Black people. You're nearly a bad as the English."

"I am English."

"English?"

"Yeah, and what's more, I'm more English than you are black, ya know?"

"Yeah, don't worry, I know wha' yeh mean. Fuck it. I'll go somewhere else. I can't be bothered with all this shite."

"Cool down. Wha' ya want?"

"D'yeh know Robin, or d'yeh not know Robin?"

"I've met him a couple of times."

"Well Robin's locked up now. I wanted to see Cyrus abou' wha' Robin used to . . . Yeh know wha' I'm on abou'?"

"I have an idea. But ya can talk to Cyrus when he gets back."

Davy sat on the bed and held his head in his hands. He wasn't sure what he would do. While he might have looked forward to the couple of days rest, he hadn't anticipated a holiday. Mickey was expecting him the following morning at the latest and while a day late might have been okay, anything longer than two . . . well it didn't bear thinking about.

"Have ya got a problem, man?" Junior asked Davy.

"Yeah, I'm meant to be back in Dublin tomorrow mornin', but I'm goin' to have to wait, amn't I?"

Junior sucked some air through his lips, mumbled something, and shrugged his shoulders. "I can get ya some tackle, to tide ya over for a couple of days, if ya need some yourself."

"Tackle?"

"Yeah, there's some nice smack around this way. Are ya clucking?"

"Cluckin'?"

"Are ya ill?"

"Aw yeah, I wouldn't mind a bit of gear, but wha' the fuck does cluckin' mean?"

"Clucking is this," said Junior, and he flapped his arms like a chicken, offering "Cluuuck, cluck cluck, cluuuck, cluck cluck" while hopping around the room.

Davy laughed hard. He laughed until a couple of tears rolled down his cheeks, he laughed until his jaws ached and his belly tightened.

Junior laughed too. He asked, "Ya like it?" then repeated the performance.

"Tha's a good one, hey?" Davy said, as he dried his face. "We call it "dyin' sick" in Dublin. Yeh should've got the part of Chicken George in Roots." He began to laugh again, but Junior didn't know what he was talking about. "So what's the story? Can yeh get me a gram?"

"Sure," said Junior, "but it'll take about an hour and I'll have to go and get it on me own. It'll cost yeh £75 and I'll be looking for a bit too, for going and getting it, just enough for a little chase."

"Yeah, I'll fix yeh up," Davy told him, and he thought for a moment. If he disappeared, Davy wouldn't have a hope of finding him on the estate. "I hope yeh're not thinking of ripping me off?"

"Don't be silly, Paddy."

Davy took a £100 bundle from his pocket and peeled off four £20 notes. "Here's £80. See if yeh can get it for £70. And by the way, me name is Davy, so don't call me Paddy, will yeh not?"

"All the Irish I know are called Paddy."

"Yeah? Well does everyone call yeh nigger?"

An ice cold rage lightened the tone of Junior's face and his eyes flashed a challenge to Davy. But Davy, while absent of any malice, also had a look that said, "Think about it." So Junior did and then he told Davy, "Yeah, I catch your drift." He smiled, before saying, "No offence meant."

"None taken, Junior, none taken."

Junior returned with the heroin ten minutes after the hour he said it would take him. After chasing a small amount to check its quality, Davy gave him almost an eighth. Junior was so grateful, he instructed the girl to escort Davy to a minicab office on Southampton Way, after Davy had asked how he would get back to Kings Cross.

"Tell Cyrus I'll be back Monda'. If you see him, that is."

DAVY APPRECIATED BEING able to sleep while he was tired and showed this with a great big smile when he woke: it was a smile of satisfaction; a smile of deep content; a smile fuelled by the memory of Junior, cluck cluck cluuucking around the bedroom in Peckham. He never wore a watch, but prided himself on his ability to guess the time accurately. Instinct was a factor, but he also listened. He could hear the time with the help of things like traffic, birds and people. All rushed in the morning; all strolled in the day; all were tired in the evening; engines, footsteps, birdsong. And he would look. The light told a distinct time too. Morning was different from evening, like the difference between being fresh and wasted. Sometimes, unseasonable weather affected his judgement, but he was rarely fooled. The final place he sought time was inside him. He usually knew what time he had gone to sleep and his body had a way of telling him how many hours, even minutes, it had notched up. Ten to seven. He got off the bed, walked to the window, opened it and stuck his head out to find the clock on the St Pancras hotel. Ten minutes to seven! It still amazed him.

Twilight Time. Out for a walk, he crossed over to Euston Station and walked until he reached Hampstead Road. That he didn't have a clue where he was going didn't matter. He was already beginning to feel a certain familiarity with London. It had something to do with the anonymity. An anonymity all in London shared, or seemed to, in a nod nod, wink wink, way. It is what he would have liked to have done, gone nod nod, wink wink, to the next person he passed. But he didn't, because that next person was a suspicious looking Asian, with dark saucered eyes. Well, one who looked suspiciously at a grinning Davy.

He passed Mornington Crescent tube station and walked on up Camden High Street. The atmosphere here was different. The shoppers were more relaxed than the anxiety-filled people of Peckham and had none of the insincerity of those who thronged the West End. They talked to each other and as they did he listened. The accents were easier to hear than some of the words. He only had to look at the Irish to be able to tell them apart. Though some, he thought, were easier to recognise than others, like those with the sideburns that big they stretshed behind the ears. Could they identify him? Probably. But it would be so much easier to disguise himself here. He'd never be one of those who went around singing about it. Mind you, it was the kind of thing, being Irish, that went in and out of fashion, so he would keep an open mind. From a table at the polished window of a Wimpy bar on Camden High Street, Davy sat and watched the slow but steady trickle of people who passed by. Were they returning home to estates like the one he had seen in Peckham? Were they returning to estates like the one he had come from in Ballymun? None seemed so depressed.

While he supped weak sweet tea, he studied the foreign girls who passed. Their non-Irishness appealed to him. They reminded him of Joan. They didn't look like her and she was Irish, but she was different. He would have to ring her. Explain to her that he wouldn't be able to see her before Tuesday, at the earliest. At least he could ring her. There was fuck all he could do to warn Mickey. They should have thought of this before he left and worked something out.

THE FOLLOWING AFTERNOON Davy returned to Peckham a day early. Junior fetched him another gram. There was still no sign of Cyrus, but Junior was able to tell him they expected him the following day.

Davy had other things to do too. He arranged to see the bookie. He was going to have to change his punts to sterling and also arrange with the bank to have easy and instant access to his cash. If he got the opportunity to score quickly, there was a slight chance of catching the night boat from Holyhead.

On Sunday evening he went wandering again and found a pub across from Mornington Crescent tube station which had a pool table. The pub had a too-old-to-locate-the-decade feel to it. Davy thought this about anything pre-seventies, and he couldn't locate the era the wallpaper pattern of dark roses on a burgundy background belonged to. He sat at a rickety table and immediatley swapped a full tin ash tray for an empty one from the solid piece of polished, moulded oak bar, which four builders were leaning against. Davy fell in with them when they began playing pool and found out they were from Longford. They offered him groundwork, at £25 a day, if he was willing to turn up at Kentish Town tube station at seven in the morning. He was going to tell them he wouldn't get out of bed at seven in the morning for £25, let alone go out and work for it, but he had already told them he was looking for a job and he would keep their offer in mind. What he also found out was the best way to get a flat. It was a way that wouldn't cost anything if he claimed social welfare. It gave him a great idea for bringing Yako with him the next time he travelled over.

Davy left before closing time, when the builders began to arm wrestle, and took some pride in the fact that he had won more pool games than he lost. When they wished him luck, he promised those he had talked with he would see them again some time and he walked back to the hotel in Kings Cross. It was a Quiet Time, even on the Euston Road, still busy with traffic. Quiet, because few people walked. The action was taking place inside passing motor cars. It was where they spoke, where they seemed to fall in love, where they sang, where they were brave and where they were frightened.

They were frightened to get out. Especially in Kings Cross, where it wasn't a Quiet Time. In Kings Cross, it was always Twilight Time. Prostitutes with fat fleshy arses and emaciated faces stood on the corners of side streets. Their high heels clacked into action when cars indicated they were turning off the main road and clacked back to corners if they were unsuccessful.

Davy stood at the main entrance to Kings Cross Station for a while. He didn't seem out of place there. Nobody did. He watched cold junkies wrapping their arms round themselves, burnt out junkies trudging up and down, waiting on an a miracle. He watched dealers, warm in padded coats, and their runners, congregate at an entrance to one of the subways. The newspaper vendor, wearing a polluted coat to match his cap, was selling tomorrow's papers full of yesterday's news. He watched bored taxi drivers drink hot drinks from flasks and eat sandwiches from lunch boxes. Davy knew they could see the dealers too. So could the couple of policemen who strolled back and forth from the station concourse. They all laughed at the screaming row a prostitute had with a transvestite. Here the extraordinary and the ordinary existed harmoniously. They met at the point where punters dipped their ordinary souls into the underworld. They blended at the point where punters got the chance to find out they're extraordinarily weird and prostitutes got the chance to find out they're extraordinarily ordinary.

Davy, after he slipped beneath his sheets in the Belgrove Hotel, recalled his phone conversation with Joan. Eighteen fucking pounds it had cost him, in 50p pieces. Jaysis. But it made her happy. Well, happier than she had been. And it made him happy too. It made him horny, though only for her, which was a pity, he smiled, because now and again he could hear the lonely clacking of heels pass below his room. She was gorgeous really. He took this as a sign, that someone like her really liked him, proof that things were getting better. Fuck it. If Mickey really didn't want to come to London, then he could take her. Well, he could think about it. They would go well together here. If London suited his desire for anonymity, it would suit too her appetite for . . . what? Well, anyone who wore a pink wig was better off in a place like this.

DAVY MET THE bookie in the Runnymede, again. A cluster of race tracks in the area was the reason he was based there. It was an alien world to Davy, more than Kings Cross could ever be. Doing business with a crooked bookie while sipping tea on the bank of the Thames as pleasure cruisers queued to pass through gate locks informed Davy his weren't the only underworlds. This, he thought, was Robin's territory, and he wondered would Robin end up in a little place like Staines running a garage. Stranger things had happened, as they say.

Davy was back in Peckham by two o'clock and it was a strange voice which called back to his knock,

"Who dat?"

"Wha'? It's me, Davy. Is tha' yeh, Junior?"

"Who?" the same voice called from behind the door.

"Is Junior there, or Cyrus?" Davy called in, as he leaned against the door frame with an outstretched arm. He was close to deciding if he didn't get what he wanted that day, he would have to go back to Dublin and figure out another way of getting it.

When the door opened, a dark skinned West Indian smiled a big friendly smile at Davy and said, "C'mon in."

"Are you Cyrus?" Davy asked, as he entered.

"Yeah, and you are Davy. Who is Junior?"

"Him," said Davy, pointing to Junior, who was sitting in a group of three.

"Junior? The man is Winston. Winston? Wha' happening?"

Winston laughed and said to Davy, "Sorry, man, but it doesn't cost to be careful."

"So your name's not Junior Brown?" said Davy.

Winston shook his head. Cyrus began to laugh. "Junior pussyclot Brown. Don't go telling no po-liceman dat. Him arrest you on the spot. Rasta."

Davy began to see the joke too. "I should have told yeh I was Paddy Murphy, yeah?"

Cyrus offered Davy a joint, which Davy refused. He explained it made him paranoid that early in the day. He was led to a room, away from the other group.

"Did Winston tell yeh wha' I was after?" Davy asked.

"Him tell me what ya say."

"Well, can yeh get me the gear?"

Cyrus didn't answer Davy's question, but asked instead what happened to Robin.

"He was reefed with a load o' gear."

"How dem arrest him?"

"I haven't a bleedin' clue. I went up to see him in the Joy, the prison, and he just said they were cleverer than him. They caught him with five ounces."

"Bloodclot! Wha' 'im do now? Stay in da jail?"

"He'll probably get bail this week and after tha', well, it's up to him. So, I wouldn't be surprised if yeh see him yourself soon."

Cyrus sat on an armchair with his legs crossed. He picked at some fluff on his brown wide cordorouy and asked Davy what he could do for him.

"Did Junior, I mean Winston, tell yeh tha' I was buyin' me gear from Robin?" Davy went on after Cyrus nodded. "Well him gettin' reefed leaves me fucked. If I buy from anyone else in Dublin, I'll kind of be under a compliment, do yeh know wha' I mean?"

"Yeah," said Cyrus, but he also told Davy to slow down when he was talking, because he couldn't understand his accent. Davy made the same request. "So ya want me to get ya the drug?"

"Of course," said Davy.

"And I can trust ya?"

"For fucksake. Robin trusted me, didn't he? At least enough to put me on to you."

Cyrus explained, in a friendly manner, that he didn't trust anyone and warned Davy about performing any "Paddy party tricks".

"Sure I don't even know London, for fucksake."

"If ya try an'thin', Davy, ya won't get to know it, me promise ya dat."

"Think abou' it, Cyrus. I'm the fuckin' stranger here."

"How much drug ya get from Robin and how much it cost yeh?"

"I was gettin' a couple of ounces a week and it was costin' me a little more than the £750 tha' he said you would charge me."

Cyrus laughed, "A little bit more than £750. So's dat wha' ya want offa me? Two ounce?"

"No," said Davy, arrogantly, "I want five ounces off yeh. That'll do me for abou' two weeks and then, sooner rather than later, I'll be lookin' for more from yeh. With Robin locked up—not that I take any pleasure from it—I'll be sellin' a lot more gear meself."

"Five ounces?" Cyrus asked, his eyes widening to reveal the bloodshot whites.

"Yeah, five ounces. Say if, when I come over the next time, I get eight ounces, will yeh do them to me for five grand instead of six?"

"Listen to me now, big spender. The price never alter and the bottom line is £750 an ounce. If ya was buyin' less than two ounces, it'd be a grand an ounce."

"Why don't yeh meet me halfway and say five and a half grand."

"Bwoy! £500 might be not much for you, but for me boy, it's enough."

"Okay, but there's no harm in tryin', is there? So, £750 an ounce. But remember, Cyrus, I was gettin' weighed quality ounces from Robin, so I hope I get the same from you."

"Ya might have been gettin' weighed ounces, but the quality won't be the same."

When Davy asked what he meant, Cyrus explained that Robin got his gear in the one parcel and cut it before he passed it on. He also explained that Robin did this before he left London by separating his parcel into ounces, but making each one up with five grams of glucose. With every five, he made another one.

Davy was resentful at first, but then realised he would have to do the same, otherwise he'd have junkies overdosing all over the place. He didn't want Cyrus to realise he hadn't suspected Robin. "Yeah, I thought he was doin' somethin' like tha'." It occurred to Davy at the same time just to sell smaller bags. If Cyrus was telling the truth, they would still be stronger than what he was selling at the moment. "Righ'. So when can yeh get me the five ounces?"

"This time tomorrow."

"Oh, for fucksake. Tomorrow? I'm goin' to be in trouble."

"Wha' cause for dat?"

"I was supposed to be back in Dublin on Sunda'. I won't get there until Wednesda' now and I've no way of gettin' in touch with the bloke I do the gear with. He'll think I've been fuckin' reefed or somethin'."

Cyrus shrugged his shoulders. The following day was the earliest he could do it. He didn't tell Davy that he wanted another day to check him out, or that he thought there was something peculiar about him. It couldn't have been his Irishness, because Robin was Irish too. It was peculiar how Robin had never said very much and Davy would never shut up. It was peculiar how someone in Davy's position was always haggling, always looking for bargains, reductions in the cost of the drug, when he was obviously going to make a lot from it. But it wasn't as if he was mean. Winston had said Davy sorted him out with a half decent chase. More importantly, Winston told Cyrus he had seen Davy smoke the smack, even if it was just a small amount. Still, he had to be careful with the Paddy, complicated people they were. Well, he could keep an eye on him for a day or so. "Wha' side of London are ya staying? North or South?"

It was Davy's turn to be wary. "I'm stayin' over near Kings Cross, wherever that is."

"Me know Kings Cross. Wha' part?"

"I don't know wha' part. It's near the train station. I'm stayin' in a bed and breakfast over there, but don't ask me wha' the fuckin' name of it is, because I haven't a clue."

Cyrus was still curious and thought the best way to find out what he needed to know was to see Davy take the drug. "Do ya wanna base some charlie?" he asked.

"Do I want to wha'?"

"Cocaine. Do yeh like cocaine?'

"Yeah, it's alrigh'," Davy said casually, "with a bit of smack."

"Me talkin' 'bout pipin' it," Cyrus told Davy.

When Davy asked, "Wha' the fuck is tha'?" Cyrus demonstrated by taking out some cocaine, which he mixed with bicarbonate of soda. He tipped it all into a baby brandy bottle, half full of water. Having tied a shoelace around the neck of the bottle, he held it in a boiling kettle and explained to Davy how the cocaine was purified and how, when it turned to oil, it gathered in small pools and crystallised into little rocks as the water cooled. This he removed and allowed to dry before crushing it with a kitchen knife to a fine powder.

Cyrus smoked some from a water pipe and offered it to Davy. "Have a little lick, man."

Davy declined. He was usually okay about trying anything once, but then felt like the wrong time and place. What he did do was take out the smack he had left and put some on a piece of foil to chase. When Cyrus tipped some of the cocaine on the foil and said, "Try dat," Davy chased it with the smack.

This was disappearing quickly enough for him to ask Winston could he score him another gram. Before he could answer, Cyrus took a few bags from his pocket and said, "Here, take some of them, ya. It's ya drug."

"Nice one," said Davy. He watched Cyrus finish his pipe and asked him, "D'yeh fancy a pint?"

"No, me don't drink in da daytime. Ya can play pool?"

"Yeah, I'd love a game," said Davy, delighted that he'd been asked.

The walk with Cyrus reminded Davy of his ignorance of geography. He asked Cyrus where he was from and when he said Jamaica, Davy was none the wiser. He knew that Bob Marley came from around that way. "Where's tha', exactly?" he asked.

Cyrus asked Davy did he know where the Caribbean was, and when Davy answered, "Not really," Cyrus asked did he know where America was.

"Of course, though I've never been there or an'thin'."

Cyrus explained that it was between North and South America, though on this side, the Atlantic rather than the Pacific.

When Cyrus asked about Dublin, Davy explained that there were only Irish people living there, apart from a few students. "Oh yeah,

I nearly forgot, they let a few of them boat people in. There's China-men and tha' with restaurants, and I suppose there's a few black doctors and students, but any of the others are just orphans. I think they were black babies."

"Black babies?"

"Yeah, yeh know, like, they were starvin', so they brought them to Ireland. We used to have to bring money into school for them. It used to drive me oul' fella mad, because he said tha' we Irish were niggers when to be black was still a novelty. He thought tha' the priests ought to have been more concerned about more important thin's."

"Is dat wha' they call us in Ireland? Nigger?"

"It's only the likes of me oul' fella. The likes of me wouldn't dream of it, d'yeh know? They're not against the blacks or an'thin', it's just tha' they don't know any different." Davy was tempted to sing to Cyrus, "In Mountjoy jail, where the niggers get no mail, and they hang dirty pictures on the wall . . ." He could tell him that's where Robin was being held, while trying to explain that racism in Ireland was only a cultural thing, but he couldn't think how to.

Cyrus learned a few things anyway. Robin only spoke when he was looking for something. It was a surprise to learn that the whole country wasn't at war. He'd imagined parts of Ireland to be like Beirut and wasn't sure if the Irish slaughtered each other because they drank too much, or if it was the other way around. He began to like Davy because Davy made him laugh.

"How come ya say Jesus all the time?"

"How come yeh say Rasta?"

They compared the price of drugs on the streets and Cyrus suggested he might move there.

"They won't let you in."

When Cyrus said that he had been led to believe that the Irish were a friendly race, Davy told him, "Oh they're not all like me, yeh know." They compared Ballymun and Brixton, which Cyrus insisted was his yard, rather than Peckham. "I take ya up there later and show ya round."

"Will I be alrigh' goin' up if I'm white, I mean, Jaysis . . ."

Cyrus laughed again. "Yeah, enough whites up there."

Davy looked forward to it and wondered what his chances were of getting off with a black bird. Just the thought of it excited him. But he thought it better to ask Cyrus his opinion.

"Well, so long as she don't belong to someone else."

"Nice one," said Davy, "nice one. Yeh never know then, hey?"

"Well, ya wanna have a very pretty white arse to have any chance."

"Don't you worry about my white arse, it's as pretty as they come."

At the pool hall, they had to wait a half an hour for a table. As well as dampening his enthusiasm, it dented Davy's good impressions of Cyrus. If this had been Ballymun, he would have fucked someone off. He told Cyrus this. Cyrus laughed.

"Will I need to wear a suit or an'thin', to get into this club in Brixton tonigh'?" Davy asked before he left.

"Just easy, man. Just come easy," said Cyrus, and he warned Davy to be back at the flat before eleven, as this was the latest they ever left.

"Alrigh', I'll see yeh later." Davy knew Cyrus had been sussing him out, but he going to give him something to think about. He was going to come easy all right.

At the hotel, he had a couple of hours sleep before he showered. He changed into the suit he bought with Mickey, the day he met Joan. The First Time. The suit was a blue/grey Irish tweed, double breasted with turned up, French-pleated trousers. He also wore a grey Italian shirt he had bought on the same day and polished, black George Webbs. After he dressed and was ready, he looked at himself in the mirror of a wardrobe and straightened his highlighted hair, with the thought, I bet yeh they don't come any easier than this.

At the flat in Peckham, Cyrus was waiting on him with the girl that Davy had seen the first day. Cyrus sucked through his lips when he saw how Davy was dressed and he said something to the girl, which Davy couldn't understand.

On Southampton Way they hired a minicab from the same office the girl had brought him to and it took them to a club in Brixton. The driver was Nigerian and laughed after everything he said, which Davy found infectious, though it irritated Cyrus. When they reached the club, Davy paid the fare and gave the driver a tip. The club looked like a derelict. A red light lit up the entrance to a hallway, and as they entered Davy saw a large West Indian and a companion body search the two men who walked in front.

Davy called Cyrus back out into the street. "Wha's the story? Yeh never said we were goin' to get searched comin' in here?"

"Ya no carryin' a knife?"

"Well, yeh should have warned me or said somethin'.."

Cyrus sucked through his lips again. "Wha' 'appen, Davy boy. Ya no trust no one? Ya have nothin' to worry about. Pass it to me and I give it back inside."

Davy looked around the street and when he was sure no one was looking, he unbuttoned his jacket and began to remove the Browning from his waistband, releasing the clip a he did so.

"Bloodclot . . . Me thought it was a fuckin' knife ya had. Cover it up, cover it up."

"Yeh should have said somethin', Cyrus. I have one of these near me in Dublin all the time." He was glad of the opportunity to let Cyrus know. "I mean, for fucksake, did yeh think I'd be strollin' around London lookin' to spend nearly four grand and not have somethin' to protect meself with?"

Cyrus didn't answer him, unsure whether to be impressed or disappointed. "Go on in dat club, go on in. Me take care of da man at da door." Cyrus greeted the bouncer with a handshake. "Cool yeah. Me do a bit of business here. He not carry nothin'—tek this and easy, yeah." He handed the bouncer £20.

The bouncer looked Davy up and down and said, "Cool, go on in."

Davy was surprised how big the club was inside. It had three levels: basement, ground and first floor. Cyrus showed him around. Downstairs, the music was mixed by DJs who spoke into mikes at the same time. Davy couldn't understand a word and was irritated by the incessant base beat. The floor was packed with people and the air thickened by weed smoke. They returned to the ground floor, which served as a bar and played background music. Upstairs, a live band played the kind of West Indian reggae Davy's ears were accustomed to and it was here that he settled with Cyrus. He quickly realised that he was the only white in the building apart from a couple of girls. Davy didn't worry. When people looked at him curiously, or got inquisitive, Cyrus always said, "Him with me."

After listening to the band for a while, they went back down the ground level, where it was easier to talk. It was getting harder for Davy to have any kind of serious conversation as Cyrus was getting more stoned, so all he began to do was nod knowingly at Cyrus every time he laughed. Cyrus noticed Davy looking at a couple of girls and asked, with a big grin, "Me thought dat ya were lookin' for a black bird?"

"I am. I thought yeh said it was alrigh'? I mean, there's no harm in lookin', is there?"

"No, but dem is a couple of crows," said Cyrus, nodding to the girls Davy was eyeing, "not pretty black birds."

"They look alrigh' to me," Davy told him.

Cyrus told him not to bother and promised he would sort something out. He didn't want "no ugly wimmin" bothering him for drinks.

Davy looked away from the girls and wondered if Cyrus would keep his promise. A black girl. Mickey would be fucking sick. It was the only thing he liked about London, the girls. Maybe if Davy got off with one and told Mickey, it would make him a bit more eager to come back. As he swept the bar with his eyes, he noticed how casually everyone smoked joints. None of this business of skinning up in the fucking jacks and blowing the smoke out of windows. The next time that Cyrus began to skin up, Davy asked him, "Is tha' grass?" When Cyrus told him it was the best weed in the world, Davy doubted him. "Is it as good as Panama Red?"

Cyrus shrugged his shoulders, flicked a few dreadlocks behind them and kept rolling.

"Grass is no fuckin' use anyway. That's wha' tha' is, isn't it?" Davy said, checking the bag Cyrus had taken it from. "Yeh can grow this in Ireland, grass, and it isn't worth the effort."

Cyrus repeated that what he was smoking was the best.

"Well, it couldn't be as good as this Nepalese black I smoked once. It had a vein of pure opium runnin' through it."

Cyrus explained that what he was smoking was as natural as life itself and was smoked as it grew. "This is sense, man."

"Sense? Wha' d'yeh mean? It just looks like grass to me."

"Sensemelia. This is sensemelia," Cyrus said, like that should explain itself.

When Davy woke the following morning, it was the last thing he could remember from the night before. For a moment. Then he remembered saying to Cyrus, "Give us a blow off it then."

Davy's head was so heavy, he couldn't lift it from the pillow. His in-built timing mechanism failed him too. Morning? He wasn't even certain of that. What was it called? Sensasomething? He felt the warmth of a body next to him and the shock helped his head leap from the pillow. He peeped at the coloured girl who lay beside him, with the sheets pulled up to her shoulders and he noticed the love bites on his stomach, before lying flat again. He recognised the bedroom. It was the same one Winston had taken Davy to the first time that he had called to the flat on the Gloucester Court. He lifted the sheets slightly, looked at the girl's curved arse and tried to remember. It was too vague, so he tried not to remember at all, in case he made memories up. It was absurd. While he had been trying to weigh everything up—the time, where he was, what had happened—his hand had reached down and gripped his prick, like that was the most important thing in the world, like all that mattered was that it was still there. As soon as his eyes opened, his hand reached down and found the reassurance comforting. For fucksake! It wasn't going to help him think, was it? What he needed was a bit of gear.

His clothes were in a heap beside the bed and he tried to go through them without waking the girl. As he looked to see if he had any gear, he wondered what he had done with the gun. Christ! His head just wouldn't work. He got out of the bed and looked around the room, frantically, desperately, but there was nowhere to look. The flat was silent. Davy put his trousers on and went to see who was there. The flat was empty. He was going to wake the girl and ask her, but he didn't have to.

She was awake when he got back to the bedroom. She lay and looked at him lazily, so he searched beneath the bed, while he thought of what he could ask her. When he surfaced, she asked first, "Is this what you're looking for?" She picked up the pillow. She didn't speak patois like he had first heard her, which disappointed Davy, but he was relieved when he saw the Browning and two bags of smack beside it. He didn't answer her, checking instead that the clip on the gun was full, before going off and returning with some foil to chase the smack.

"I hardly slept a wink last night," the girl said to Davy. "I kept finking that bleedin' fing was going to go off."

"Don't worry abou' it," Davy told her. "It has a safety catch." It didn't reassure the girl.

Davy sat on the edge of the bed and began to chase the gear. "What's your name?" he asked her.

It was the girl's turn to be disappointed. "Can't you remember? You thought it was right hilarious last night."

Davy tried to think and when she could see that he was getting nowhere, she told him, "Cynthia."

Davy was puzzled. What would he find funny about that?

"Get tha' into yeh, Cynthia. That's what you kept saying last night."

Davy buried his embarressment in his hands and laughed until it began to hurt.

"What's funny about that?" She asked, laughing too.

When he could speak, Davy said, "Don't worry abou' it. It's nothin' personal." He offered her a chase from the gear.

"What is it?" she asked.

"Smack," Davy told her and realised that if she didn't know what it was, she wouldn't want any.

She declined with a request of her own, "Have you any more sense?"

"Sense? Aw, sense. Jaysis, don't be talkin' to me abou' sense. Wha' was I like last nigh'?"

"Oh, you were sweet," she said, stroking his arm.

"No, I didn't mean . . . Like, was I out of me head?"

"You were funny."

"Funny? Wha' do yeh mean, funny?"

"You have a rude laugh," she told him, and gave him a chance to hear her own.

"I see wha' yeh mean."

When he finished smoking the smack, he lay down beside her and crawled beneath the sheets. Her black soft skin was gorgeously silky, her young breasts full and firm, her giggle deep and delightful. But none of these were enough to make Davy hard for long. It must have been the combined effect of the gear and the night before. He was going to stay beside her until it passed, or more to the point, returned. But when she muttered, "Not again," he got up and got dressed.

Winston, who had slipped out to the shops, returned just after Davy had risen and told him Cyrus left a message to say he would have what he wanted at four. It was only midday, so Davy had plenty of time to return to Kings Cross and get changed before picking up the money. He wet his face in the flat and found out from Cynthia how he might contact her the next time he was over. She told him he only had to ask Cyrus.

It was a Sad Time for Davy. Time to leave London, again. He wanted to take it out on someone.

THREE O'CLOCK IN the morning is an Easy Time and it was that kind of time when Davy Byrne stepped on to the ferry taking him back to Ireland with five cheap ounces of heroin. He had spread the ounces around the pockets of his jeans and the jacket of his suit. No one said anything, apart from checking his ticket, as he boarded the boat. They were more likely to at the other side. It'd be easier then, when he'd feel even more tired.

He dozed on the voyage, to a state where he could half think and half sleep. He would have to go back to London soon and get a flat. Take Yako. Take Joan? Would she live there? Maybe he could run the whole thing from London. Never get reefed then. Jaysis. That'd be the business. But who could he trust? Mickey would go to bits on his own. Jamesie Riordain, maybe? No. He didn't know him well enough. He was going to have to trust somebody. Joan? He didn't trust her. She fucked too well for his liking. Too good to be able to do it like that without practice. Had someone been getting it into his little Cynthia when he was away? Wouldn't put it past her. Something about her though.

It was so easy for Davy going through customs in Dublin it

tickled him. He had carried the gear in his pockets, just in case they searched his bag, but they hadn't even looked at him. It warmed the cockles of his heart when he walked past two coppers on his way to the taxi rank and thought, if only they knew.

He found Mickey asleep on the couch in Anne's. "Get up, for fucksake," he called, prodding him in the chest with his foot. "I though' you would have been up waitin' on me."

"Davy? Yeh oul' bastard. Wha' happened? Did yeh get the gear?"

"Yeah, I got the gear, but yeh wouldn't believe the runnin' around I had to do."

"Tell me abou' it. All the gear's been sold here and the money's upstairs in Burke's. And, I have a few dike left for yeh. I scored some off Breen, just before I ran out."

"Well let's sort everything out before I have a hit. I'm tha' fuckin' knackered, I'll crash out before I get the works out of me leg."

"Yeh can sleep here if you want to," Anne told him as she handed him a cup of tea. "The babby's up now, so yeh can have my bed."

Davy didn't let Anne know how he felt about the offer.

When Mickey was ready, they went upstairs to Burke's flat to get the Diconal. Davy managed to tell some of what happened in London. He was disappointed Mickey wasn't impressed about Cynthia. He remembered to tell him to try and get Jamesie to meet them that night, but after that, all Davy could do was give Mickey the gear, warn him how strong it was and then fix five dike.

Davy didn't wake until six that evening, though Mickey checked him a few times to make sure he hadn't gone over. It was on such an occasion that he woke and saw Mickey sitting on the floor of the bedroom, reading a newspaper. Davy closed his eyes again before Mickey noticed, to give himself time to acknowledge the quality of the sleep he just had. While doing this, he remembered bits of a dream and tried to recall it all.

Middlesex, England. How did he know? He just knew. Wembley football stadium. It was packed. Ringo was with him, but they couldn't get a touch anywhere. An airship, flying above the stadium. Bursts into flames. Everyone runs. Ringo too. Davy pulls him back. Tells him that they'll get a few bob in the crush. Ringo is horrified, looks at Davy like he's mad.

Davy chuckled and opened his eyes.

"Wha' a'yeh laughin' at?" Mickey asked him.

"I just had this mad fuckin' dream. Wha's the story?"

"Yeh wouldn't believe wha's in the paper."

"Wha'? Not more bad news," said Davy, sitting up and leaning on his arm.

"There was a busman robbed down in Shanghan last night."

"Another one?"

"Yeah. But listen to this. 'A youth wearing a pink balaclava robbed a busman of £3.54 last night. The youth, armed with what police now believe may have been an imitation firearm, told the driver of a 36A in Shanghan, Ballymun, "This is a stick-up," before demanding money. When the busman refused to hand over any, he was battered about the head and had his takings stolen before the youth made off on foot. The busman was later released from the Mater hospital after having a number of stitches inserted, to repair a head wound.'"

Davy started to laugh at the image of someone in a pink bali' saying, "This is a stick-up," but Mickey said, "Hang on, this is the best bit. 'Police said the assailant told the busman that his nickname was "Buckets of Blood" because this was usually the state his victims were discovered in. While they suspect it may have been a diversionary tactic on the part of the thief, they believe he is dangerous and should not be approached by members of the public.'"

The tears were beginning to roll down Davy's face, even before Mickey had finished. He laughed so hard that Mickey had to wait until he had stopped. "Do you know who it was?"

"Who wha' was?"

"The fuckin' robber?"

"Who was it?"

"Yako."

"Yako?"

"I told yeh he was a fuckin' lunatic. Mind you, tha' bleedin' brother of yours, Jojo, put him up to it. I only found out abou' it while yeh were asleep."

"Who told you?"

"Yako did. The gobshite couldn't resist it. 'Guess wha', Mickey? That's me,' he says, proud as yeh fuckin' like and he hands me the paper."

Davy curled up in the bed laughing. "Buckets of fuckin' Blood, wha'? He should have been a comedian, do yeh know tha'. Where is he now?"

"He should be in the snooker hall with Jamesie Riordain. I sent him out to get him earlier and gave him the money for a taxi, yeh know, just in case he robbed the fuckin' busman."

Davy grimmaced when he laughed. "Don't tell me any more, for fucksake," he told him, when he could catch his breath.

Mickey took the opportunity to fill him in on what he had managed to organise while Davy had been away.

"No more overdosin' then?"

"C'mon, Davy, tha' was a one off."

"I know. I couldn't resist it. So wha's the score with these flats then?"

"They're alrigh'. All legal and tha', the people tha' rent them don't stay there. I'll tell yeh though, I don't why Yako doesn't creep gaffs. He doesn't just fuckin' know everyone, he knows when they're in and when they're out. It was him who helped me get the gaffs. They all belong to mots tha' are split up with their fellas, but who stay with their oul' wans."

"Nice one," Davy told him. "Wha' we'll have to do now is start keepin' different things in different gaffs. The oney ones who are to know where they are, are me, you and Yako. Nobody else, okay?"

"Yeah, sure."

"Get Yako to bring the pieces over tonigh' to one of the gaffs. We'll keep the money split between two of them. And in the other one, Jamesie can bag up the gear for us. Righ', we're on the pig's back. Where's the gear and we'll have a turn on," said Davy, as he hopped from the bed.

"I thought yeh'd never ask."

When they met Jamesie in the snooker hall, they hired him. Davy had worked out a complicated commission system. Jamesie thought he was going to make a fortune. Mickey knew it just meant he would get his gear every day, if they sold enough, and maybe the price of a few pints. Jojo was told he was going to have to move into town for a while.

"Why do I have to go in? Why don't yeh get Skinnier to do it?"

"If yeh don't want to do it, then forget it. But I mean forget it."

Jojo didn't argue further. Davy called Yako aside and asked him what happened with the busman.

"He wouldn't give me the money, Davy, so I let him have it."

"Yeh let him have it?"

"Yeah, I gave him the gun across the head. Jojo told me to do it, if he laughed at me."

"Did he laugh at yeh?"

"Yeah, well when I told him me nickname he did."

Davy nearly pissed himself. He went so red, Mickey thought he was having a heart attack. He laughed even more when Yako explained, "Of course, I was after makin' it up . . ."

"I have to get out of here," Davy told Mickey. "I swear, tha' Yako crucifies me."

"Where are yeh goin'?"

"I'm goin' into town to see Joan. She gives hairdressin' lessons to juniors on a Wednesda' nigh', so I'll probably catch her, if I leave now."

"I thought yeh would have hung around here for a few pints."

"I'm dyin' for me hole, Mickey."

"Wha' abou' tha' nigger yeh were with?'

"It's not the same, is it? Look, I'll catch up with yeh tomorrow and we can have a few pints then, yeah?"

"I suppose so."

Davy spotted Joan's pink wig from the street. The door to the salon was locked and Davy had to knock hard on the plate glass to catch her attention. She turned, and when she saw it was him, put one hand on her slight hips and raised two fingers to him with the other. Davy thought she was serious, until she smiled and walked to the door. She opened it, still smiling and with one hand still on her hip, told him, "You've some neck, do yeh know that?"

"Yeah, I have, like a jockey's bollix, so I'm told. Wha's the story? Wha' time do yeh finish?"

"Not until half nine."

"Half nine? It's oney half eigh'. Can yeh not leave here now?"

"Don't turn up here a half a week late, Davy, and tell me yeh can't wait an hour."

"Yeah, righ'. I'll call back. Okay?"

"Okay, stranger. I'll see yeh then."

The idea of a walk appealed to him. He had nowhere particular in mind as he strolled towards College Green, just that it should take an hour. Luminous Dublin was attractive at night and when there weren't many people about. A few drunken students. What were they celebrating? Surely it was too early for exams. He didn't like them when they acted the gobshite. Always acting they were. The way they talked; the way they walked; the way they gawked. Fucksake. There'd be a good excuse for it if they were culchies, but most of them were snobby bastards. You could tell by the accents. Him and Mickey used to mug them, just for a laugh, because the fuckers never had a shilling. They used to frighten the living shite out of them. That was another thing, never had a penny and yet were always smoking dope and drinking. Liars, the fucking lot of them. Telling lies. Is that what going to school was all about? Trinity College Dublin. Exporter of some of Ireland's finest. Those who failed the test, who didn't pass the exams, were made honorary gobshites instead. Only thing was, nobody told them.

Thinking of gobshites helped him realise he was approaching Pearse Street Garda station. He avoided it by crossing the road and walking towards Townsend Street, then chanced a bit further left and on down to the quays. A bit of peace and quiet there. A bit of peace.

Past the Guinness boats, ready to set sail and invade England. Liberator of many a culchie's thirst. Lost a few casualties on the way, broken hearts and swollen livers. Patriots, each and every one, dying for a cause yet to be properly defined, dying for a fucking pint. Something the Irish and Guinness had in common, neither travelled well, with the odd exception, of course, like yours truly. On the north side of the Liffey, he could see the Custom House, and as he headed east, Mulvanney's pub, the Jetfoil. Sheringham was probably in there. His territory. His nose should be better by now. He walked on past the Eight Bells, along the edge of the quay wall, which the Liffey slapped relentlessly.

In Dublin's fair city
Where the smells are all shitty,
I made up me mind to get the fuck out.
As I moved like an arrow
Through seagulls and sparrows
Crying . . . I cried his story, my story,
History and mystery, are nightmares
From which I am trying to awake.
Aloney, aye o,
Aloney, aye o,
Crying, crying, crying, crying.

A couple of rusty old boats were parked along the quay wall like abandoned cars. He toyed with the idea of exploring one, but thought, with his luck, they would choose the moment to sink. On past redundant coal cranes, away from the Liffey and on to the last of the locks of the Grand Canal. It was time for a rest. He sat again, hung his legs over the edge of the basin wall and lit a smoke. With the cigarette in his mouth, he leaned back to rest on his hands and gently kicked the sides of his feet together. An old man passed and asked if he was all right. Davy had forgotten. He was sitting, staring into Ringsend's suicide spot. He smiled, and said, "Yeah, I'm great. And yeh?"

"Not a bother," the oul' fella replied. "Not a bother, thank God."

Had he thought that Davy was going to fuck himself in? Did he look that depressed? He might have done. It's hard to see it in yourself, so they say, until it's too late. Fuck that. As bad as it was being back in Dublin, he wasn't going to fuck himself into the basin because of it. Nothing was that depressing. Depressed? What in the name of fuck did it mean, horrible Jaysis word that it was? Depressed? Suffering from depression. Fucked himself in the basin. Lost his job. Thought he would never work again. That was true. Some of the excuses. Gobshites. One of life's little delights, having no job. Who in their right mind would want to work? Not himself, that was for sure. And nobody could say fuck all to him, because he didn't sign on the labour. There had to be more to it. Secrets. Torments. Why else? Exhaustion. He could believe that. Dying . . . Jaysis. he got up and walked across the foot bridge on the lock gates and around by the mouth of the Dodder. Filthy fucking river. Dirty oul' Dublin is right. Dirty rivers. Dirty secrets. Pure torments. He walked up the steps at Ringsend Bridge and down Ringsend Road, back towards town. Shelbourne Park was silent. No dog racing there. Harolds Cross maybe, that's where Ringo would be. The gear was starting to wear off. A chase would be nice. Go into a pub and chase a quarter in the toilets. Where was the nearest pub? Must be the longest road in Ireland without a fucking pub. He had to cross over Bolands Bridge and stroll down into Pearse Street before he came to one.

After he had spent as much time as he could bear in a jacks with a shit covered toilet, he continued and picked from the front of his teeth sticky crumbs of smack that had crystallised and stuck to them. To avoid Pearse Street Garda station again, he veered left when he reached Westland Row. The quarter he'd chased was helping him to feel better. Fuck it. Wouldn't be here for much longer anyway. He'd be rich soon. The money was going to keep rolling in and it was going to get easier and easier and easier. What would it take to fuck it all up? A terrible dose of bad luck. It couldn't go that wrong.

JOAN WAS READY to leave when Davy arrived at the salon. He told her he would prefer it if they went straight to the flat. "Sure," she said, eager that they get on.

He was tired again. She could tell. She could tell this when they showered together and he didn't get horny. "I thought yeh'd be glad to see me."

"For fucksake, I am. Wha' is it about yeh? Are yeh a sex maniac or somethin'? Wha' is it abou' women? Jaysis."

"What women?"

He laughed, "Oh, c'mon, don't start tha'."

"I know what I'll start," she told him, as she forced a smile, a testing smile, and tugged him towards the bedroom.

"Well, go easy, I'm jaded. I oney got back today, yeh know?"

"Yeah, yeh told me, remember?"

Still, he liked her touch. He liked her softness. He didn't want her to make him hard, but she managed it anyway. "I won't be long," she told him, "I promise." He believed her and didn't really care anyway, when she sat on him. His groin got wet, got warm, he was hard but he wasn't horny. He got angry. He wanted her to hurry, so he closed his eyes and thought of Cynthia and smiled. "Are yeh enjoyin' it now?" she asked.

"Yeah, it's lovely," he told her, and he almost laughed. He stopped smiling, opened his eyes. Hers were closed, her mouth open, as she pushed into him, hard, deep.

"D'yeh think blind men enjoy sex more?"

"What?" She stopped. "You're fuckin' strange, do yeh know that?"

"I was just wonderin'. Well, wha' d'yeh think?"

"How would I know what blind men think about sex?"

"I though' yeh probably knew wha' most men though' abou' sex."

"What's that supposed to mean?"

"Nothin'."

"You're a creep sometimes, yeh really are."

"I was oney jokin'."

"No, yeh weren't."

"I was. C'mere." He pulled her underneath him. "Don't listen to me. I'm bad humoured and bollixed." He was still hard, but didn't want to stay hard, so while he pushed, he thought of Cynthia and what he would have liked to have done and what he would do the next time. While he pushed, he buried his head in the pillow so he wouldn't have to look at Joan's face. She held the back of his neck anyway, after he came.

As he smoked some heroin, he told her. "There's somethin' wrong."

She had been waiting on the change. "What's that?" she asked.

"I don't know. I keep feelin' tired. Can't get rid of the fuckin' thing, even after a good kip. It's even beginnin' to affect me horn."

"Do yeh think yeh might have somethin'?"

"Wha' are yeh talkin' abou'? The germ?"

"What's that?'

"AIDS. Are yeh askin' me have I got AIDS?"

"I'm not askin' yeh have yeh got anything in particular. I should really be thinkin' of myself. I'm mad not to be usin' anything and just hopin' from my period that I get the safe times right."

"What's a safe time?"

"Exactly."

"Well, anyway, as I was sayin', somethin's not righ'. I'm fuckin' knackered and I can't relax. D'yeh want to go for a walk?"

"What? Now? At this time? I thought yeh were knackered?'

"I'm talkin' abou' me soul, not me body. Wha' a'yeh laughin' for?"

"Nothin'. It's just, well I never heard yeh talkin' about things like that."

"Wha'? Do yeh think that because I come from Ballymun, I mustn't have a soul."

"I never said that."

"C'mon then. D'yeh want to go for a walk. It'll be lovely now, down be the strand."

"Oh, all right."

"Well, get ready, while I finish this."

It was a five minute walk to the Martello tower, and although the tide was in, they could only see the sea in the distance, where light reflected on its surface. They could hear it close by, rushing at the sands and then away again. And they could feel the chill wind whipping at their faces as they walked towards Irishtown. Joan had snuggled beneath Davy's arm, to keep warm, so he held her close. It was easy to gather her in, wrap her up, like the way he might throw his arm around a child's shoulder. She smiled when he did this. It made up for things.

As they walked past the rear of the Star of the Sea school, a car passed and Davy recognised the front seat passenger. He caught Davy's attention because he was staring at him from the car, which braked smoothly to a stop. Davy uttered a prayer of relief, thankful he had left the gear in the flat. Then he remembered to warn Joan, "Wha'ever yeh do, don't give them your address. Give your oul' fella's. Okay? Don't give the address of your flat."

Before she had time to ask him why, an occupant of the car had caught up with them. "Well well well, Mr Byrne. This isn't exactly your neck of the woods, is it?"

"So?" said Davy. "Wha's tha' got to do with yeh?"

"What are you doin' over here, you cheeky little bastard, and who's this young lady? I don't know you, do I?" he asked Joan.

"No, yeh don't know me," she told him, "and I don't know you."

"I wouldn't be able for yeh, Byrne, accompanyin' a young innocent. I'm Detective Garda O'Toole, from the Garda Task Force. Now, who are you and what are you doin' with him?" O'Toole asked, as he nodded towards Davy, who by then was being searched by the other Garda. Joan told her name and explained they were just out for a walk. O'Toole asked for her address. When she gave him her father's, he turned to Davy and said, "Well, we really are goin' up in the world. I've been hearin' a few stories about you lately."

"That's all yeh ever hear abou' me, stories, isn't it?"

O'Toole smiled sarcastically and turned to the other Garda, "Mother of God. We got a statement off Mr Byrne." He smiled at Joan, "Usually he tells us he has nothin' to say."

Davy didn't react.

"What's he got in his pockets?"

"Almost two hundred pounds and a set of house keys."

"Are they the wages of sin?" O'Toole asked Davy.

"A'yeh jokin' me? That's just a few bob spendin' money," said Davy, taunting O'Toole, who stepped angrily towards him.

"Ah, ah," said Davy, stepping back. "Don't forget the witness."

O'Toole stopped and turned to Joan again. "Did he tell you what he does for a livin'? He kills kids."

Joan looked to Davy, who had looked away from everyone. O'Toole went on. "Didn't he tell you? Yeah, he sells heroin. Aw, Jaysis, have I let out a little secret?" Davy didn't respond. Joan was shocked.

"Give him back his money," O'Toole told his colleague. The two Gardaí walked away without saying anything else until they had started the car. They slowed as they passed. "See you soon," O'Toole called out to Davy and then said to Joan, "I hope I don't see you again, miss."

Davy sighed and said to Joan, "C'mon, we better walk back."

Joan, still stunned, began to walk with Davy. When he went to put his arm around her, she stepped back and asked, "Is that true what he just said?"

"Don't be fuckin' stupid, Joan. It's just wha' happens when yeh live in Ballymun. I buy drugs for meself, okay? Now and again I might get a bit of hash for someone, but that's all."

"So why did he say all that? He wouldn't just. . ."

"He said it because the bastard doesn't like me. I've one foot out of the gutter and they can't handle it."

"Maybe," she said, "it's still having one foot in the gutter that bothers him."

"What's tha' supposed to fuckin' mean?"

"Well, he wouldn't just pick on yeh for nothin'."

"Yeh really believe tha', don't yeh? I suppose your daddy told yeh tha', or your poxy friends in Davey Byrnes. Them tha' think the likes of me is only good for pissin' on. Is tha' it?"

"Don't take me for a thick and don't start goin' on like a child. I'm not one of those sluts that you go out with."

"Wha' a'yeh talkin' abou' now."

"You just lie to me, don't yeh? I saw the bites some cow left on your stomach and you had the gall to be questionin' me about what is my business?"

"Love bites? Is tha' wha' yeh think they are? They're fuckin' flea bites, from Mickey's dog. Actually, they were hoppers, though I don't suppose yeh get them in Sandymount, or poxy Dalkey, or wherever the fuck it is yeh come from."

"Flea bites?" Joan asked, flabbergasted. "Do yeh really think I'd swallow that?"

"Well, just shut up then," Davy said, clenching a fist and raising it to his mouth. "Just shut fuckin' up." They walked back to her flat in silence where Davy fetched his gear and turned to leave.

"Where are yeh goin'?" she asked him.

"I'll see yeh later."

"No, yeh won't. If yeh walk out of here now, don't come back. I mean it, don't come near me. I won't be treated like this."

"Okay then."

"What does that mean?"

"Tha' means tha' I hear wha' yeh're sayin'. I don't want to be near anyone tha' doesn't trust me."

"Davy, I don't trust yeh because you're a fuckin' liar. What do yeh expect? I'm tellin' yeh. I don't know what you're used to, but I won't put up with it."

"See yeh later."

"Oh, fuck you then." She slammed the door behind him and cursed until he was out of the building. Then she cried. Why hadn't she listened to Jake? Now, even though she wanted to run after him and apologise, it was too late. He was gone. She wanted to apologise to him because he lied to her. She didn't care. It didn't matter. He probably wouldn't do it again, if she did whatever it was that he wanted her to do. Why had she let him? Why did she allow him to charm and smarm all over her? The dirty lying bastard.

Davy was relieved to get away. He'd give her a ring during the week. It just wasn't the right time to be with her. A rest was what he needed, not some nagging cunt asking, asking, asking. Jaysis. They never let up sometimes. It always happened. As soon as he felt safe enough to expect things from people, they disappointed him. He walked back towards the Strand Road, hoping to find a taxi. She baffled him a little bit, the way she went on. Frightened him. Jaysis, she was a bit like, you know, she sounded like she meant she wouldn't have any of it. Fuck her.

A couple, walking arm in arm, approached him. As they passed, Davy asked the unsuspecting boyfriend, "Wha' a'yeh fuckin' lookin' at?"

The young man didn't answer. He hadn't time, before Davy lashed out with a kick and caught him on the top of the leg. His bewildered girlfriend jumped in front and told Davy, "We're sorry, we're sorry. We didn't mean an'thin' . . . Honest."

A PRODUCTIVE TIME arrived. No room for love and shite like that. Or at least, productivity came at just the right moment. A chance to only think, to only worry. It was when Davy was at his best. It was when Mickey behaved. When they worked together. A bit like the good oul' days.

It filled a few weeks, this Time. Jamesie Riordain settled into his new role. He worked with Yako, collecting gear, bagging it, getting it to Jojo, Skinnier, Eamo and Mick and depositing the money with Davy and Mickey. Jojo didn't need to work in town for more than a few days. A drought on the South Side ensured an influx of junkies from that part of the city, and Ballymun became what Davy wanted it to be: a centre of demand. With Mick Murtagh knocking it out, some of the attention was kept away from the snooker hall, and Eammo Thompson did his hippy little bit and knocked out twenty quarters a day.

Mickey seemed easily pleased at this time. It seemed all he had to do was get stoned, though he and Davy found themselves back in London a week after Davy had left, to take more money. It pleased Mickey, but Davy was giddy with delight. He told Mickey, when he left the country with money, it felt like he was walking away from a stroke with the snatch. The same feeling, without the risk. You just had to smile at the nice custom officers and think, "Kiss me emerald green Ballymun arse, ha ha ha."

They rented a bedsit off Arlington Road in Davy's "favourite part" of London. The Greek landlady seemed very concerned that they should feed themselves properly, especially if they were going to work as building labourers. She seemed especially worried by Mickey. "You sure you work the buildings before, hey? Isa very hard, yeah? Need to be big and strong, yeah? Not small and how you say, skinny?"

When Davy laughed, she said, "Isa no joke, you know. Very dangerous. Very very dangerous. Lots of young boys hurt."

"Where would yeh get it, Mickey, hey? A gaff in London for £180 a month. And someone to look after yeh into the bargain. Jaysis!"

"Gaff is righ'. D'yeh know wha' I just seen down in the jacks? A fuckin' cockroach. I thought they oney had them in America."

"How d'yeh know tha' it was a cockroach?"

"What else would it be? It was fuckin' huge. Yeh have to share them bleedin' toilets as well. There's somebody else's washin' hangin' on a line over the bath."

"For fucksake, it's just so we have somewhere to stay when we come over."

"I'd watch tha' oul' wan as well. She could report us to the Filth."

"For wha'?"

"We're suspicious Paddys, aren't we? I'm tellin' yeh, they're always told to be on the look out. She's goin' to find out tha' we're never here. Workin' on the buildin's? With softer hands than her own?"

"She's not suspicious. Did yeh hear her, she's just worried abou' yeh . . . 'The little boy shouldn't go on the buildin's' . . . Ha ha ha."

This time they took four ounces back with them and carried two each. They didn't carry them as Davy had done, loose in their pockets. This time, both parcels of smack were wrapped tightly with cling film, lubricated liberally with Vaseline, and slippery slipped up their emerald green Ballymun arses.

"It's amazin' this, isn't it?" said Mickey. "Once it's up, yeh can't feel a thing. I keep wonderin' if it's fallen down."

"You must be used to havin' your arse filled, if yeh can't feel an'thin'. Every time I move, I feel it draggin' against the wall of me back passage. Jaysis!"

"Yeah, well, I thought we weren't goin' to have to worry abou' an'thin' like tha', yeh and your 'We wont have to carry an'thin'' talk. Wha' happened to all tha'?"

"Listen, it's a fuckin' cinch. I told yeh, I walked through with it in me pockets, the last time."

"The last time? Some time will be the last time, d'yeh know tha'?"

"Righ' then. This will be the last time, I swear. One more time, righ'? After this time, that's it. We'll get someone else to carry it."

"It better be."

It was a cinch. The kind of cinch which cultivates complacency and encourages recklessness. The worst kind of recklessness. The sort of recklessness which doesn't just ignore danger, it invisibilises it.

The money rolled in, though not, Davy suspected, as fast as it might have if it hadn't been rolling out at the rate it was. They all needed paying. Jojo seemed to expect £30 expenses a day on top of what he earned. He got this idea, Davy learned, from Jamesie who pacified the concern of anyone who expressed it with a "Davy won't mind." His philosophy was infectious. Skinnier copied everything Jojo did and was cute enough to make a few bob on top of that. As was Murtagh, who tried to persuade Davy that every junkie who scored from him was four quid short for a bag. Yako, by then, had a half gram a day habit and he too had been brainwashed by Jamesie. "Have you joined the 'Davy won't mind' brigade, Yako?" Davy asked him once. Yako, who now thought, since the busman incident, that Davy was having a laugh every time he opened his mouth, simply laughed too in response and said, "Yeah." Eamo Thompson was the only one who always had the correct money and Davy knew why. Eamo still remembered the last hiding he had.

Enough money came in to travel to London again ten days later. They would look for a donkey this time, so Davy said. They travelled executive class, Aer Lingus. They sat in the company of some of Ireland's finest, the crème de la crème of hustlers, and discussed future strategies in relation to their own objectives.

"If it turns out tha' we don't find anybody, for whatever reason, I'm not carryin' it back. And if you carry it, I'm not goin' with yeh. There's somethin' up. I haven't even seen a copper in the last few weeks, let alone been stopped by one. Neither have you. Now yeh know wha' tha' means. They're goin' to try and bust us soon. If we get reefed for an'thin' like this, well, we'll be pickin' up a pension by the time we get out," Mickey told him.

"D'yeh know wha' we ought to get?" said Davy.

"Wha'?"

"We should try and get our hands on one of those computers."

"I can't believe it. You're fuckin' serious, aren't yeh?"

"Listen, till I tell yeh. I saw this thing on the telly the other nigh'," Davy said, explaining with simple hand gestures. "Yeh can give them things a password, righ'? And if yeh don't know wha' the password is, yeh don't get in. Now think abou' it."

"Think abou' wha'? Wha' difference do they make? Yeh can't get one of them to bring the money over and the smack back, can yeh?"

"Okay, smartarse, I'm not talkin' abou' tha'."

"Wha' a'yeh talkin' abou' then?" Mickey asked, irritated by the change of subject and the manner Davy used to express his lunatic, imbecile fucking fantasies.

"I know it sounds mad, but we could put everything down on it and we have to do somethin'."

"Abou' wha'?"

"Abou' the fuckin' money. Even Yako is at it."

"At wha'?"

"Well, every time I've to collect money off them, they all have some excuse for bein' short. Yeh know, it's 'I gave Jojo this and he said tha',' or else 'Jamesie said he would sort this tha' or the fuckin' other,' or else 'Skinnier owes me this, so when I get tha'.' By the time I get round them all, I forget wha' they told me in the first place. The fuckers are rippin' me off left, right and centre."

"Jaysis, Davy. We're loaded, bleedin' loaded. Wha' we should be worryin' abou' is gettin' the gear back. I worry abou' yeh sometimes, do yeh know tha'? I really do."

Davy knew Mickey was right. They would have to get someone to carry the gear over. Everybody in Ballymun knew they were knocking it out and the Filth would have known before most. It excited him that he could have been caught before, carrying the gear in. But he hadn't. Now it was too late. He would have to tell them. How? Let someone know, then word would get around. Drive Langley and Maskey around the bleeding twist.

It'd be easy to get someone to carry it back, but getting someone who wouldn't be caught was going to be hard. After they arrived in London, banked their money and arranged to pick up from Cyrus, Davy decided it was time to find a donkey.

"I though' they were called mules?"

"Wha' are?"

"Donkeys. Tha's wha' they're called in the films, 'mules'."

"Well they're called donkeys in Ireland."

"So how are we goin' to get one? Put an ad in *The Evening Standard*?"

"You can if yeh like, but I know a better way."

Mickey discovered this meant doing a tour of the pubs in Camden Town, though they started around the corner in Mornington Crescent and ended up working their way as far as Kentish Town, without success. The following evening they began in Kilburn and ended up in Biddy Mulligan's on the Edgware Road. By this time, Mickey still wasn't sure what Davy was looking for. He had talked to what seemed like hundreds already, but always said, "No, it wouldn't work. They're not righ'."

In Biddy Mulligan's, Mickey was ready to volunteer if it meant they could leave London the next day. He'd only really gone along again because Davy swore he would get him off with a black bird.

He wondered was this something Davy secretly wanted, for Mickey to volunteer to carry the gear? To say something like, "Why don't we carry it ourselves until the next time we come over. Yeah, make this the last time."

But Davy met who he was waiting to meet in Biddy Mulligan's. She was from Malahide and had told her parents she was working as a receptionist for a financial institution in the City of London. They didn't know she couldn't afford a break home on the wages she earned waitressing in a French cafe in Islington. Her mother, who was at her wits' end, was threatening to come and visit her if she didn't see her daughter home for a holiday soon. The idea of her mother coming was bad enough, but the trouble was the girl was living in a squat and God only knew what her mother would do if she ever saw it. Even worse, say if the father decided to come too. It was well for Davy, being able to afford to travel back and forward as he pleased. What was it he did for a living again?

She smoked a bit of dope and liked to be cool about it. Perfect. He'd be willing to buy someone a ticket and give them a few bob spending money, if they carried a bit home for him. He didn't know what it was that made him so nervous, especially when it was only dope.

If only he was serious, her prayers would be answered, she told him. He told her, too, he hadn't really thought about it. It was something to think about, this idea of hers, especially if she was the kind who didn't get nervous. But then, there was loads of problems too. She was bound to tell someone, her friends, wasn't she? No, she swore. She hadn't really got close friends anyway. Davy was convinced this kind of thing got around quickly. And you know what they're like in Ireland. They think that hash is a drug. They're such hypocrites. She agreed. Their attitude towards alcohol and hash, well it was enough to make you, you know. It wasn't that she didn't enjoy a drink with the rest of them, but each to their own and all that. One man's meat, yeah? It was a pity, Davy said, that he was going back the following day. Otherwise he would have seriously considered buying her a ticket. And giving her fifty quid spending money. He couldn't buy the draw he liked in Ireland. Sense. Sensemelia. Had she ever heard of it. Oh yeah, Jamaican weed. Davy was right, as far as she knew. Well she had never come across it in Ireland. It'd be gas, wouldn't it, if she just turned up and said she was home for a surprise visit. She hesitated. It might be hard to get off work. Just phone in sick. Fuck them. You could get a job like that any time. The same couldn't be said about a free flight home and fifty quid. He even told her if her squat was gone when she came back, he'd put her up for a while. He was minding a flat for his brother who had gone to work in the States and wouldn't be back for a year. Jaysis. Get in there, while you can. Pick you up tomorrow then, yeah?

"I couldn't believe it, when yeh were comin' out with it. Yeh'd talk the knickers off a nun, d'yeh know tha'?"

"No I wouldn't talk the knickers off a nun. There's some things I wouldn't do. I'm not like you, yeh know?'

"How much a'yeh goin' to get her to carry?"

"Eight ounces."

"Jaysis! Make sure I'm not on the same plane. A'yeh goin' to use her all the time now?"

"I dunno. But think abou' it. Oney me and you know her. We'll just call out to her in Malahide on the bike and pick up the gear. Fuckin' simple. But we'll just take each trip as it comes, okay?"

"Yeah, clunk click every trip. Ha ha ha."

"Her ma's a teacher. Her oul' fella's some kind of inspector with the Corpo. Can yeh believe it? Yeh wouldn't have anyone with better qualifications, even if yeh had put an ad in *The Evenin' Standard.*"

"Ha ha ha."

"Three cheers for Biddy Mulligan's on the Edgware Road."

Davy showed her his ticket and Mickey's, to prove they were already booked on a flight before her. She got a little nervous. That was to be expected. But don't worry. Davy would own up that it was his, if they caught her. It was only a bit of dope. Here, take one of these. What was it? A Valium. It would help her relax. Did she fancy going out for a drink, or something like that, when they met up in Dublin? Or maybe in London? Davy told her it was her sense of humour, her personality. She was great company. Maybe they could arrange something when they met in Malahide. That'd be great.

DAVY AND MICKEY didn't want anyone to know they were back, not before they had picked up the gear from the donkey. Davy didn't want to leave her with it too long, in case the donkey got too nosy.

"Maybe one of us should've hung around the airport and made sure tha' she came through alrigh'."

"A'yeh fuckin' mad? Say if she got reefed?"

"Yeah, I suppose so. Mind yeh, if she is reefed, you'll have to get offside for a while." Mickey chuckled, "I mean, it was yeh who gave her the gear. Ha ha ha. She can't grass me up; I knew fuck all abou' it."

"And yeh find tha' hilarious, d'yeh?"

It was Davy who picked up the smack. It was so easy, she was keen. "Any time you like. I mean it, it's no problem." Davy told her he would give her a call when he got back to London. She looked forward to it.

After he stashed the parcel in Santry Woods, he went back to Balcurris to give Mickey the good news. "We can take Jamesie to collect it later and he can cut it up with Yako."

"What'll we do now? Go over to the snooker hall?"

"No. Let's go over to Anne's. We can have a turn on up in Burke's first. Then Anne will tell us all the gossip."

They walked around the back of Balcurris, across the end of the dual carriageway and through St Pappin's Church, along the side of Coultry, past the fenced off power station and by McDonagh Tower. "There's a weird fuckin' atmosphere, isn't there?" said Mickey.

"It's a bit quiet, alrigh', for a Monda'. Though that's the worst abou' bein' away for a few days."

"Wha's tha'?"

"Well, yeh get kind of paranoid when yeh come back. Seriously. Have yeh never noticed it?"

"Are yeh windin' me up?" Mickey asked. Before Davy had time to deny it, Mickey saw a small funeral cortège crawl towards the Virgin Mary Church. "Look, there's a funeral," he told Davy, and he blessed himself, for luck.

They crossed Shanghan Road and used the lift in Pearse Tower to go to Anne's and laughed while they waited for her to answer the door. They laughed about the donkey and her hippy cool attitude.

"It's cool, man. I don't show my nerves on the outside."

"Who is it?" Anne called from behind the door.

Mickey pretended to be irritated because she hadn't recognised their voices. "It's us, for fucksake."

Anne opened the door and stood in the threshold, before swinging it back and walking ahead of them. Davy thought she looked terrible. Maybe it was the shade from the door, but she looked grey. She looked like she was strung out to bits. Mickey knew that there was something wrong. He knew his sister well enough to recognise that she had never looked the way she did now because of the gear. Davy wondered too might it be something else. He wondered was it safe to enter the flat, but Mickey was already pursuing her down the hall. "What's wrong, Anne? What's wrong?"

Davy had a look over his shoulder, back on to the landing, and followed them in. Mickey had his hands on Anne's shoulders. He was trying to hold her steady while she stood with her hands to her face, tears running over her fingers. Áine sat on a blanket on the floor and looked up sympathetically. She looked up with wide sorrowful eyes, with the lips on her chubby little face turned down and her hands joined. When she heard Anne cry, she sobbed too and clapped her hands until her mother picked her up and they held each other tight, while her Uncle Mickey listened in disbelief .

"A'yeh fuckin' deaf? Yako's dead." Anne buried her tears in Áine's cardigan.

Mickey smiled. He always did when someone died. He couldn't help it. He just stood there and smiled. Davy panicked, mentally. "How? When? Why?"

"He overdosed, by accident. He'd been drinkin' beforehand. He drank too much. He must have went mad. Jude said he told her he needed £40s worth of smack, just to keep him together. She said he fell asleep and she did too. When she woke up, he was dead."

"When?"

"A couple of days ago. Just after yeh left. He's goin' to the chapel tonigh'. He should be there now."

"Where? The Virgin Mary? Jaysis Christ! We just seen it drivin' in. Tha' was Yako in the coffin? Do yeh hear tha', Davy? Tha' was Yako."

Davy was still trying to think. Yako had overdosed on their gear.

"I don't believe it. I don't fuckin' believe it. Where did he get tha' much gear?" Mickey asked. Before anyone could speculate, he went on, "It's Jamesie's fault. He was meant to be lookin' after the gear. He should have been lookin' after him."

"How come yeh didn't go to the chapel?" Davy asked.

"There's been all kinds of rumours flyin' abou'."

"Wha' kind of rumours?"

"His uncle has somethin' to do with Sinn Féin and there's rumours goin' around tha' whoever sold him the gear is goin' to be shot."

"Nobody sold him any gear."

"They don't know tha', do they?" Anne said, looking straight at Davy. "The Concerned Parents are havin' a meetin' in the Holy Spirit on Wednesda'. Everyone's already sayin' tha' they know who the pushers are."

"Who's everybody?" Davy asked.

"Yeh know," said Anne, "everybody. Yis'll have to stop comin' up here for a while. Yeh know wha' they did to Rita Keogh. She was oney goin' out with someone who was sellin' the gear and they still fucked her out of her flat, after they thrown all her furniture over the balcony."

"Well tha's fuckin' great," said Davy. "And after all tha' we done for yeh."

Anne started to cry again. "Jaysis, Davy, if wha' yeh're talkin' abou' is the few bob tha' yis gave me, well don't worry. I'll pay yis back. I have to think of the babby, yeh know. And look at wha' I have? They wouldn't have to fuck much over the balcony to leave me with nothin'."

"Don't worry abou' it, Anne," Mickey told her. "She's righ', Davy. We'll have to keep away from here."

"I know we have to stay away," said Davy, "but it's the way she goes on abou' it. It's fuckin' typical."

"Where a'yeh goin'?"

"Why?" said Davy, walking towards the door. "Once we're out of here, that's all tha' counts."

"For fucksake, Davy," said Anne. "What else can I do?"

"Oh, it doesn't fuckin' matter. Listen," Davy said to Mickey, "I'm goin' over to the snooker hall and then I'll be over in Balcurris."

"The snooker hall? Yako's dead, Davy. I wouldn't go near them fuckin' shops if yeh paid me."

"Yeah? Well, you do wha' yeh fuckin' like. I have to go upstairs first and have a hit, before I go anywhere." Davy said this to himself, more so than to Anne or Mickey. He felt it too. He felt how important it was that he had a hit before he did anything else. Even thinking about it helped him forget what was waiting on him. It hung there, just outside his face, like a soft toy monkey on a string, dangling. Fucksake, Yako. For fucksake.

After the hit, Davy went over to the snooker hall. Mickey had a fix with him, but he went back down to Anne's for a while. Davy told him to give her fifty quid. As he walked to the snooker hall, he nodded to people he met and those he knew. They replied in their usual way, but he wondered whether they were secretly blaming him for Yako's death. As he walked into the snooker hall, he realised it still hadn't clicked yet. He couldn't determine if it was because of the hit, or despite it, but the penny hadn't dropped. It started to fall when he stood at an empty pool table, because the first person he looked for to set up the balls was Yako. Jojo and Skinnier were in the snooker hall. They came over and asked had he heard. Davy nodded that he had. Jojo was cautious. He knew Davy well. Skinnier was reckless.

"Did Jamesie tell yeh tha' we used a few bags when we heard abou' it? He said yeh wouldn't mind."

The penny stopped still and Davy's fist hit Skinnier's mouth with enough force to burst his bottom teeth through the skin just below his lip. He sat trembling, at the bottom of the wall he collided with, while Davy stood above him and said, "As it goes, Skinnier, I do fuckin' mind." In the short time it took Davy to turn around, Jojo had disappeared.

They held the post-mortem in Balcurris. Mickey and Davy were the only two present, because they didn't need to hear evidence from anyone else. They recorded death by misadventure. There was nothing anyone could have done about it. The city coroner would agree with them, but he would be about the only one. Especially in Ballymun, where it was so dangerous, Davy and Mickey agreed, they better keep out of sight for a while. Just in case someone, everyone, started screaming, "Tha's them. They done it."

Of course, this meant they couldn't attend Yako's funeral and they had already missed his remains being removed to the church. Mind you, they had seen them driving down Shanghan and Mickey had blessed himself out of respect, remember? The funeral. That was a day to get offside. Mickey lay low out in Eamo Thompson's. Davy went in search of Joan. He called into her at work. He told her he needed to see her and before she could say no, he told her a friend of his had died. He didn't have to say any more. She knew he needed her. She left work early and took him home where she could help him grieve. She lay beside him and stroked his hair. She listened for ages. All about this kid. Davy had adopted him. Took him under his wing. In Ballymun, this was everything. Joan wouldn't understand this. She only knew what she had read in the papers. Had only heard the rumours. None of which could possibly reveal the reality. Davy had saved him, effectively. But this Yako still hung out with his old crowd. Nothing Davy could do about it really, she told him. It seems it's what this Yako wanted. No. Not to die. She didn't mean that. What she meant was, who he wanted to be had to die. Nobody could do anything about that. Davy agreed. But still, he was going to miss him, was missing him already.

So he grieved Yako by fucking Joan. And he grieved a little differently when halfway through, he ran his tongue around the outline of her lips, along the length of her torso and up and down each groin, before sinking down, burrowing down, and burying his tongue deep between her piss flaps. He grieved so hard, she nearly pulled the ears off the side of Davy bleedin' Byrne's head.

Jamesie Riordain grieved Yako by bagging up the gear on his own. There was no point in trying to replace Yako. Sure there was no one like him.

Somehow or other, Jojo managed to find himself grieving with Jamesie.

Skinnier stayed at home. He needed eight stitches to put his lip back on to his face, so he recuperated with the woman who loved him more than any other, his oul' wan.

Two women loved Yako. One was really a girl. Jude was fifteen when they buried not just her first love, but what she was certain would be her only love. Two of her friends, Sharon and Aileen, accompanied her to the funeral. The heels of their black stilettos clacked in unison as they walked along the weedy paths of Glasnevin cemetery. Their split black skirts had been pressed creaseless and they managed to keep them like that when they travelled by taxi to the funeral. There was nothing they could do to stop the mascara running the length of their blotched faces, carried by tears that had fallen throughout the day. They flowed, buckets full, when the wail went up from the other woman in Yako's life at the sight of his shiny brown coffin being lowered into a fresh mucky grave. The cry came from the pain in his mother's chest. A pain deep behind her cancerous breasts and struck by the loss of the man in her life, the death of her little boy. Bent in black, her face veiled by a lace scarf, her head shot back when they lowered him down and she screamed towards the sky a howling, piercing wail of despair.

A FEW THINGS convinced Davy it was a Low Profile Time. The first was Jojo being skull dragged from the snooker hall a week after Yako died. Jojo was interrogated by a citizens' committee of Concerned Parents. His name, they informed him, had cropped up at a few of their meetings and some of the members thought it was about time they did a bit of snookering themselves. Jojo could only swear, on his mother's good health, that he had never sold drugs in his life. He said he didn't know why so many people would say such a thing, dirty filthy liars, whoever they were.

Davy laughed when Jojo told him about it. "Two big mullahs, I'm not jokin' yeh, Davy, they reefed me over to St Joseph's. I nearly shit meself. I had to get up on the stage and answer their questions. There was two oul' wans in the mob shouting, 'Take him out the back and give him a bullet behind the knee.' 'Don't waste it on his knees,' the other one says, 'give it to him in the head.' Then yeh had this big 'RA head, he was the fuckin' chairman or somethin', sayin', 'We're not like tha'.' I knew then there must have been somebody from the *Herald* in the audience."

"Wha' happened then?" Mickey asked. He didn't find it as funny as Davy.

"Well, I had to tell them I was a junkie. Tha' was me line of defence, d'yeh know, sayin' I took drugs, but I didn't sell them. So, they says tha' if I can't give them up on me own, they'd be sendin' me to a rehab, in France."

"In France?" Mickey asked.

"Yeah. It sounds great, doesn't it? Phil Kearney was tellin' me tha' they sent him there and it was fuckin' terrible. It was full of Spaniards and some Arab kept tryin' to ride him. And nobody spoke any English. Can yeh imagine it? He was tryin' to tell this Arab he wasn't like tha'. In the end he had to escape and walk back to Ireland. He said the next time he's goin' to let them shoot him. It's not really tha' funny, Davy."

Even Mickey was beginning to smile. "How did yeh get away?"

"Tha' was the worse. These two oul' wans said they wanted to have their say. I swear, I don't know where they turned up from. They must've let them out of Brendan's for the day. Anyway, one of them shouts up, 'Whose great idea was it to send these druggies to France for a holiday.' 'Yeah,' the other one shouts up, 'especially as him's probably the same sleeveen bastard tha' robbed me handbag last year and I haven't even got the bus fare to Bray.'

Mickey laughed hard at this, with Davy, until Davy suddenly stopped and asked, "Why wasn't Skinnier dragged over?"

"He wasn't in the snooker hall when they came up."

"Where was he?"

"He went into the hospital to get his stitches out and I haven't seen him since."

The following day, Davy was relieved to get off to London again. Mickey stayed in Dublin. No need for him to go over there. "Sure amn't I great at keepin' me head down? You're always the one who gets reefed."

Jojo went back to work in the snooker hall with Skinnier, who turned up the following day. On his way to the airport, Davy came up to see if Skinnier was there.

Skinnier could see that Davy didn't believe the reason he wasn't about when Jojo got tore out of it was because he was getting his stitches out. If it hadn't been him who bursted his mouth, he wouldn't have believed that Skinnier had had any stitches in the first place. Davy didn't say much. He just looked at Skinnier in a way that told him, convinced him, the best thing to do from now on was box clever, because he could tell that Davy was capable of blaming him for everything.

Fuck him, if that's how he feels abou' it. He obviously doesn't appreciate all I've done for him, especially the way I do be looking after tha' gobshite of a brother of his. Fuck him. I'm just goin' to look after meself from now on.

The stretched scar beneath Skinnier's lip stood out. He saw it as soon as he looked in a mirror and it frightened him even to secretly feel angry at Davy. So he forgave him, or at least forgot him, by blaming Mickey.

All of this was that bastard's fault anyway. If he hadn't ripped me off in the first place.

After Davy left, Mickey was swift to leave too. Jamesie popped in now and again and collected the few bob. He told them where they could pick up and at what time. Skinnier watched Jojo work. He watched him get stoned. He watched him get careless, because Jojo too was frightened. Skinnier knew it was a time to be careful, so he gave his gear to Jude and told her to stash it down her knickers. Skinnier watched when a junkie came in and scored off Jojo. Jojo kept looking over to the door. He was expecting something too and was looking away, he was looking for danger somewhere else, when the junkie copper took his handcuffs out and snapped them shut round Jojo's wrists. Before Skinnier knew what was happening, there were coppers everywhere. He was close enough to Jojo to hear the copper who busted him laugh. "I never seen anyone's face change colour so quickly, d'yeh know tha'?"

Skinnier wasn't busted. He didn't have anything on him. And they hadn't found the gear on Jude, because they didn't search her. She looked so young they sent her home.

Davy heard the story from Mickey when he returned to Dublin a week later. Jojo had been caught with thirteen quarters. He was pleading guilty because he hadn't a hope of getting bail, not unless he agreed to set his brother up. He decided instead to do the five years on his back. He was sick of it all anyway. Maybe when he came out those Concerned Parents would have disappeared and Davy would have some better ideas. There had to be an easier way to make a few bob. Give up the gear, which always seemed like a great idea, until he thought, . . . What then?

Jojo took the test when he went into the Joy. It was the best way to get detoxed on the Physeptone. They told him ten days later he had tested positive. It didn't feel any different having the germ.

The welfare officer who disclosed the results of his tests wondered again. She wondered why their eyes always sparkled with pride when they heard the news. It had to be one of the saddest things she would ever see. Why did their self-esteem increase when their self-destruction managed to reach new depths? Why did it satisfy them, the more painful their pain became? Was it the only way they knew how to compete? Measuring their suffering against each other? When Jojo told her that he came from Ballymun, it was like he was expecting extra points.

Davy was relieved. He hadn't used with Jojo for years, so he hadn't a hope of having the germ. He took great pleasure from the fact that Skinnier would have it, must have it, because he used with Jojo all the time. He bit his hand when the thought occurred to him that Skinnier might have given it to Jojo in the first place. He remembered how Skinnier had got away with it, twice. He had missed the Concerned Parents. And for some reason, there could only be one really, he had missed getting reefed by the Filth when Jojo got busted.

There is nothing quite like the power of resentment, and to this young resenter, it meant nurturing an air of intent.

HE COULDN'T BELIEVE it really, the way she just came out with it. She took a deep breath before she asked, though this wasn't because she was frightened. No, it was more like she found the ordeal an effort. "I need some money, Davy. Do yeh think yeh could give me some."

"Why? What's wrong? Have yeh had a row with your oul' fella?"

"No, I just don't want to ask him."

"How much do yeh need?"

"Four hundred pounds."

"Four hundred quid? For wha'? You're not on the drugs, a'yeh?"

"Very funny, Davy. No, I'm not on the drugs. I need to go to England."

He didn't get it when she said it. Excitedly, he told her, "I've been meanin' to bring yeh over there for ages. Yeh said yeh were there before, when was it? A couple of years ago? You'll love it there with me. I can get us into the black clubs and everything. Jaysis, it's strange the way I've been meanin' to ask yeh. Wha' d'yeh need to go for anyway?"

"I have to have a termination."

"Wha' the fuck is tha'?"

"Jesus, yeh don't make it easy, do yeh?"

"Wha' a'yeh on abou'?"

"I need to have an abortion. I'm pregnant."

Davy jumped up from the bed. "Pregnant? With a baby?"

"Well I'm only guessin', but that's wha' I think it is."

"Holy Christ. How can yeh joke abou' somethin' like tha'? Pregnant? Yeh can't have an abortion, Joan."

"Of all the things I took yeh for, a family man was never one of them."

"It doesn't matter wha' I am, or amn't. Yeh can't have an abortion. It's as simple as tha'. A'yeh listenin' to me?"

"Who's goin' to stop me?"

"Joan, I don't want to argue with yeh. Think abou' it. It can fuck yeh up and interfere with yeh havin' children in the future."

"What are yeh talkin' about?"

"It can mess with your insides and stop yeh ever havin' children."

"How come it didn't stop me gettin' pregnant this time?"

"Wha'? Yeh mean you've had one before? Jaysis! Wha' am I with?"

"Take it easy, Davy, for Christsake."

"I'll tell yeh, Joan. I'll tell yeh how it'll fuck yeh up havin' children in the future. If you have an abortion, I'll wrap me boot so hard around your fanny, there's a chance yeh won't even be able to ride again. That baby could be me."

THINGS REALLY HAD quietened down to Mickey's liking. Davy was away in London again, but it didn't matter. With Jamesie doing this and Jamesie doing that, all Mickey had to do was look like he was important. What do they call them? The sleeping partner? The silent partner? Something like that. It just meant he had to do fuck all, though he'd sometimes pretend the others weren't doing it right and they needed him to give guidance, direction. After Jojo got locked up, Skinnier was given an apprentice, Tommy Reynolds. He still wasn't himself, Skinnier. Not since he heard Jojo had the germ, but he didn't go and have a test. He said he didn't want to know. Not yet. Whatever the fuck that meant.

Mickey still had time for Skinnier. He was all right, if you treated him properly. He knew Skinnier was convinced Davy had it in for him, but Mickey wouldn't let anything happen. He couldn't help it when Davy bursted his lip, because he wasn't there that day. And anyway, it was stupid of Skinnier not to realise the kind of mood Davy was in. So, when he called over to Mickey and said he was out of bags, said he was dying sick, said Jamesie hadn't any gear either and was waiting on Mickey to get him a quarter, said he couldn't wait because he really was dying sick, Mickey relented and said, "Okay, for fucksake," and he took him with him.

Usually Mickey would get Jamesie to do it, but he didn't mind helping out. Hadn't been himself really, Jamesie that is, not since Yako's death a few months ago. Amazing how long it takes people to get over things and yet life goes on. Life goes on. And Time flies.

Mickey took Skinnier to the exact same place where Davy and he had buried the gear in Santry Woods, the First Time. He was in the humour of reminiscing and recalled it for Skinnier. The weather was just as cold then, though a lot wetter. And of course, it was pitch black. He laughed when he remembered Davy and the light from the silvery fucking moon. Skinnier didn't seem to get the joke. Maybe it was because he was sick. Maybe he should have given Skinnier a bit out of his personal before he brought him to the woods. But Mickey wanted some company. It got a bit lonely sometimes, especially since Davy seemed to be away more often than he was at home. It had been like that since he split up with that bird, Joan. Davy didn't even tell Mickey much about that. It was strange. He thought Davy really liked her. Then it was over.

Maybe Skinnier wasn't laughing at the joke because he was lonely too. Probably missed his good oul' buddy, Jojo. Not to worry. He would give him a nice big turn on. That would cheer him up.

Skinnier didn't find it funny because Mickey was joking about a Time when he should have got his proper share. Instead, while Davy Byrne was flying back and forward to London and the gobshite, Hughes, was falling around like a fool, Skinnier had to keep his wits about him. If he wasn't on the look out for the Filth, he was looking over his shoulder for the vigo's. Even lately, there were lunatics with the germ robbing people carrying gear, because they didn't give a fuck. If Mickey Hughes hadn't ripped him off, everything would've been all right. He wouldn't be wondering if he had got the germ off that bollix, Jojo, who was now sending out all sorts of threats from the Joy. And it really was Mickey's fault. It was him who had made all the promises. At least you knew where you stood with Davy Byrne. Out of the fucking way, if you could help it. No joke. No, he didn't find it funny at all. Apart from intent, there is nothing, nothing quite like the power of resentment, because it never lets you forget. And to this young resenter, this meant being constantly reminded over and over again by the gobshite, Hughes, of all those things that should have been his all along.

Mickey wondered was it the same fence post where they had buried the gear the First Time. He mentioned it to Skinnier and told him that it probably was. Who would have thought so much could happen in such a short space of time. Did he, Skinnier, believe it? No. Mickey wasn't surprised.

"Here, you carry the gear back, seein' as you're so anxious for a turn on."

Skinnier took the package from Mickey. Another fucking worry. Another resentment. It was too big to put in his mouth, so he was going to have to carry it and just leg it if they got a pull. Best thing to do was pray first that this didn't happen. "Where are we goin'? Straigh' over to Jamesie?"

"No. I'm goin' to take yeh to this gaff in McDermott Tower. I want to take some gear out for meself. I'll give yeh a turn on out of it, then yeh can bring it over to Jamesie to bag up."

Skinnier was relieved. With Mickey this stoned, and likely to have another fix, there was a good chance he would get a decent turn on. But it was typical of the bastard. He wasn't going to carry anything, was he? No fear of him taking the gear over to Jamesie where, if the Filth were watching anywhere, it was there.

"Don't tell anyone where this gaff is, Skinnier. D'yeh hear me?"

"Don't worry, I won't tell anyone."

"I mean it. Davy'll go bleedin' mad and I'm talkin' abou' crazy bleedin' mad, d'yeh know?"

"Yeah, I know," said Skinnier, while he thought, Yeh stupid, stoned gobshite. Look at the fuckin' state of yeh. I don't know how yeh get away with it. Yeh haven't a bleedin' clue any more and yeh know wha' tha' means: you're goin' to get reefed one of these days. Davy'll stay in London and I'll start knockin' the gear out with Jamesie. I'll get wha's comin' to me. As they walked into the lift in McDermott Tower, Skinnier told Mickey, "Yeh know wha' I'm like, Mickey."

"Yeah, I know wha' you're like, Skinnier," Mickey said, unambiguously.

Skinnier thought it strange. It was the first time Mickey had ever said something like that. He was treating him like a friend. Fuck it. It was probably because he was stoned. Mickey gave him a nice turn on, there must have been a weighed quarter and this was before Jamesie had got his hands on the gear and cut it with glucose. Skinnier already had his works out. He carried it about, wrapped in tissue and stuffed down his sock.

"Here yeh go, Skinnier. Is tha' alrigh'?"

"Nice one, Mickey, yeah, that's great. Can yeh just put another little bit on it. Just a speckle."

Mickey had lifted the heroin from its wrapping with a piece of cardboard he had torn from a cigarette packet. He stuck it in again and shovelled out a little bit more. "Jaysis, Skinnier. You're never satisfied, a'yeh?"

Skinnier grinned.

"Here, get tha' into yeh and leg it over to Jamesie. He'll be wonderin' wha' the fuck's goin' on."

Mickey pierced his groin for the second time that day, the Last Time, as Skinnier was removing his syringe from his arm. While Mickey stood crouching from the impact, Skinnier stood at the sink and wondered, as he rinsed out his syringe, was he squirting hundreds of antibodies down the plug hole. Mickey had removed his from his groin and was heading towards the sink just as Skinnier finished.

"Wha' a'yeh waitin' for?" Mickey asked him. "Hurry up and get the gear over to Jamesie."

"I'm goin', I'm goin'. Gimme a minute."

"Why does it take yeh all day? For fucksake, c'mon."

As Skinnier left and walked to the lift, he wondered what had caused the change in Mickey's mood. Oh fuck him, he was always a prick when he got stoned. Shit. Skinnier remembered, he had forgotten to call Mickey to double-lock the hall door after him. Well, it was too late now, the lift was on the way up. He could hear it chugging along and anyways, Mickey would probably start moaning at him if he went back. As the lift doors opened, Skinnier lifted his head back to avoid the smell of piss. He had already taken a deep breath to avoid breathing in the lift. He didn't manage to hold it in for the length of time it took to reach the bottom. That was something he could never manage. One of the little mysteries in Skinnier's life. He wondered was it panic? The lift doors opened and Skinnier stepped into a fresh breeze that blew through the tower. He decided to cut back, to walk beneath the block. It was much shorter to Jamesie's that way. As he passed the back stairs, just as he was about to leave the tower, Skinnier Martin got the fright of his fucking life.

Mickey was still standing at the sink, trying to figure out why he was so tired these days. He could feel his eyes closing and when they did, he drifted off. For a moment, he dreamed about the things he wanted to do. It was a Weird Time to do it, to start one of those smack induced fantasies about settling down with a decent bird and having a few kids. To dream about getting away from it all. Jaysis. He was starting to sound like an oul' fella. Maybe there was something in it. Had to be. He had said something to Davy about it. They had talked about it. Discussed and joked about it. Davy suggested they move to London, or something like that. When was it? The Last Time?

He heard the knock at the door and for some foolish reason began humming the words of a song to himself. *Somebody's knocking at the door, somebody's ringing the bell.* He was only halfway down the hall when the door came off the hinges.

THEY GRABBED DAVY as he left Dublin airport and was just about to step into a taxi. He knew they weren't normal coppers after he convinced himself that they were coppers. You see, that's how different they were.

Davy was sure that the fucker who threw him against a car to put handcuffs on him had lifted him clean off his feet. He'd done this effortlessly.

"Wha' the fuck's goin' on?" said the sometimes silent Davy bleedin' Byrne, as he was bundled into the back of an unmarked Garda car.

From the airport, they drove straight to Ballymun Garda station. The detectives didn't tell him why he was being arrested. Well, not specifically. They said something about the possession of firearms and used the flexible act. During the drive, they asked him where he had been and what he had been doing. They were impressively patient. Confidently patient. The very idea of it terrified Davy. This lot looked like real IRA hunters. So what the fuck did they want with him? He wondered had Mickey done anything? Probably hadn't even been reefed, the jammy bastard.

When they arrived at the Garda station, the three detectives escorted him to the desk sergeant. Davy was dwarfed by their height and build. They all wore dark, crumpled suits which looked a size too small. All wore their ties and collars loose and the three of them still ambled along with John Wayne confidence. They didn't play any games with him. It concerned him. What would he do when they asked him whatever it was they wanted to know?

At the desk one whose suit was a little less crumpled and whose collar was a little tighter than the rest, told the desk sergeant, "When you're finished with him, send him through to me. I don't want anyone else talking to him first. Nobody."

Another of the detectives removed Davy's handcuffs and briefly explained to the sergeant that Davy had been arrested at Dublin airport under a Section 30, and he followed his superior deep into the station.

The sergeant noticed Davy's eyes darting about more than usual. He told him to empty his pockets and when Davy had done this, he asked, "Do you know why you're here, Byrne?

Davy shook his head. It was a slow, distinct shake, an attempt to convince the sergeant that he cared even less.

The sergeant resisted the temptation to tell Davy and escorted him to the interrogation room where two of the detectives who had arrested him were waiting, one sitting, one standing. Davy was ordered to sit. When he didn't do this quick enough, one of the detectives took him by the scruff of the neck and slapped him into the seat.

"Wha' a'yeh fuckin' doin'? Do tha' again, yeh big culchie bastard, and I'll fuckin' sue yeh."

"Hit him harder," the sitting detective instructed his colleague.

By the time he had finished, Davy was no more than a bewildered heap in the chair. His nose and his lip bled, his jacket was torn and the tail of his grey Italian shirt hung out over the arse of his trousers.

"Okay, Byrne. Now I'm goin' to ask you a few questions. Can you hear me?"

When Davy looked at him and didn't answer, the detective looked to his colleague. This encouraged Davy to say, "Yeah, I hear yeh, for fucksake."

"Good. Do you know why you've been arrested?"

"A Section 30."

"In relation to . . .?"

"The possession of firearms."

"Top of the class. What I really want to talk to you about, Byrne, concerns the fatal shootin' of Michael Gerard Hughes on the 1st of November, at Sean McDermott Tower, Ballymun. Did you know Michael Hughes?"

Davy tried to let the words form some meaning. While he waited, the room began to reel and he had to hang on to the side of the chair, in case he fell from it. He thought for a moment that he was going to be sick and it seemed to take an age before he could ask, "A'yeh talkin' abou' Mickey?"

"Mickey Hughes. That's what everybody seems to have called him, yes."

"Wha' a'yeh sayin'? He's dead?"

"That's what fatally shot usually means, yes. You hadn't heard?"

Davy shook his head.

"Where were you on the 1st of November?"

"When was tha'?"

"Three days ago."

"London. Who shot him?"

"Where did you stay in London and what were you doin' there?"

"I stayed in a bed and breakfast. I wasn't doin' an'thin'."

"Okay, Davy. I want to get one thing straight. I'm from the murder squad. I'm only interested in findin' out who killed Michael Hughes. Now, I know you and Mickey were sellin' drugs together. I couldn't give a tu'penny fuck. I'm not even askin' you to make any statements about that, but I would appreciate you not wastin' me time tellin' lies. Comprendo?"

Davy nodded again. He remained stunned and thought it might be best to just go with the flow of what seemed like a bad dream.

The detective recognised this as shock, or a very good impression of it. "I've heard a couple of things, Byrne."

Davy waited while the detective asking the questions, the one who was seated, picked a piece of dead skin away from the edge of his thumbnail. The third detective had joined his colleagues and remained standing. There were only two chairs, one on either side of a small table, and nothing else in the room. Both standing detectives leaned, with arms folded, against a wall each.

"I've been hearin', Byrne, that you were pissed off with Hughes because he was takin' more drugs than he was sellin'. Is that true?"

"For fucksake."

"Just answer the question."

"No, that's not true."

"You see, I've a fair idea that you didn't shoot Hughes. But I've a fair idea who did and if I'm right, they're the kind of people who charge £2,000 a time. So, I'm kind of thinkin' to meself, to a big drug dealer like yourself, £2,000 would be nothing. Is that right?"

"Yeh can think whatever the fuck yeh like, yeh dirty big fuckin' bastard. I had nothin' to do with Mickey gettin' shot. And anyways, I don't fuckin' believe yeh. In fact, I must've been bleedin' mad even

---

listenin' to yis. And I don't know wha' you're lookin' at," Davy said to one of the detectives who stood against one of the walls. "Yeh can't do an'thin' to me. Do yeh think I'm frightened of a few slaps? C'mon then. Wha' a'yeh goin' to do if yeh hurt me? Say I was tryin' to escape?"

The detective who was seated still picked at his thumb when he said to Davy, "You're in Ballymun now, Byrne, not South Africa. Tryin' to escape? Listen to me, you gobshite, there is nobody in this world who gives a true fuck about you, apart perhaps from your mother and she can't do anything for you at the moment. Now I, if I wanted, could push your balls up your arse and all I'd get would be a round of applause. I want you to tell me everything."

"I've nothin' to say, and this is the last time I'll say it, unless it's in the presence of a solicitor."

The detective opened a beige cardboard file, which had been lying on the table in front of him. An assortment of colour photographs fell out and he began to sort through them. He chose one and handed it to Davy. "Have a look at this."

Davy tried to resist taking the photograph. For a split second before his hand reached out, he knew what he was going to see. He didn't anticipate the image, but rather the information, the news. He knew he was never going to forget this moment for as long as he lived. As his hand reached up, he felt his insides shudder, could feel them tremble uncontrollably, and then he saw the picture. He saw the blood and made out poor Mickey lying in a heap. It was a full length photograph. It was him. Jaysis, it was him, with one side of his face covered in blood. The detective handed Davy a close-up of Mickey's face. Davy thought the bloodied eye was opened and then he realised it was a hole where his eye should have been. He couldn't breathe. His heart felt like it was going to arrest. But still, he couldn't stop looking. Mickey died trying to mouth something. You could see this. He looked like he died before he could say it. Mickey died terrified. You could see this too. You could see the fear on the grey unbloodied side of his face.

"Is this what you paid someone £2,000 to do?"

Davy couldn't speak. One of the detectives leaning against the wall came over and took the photographs from his hand.

"Did you pay someone to murder Michael Hughes?"

His stomach felt like it had seized. He felt like he was going to throw up. He shook his head.

"If you didn't have anything to do with the death of Michael Hughes, then you must know who did. You won't be going anywhere until you tell me what you know."

They took Davy to a cell and gave him a cup of tea. It gave him time to think, but he couldn't do it properly. Every time he tried to work something out, every time he tried to understand what had happened, he walked into a wall of feelings. It was almost as if he could stay numb, or else he could disintegrate. He had nothing on him, no smack, and while he hated to think of it at a time like this, there was no alternative. It was going to start affecting him soon. He had to get out of there, would have to tell the coppers something. Tell them everything. He couldn't. Who shot him? Jaysis! Shot? Mickey was dead. No, no, no. They were going to blame him. Everyone was going to blame him. Tell the coppers something. Anything. They're going to keep you for two days anyway. Tell them nothing. Tell them nothing.

DAVY WALKED AWAY with a whole new understanding of the phrase "dead and buried". Mickey had been dead for a week and buried for two days. His funeral was held the same day they arrested Davy. He couldn't go. It wasn't right. The thought brought a tear to his swollen eye as he walked past the side of the Garda station and headed for the gear. Christ, he was sick. Dying sick. As sick as he had ever been. A couple of hours before letting him out, they allowed his ma in to see him. Anne was with her. They told him that Mickey was buried. Anne's ma and da wanted to get the funeral over and done with as quickly as possible, as soon as the autopsy was finished and they had permission. He couldn't believe it. Anne only came to see him because Jamesie wouldn't give her any gear until Davy said it was okay. She couldn't answer any questions, wouldn't answer, except that Skinnier had been with Mickey before he was shot.

"Wha' happened to Skinnier?"

"Nothin'," Anne answered.

When Davy heard this his face ached all the more. It was already sore from where it had been slapped, even punched once or twice, over the two days he was detained. The coppers told him, "It's your fault that Mickey got shot in the head."

Was it? Davy walked on down the side of the dual carriageway, towards Santry Woods. It was Yako's fault, for going and dying. It was the fault of the bastards who shot him. Skinnier Martin definitely had something to do with it. It was Mickey's fault for not listening. He never listened, did he? Jaysis, it drove Davy around the twist, it really did. Why did Mickey never listen? Why?

Davy needed a bit of gear. It was fucking freezing and he was sweating. He stopped at a shop at the end of Santry Lane and bought what he would need: forty cigarettes; four boxes of matches; a roll of tin foil and six small bottles of Lucozade. The young girl who served him stared. She was frightened by Davy's half closed eye, his bruised nose bridge and his cut lip.

He filled the pockets of his tweed jacket, which he carried across his shoulder, and walked over to the woods. He smiled when he found the heroin and compromised seclusion for the sake of necessity when he sat his arse down at the damp base of a tree. The ground was winter damp, but not wet. It gave him some Thinking Time. Time alone. It gave him time to indulge in the relief he felt which, when he realised the pleasure of it, he tried to deny. Well, it wasn't very appropriate, was it? With Mickey dead and that. But what could he do? He was sick and the smack he held in his hand made him smile. His hands were cold and it took him longer than he wanted to undo the wrapping. He carelessly poured about a gram on to a strip of foil and took his first long drag. Lumps of powder came up the tooter and stuck to his tongue and the palate of his mouth. He was smoking too anxiously, was in too much of a hurry.

He was in too much of a hurry because the tears were streaming down his face and he really didn't want to cry just yet. Christ! Not yet. He chased again and felt the smoke hit the back of his raw throat. He tasted the sickening bitterness as it enveloped his mouth, swallowed as much as he could into his reluctant lungs and held it there for as long as possible. Long enough to have to cough it out. Immediately, the aches begin to disappear. The pain began to go, but the unease of this comfort lingered longer. He burnt his fingers when he chased again, for some stupid reason. Maybe because he couldn't see the flame from the matches below the foil. Sometimes he forgot his fingers were there. Sometimes the flames licked along the foil hungrily and caught him unexpectedly. He cursed and then inhaled another long, deep drag.

When he finished, he dragged his legs to his chest to keep himself warm and to think again. When he began to feel the hurt he chased again. He chased until he couldn't hurt, but by then he couldn't think. By then he had dreams that began as thoughts.

Of London again, of the long wide Thames. A Night-Time Thames, with riverside lights chasing the waves of an easy swell. Lights shone from the gantry of Tower Bridge. He stood on the west side and looked down, against the tide, on to Traitors Gate. He heard Joan call, "Davy? Davy? Davy bleedin' Byrne!" She was approaching from the Bermondsey side of the bridge. It brought a smile to his face just to hear her, and he turned to greet her. Oh, she looked lovely, lovelier than ever, until she spoke and sounded like Anne. This strangeness made Davy hesitate, but he couldn't resist when she held out her arms and offered him a baby wrapped warm in a blanket. "Come and see your son."

Davy laughed. He laughed with relief, like he'd been holding his breath. He laughed with gratitude. Joan laughed too, with the same kind of feeling, the same kind of sincerity. They both laughed on Tower Bridge, with the relief of lovers who had just made up. Davy put his hand behind Joan's neck, to pull her towards him, to kiss her. Their lips touched, just enough to stick. He peeled away and bent a little to kiss the infant. A blanket covered the baby's head, so Davy used both his hands to gently unfold it, while Joan smiled on with a pride common to all new mothers. Davy searched for the source of the gurgling noise, then used his fingers to probe carefully, until he found the little face. Jaysis! It took his breath away.

The round, almost featureless face of a lifeless foetus. Davy cried out, shuddered for breath and pulled his hands off the blanket. It fell open, causing Joan to laugh hysterically. Holding the bundle sacrificially, she offered it to Davy. He stepped back, far enough to see the trail of blood that had fallen from where Joan had haemorrhaged between the legs.

Davy wanted to run past her, but Mickey and Yako arrived and blocked the way. They were laughing too, pointing fingers, saying, "Now, now, now." He couldn't get past Joan who was beginning to shuffle forward, dragging her legs free from the blood which had coagulated around her feet. Mickey was right behind her and still bled from the wound in his right eye. Yako didn't look too well either. He was grey, with blue lips, and Davy just couldn't believe the bleedin' cheek of him. But still he stepped back while Joan stepped forward, until, that is, she flung the foetus over the bridge rail. Davy rushed towards her, but it was too late. He couldn't stop it and only reached her in time to look over and see the foetus smack the water below. While he watched it float beneath the bridge, Joan clung to him and began to cry. It was an effort to push her off, especially with Mickey and Yako pointing fingers. Every time he managed to pull away, Joan would grab at him again, before he had time to run off. And it was all he wanted to do, to run off. But he couldn't, not with Joan hanging on to his ankles and Mickey and Yako in his face. Jaysis! He wanted to punch Yako, but he couldn't. He couldn't swing properly. He couldn't aim the way he wanted to. Even when he finally kicked himself free of Joan, he hadn't the strength left to hit Yako. He stumbled, couldn't seem to pick his legs up, couldn't seem to get into his stride. Yet before he knew how he got there, he found himself running down a deserted Old Kent Road, through Burgess Park and towards the north Peckham estate. He was looking for Cyrus, because Cyrus would look after him. Cyrus would understand.

As he ran, Davy felt like each step would have to be his last, but there always just seemed to be enough energy for one more. Then he was with Cyrus and asking for smack, a chase, anything to take the fear away. Cyrus laughed, in his easygoing, irritate-the-fucking-arse-off-you kind of way. Davy demanded, "C'mon, c'mon, where's the gear?" Cyrus was trying to tell Davy he didn't understand. Cyrus smiled when he didn't have to explain any more. He shrugged his shoulders, indifferently, when a dripping wet placenta wrapped foetus landed at Davy's feet and Joan, Mickey and Yako burst through the door and rushed around him, still laughing, still pointing, still clinging. Davy tried to rescue the foetus, or at least reach it, through the bodies of those around him. They poked as they pointed and this distracted him. "Wait," he tried to say, but nobody listened. He was too tired to stop them, too weak to push through them and was painfully powerless when the resentful foetus began to whine and point and poke with the others. When Cyrus began to laugh and slap his fingers together, Davy tried to scream.

He opened his eyes in the pitch dark and couldn't be sure if he had screamed. Had he been asleep? It took some moments before his eyes became accustomed to the dark and for him to realise where he was. He felt a bone-stiffening cold and his joints ached as he reached and searched for the matches. His damp clothes depressed him and when he tried to lift his legs to his chest for comfort, he noticed he needed to piss. Jaysis! His knees throbbed as he stood. Just piss, he told himself, and then have another chase to take the pain and cold away.

Having made sure that the matches, cigarettes and heroin were in his pocket, Davy inched his hand up the cracked wet bark of the tree and took a couple of tentative steps forward. It hurt to piss too through a hard shrivelled prick. As soon as he began, he felt rods of pain shoot from the prostrate gland below his swollen balls. He was pissing into darkness. He knew there wasn't much distance between where it fell and his feet. He directed the flow by letting his prick rest across the first two fingers of his right hand. At the same time, he cupped his balls in the other. While the pain lasted, it made Davy grind his teeth. It made him feel sick, but as soon as it passed, he managed to smile. As his balls sat in his hand, he remembered Joan's description, chicken-skinned balls. That's what she called them. It made him smile at the time too.

Davy put his prick away and felt a few warm drops go cold as they dribbled down his leg. Having edged his way back to the tree, he sat again and chased. He smoked carelessly, inefficiently. It hardly bothered him that the heroin was almost moist, that it was difficult to smoke, difficult to get it to run, but he was careful not to burn his fingers again. That he couldn't concentrate was the real source of his apathy, the reason he was wasteful. He couldn't settle in the dark and the cold, and wanted to be home in bed. He wanted to be wrapped in warmth. It was too dark to leave. No lights from the stars or the silvery fucking moon on this night. Sitting with his back against the soft bark of the tree, his legs stretched out and crossed, the lapels of his tweed jacket turned up to shelter his neck and with his hands in his trouser pockets, he waited.

STAND UP, DAVY Byrne, and Explain Yourself is a one-scene, one-act, one-part play. Davy Byrne plays himself. The other voice you hear is Davy's conscience. It transcends everything, because it has little wings. With these, it speaks from a point of advantage, privilege. It speaks to Davy in a place where he needs candles. The result is a flower in a fucking desert.

Stand up, Davy Byrne, and explain yourself. Tell them why.

(The scene is a sparse field, hedged, with a solitary oak tree in its centre. Davy Byrne sits at the base of the tree. It is a brilliantly sunny day, which contrasts sharply with Davy, who looks like something the cat dragged in. When he stands and steps forward, his two piece, double-breasted, blue tweed suit looks like it has been slept in. His gathered tie hangs untidily from his breast pocket. The jacket is closed and pushed up slightly, allowing Davy to stand with his hands in his trouser pockets. He steps away from the visible, tangled roots of the tree, but stays beneath the shadow of its crisp green leaves. His hair stands up and against how it naturally hangs. He looks shy, embarrassed, even agitated. Nevertheless, when he speaks, he does so confidently, authoritatively.)

Fuckin' explain meself? Why should I bother? Yeh know wha' the story is. I hadn't a bleedin' choice in the matter, had I? It just turned out the way it did.

(He looks to the ground, pauses and then looks up and starts again, from the same position.) I know why I'm bein' asked to do this. It's because I'm gettin' the blame for everythin'. I always do. But I couldn't give a fuck. Yeh see, none of it's my fault. Not Mickey. Not Yako. Not Jojo gettin' reefed. None of it. If they'd listened to me, there'd have been none of this. Take Jojo, for a start. He wanted to get caught. He shit a brick when them vigo's caught hold of him and gettin' reefed was his oney way out. He hadn't the bollix to turn around and tell me tha' he didn't want to knock out the gear any more. Hang on (Davy holds up an open palm), I know wha' yeh're thinkin', tha' I got him strung out to bits, and if tha' wasn't enough to stop him tellin' me he didn't want to knock out the gear any more, you're thinkin' tha' I would've asked him for the money he owed me. Too fuckin' right I would. Wouldn't yeh? Yeh don't get nothin' for nothin' in this world. I mean, it's not as if he was a thick or an'thin'. He knew wha' the story was, righ' from the very start. Okay, I mean I was beginnin' to wonder meself if he was thicker than I thought, when he went and tried to sell gear to a copper, but tha' wasn't him bein' stupid. Tha' was him bein' careless, on purpose. Tha' was him temptin' fate and there's no room for an'thin' like tha' in this game. It gets on me bleedin' nerves, it really does. Here am I standin' up to explain meself and it shouldn't be me who's explainin' an'thin'. Think abou' it. He owed me £700. Seven hundred fuckin' pounds, tha' he robbed on me. Tha's a lot of money to me, somethin' I risked me liberty for. And really, when yeh think of it, not oney did I let him off, which in a way I did, because I never saw a shillin' of it, I even went and gave him the chance to make a few bob. He was makin' £160 a day. It was his choice to put all tha' up his arm, but we're missin' the point here; £160 a day is the bleedin' point. There isn't many in Ballymun earnin' tha', I can tell yeh, £160 a day? Jaysis! But anyways, the other point I'm tryin' to make is tha' he fucked up because he was frightened and wha' could I do abou' tha'? I know he's me brother and I'd do an'thin' for him, I would, but yeh can't give tha' kind of stuff away. Yeh either have it or yeh haven't. And at the end of the day, Jojo hadn't got it. He hadn't the balls to see it through, so he got himself reefed. Five years won't kill him. In fact, it might even do him a bit of good, give him a bit of sabby, who knows?

(Davy pauses again and this time takes his hand from his pocket and points a finger.) I know Yako wasn't frightened, but he wasn't the full shillin' either. Mickey said tha' abou' him often enough, didn't he? He wasn't all there. Sure he even said it himself. He told Mickey he thought everyone else came from another planet. Tha's real bleedin' madness, tha' is. It was sad though, because I liked him anyway. I mean, when he robbed the bleedin' bus: "This is a stick-up", ha ha ha. "Tell them me name's Buckets of Blood", somethin' like tha' he said, ha ha ha. He was a real character, wasn't he? Even if he was a fuckin' nut case. I wonder was he ridin' tha' Jude one? He used to smile if yeh asked him, with tha' dim fuckin' grin of his. I felt a bit sorry for his oul' wan too. I did! Cancer of the tit she has. Yako told me one nigh', like he was tellin' me a secret, like he was lettin' me in on somethin' tha' he done wrong. They say when they dropped his coffin down, she let out a scream tha'd waken the dead, a scream like she'd just died herself. Yeh see? I feel fuckin' terrible. I feel just as bad as anyone. But wha' did I do? I gave Yako a chance, that's wha' I did. Wha' did you do for Yako? Yeah, caught yeh on the fuckin' hop there, didn't I? Did yeh give him a chance? When yeh walk by the tappers outside the Post Office, and tha's wha' Yako was, do yeh even look at them twice? I gave Yako a chance to get away from all tha'. I even dressed him, for fucksake. Didn't yeh see the lovely leather jacket I got him? The oney problem was, it was too late. Yako had already gone mad when I met him, though I didn't know tha' at the time. And when I did, I still put up with him. Actually, I more than put up with him: I accepted him; I appreciated Yako for who he was; I looked after him, despite the fact tha' he was fuckin' mad, not because of it. I was willin' to live my life in the company of a lunatic. The fact tha' he overdosed, well tha' was all just a part of the mad little world he lived in. An occupational hazard. In fact, he probably thought he was a cross between Ian Curtis and Che Guevara, d'yeh know? There's no understanding the likes of Yako's mind, but least I allowed him to be Yako. Okay, I know he used to run around doin' things for me, but he liked it, didn't he? Think abou' it. He wouldn't have got so much as a second glance from tha' Jude one, let alone a dart, if it hadn't been for me. If it hadn't been for me, he'd still be standin' at the bottom of the snooker hall with the rest of the 20p brigade. Yeah, he'd still be alive. But d'yeh call tha' livin'? If yeh do, then you're more out of your fuckin' mind than Yako was. Tha's not even an existence. I'm not a gobshite. I realise tha' there's many who'd like to keep the likes of Yako righ' where they are, have them stand as a reminder tha' things could be worse. Yeh don't believe me? Well ask yourself why someone like Yako jumped at the chance to get away from it. If you're too dishonest to answer yourself, go and ask the 20p brigade. Yako was, and still is, a fuckin' hero to them. Yako is the oney bleedin' hope they have. D'yeh get the gist of this? Nobody offers them any hope, not because they haven't any to give, but because at best, they couldn't give a fuck and at worse, they need them where they are. That's why the 20p brigade looked up to Yako. They saw him lean against the post box with his twenty Major and his leather jacket. They used to see him fuck away a cigarette before it'd been sucked clean to the butt and remember the days he divebombed on someone else's. They saw Jude rest her head on Yako's T-shirted chest, saw her wrap her thin arms around his thin waist, watched her diddys lift up when she took deep breaths and watched them fall away again, slightly, after she sighed contentedly. They knew all abou' those diddys, because Yako told them. He told them abou' her inverted nipples and how she used to ask Yako to suck them for her in the hope tha' one day they'd pop out. They knew abou' the wail Yako's oul' wan let out when they dropped him down and they hoped one day someone migh' wail like tha' for them, because tha' was all the fuckin' hope they had.

I know Mickey was neither frightened nor mad. I'm not goin' to make excuses. I'm not goin' to breeze over this and cover up the truth with lies. I've nothin' to fuckin' hide anyway. Me and Mickey were like blood brothers. In fact, we were goin' to do it once. We were goin' to cut our hands and mix the blood with a handshake, but Mickey had the hep' at the time and I hadn't caught it yet, so it didn't seem like a good idea. We must have forgot all abou' it after tha', but it's the thought tha' counts, isn't it? See, tha's the type of blokes we were. I wish he were here now, because he'd be able to tell yeh better than me wha' I mean. He'd explain it well. Alrigh', we mightn't have seen eye to eye on it, we migh' have even argued over it, but we understood each other. I'll show yeh wha' I mean. We were doin' this snatch one day. It was one of the first ones we ever did. It was the money they made at the bingo. An oul' fella used to take it from the church to the bank the mornin' after. I wanted to take him at the church, but Mickey said it was bad luck and he refused to do it there. He'd oney do it at the bank. We were on foot at the time, which shows yeh how long ago it was. We couldn't even ride a bike, let alone rob one. Anyway, as much as I argued, Mickey wouldn't listen and we had to rob the oul' fella at the bank. Wait until yeh hear wha' happened. Me and Mickey are standin' beside the wall of the underground, at the side entrance to the Penthouse, when the oul' fella pulls up in his car. We're just about to move on him, when guess wha'? A fuckin' pig car drives past. Of course, by the time it's out of sigh', the oul' fella's at the top of the steps to the bank and there's no way we can take him there. The staff'd see us and set the alarms off. I'll tell yeh, it done me fuckin' head in so much, I turned round and let a roar at Mickey. "Bad Luck?" I says to him. "You're a fuckin' gobshite, yeh are." That's the oney thing he hates bein' called, yeh know, like, if you're serious with him. So he turns around and says to me, "If yeh call me tha' again I'll punch yeh in the fuckin' mouth," and he goes and raises his closed fist to me. Yeh wouldn't believe wha' happened next. The oul' fella hears us and turns and comes back down the fuckin' steps sayin', "Aw, c'mon, lads, there's no need for all tha'." It was like somethin' yeh'd see in a film. As soon as he was close enough, "Shake on it, lads," somethin' like tha' he was sayin', Mickey slapped such a bleedin' loaf on him, I thought the oul' fella's face was goin' to crack open. He hadn't hit the deck when I had the pouch out from under his jacket and we were off. Tha' got on Garda Patrol, yeh know? It was the first time we were on it. They even said the argument was a diversion, can yeh believe it? Anyway, the point I'm tryin' to make is, was tha' two blokes who understood each other, or wha', huh? Me and Mickey were a good team. We were partners. I shouldn't have to stand here and explain why he was shot in the head, as if I'd somethin' to do with it. It's the bastards who shot him tha' yeh should be askin', though it wouldn't surprise me if some day they name a fuckin' tower block after them. Wha' abou' Yako and Mickey, hey? Wha' kind of monument d'yeh think they deserve? With no speech from the dock to remind yeh, who will remember? I fuckin' will, I can tell yeh tha'. Yako was a breath of fresh air in me life, and as for Mickey, well, I loved Mickey. There, I'm not afraid to say it. I loved him. Not in a funny way like, d'yeh know wha' I mean? Like brothers, tha' kind of thing. There'll never be a time when I forget him, or any of the others.

C'mon, Davy Byrne, that's not good enough. You'll have to do better than that.

(A flash of rage crosses Davy's eyes. He removes his hands from his trousers pockets and clenches them into fists.)

Well, if they ever build a statue of me, at the Glasnevin end of the dual carriageway, yeh know, as it heads towards Ballymun, I want to have somethin' like this on it:

Gimme those who consent and those who won't,
All willin' and unwillin' prey.
I'll ride every las' bleedin' one of them,
Then see wha' yeh have to say.

D'yeh think I'm jokin'? Why don't yeh ask Deirdre then? See wha' she thinks. Why is it, every time I open me mouth and try to do me best, the fuckin' worst is dragged out of me? (One hand goes back into his trousers pocket, the other scratches the back of his head before dropping to his side.) I oney mention Deirdre to make a point. She rode me first. D'yeh know tha'? We were over in the Towers one nigh', drinkin' separately. Anyway, she comes over and asks me, if I'd nothin' better to do, would I mind walkin' her home. I didn't think much of it. Billy was locked up at the time, so I agreed. When we got to their place, she asked me in for a cup of tea and I still though' nothin' of it. To make a long story short, I'm sittin' there drinkin' me tea and in the middle of it I decide to go for a piss. When I come back, she's oney lyin' on the sofa, her skirt up around her hips and she's stretchin' her knickers between the lips of her fanny. This isn't a word of a lie. "D'yeh like this, Davy?" Somethin' like tha' she said. Needless to say, I gave her a dart, after me eyes popped back into me head, tha' is. Now I would have just forgotten abou' it, yeh know? I would've just left it at tha'. But one nigh', after he got out, Billy comes over to me, after I bumped into the pair of them in the pub, and he says to me somethin' like, and he's all sincere mind, "Listen, Davy, thanks for wha' yeh done. Deirdre says yeh kept an eye out for her when I was locked up." I looked over to the Deirdre one and she's oney sittin' there smilin' at me. Can yeh believe the little cunt? I don't know where she got the barefaced fuckin' cheek. Yeh know, I'm left sayin' to Billy, "Don't worry abou' it," and he says somethin' to me like, "Yeah, I suppose that's wha' brothers are for." I don't know abou' you, but when people treat me like tha', well, I know one thing, she won't do it again in a bleedin' hurry. If I'd known at the time tha' Jojo had the germ, I'd have gotten him to give her a dart up the arse, though I suppose tha' wouldn't have been fair on Billy, in a way, because he would've probably caught it then too. But as Mickey used to say tha' they said in Russia, life is tough sometimes, life is fuckin' tough.

(Davy puts the loose hand back in his trouser pocket and walks anti-clockwise around the tree, until he completes a circle. He begins to speak and it's obvious he's clenching his fists in his pockets.) Tha' Skinnier bastard. Jaysis! He gives me a heartburn on the fuckin' arse, I swear. He's a fuckin' dirt bird, a scumbag. D'yeh know, if Sean Graham had opened a book on who was goin' to catch the germ first, he'd have made Skinnier Martin the odds on fuckin' favourite. I should have given him fuck all, apart from a kick in the bollix, righ' from the fuckin' start. I bet yeh the bastard knew he had the germ and he gave it to Jojo on purpose. They're sayin' these days tha' it started off in monkeys. Tha's probably how he caught it, from ridin' a fuckin' monkey in the zoo.

Okay, I know this is a long-winded way of gettin' around to explainin' meself, but bear with me. It's just tha', sometimes it's important to say other things too. (A mischievous grin crosses his lips.) They make sense later on.

Righ'. So I had an idea. I thought of a less risky way of makin' a few bob. There was nothin' new abou' it, but I went for it. I had to. Those days of somebody robbin' a chemist shop and sharin' out the gear are long gone. That Time is over. I didn't change it and I'd have been happy if it was it still like tha'. But it isn't. As I say, I went for it. I know wha' you're thinkin'. I made a few bob in a way tha' was less risky alrigh', less risky for meself. While it meant Jojo gettin' reefed, and the germ, Mickey gettin' shot, Yako overdosin', Anne gettin' strung out to bits and fuck knows wha' else, I was left with nothin' better to do than shake the creases out of me lovely two piece tweed suit and fuck off somewhere else. Well, you're absolutely fuckin' righ'. Otherwise, I'd have ended up at worst like me oul' fella, or at best like one of the 20p brigade. C'mon? Would you be happy with tha'? Yeh know, I'd lovin' to have been born with brains to burn and do all tha' readin' and tha'. I'd lovin' to have been born in Ballsbridge or somewhere and have everything handed to me on a plate. Yeh think I have a chip on me shoulder? Well yeh should come and try this for a while. Come and see wha' yeh'd do. Don't get me wrong. I'm not complainin'. Fuck it! Life on life's terms does me. I don't think I'd change a fuckin' thing, though I don't pretend to speak for anyone else. Do yeh know wha' I mean?

Regrets? No none at all,
But then again, there's one
That I should mention.

Tha' I didn't wear a condom, a ribbed condom, when in 1979, on St Valentines Day, at the tender age of 14 and havin' taken one by the tail first, I rammed me prick up the sausage pink arse of a stray black mongrel. When I told Mickey this, he said he didn't regret not wearin' one when he rammed his down the neck of a headless chicken his ma had left out to defrost one night. He didn't even regret it the followin' day when he had to say he couldn't eat his dinner because of the woeful hangover he had. Not even when his oul' fella said, "Can I have your meat then, son? This chicken looks lovely, Mammy. It's much juicier than usual." In fact, Mickey said it was worth every fuckin' minute of it when, after his ma said it was the same kind of chicken she usually got, his oul' fella asked, "Did yeh stuff it any differently?"

Step forward, Davy bleedin' Byrne, and take a bow when you hear the roar of applause.

IT WAS MIDDAY when Davy woke, shivering. The cold had set in and he felt it gnaw at his bones. For a moment, he wondered if anyone had called him awake. Something woke him. It felt like Mickey or Yako. Well, it felt familiar. But there was nobody there. When he tried to straighten his arms, they ached from the effort. They needed warmth, they needed a dry bed. When he stood, it seemed he couldn't straighten his knees and his arse tingled as blood poured back into blood vessels, chilled by the pressure of the cold, damp ground. Rubbish lay strewn at his feet: empty Lucozade bottles; cigarette butts; strips of kitchen foil with burnt track marks; used matches.

Davy knew he was in a state. He knew he needed to sort himself out, but he wasn't ready just yet. He didn't particularly want to get his head together, thank you very much. If anything, he found his confusion appealing. He wanted to be chaotic. The control could wait until later. For the moment, Davy just wanted to feel. He wanted his anger, his sorrow, his pain, to feel him, in a beautifully perverse kind of way. When he walked to leave the woods, it was hard to keep moving. Having got so cold, he thought he would never get warm again. But it got easier. He wasn't sure why, or how. Maybe it was because he was moving from the shadow of trees out into the winter sunshine. At the edge of the woods, he carelessly stashed the remainder of the smack, crossed the road to pass the gypsy camp and had to walk round a snapping, spiteful looking dog. Davy had been concentrating so hard on the threat from the dog, trying to look just as spiteful by glancing sideways down his cheek at it, he didn't hear the car coming. He hadn't even bothered to consider the blue Maestro until it pulled right up beside him.

When the passenger window opened, Davy, wholly out of character, spoke first.

"Wha' the fuck d'yeh wan'?"

"Byjaysis," said Maskey, chuckling, "how the mighty fall, hey?" He was still laughing when Langley called across from behind the steering wheel, "I hear you're next on the hit list, Byrne. Is that right?"

"D'yeh think I give so much as a monkey's fuck? I've been on your poxy hit list for years and wha' fuckin' difference has tha' made?" It was Davy's turn to laugh. "Not a fiddler's fuck, has it?"

"Well, you're playin' a different ball game now, Byrne."

"Yeah," added Langley, "and there's no rules, except those that suit them. And you know what that means?"

"Yeah, tha' yeh're full of shite," said Davy.

"Would you listen to the gobshite," said Maskey. "Do you know something, Byrne? You're nothing but a parasite."

"A wha'?"

"A leech. A bloodsucker."

"I am, am I? Well tell me then, yeh bollix, where'd yeh be without the likes of me? Wha'? Yeh'd be pickin' potatoes in the arsehole of Leitrim, or somewhere like tha'. I don't even sign on the labour, do yeh know tha'? The poxy £30 a week tha' I'd get wouldn't be enough to blow me nose on. And as for your poxy wages, I wouldn't wipe me fuckin' arse with it."

"I pity you, Byrne, I really do," said Maskey.

Davy stood shocked for a moment, then the rage shot through him. It filled him with enough energy to run after the car as it pulled off and scream, "Pity me? Come back, yis bastards, and I'll show yis pity." By the time he reached St Pappin's, the car was disappearing out of sight.

Davy sat on a stone wall in front of the church to gather his breath. His exertions had invigorated him, made him giddy with appetite. It was great to be angry again, angry in a way that made him want to kick the living shit out of something. It lifted him down from the wall and propelled him towards the shopping centre. He crossed the dual carriageway as if immune to the speeding traffic and felt his pace increase, felt his height rise monumentally. He wasn't sure what he was looking for until he collided with it outside the post office. A member of the 20p brigade recklessly requested odds and got a bloody nose instead. Davy grinned, a dim-witted Yako grin, then marched up the stairs of the snooker hall where about a dozen young men were playing snooker and pool. Davy was rampant. All heads turned to look at him, even those bent at tables. It gave Davy the opportunity to challenge, "Wha' are yis looking at? Yis shower of parasites." He leaned the palms of his hands on the first vacant snooker table he came to and glanced around the hall. "Yeah, tha's righ', parasites. Fuckin' bloodsuckers."

There were a few, like Tommo Kane, who didn't know Davy. When Tommo innocently, adolescently sniggered, Davy descended on him like a gale. Tommo, took flight around a snooker table, with Davy in hot pursuit. It was a howl. Others found it funny too, especially when Davy began to throw snooker balls at Tommo. Some found it hysterical, until one of the snooker balls connected with the side of Tommo's head and dropped him to his knees. It enabled Davy to stroll up and plant a boot deep into Tommo's stomach. He continued to kick him, in the head, in the ribs, until he was too tired to go on kicking. Then he stamped on him until he couldn't lift his leg. Nobody interfered, though afterwards, some said they regretted this.

Davy gathered his breath in gasps, while leaning his hands on another vacant table. In between sucks he shouted, "Righ', is there any more of yis bastards . . . who want a good laugh?" Everyone of them looked at Davy, until he looked at them, when none would look him in the eye. "Fucking parasites," he said, as he pushed himself away from the table and left the snooker hall.

He tried to straighten the creases in his jacket as he walked down the mall, but laughed at the futility and abandoned the attempt by the time he reached the centre. Groups of people cluttered together to chat. He noticed they were mostly women with children in tow, and they were concentrated in the heart of the shops at the entrance to the only supermarket.

It was here Davy stopped to laugh. It was here where people turned to glance. Vera Collins was one who stared. She had just left a prescription in the chemist and was on her way down to the post office when she bumped into Bridey Kavanagh. She hadn't meant to stop long, because of the kids, especially Burt, a very needy child, who was tugging at her coat. She noticed Davy when she turned to smack Burt, who had tugged once too often, and she could hardly take her eyes away. The only time was to glance and see if Bridey had seen him too. She tried to explain it to her sister afterwards why she felt compelled. "There was somethin' funny abou' him. Not funny ha ha, do yeh know wha' I mean? I mean, he had the look of a madman. I swear, if this was America, it wouldn't have surprised me if he had opened up and shot us all dead. Of course, we realised for definite tha' he wasn't all there when he started tha' roarin' and shoutin'."

Davy had tried again to pull the creases from his jacket, before spinning a slow circle on his feet and focusing on those who looked back at him. He spun a twirl and stopped to curtsy, flamboyantly, to oul' Bridget McMann. She smiled a loose dentured grin to him and waved him up to his feet, where he stood straight and erect. He smiled back to her and turned and looked to more.

"Well, a'yis satisfied? Yis shower of fuckin' whores." This was unexpected and caused a muffled movement of mouths amongst the crowd. "So Mickey's dead, yis murderin' fuckin' bastards. Yeah, tha's righ'," said Davy as he turned on his feet and pointed a finger randomly. "Yeh lot killed Mickey just as much as those who pulled the trigger."

"Who's tha', Bridey?" Vera muttered through tight lips.

"I haven't a bleedin' clue, Vera, but whoever he is, he belongs in the Gorman."

"Yeh lot as good as fuckin' killed him, because yis love to be judge and jury, egged on by the likes of the bastards who paid to have Mickey shot. And now, so I'm told, I'm next. Well, c'mon then. Who wants to have a go? Which of yis has the bollix?" Davy, still turning, appealed, arrogantly. No one responded. He slowed, because he was beginning to see less and less through tears which welled up in his eyes. When he fell to his knees, his arse fell back on his heels. "Yis shouldn't have done it," was the last thing, so somebody said, that Davy said, before the police arrived. Davy's head had fallen to his chest.

"You take one oxter, I'll take the other," said one Garda to the next, and they carried Davy out of the shops and around to Ballymun Garda station, his legs dragging lamely behind him.

THEY DRAGGED DAVY to a cell and dropped him there, while they went to consult with a sergeant about what might be the best thing to do with him.

Davy cried hard, unceasing, an unrelenting flood of tears, which washed snots down his face. They fell from his chin in long lines and gathered in little pools on the concrete floor. He cried until his skull ached violently at the forehead. He cried through the periods when Gardaí came to pry and pity. He cried until there were no tears left, until all he had were those short sharp involuntary gasps for breath which he hadn't experienced since childhood. He cried until he couldn't cry any more, until he arrived at silence.

When he first became aware of his ma's feet, he looked up to see her standing over him, bent almost, as if the very sight of him crushed her. Her hands covered her mouth and prevented her sobs coming out in one great groan.

"What's wrong, Ma? Wha's the story?"

"Oh Davy . . . they think yeh ought to go to hospital and have a little rest."

"A rest? In wha' fuckin' hospital? Wha' a'yeh talkin' abou'?"

"The doctor's had a look at yeh, and he thinks it migh' be best as well. He says tha' you're traumatised. Tha's all it is, son. It's the trauma of it all. I'm goin' to sue these rotten bastards," said Mrs Byrne, jerking a thumb in the direction of two Gardaí who were looking on. "If it's the last thing I do. I swear, first thing in the mornin', I'm goin' in to see the solicitor. As God's me witness, I won't rest if an'thin's permanently the matter with yeh."

"There's nothin' the matter with me. And will yeh answer me, wha' hospital are yeh talkin' abou'?"

"Well, Brendan's, but it'd only be for a rest. It'd oney be for a day or two. And yeh wouldn't be locked up, I made them promise me tha'."

"Don't sign me in, Ma. I'm alrigh' now, honest. I just need to go home and lie down. I'm wrecked, that's all it is. Get tha' fuckin' doctor back in. Trauma? Jaysis! Get him to tell them he's going to give me a couple of barbs and tha' tha's all I need, just to sleep it off. But I'm warnin' yeh, Ma, don't sign me in."

She knew she could get him home. Nobody had complained about Davy. The police said they had only taken him into custody because they feared he was a danger to himself more so than society. She told them and the doctor what was best: a good meal and a decent night's sleep, in his own home.

Davy woke refreshed and was almost enthusiastic about a plan he began to formulate in his mind. It took half an hour, lying on the bed, gazing through the only window in the room. He had pulled the curtains back the evening before, because he wanted to wake up and see the sky. It was hard to concentrate, but some things helped, like a diet of cigarettes on an empty belly. He smiled when he realised the plan would be complete in time for him to catch the last plane from Dublin to London. Fucksake, what time is it now?

"Ma?" Davy roared, at he top of his voice. When she didn't answer immediately, he roared again. "Ma?"

"Yeah, Davy, wha' is it?" she asked, galloping towards the bedroom.

"C'mere for a minute," he called out, before she got there.

Mrs Byrne walked straight into the room and asked Davy, kindly, what it was he wanted.

"D'yeh remember tha' bit of gear I gave yeh to stash?"

"Wha', in the packet?"

"Yeah, tha's it. Get it for me, will yeh? I'm dyin' sick and I need it now."

"Did those tablets the doctor gave yeh not do any good?"

"No, they were for me nerves."

Mrs Byrne went to her bedroom and removed the trousers of her husband's only suit from the wardrobe. She felt the end right leg until she located a small packet and then wrapping the thread which hemmed the bottom of the trouser leg around her hard bony finger, she tugged and snapped it. Having retrieved the packet, she dutifully returned it to Davy.

As she handed it over, Davy told her, "Get me some foil as well, will yeh? And some more matches." These too were returned with dutiful efficiency and then she was dismissed, with a raised nod of instruction.

Davy thought, as he chased. He needed a bath. "Ma? Ma? Fill the bath for me, will yeh?" He lay on the bed listening to the water running and didn't get up until he heard his mother call that it was ready. He took with him what heroin he had on the foil to the bathroom and on the way picked up a couple of fresh towels from the hot press in the hall.

"I was just abou' to get them for yeh, Davy," she said, when she met him on the way.

Davy tested the water carelessly, because it burned his arm which he casually dropped in after his hand.

"Jaysis!" he called out. "Wha' a'yeh tryin' to do, Ma? Scald me to fuckin' death?" The chain on the stopper had snapped off years ago and the bath was too full for him to try and reach down to pull it out with his fingers so he went in search of a pot.

"Wha's wrong?" his mother asked, when she bumped into him in the hall again.

"The fuckin' bath's too full and the water's scaldin'. I'm goin' to have to empty half of it out meself."

"Here, let me in. I'll do it."

"It doesn't matter, for fucksake," and he threatened to push her out of the bathroom if she tried to come in. He didn't see the look in her eye as she walked away. The humiliation. Worse, the familiarity of it and the futility of dissent.

Davy got fed up pouring pots of water down the sink from the bath. He decided, while he waited on the water to cool, to wash his hair in the hand-basin. He used the same pot to rinse his hair and was reminded of his childhood, how he used to stand, holding a towel to his eyes, with his head bent into a sink, while his ma's hard nails and strong fingers seemed to tear into him as she scrubbed his scalp. More often than not, she wouldn't have any spare towels, so he would use the trunks he had just taken off and had been wearing for a week, to protect his eyes. He would manoeuvre these round his nose to sniff the different odours: the cabbagey smell of crayon brown skidmarks, which Billy said were caused by the blasts from farts; the sour smell of corn yellow stains from piss trapped in the pouch of his foreskin. He had to scratch for them though, bury his nose deep in the trunks to find them.

Davy towel dried his hair, quickly and vigorously. He removed the Mickey Mouse boxer shorts he was wearing and carried them, pressed in cupped hands, to his nose. He still found the smell appealing. He still couldn't understand it, why he was so attracted to his own stale body odours, the older the better.

He tested the bath water with his big toe and pulled it away quickly. The water was still too hot and although there was room to run some cold water, he decided to shave first, another thing he didn't like doing. Especially with the only razor available, a blunt Bic disposable and a lather from a bar of Shield soap. But he had a three day growth and it was going to have to go. The razor scraped rather than shaved the stubble and left dry, burning sensations all over his face. He had "gallons" of expensive aftershave which Maree Whelan had swapped him for gear, but none of it was at his ma's, so the best he could do to comfort his face was rinse it with cold water. As he towel dried his neck, he noticed himself in the mirror. Jaysis! His face was getting thin. And they're big black fuckin' coal sacks under me eyes, not bags. It was a junkie's face, he agreed with himself. The image brought a stab of pain across his chest and

Mickey's name came to his lips. He mouthed it to his reflection. They showed me the pictures. Oh Jaysis, Mickey.

He pushed the name away, but not before promising Mickey, wherever he was, that it was only until a time when the pain became bearable. It was only until the name might reflect any time other than a Painful Time. And this didn't mean a Made Up Time, a Time that had never existed. Any Other Time was any Time at all, other than that One Time. Any Other Time was every Other Time, apart from that One Time.

Davy jumped into the bath, disregarding any concern he might have for how hot it was. He needed to think of something else, so he thought of Joan. He hadn't seen her since the night she asked for the money. It still puzzled him, why she had asked at all, when she could have got it somewhere else. Why she seemed to take a certain pleasure, not in telling him she was pregnant, but that she was going to get rid of it. It didn't matter any more. It was too late now, bound to be. When he remembered their sex, he lifted his balls and crossed his legs. Lying back in the bath, he took hold of his prick and pushed and pulled his foreskin. He recalled Joan, her chuckle, the way her tiny fist took hold of him when she'd bend to take him in her mouth. He slapped the bath water to splash round his genitals, but nothing was happening. He remembered her in positions that once had shocked him, remembered her say, "Ram it up me, Davy Byrne." He pulled and pushed, faster and faster, but still nothing, so he slowed and began again. He introduced more women. Fat ones. Skinny ones. Some he knew and some he didn't. He introduced more men, took all the women away, except Joan. She sucked one, wanked two more, sat on another, so he would go straight up her fucking hole. Jaysis! Still nothing but a raw prick. He was going to give up the gear when he got to London.

Davy stepped one foot out of the bath and reached for the heroin on the foil and the matches on top of the cistern and stepped back into the bath to chase some more. Not long after, his ma was banging on the door, asking if he was all right. It was long enough for the water to have gone cold. It was time to get ready to visit Jamesie. He wanted to get ready for another reason too. It was important that he looked well, especially after what happened the day before. It was essential that he return to the scene looking as well as he had ever done. Where he could, if he wanted, do another twirl for oul' Bridget McMann, though she wouldn't be there. Neither would Bridey Kavanagh, or Vera, though it really didn't matter. Someone would tell them. It didn't matter either that he had to wear the gaunt face of a junkie. It didn't matter that his mouth hung open when he forgot to keep it shut. What mattered was, someone would witness how he walked, how he swaggered with a broad swing of his shoulders. How, when he got to the middle of the shops, he would, with skilled exaggeration, brush an imagined piece of fluff from the sleeve of his black, two-piece Italian suit and straighten his thin, red leather tie. How he would run a hand over the shape of his hair, pat it reassuringly, and scratch behind his ear. And then, with a wink and a nod, he would toss ten bob into the grubby hand of a tapper, and licking the tip of his index finger, run it along the eyebrow of his right eye. And take a bow. Turn and take a bow before he descended the steps at the post office. Jaysis! That was a great idea.

"Ma? Ma? Where's me white shirt?"

"Which one, Davy?" Mrs Byrne replied, coming down the hall again and stopping outside the bathroom door.

"Me good one, Ma. The one tha' I got in London."

"It's in your wardrobe, in the bedroom. D'yeh want me to run the iron over it, to freshen it up?"

When she returned with the pressed shirt, Davy was standing in front of the wardrobe mirror, dressed only in a pair of boxer shorts. "Here," he told her, "run the iron over the trousers of me suit as well, will yeh?" She handed him the shirt and left with the trousers. By the time she came back, he had his shirt and tie on, a pair of socks, and was happy with his hair.

"A'yeh goin' out, Davy?"

"No, Ma. I'm goin' to bed. Jaysis! Of course I'm goin' out. Wha' does it look like?" He saw her anxious features reflect in the wardrobe of the mirror. "Don't worry. I just have to sort out a couple of things. I'll be goin' away for a little while then. D'yeh know wha' I mean?"

She knew what he meant. "Yeah, Davy. It's probably for the better," she told him and her eyes started to fill with tears.

"Jaysis. Don't start cryin', for fucksake. I knew I should've just fucked off," he told himself in the mirror.

"For Godsake, Davy, it's just tha' I worry abou' yeh. It's oney natural. Any mother would," she told him and she tried to make sure, for his sake, that no tears fell.

"Amn't I after tellin' yeh tha' I won't be gone for long? Listen, anyway. I'm either goin' to send a taxi here to pick up a suitcase for me or else I'll collect it meself. Either way, make sure yeh have it ready, won't yeh?" He neither looked, nor waited, for an answer. "I'll have a few bob for yeh too, so don't worry."

"That's the least of me worries, Davy," Mrs Byrne told him, before she asked what it was he wanted packed.

Davy told her, as he took a last look in the mirror. He was pleased with what he saw. The suit jacket sat well on him, his tie hung straight and his trousers looked stylishly baggy. He couldn't see his shoes in the mirror and when he looked down, he realised he hadn't put any on. Fuck! It made him to chuckle. The thought of walking through the shops like that. Jaysis! They really would put him away.

From the bottom of the wardrobe, he chose a pair of flat black brogues. While loosening the laces, he found a gold watch inside one shoe. Jojo must have stashed it there and forgotten it. He tossed his ma the watch and said, "Here, give this to the oul' fella." He smiled at the thought that his oul' fella might wear it for a day or two. He laughed when he thought he might get reefed for receiving stolen goods.

Davy felt better than ever. He left his ma, telling her, "See yeh later," and walked straight out and across to the shops. Although late in the evening, there were still a few people about. Some recognised him, some didn't. The two Gardaí who stood outside the Penthouse did. He spat on the ground as he passed, while looking straight ahead. His bravado thrilled him and though he didn't need to, he fiddled with his tie as if to straighten it. His heel capped brogues clicked clacked clicked on the concrete paving slabs and echoed in the silent parts of the shops. Outside of the supermarket, he felt uneasy, especially when he stopped and looked down on the spot he had been carried from. It was like coming across the location of a film he'd seen. He quickened his step until he reached the snooker hall where he went upstairs for a smart, informal scout.

"Wha's the story?" he asked a couple of the 20p brigade after he came back out.

"Did yeh hear abou' the factory gettin' blagged for naps and difs, Davy?"

"Yeah, but don't worry, it had nothin' to do with me," he laughed, before making an unsolicited contribution. He took one final look through the shops before descending the steps and was too shy to take a bow. He chose the route to avoid walking by the window of the police station. He'd had enough bravado for one day. At the bottom of the steps he swerved sharply and headed for the taxi rank.

A line of five taxis waited for fares and behind these, a row of four. Arthur was third in the queue. Davy always used him when he could, and if other drivers complained Arthur told them he was taking Davy on tick. When offered the same opportunity, they always refused.

"Wha's the story, Arthur?"

"Not bad, Davy. It's a bit quiet, but I can't complain."

"Yeah, I wouldn't complain either if it was quiet and I had a lovely little gaff to go home to on the Navan Road. D'yeh know wha' I mean?" Davy smiled.

Arthur pulled his peaked cap a little lower and smiled too. Davy was always asking why taxi drivers complain so much.

"Listen, take me to Jamesies, his oul' wan's, I mean."

Arthur pulled the taxi out and headed north down the dual carriageway, towards Santry Lane. While he drove, Davy gave him further instructions. "When we get out here, I want yeh to wait on me. Then I want you to drop me back in the Mun. After yeh do tha', go and collect a suitcase from me oul' wan's. Have yeh got tha'?"

Arthur nodded. "What'll I do with the suitcase?"

"Wait on the taxi rank for me, okay?"

"Will it take long, Davy? Yeh know wha' the missus is like. If I'm not in by midnigh', she's ringing' the hospitals. There's been so many late night robberies recently."

"Don't worry, Arthur. I'll be finished with yeh before ten and I'll fix yeh up for everything."

"Okay then, Davy. Listen, I meant to say to yeh, I was sorry to hear abou' Mickey. It was a terrible tragedy and must have been hard for yeh, because I know you and him were like brothers."

"Yeah, well . . . yeah," said Davy.

Arthur tried to lighten it by saying, "As thick as thieves, hey?" but it didn't even bring the hint of a smile to Davy's lips. Arthur couldn't say a bad word about either. They were always game ball with him. "I know this is a sad thing to say, Davy, but maybe it was for the best. He was lookin' woeful lately, I'm not jokin' yeh."

When Davy shot Arthur a curious glance, Arthur decided it was time to stop talking about Mickey. He waffled on a little bit, but Davy didn't say much before they reached Jamesie's.

"Okay, wait here. I'll oney be a few minutes."

Jamesie's ma answered Davy's knock. "Wha' do you want?"

"Tell Jamesie I want him for a minute, will yeh?"

"He's not here now and I don't know when he'll be back."

"Who's tha' at the door?" Jamesie shouted from upstairs.

Davy grinned.

Mrs Riordain looked to the heavens before shouting back up, "It's tha' Davy Byrne fella."

"Tell him to come up, will yeh?" Jamesie shouted down.

Mrs Riordain dropped her elbow from her hips and allowed Davy to walk past her and up the stairs. When he was inside, she looked out, checking to see had anyone seen him enter.

At the top of the stairs, Jamesie greeted him. "Wha's the story, Davy?" He was surprised Davy wasn't in mourning.

"Nothin' much. Have yeh got me money here?"

"Yeah, well, I've got eighteen hundred, Davy. I'm still owed a few bob, but don't worry. I can trust them, so I'll definitely get it. They never let me down."

"How much gear have yeh got now?"

"I've half an ounce, but it's cut into four eighths. It's stashed as well."

That was clever, Davy thought. Jamesie had sussed straight away to make sure he kept the gear safe. Safe enough for him to be all right for smack if anything happened. "Alrigh', gimme the money then."

Jamesie went downstairs and was back quickly with the money.

Davy counted it. Twice. "For fucksake, Jamesie. Didn't I tell yeh not to be doin' tha'? There's only £1,740 here."

"Aw yeah. I meant to say nearly £1,800."

"Nearly £1,800? There's nearly £1,700 here."

"Well, there's more than £1,700, isn't there?"

"Listen, forget tha', for now. I have to get a new suss. Somethin's happened, so I migh' be away for a little longer than usual. Now wha' I want yeh to do, after you've sold tha' gear, is to drop the money out to me oul' wan's. And don't be short of any of it, okay?"

"Jaysis, Davy. Have I ever let yeh down?"

Davy sighed patiently. "I mean it, Jamesie. Don't fuck abou' with it."

There were a few things that Jamesie wanted to ask, but even more, he wanted to be rid of him. "Okay, don't worry. I swear, everythin'll be alrigh'. When I sell the gear, I'll take the money out to your ma."

Davy left flinging a cheery good-bye to Mrs Riordain. He counted out £440 of the money in the taxi, and handed it to Arthur. "Here, give this to me ma, will yeh? Tell her it's for herself and tell her tha' Jamesie's goin' to be droppin' round a few bob, but she's to put tha' aside for me. Make sure she doesn't get confused abou' the two, do yeh know wha' I mean, Arthur?"

Arthur nodded.

Davy realised he had £1,300 left. Unlucky for some. Having counted out another £100, he asked, "Is this okay?"

"Sure," said Arthur, without checking it and he put it away in his breast pocket.

"If it's not enough, yeh can tell me later."

"It'll be grand," said Arthur. "Don't worry about it."

"That's great then. Listen, drop me at St Pappin's Church. I don't want to drive through the Mun. And don't forget, wait for me at the rank, okay?"

Arthur nodded again, solemnly.

After he'd been dropped off, Davy watched Arthur drive out of sight before walking across the dual carriageway to Balcurris Road. He crossed and walked along the edge of the flats until he reached the second last lift in the last block. Pausing outside, he sucked a determined breath and walked in.

There is nothing, nothing quite like the power of intent, and when this young intender had marched the fourteen flights of stairs, he turned right on the seventh floor landing and walked to the one-bedroom flat. Before he knocked, he pushed the door quietly, slightly, and realised there was something holding it tightly closed from the inside. There was someone in.

Rapping the small door knocker, he called through the letter box, "It's me, Davy. Let me in."

While he waited for a reply, he looked around at the silence of the empty balcony and the quietness behind the other three doors on the landing, a quietness eager to mind its own business.

Just as he was about to call through again, the silence was broken by Skinnier's nervous voice whimpering from behind the door, "Is tha' you, Davy?"

"Yeah," said Davy. "Open the fuckin' door, will yeh?"

The impatience comforted Skinnier. It reassured him that Davy was his usual self, especially when he pulled back the door and Davy brushed past.

Skinnier had removed one of the long doors from the airing cupboard and wedged it between the hall door and the facing wall. It was as much as he could do to stop anyone kicking the door in.

"Is anyone with yeh?"

"A'yeh mad? I didn't even think anyone knew I was here."

"Yeh look terrible. A'yeh sick?"

"I'm fuckin' dyin'. I haven't had a bit of gear in nearly three days."

"Yeah, you're not lookin' the best. Get a spoon and a bit of citric."

"I haven't any citric, Davy, oney vinegar."

"Tha'll do."

Skinnier went and fetched what Davy wanted. When he returned, Davy was sitting waiting on a rotten settee.

"D'yeh want a bit of gear?"

Skinnier was hesitant, suspicious. Maybe Davy was thinking of poisoning him. "Em, yeah, . . . go on then, if yeh have enough. I was goin' to try and give it up, but fuck it," Skinnier shrugged. "Though you have yours first. After three fuckin' days, it won't kill me to wait another couple of minutes, will it?" Skinnier slapped his hands together and rubbed them warmly.

Davy could hear Skinnier's fear. He could taste his greed. As he fixed just over a quarter, he studied him as he knelt in front of a table made from two milk crates stacked on top of each other. The flames from a few old candles, wedged tight between gaps in the crates, brightened his face and flickered some light in his sunken eyes. You could almost forgive him.

The sight of Davy fixing almost cleared Skinnier's withdrawals and anticipating a hit made him euphoric. Yet, he remained careful. Davy was calm, and experience dictated that such calmness was often the beginning of something he would come to regret. He wondered if Davy was going to give him a hiding. If he had discovered where he was staying, then he'd probably managed to find out everything else too. Maybe Davy would let him get stoned first. He didn't care what happened after that. He just needed a bit of gear. Surely Davy owed him that much.

When Davy was finished, he put a fiver's worth on the spoon and said, "There yeh go."

"Jaysis, Davy. Tha' won't do an'thin' for me. Can yeh give us bit more? I know I haven't got any money, but I'll pay yeh back when I get me labour, yeh know I will."

"It's strong gear, Skinnier. Get tha' into yeh first and see wha' yeh think."

Skinnier was about to argue, but took some hope instead from the way that Davy had offered the hit. If the door of generosity was closing, he might still get in through the window.

Davy watched him as he fixed, concealing well his delight that there was just about enough on the spoon to make Skinnier feel worse. After he'd finished and before he'd time to complain, Davy asked him, "Have yeh any foil here?"

"Yeah, I'll get it for yeh." Skinnier fetched the foil for Davy and watched him pour another half gram. He watched him chase carelessly, watched the smoke wisp away from the heat beneath the foil.

Skinnier saw Davy doze, stoned, but what he saw wasn't real. Davy wasn't dozing and Davy wasn't stoned. From the moment he'd exhaled his last drag he was acutely aware of how Skinnier was suffering. The horrible, twisted, disloyal, lying little bollix. Davy pretended to stumble from the doze and asked, "D'yeh want a chase, Skinnier?"

"To tell yeh the truth, I wouldn't mind another fix. I didn't get a fuckin' tiddle out of tha' last one, honest to Jaysis."

"Is tha' righ'," said Davy, like he was concerned and he poured some more on the spoon. "Here, is this alrigh'?"

"That's lovely," said Skinnier to the quarter gram and he couldn't get it into himself quick enough.

Davy watched the tension leave Skinnier's features, waited until he was finished and then asked what it was he came to find out. "Wha' happened with Mickey, Skinnier?"

"It wasn't my fault, Davy. There was nothin' I could do abou' it." The tension returned, concern for himself, but because he was stoned, all sincerity was lost and this made it so much easier for Davy.

"I'm not sayin' it was your fault and don't worry, I'm not goin' to do an'thin' to yeh. Just tell me wha' happened."

The reassurance sliced through Skinnier like a sliver of glass. "None of us had any gear and Mickey went over to Plunkett Tower to get it, for Jamesie to bag it up. He told me I could have a turn on up there with him, because I was dyin' sick."

Davy knew Mickey would have said no, but Skinnier would have begged and pleaded with him.

"We went over to the gaff and had a turn on each. After tha', Mickey said he was stayin' for another one. Yeh know wha' he's like. Em . . . was like. He told me to go and tell Jamesie he'd be over later, so I left and tha's when it happened."

"Wha' fuckin happened?" The change in tone frightened Skinnier and reminded Davy to remain calm.

"Well, as I was walkin' out of the tower, these two blokes stopped me and asked me which flat Mickey was in. I asked, Mickey who? and one of them took out a gun and said, "Mickey fuckin' Blue! Who do yeh think?" I tried to give them the wrong address, but one of them said he was takin' me with them and if I was lyin', they were goin' to shoot me too." Skinnier was desperate to sound sincere. He was sincere, but the gear had numbed him. He wanted to cry when he told Davy, "I swear, there was nothin' I could do abou' it. I even thought at first tha' they were just goin' to rob the gear. They even asked me where you were and I told them I didn't know, because I didn't. I swear, Davy, they would have killed me too if I hadn't told them."

"D'yeh know who they were?"

"No. I could just tell tha' they were from the North. I could tell from their accents."

Davy enjoyed Skinnier's anxiety. "D'yeh want another bit of gear or a'yeh alrigh' now?"

"I wouldn't mind another pinch, yeh know?" said Skinnier, rubbing his nose. "Just enough to sort me out."

Davy poured another quarter gram on the spoon. As soon as Skinnier fixed it, he began to mumble. "They're goin' to kill us, Davy. They're goin' to kill yeh."

"Aw, don't worry abou' me. I'll wait, and die tomorrow," he chuckled.

Skinnier began to goof. Sitting forward on the settee, he threatened to fall from it. Now and then, when he leaned too far forward, he would jump back, open his eyes and scratch his face, before repeating the whole procedure. Davy put another quarter gram on the spoon and cooked it. When he'd finished, he sucked it up with Skinnier's syringe and knelt at his feet. Locating a ripe vein on Skinnier's hand, he slid the needle in.

"Wha's up, Davy? Wha's up?" Skinnier asked, startled.

"Yeh're goofin' off with the works in your hand, for fucksake. I'm just goin' to flush it for yeh."

"Aw, nice one, Davy. Nice one."

Skinnier was goofing again before Davy finished, so Davy pushed him back in the chair and stood up and walked out to the cool air on the inside balcony. From there, he looked out to a Quiet Time, a silence below and the many lights from the flats in Balcurris which swung round from his left. Flat lights shone too from Balbutcher and Sillogue and all stayed quiet, apart from distant, irregular traffic and the footsteps of a couple who walked directly below. When they passed, Davy went back inside and saw that Skinnier was as still as silence. To check, he put his fingers beneath his nose and could feel the warm breath falling softly, almost imperceptibly. Davy pulled him up and threw him across his shoulder.

Jaysis! The weight of him! Even his name was a fucking lie. Was he saying something? Or was that just a cough?

He carried him to the cool air of the balcony. When the empty clothesline got in the way, he put him down and lifted him under. Then, instead of resting him across his shoulder, he rested him across the parapet of the balcony wall and looked over on to the same quiet scene. It was the same except now nobody walked below. When he was certain of this, Davy bent, and taking Skinnier by the ankles, stood and toppled him over the side, with the hope that Skinnier would open his eyes some time before the bottom and know.

Davy didn't look because he didn't want to see him fall. He didn't want anyone to see him either, watching him fall, but when he heard Skinnier collide noisily with the wall of the balcony on the floor below, so loud it almost took Davy's breath away, he almost threw himself over in his anxiety to make sure that Skinnier hadn't fallen inside. But all he saw was Skinnier somersault once to a harmlessly dull thudding stop, seven flights below, and then lie motionless on the raised cobblestones which bordered the walkway to the block of flats.

Wait, he told himself, his heart thumping, straining. Don't run, for fucksake, don't run. When he walked inside, he left the balcony door ajar and he couldn't believe it. Jaysis! He couldn't believe that he half expected Skinnier to be still sitting in the settee. Get out of here, get out of here.

He'd already put away his syringe, so all that was left to do was quickly wipe anything he'd touched: the spoon, Skinnier's syringe, the glass. Christ! Someone was goin' to start screaming soon.

As he walked from the flat, he let the cupboard door drop behind the hall door and wedge tight against the wall, or at least it would when someone tried to open it. This he did cleanly too, safely, and as he walked down the stairs, he tried to count how long it was taking him. He left the back way, to avoid the corpse. How could he forget? And headed straight for the taxi rank.

By the time he reached the subway in the middle of Balcurris Road, he was out of hearing range, but he still waited on the screaming to begin. It was an expectation neither time nor distance was likely to effect.

Arthur drove the taxi down the back roads to the airport because it was more convenient. As they drove past St Pappin's Church, between St Margaret's Lane and Santry Lane, Davy thought about how Ballymun ended there. Nothing had been built to the north of it, though the airport, as it lay directly in front, was a good enough reason for that. To the north-west nothing had been built either, while north-east, the city stretched as far as Swords. No one wanted to live there, he supposed. Fuck it! What did it matter anyway. He wouldn't be coming back, especially after Mickey and that. Fuck them! *Tiocfaidh Ár Lá. Slán leat saor bleedin' Éire agus Éire Nua.*

ÁINE SAT ON the living room floor in the middle of the woollen cot blanket. She squeezed the tennis ball between both of her tiny, chubby hands. She squeezed it like she was just about to give it a great big kiss. It was her favourite toy that day. There was something about the hairy feel to it, something about its weight and because of its roundness it sat easily in her hands. She loved, having tossed it into the air, to scurry after it, as it bounced away. She loved to scarper on her hands and knees and stick her head beneath armchairs. She got giddy when she arrived at floor length curtains and absolutely shrieked with unrestrained delight when she found the ball behind them. There is nothing quite like the beauty of babies, especially when they play uninhibited. To this young infant, it meant with an air of undisguised content.

Anne kept an eye on Áine from the kitchen. There are no doors or walls to separate the living room and kitchen in the one-bedroom flats in Ballymun, but it's easy to see that the kitchen begins where the carpet on the living room floor ends. Anne kept a balanced eye on Áine, as she played on the living room floor. The child needed to see that Anne was there if she checked. Anne had to be careful though. She had to disguise the fact she was paying the baby any attention, because if the baby knew this, she would simply demand more and more. But even babies get used to routines, so all Anne had to do was seem busy.

She was busy. It was hard getting the hit together beside the cooker. It was hard because she'd been waiting for three hours for Jamesie to come back with the gear. At one point she worried he might have been reefed, but almost immediately suspected this might be an excuse he'd use if he wanted to rip her off. She prayed he wouldn't, because there was nothing left in Kathleen Burke's flat worth selling. She'd had to wait in some dive of a flat in Coultry, because Jamesie was nervous and wouldn't come to her place since they'd shot Mickey. When Anne finally returned, her ma told her it was the last time, because Anne had said she would only be a half hour, an hour at the latest, not three. She wasn't going to mind the baby again. She also told Anne she ought to be ashamed of herself, the state she was in, thinking she could look after a baby properly. If she wasn't careful, the child would be taken off her. But her ma didn't understand. Anne wasn't stoned, she was sick. To make matters worse, the few Valium she'd dropped and the naggin of vodka she washed them down with only made her feel worse.

The gear Jamesie brought back looked filthy. It looked like it had been cut to bits. Grey gear? It looked like ash. She prayed he wasn't ripping her off. He had told her the gear was lovely and not to use too much of it in the one go, but that was the kind of thing he would say. Then, if she complained, he'd probably say she'd fucked it up by not using enough in the first place. Anne had considered using half of the bag and keeping the other half until later, but she needed a little more than half. A funny thing happens when you mix Valium with alcohol. A funny thing which made Anne throw caution to the wind. What was the point in keeping less than half, if she needed more than half to get a hit? Anne tipped all of the bag on to the spoon.

On top of the gear, she poured a few drops of vinegar and squirted in carefully one and a half mls of water from her two ml syringe. In the process, she washed speckles of smack from the side of the spoon to a more manageable heap in the centre.

Anne delayed and checked Áine again, after she had heard her shriek from the living room. She saw her clapping her chubby hands and it touched her, briefly, the beauty.

Having picked up the spoon, she swirled the liquid and powder together. She did this with the kind of easiness that comes with experience and then held it over a low flame on the cooker, allowing it to heat slowly. She let it heat until it began to splash boil and was surprised when it cooked clear at the first attempt. Maybe whatever it was that they cut it with dissolved easily. Something like that, she thought. Using the syringe to draw up the liquid through a clean piece of cigarette filter, Anne sucked the spoon dry.

It wouldn't matter, in a minute, if Áine wanted attention. By then, Anne would be able to give her all the attention she'd need. But she still pretended to ignore her when she sat on an armchair in the living room, having fetched one of her late brother's ties. Well, it was his only tie. It was the one that he bought with Davy Byrne that day, when they both bought loads of clothes and got all dolled up. For what? For getting stoned? Davy bleedin' Byrne. Nobody had heard so much as a whisper from him in over two months. The bastard wasn't worth thinking about.

Anne looped the tie around her arm and pulled it tightly. Her hits were becoming harder to get. When the last of her veins in her arms collapsed, she would give up the gear. There was no way she was going to start fixing in her groin the way Mickey did. Even the thought of it was enough to turn her stomach.

Having flexed her fist a few times in the tightened tourniquet, she closed the arm and saw on the far side the vein just below her elbow. That would do. She just had to encourage it to get a little bigger. Holding the syringe between her teeth, she slapped the vein and knew when it was ready. With the tourniquet still knotted tight, Anne slid the needle in and drew back the plunger. She almost choked on the sigh she felt as she saw the blood shoot into the syringe and almost as quickly she loosened the grip of the tourniquet. With the appetite of an addict and the shame, her thumb pushed the plunger of the syringe forward.

Áine had stopped playing with the ball. She had stopped clapping her hands, until Mammy came home, cake in her pockets for Áine alone. She sat again, in the middle of the cot blanket and watched her mother, dispassionately.

Anne knew, when only half of the gear had gone in. She knew, because her heart felt like it was going to erupt. But do you know, for the life of her, she couldn't stop pushing the plunger. Do you know, it seemed there was even more of an urgency, that she should get the hit into her all the quicker.

Áine sat and watched the emotions on her mother's face. She saw the hunger. She saw the feeding. She saw the horror. She saw the peace. The peace was something she would never forget, even long after she had stopped remembering it. She saw her mother sitting stretched out on the armchair, saw the tie hanging loosely from the arm that had dropped to the side of the chair. The arm which a syringe still protruded from.

Áine couldn't see the very thing that she wanted, but more than anything else, she knew it was there. She crawled, scurried towards her mother's legs, and climbed up into her lap. Gripping first with her tiny fists, her mother's T-shirt and then her bra, she pulled herself up and buried her head down between her mother's breasts and listened. She listened for the very thing she wanted to hear more than anything else. She listened for, and heard, her mother's heartbeat. She heard it boom, felt it pulse into her chubby cheeks. She heard it boom again and pulse into her face again, so she carried her thumb to her mouth and licked a suck of satisfaction. The beat of her mother's heart lulled her. It drew her towards a sleep.

In a tower block, high in the heart of Ballymun, but from another world, a world of her own, Áine heard her mother's heart beat for the very Last Time.

Acknowledgements

A first draft of this novel was written in 1988. Its history since is probably less believable than its plot. While I cannot blame anyone else for its shortcomings, it would never have seen the light of day if it weren't for the support of others at crucial times.

Irene for nourishing me.

Mick O'Brien for being the first to professionally appreciate my endeavours and for crying when reading the parts I had cried writing. His belief sustained me long after he died and it was as a gesture of respect for him that I harassed Steve MacDonogh into taking a risk with it.

I would never have arrived at this point without the encouragement of Sue Habeshaw at the University in the West of England, nor the practical help of Claire Williamson, Mel Nortcliffe, Adam Butcher, Steve Cooke, Rory and Nuala O'Connor.

All my family for carrying me.

Becky for tolerating me.

The crew at Craftprint for their help with the original promotional copy, including John Lawless for setting it out. Maurice Lawless for running it out and calling in all his favours. Derek Fagan for keeping an eye on him to make sure he did it properly. Alan Murtagh for the unpaid overtime. Rock for making the tea and David Fagan for the marketing.

Delroy Smith, wherever you are!

Aileen for always being there.

Sarah and Niall for still loving their oul' fella when they were all he had left.

Paddy Graham, without whom I would never have written a word.

FICTION
from
BRANDON

JOHN TROLAN

Slow Punctures

"Compelling. . . his writing, with its mix of brutal social realism, irony and humour, reads like a cross between Roddy Doyle and Irvine Welsh." *Sunday Independent*

"Three hundred manic, readable pages. . . *Slow Punctures* is grim, funny and bawdy in equal measure." *The Irish Times*

"Fast-moving and hilarious in the tradition of Roddy Doyle." *Sunday Business Post*

"Trolan writes in a crisp and consistent style. He handles the delicate subject of young suicide with a sensitive practicality and complete lack of sentiment. His novel is a brittle working-class rites of passage that tells a story about Dublin that probably should have been told a long time ago." *Irish Post*

ISBN 0 86322 252 8; Original Paperback £8.99

KITTY FITZGERALD

Snapdragons

"A unique and extremely engaging story of two sisters, each of whom is looking for love and salvation in their different ways."
Irish Post

"An original, daring book." *Books Ireland*

Sometimes shocking, frequently humorous, often surreal, *Snapdragons* is a unique and extremely engaging rites of passage novel about a young woman who grows up unhappily in rural Ireland after World War II. She is disliked – for reasons she cannot understand – by her parents, and has a running feud with her sister. Yet the mood of this story is strangely light-hearted, frequently comic and absolutely memorable.

She makes her escape to the English midlands, and works and lives in a pub in Digbeth, Birmingham, where her sister has settled with her husband. Her already difficult relationship with her sister is further strained when she discovers how she is living. She also learns the sad reason for her parents' hostility towards her.

A captivating story of a young girl in Birmingham and the North of England in the 1950s, its main protagonist, Bernadette, who carries on a constant angry dialogue with God, is one of the most delightfully drawn characters in recent Irish fiction.

ISBN 0 86322 258 7; Original Paperback £8.99

THE NOVELS OF J. M. O'NEILL

Duffy Is Dead

"A book written sparingly, with wit and without sentimentality, yet the effect can be like poetry. . . An exceptional novel." *Guardian*

"The atmosphere is indescribable but absolutely right: as if the world of Samuel Beckett had crossed with that of George V. Higgins." *Observer*

"Not a single word out of place. . . Every word of it rings true." *Daily Telegraph*

ISBN 0 86322 261 7; Paperback £6.99

Open Cut

"A hard and squalid world depicted economically and evocatively. . . the tension in the slang-spotted dialogue and the mean prose creates effective atmosphere." *Hampstead & Highgate Express*

"A powerful thriller." *Radio Times*

"O'Neill's prose, like the winter wind is cutting and sharp." *British Book News*

"Fascinating." *Yorkshire Post*

"An uncannily exacting and accomplished novelist." *Observer*

"Exciting and dangerous, with a touch of the poet." *Sunday Times*

ISBN 0 86322 264 1; Paperback £6.99

Rellighan, Undertaker

A dark, intriguing modern gothic tale. The final novel by a writer who was a master of his craft.

In a small rural town in Ireland, nothing is as it appears. Ester Machen brings with her a mystery, and death is stalking the young people of the town. Though 'the town is talking', the only person determined to get to the bottom of the mystery is the detective Coleman. He has few allies, but Rellighan the undertaker gradually assists him in attempting to reveal and rid the town of the terror that has grown within it. They both risk death but unfalteringly continue to unveil the mystery, becoming deeply embroiled in the dark world of the occult as they strive to eradicate evil.

ISBN 0 86322 260 9; Original Paperback £8.99

Bennett & Company

Winner of the 1999 Kerry Ingredients Book of the Year award

"O'Neill's world owes something to the sagas of Forsyte and Onedin, and his plotting has, at times, some of the pace and complexity of John Buchan, but the novel is, nonetheless, uniquely Irish with its sanctuary lamps, street-children, moving statues and bitter memories, and it is a contribution to an overdue examination of Irish conscience. The poor and the middle classes are indeed those of Frank McCourt and Kate O'Brien, but O'Neill's is a strictly modern and undeluded vision of the past. The writing is shockingly credible." *Times Literary Supplement*

"He is an exceptional writer, and one we must take very seriously." *Sunday Independent*

ISBN 1 90201 106 6; Original paperback £7.99

THE NOVELS OF WALTER MACKEN

I Am Alone

Banned in Ireland when it was first published, *I Am Alone* tells the story of a young Irishman, who leaves behind the grey stone and green fields of Galway for the bright lights of pre-war London.

ISBN 0 86322 266 8; hardback £12.99

Rain on the Wind

"It is a raw, savage story full of passion and drama set amongst the Galway fishing community . . . it is the story of romantic passion, a constant struggle with the sea, with poverty and with the political conservatism of post-independence Ireland." *Irish Independent*

ISBN 0 86322 185 8; paperback £6.99

Sunset on the Window-Panes

Careless of the hurt he inflicts, Bart O'Breen waslks his own road, as proud as the devil and as lonely as hell.

ISBN 0 86322 254 4; paperback £6.99

The Bogman

"Macken captures the isolation and poverty of the village – its closed attitudes, its frozen social mores . . . and its deeply unforgiving nature." *Irish Independent*

ISBN 0 86322 184 X; paperback £6.99

Brown Lord of the Mountain

"Macken knows his people and his places, and his love of them shines through." *Examiner*

ISBN 0 86322 201 3; paperback £5.95

Quench the Moon

A romantic story of the wild, hard and beautiful land of Connemara.

ISBN 0 86322 202 1; paperback £5.95